"The Civil War is seared into American mem_____ __.__ors of the battlefields, North and South. Mary Calland's *Consecrated Dust* brings the tragedy to the northern home front and Pittsburgh – the Arsenal of the Union – which experienced in a single day the greatest death of civilians during the four year conflict. On September 17, 1862 a mysterious blast leveled the ammunition laboratories at Allegheny Arsenal and devastated families at the same time great armies struggled on the field of Antietam – just over 100 miles away – the bloodiest day of the war."

> ANDREW E. MASICH, President & CEO of the Senator
> John Heinz History Center, Pittsburgh, PA.

"For nearly 150 years the story of the September 17, 1862 tragedy at the Allegheny Arsenal has been shared among historians who understand the important place the catastrophe holds in American History. Mary Frailey Calland bridges the gap between historian and storyteller, adeptly using characters to walk the reader through the times and events in 1862 Pittsburgh where life and the consequences of war collide. Rich in historic detail, *Consecrated Dust* is a narrative window to the past."

> MICHAEL KRAUS, Curator of Soldiers & Sailors
> Memorial Hall & Museum, Pittsburgh, PA, and military
> consultant to the films *Gettysburg* and *Cold Mountain*.

"*Consecrated Dust* eloquently portrays a family struggling through the Civil War in a way that transports the reader back in time to the home front and battlefield."

> 9th Pennsylvania Reserves Civil War reenactor,
> Cpl. KEN BOWMAN.

"Mary Calland's novel has brought to life the little known Civil War period in Pittsburgh's history, and in particular the iconic Allegheny Arsenal in Lawrenceville. I applaud her effort in 'imparting a voice' to those ordinary folks, on both the home-front and battlefield who lived through and survived the most turbulent period in our nation's history."

> ARTHUR FOX, Professor, World Geography, CCAC,
> author of *Pittsburgh During the American Civil War,
> 1860-1865*, and *Our Honored Dead, Allegheny County, PA
> in the American Civil War.*

Consecrated Dust
A Novel of the Civil War North

By
Mary Frailey Calland

First published by Dog Ear Publishing
4010 W. 86th Street, Ste H
Indianapolis, IN 46268
www.dogearpublishing.net

dog ear
PUBLISHING

ISBN: 978-145750-501-0

This book is printed on acid-free paper.

This book is a work of fiction. Places, events, and situations in this book are purely fictional and any resemblance to actual persons, living or dead, is coincidental.

Printed in the United States of America

For Dean, always

ACKNOWLEDGEMENTS

ALTHOUGH FICTIONAL, *CONSECRATED DUST* IS based on true events, and great care has been taken to ensure the historical accuracy of the places, people, and battles portrayed. My sincere thanks go to the following experts who lent their time and expertise to ensure that the book represents as closely as possible the experiences of both the soldiers of the 9th Pennsylvania Reserves regiment and the civilians of Civil War Pittsburgh: Arthur B. Fox, Pittsburgh author, professor, and Civil War historian (*Pittsburgh During the American Civil War, 1860-1865* and *Our Honored Dead*); Michael Kraus, curator of Soldiers & Sailors Military Hall & Museum in Pittsburgh, and military consultant for the films *Gettysburg* and *Cold Mountain*; Andrew Masich, President and CEO of the Senator John Heinz History Center in Pittsburgh; David Haalas, former Director of the Center for the French and Indian War at the Senator John Heinz History Center, past Director of Library and Archives, and past Director of Publications; Kenneth T. Bowman, a corporal and former president of the board of the 9th Pennsylvania Reserves Civil War reenactment group; Dr. James M. Owston of Mountain State University; and Jude Wudarcyk of the Lawrenceville Historical Society. Their suggestions and corrections to earlier versions of the manuscript were invaluable and any errors that remain in the final version are attributable solely to the author.

A number of dedicated individuals and organizations contributed to the authenticity and historical accuracy of this novel. Thank you to the staff of the library and archives of the Senator John Heinz History Center in Pittsburgh, Pennsylvania; the staff of the National Museum of Civil War Medicine in Frederick, Maryland; the staff of the Antietam National Battlefield, particularly the very knowledgeable park rangers of the National Park Service who conducted a walking tour over the actual ground of The Cornfield; the members of the 9th Pennsylvania Reserves Civil War reenactment group who allowed me to observe their campsites at Antietam and on the grounds of the Soldiers & Sailors Memorial Hall & Museum in Pittsburgh and provided valuable insight into the daily life of a Union soldier; the staff of the Carnegie Library of Pittsburgh, Main Branch; the staff of the Captain Thomas

Espy G.A.R. Post #153 at the Andrew Carnegie Free Library in Carnegie, Pennsylvania; and the staff of the Soldiers & Sailors Memorial Hall & Museum in Pittsburgh, Pennsylvania. All of these people and institutions do a tremendous service by preserving our treasured past and honoring the men and women who fought in the American Civil War.

Consecrated Dust also benefited from the input of four very special book clubs who agreed to act as "test markets" for an early version of the manuscript. Their insightful comments and suggestions helped make this a better book and gave the author a very enjoyable experience of interacting with the readers. I'd like to say a special thank you to all of these "editors":

In Boston: Rosalind Bunnell, Cindy Lynes, Nancy Mooney, Rooney Russell, Joanne Scheuble, Carolyn Williams;

In Chagrin Falls: Joyce Bloom, Lorrie Clasen, Justine Coticchia, Ann V. Faist, Tamara Fallon, Stephanie Goodman, Debbie Gratto, Mary Beth Hubert, Carol Andress Kimes, Sandra Lewis, Connie Lowman, Jennifer Molner, Margaret Ringness, Karen S. Wamelink;

In Pittsburgh: Arlene Carbone-Wiley, Barbara Clements, Patricia Davis, Michele Domeisen, Lu Donnelly, Nancy Geer, Julie O'Hara, Peg Showalter, Susan Showalter, Nicki Ubinger;

In Pittsburgh: Bob and Didra Kirschner, John and Susan Kudlik, Howard and Jane Voigt.

A final thank you goes to my talented "cartographer"/daughter, Grace Calland. Her patient and skillful rendering of the maps in this book contributed greatly to the reader's understanding of some complex campaigns and battles, and proved to her parents the value of all those tuition payments.

INTRODUCTION

ON THE EVE OF THE American Civil War, the city of Pittsburgh, Pennsylvania, stood on the threshold of its industrial might. Its smoke-laden skies had already been likened to "hell with the lid off," a label that belied the beauty of its natural setting where the Allegheny and Monongahela Rivers cut through wooded mountains to meet and form the Ohio River. This gateway to the west, which had seen Lewis and Clark start on their journey of discovery, remained a stepping off place for pioneers, entrepreneurs, and dreamers who saw their futures, not in the lands beyond the horizon, but in the factories and mills that glowed at their feet.

In these years before the big money, when Andrew Carnegie was still just a telegrapher, before the Fricks and the Mellons made their names, Pittsburgh churned with the natural resources of coal, water, and people. The city combined the raw material of the land with the ingenuity and strength of the native born, the immigrants, the old money and the new, and fired them in the rough furnaces of its mills, its churches, and its fledgling society. What emerged was a hardened, distinctly unique product – an American. The people, like the land, were both rugged and beautiful.

As war approached in the winter of 1860, Pittsburgh vibrated with a mix of patriotic fervor and opportunistic greed. Under dark skies, its factories labored to produce the rails, cannon, ships, guns, and bullets that would be needed in the conflict to come, and would earn the city the name, *Arsenal of the Union.*

Beneath this industrial might were the everyday working people of Pittsburgh – the seamstresses, glass blowers, mill workers, clerks, housewives, shipbuilders, grocers, and dock workers – who powered the machinery, manned the regiments, and dedicated their lifeblood to the cause of freedom. Through their determination and sacrifice, at home and on the field of battle, they helped to right the steps of a faltering nation.

This book is dedicated to them.

Lawrenceville, Pennsylvania
Two and a Half Miles Northeast of Pittsburgh
May 1915

THE OLD WOMAN TURNED DOWN the kerosene lamp until only a soft light suffused the sickroom. The house was quiet now. All day there had been a steady stream of visitors hovering by the bedside, saying their goodbyes, gently pulling her aside to ask if there was anything they could do for her, anything at all. But, now, even her children had left to go home and tend to their own children. She was glad. For so much of his life, she'd had to share him – with his family, his work, his memories. Now that his life was ending, she wanted this time with him, alone.

She bent over the old mahogany bed and stared down at her sleeping husband. The contours of his face had been honed to angles and hollows by the slow wasting of his illness. With each hour that passed, he seemed to be melting away, becoming smaller and smaller against the white sheets until she feared one moment she would turn to find him gone altogether. Tenderly, she ran her finger along the faded scar that stretched across his cheekbone and imagined she saw the furrow in his brow relax. She lowered herself into the chair next to the bed, took his hand in hers, and waited.

The soft chiming of the clock over the fireplace jolted her awake. She had dozed for almost fifteen minutes. In a panic, she pressed her hand to her husband's chest. His heart pulsed against her palm and she let go the breath she had been holding. When her own heartbeat returned to normal, she rose and hobbled to the front window. She drew aside the heavy velvet curtain and rested her forehead against the coolness of the windowpane. People and carriages hurried by in the rain-slick street below. How strange, she thought, that they went about their business, unaware of the momentous event taking place in the room above them. How unimaginable that their lives could go on unchanged while hers was ending; ending with her question gone unasked, unanswered.

The air in the room felt suddenly close and stale. With a quick glance at the still form in the bed, she placed the palms of her hands on the underside of the window jamb and hoisted the glass a few inches. At once, a gentle breeze ruffled the lace collar of her dress. The spring rain had temporarily washed the air clean of its perennial soot, and the breeze held a touch of the sweetness she remembered from her youth. She closed her eyes and breathed. Immediately, the memories swirled; beckoning, pulling. Ah, old woman, she silently scolded herself, don't look back. You can get lost in the lookin' back.

Returning to her bedside vigil, she sank into the chair and folded her hands in her lap, her good hand automatically covering her bad, the habit of many years. The soft patter of raindrops on the windowsill had a soothing, timeless quality, and she almost believed that, if she held very still, she could stay in this moment forever. But the future loomed, empty, unthinkable. She closed her eyes against it. She was tired, so tired. A carriage rumbled by on the cobblestone street below and, once again, long-ago memories assailed her. This time, she let them come.

CHAPTER 1

Lawrenceville, Pennsylvania
December 1860

A CARRIAGE RUMBLED TO A halt in front of the red brick row house on Allen Street, just off of Butler. Mrs. Ambrose glanced up from her sewing and checked the rosewood clock on the mantel. Only 9:20 p.m. She frowned and cast a knowing look at her husband who sat reading in the armchair across from her.

"Now, Laura," he cautioned, lowering his medical journal, "give the girl a chance to explain."

The front door opened and closed softly. Mrs. Ambrose waited.

"Clara?" she called out at last.

Their seventeen-year-old daughter, foiled in her attempt to tiptoe past the parlor unseen, appeared in the doorway. Her blue eyes warmed when she saw her father. He smiled in return, still unused to the beautiful woman his little girl had become.

"You're home early, dear," said her mother. "Come sit and tell us about the party."

With a sigh, Clara entered the room, her silk skirt and crinoline swaying. The cold had lent a rosy glow to her complexion and a few stray snowflakes clung to her chestnut hair. She untied the neck ribbon of her heavy wool cloak and swung it from her shoulders. Hugging the garment to her bodice, she sat on the floral divan opposite her mother and steeled herself for the interrogation that was to come.

"Well?" said Mrs. Ambrose.

"It was fine," Clara replied, avoiding her mother's eyes.

"You didn't stay very long."

"I had a headache, so Mr. Gliddon brought me home."

"A headache?" said her father.

"Just a little one. I'm fine."

Mrs. Ambrose raised an eyebrow. "And how is Mr. Gliddon?"

"Oh, Mr. Gliddon is ... Mr. Gliddon."

"Oh, Clara," said Mrs. Ambrose, the exasperation plain in her voice, "Edgar Gliddon is one of the most eligible young men in Pittsburgh. You promised me you would try this time."

Clara dropped the evasive tone.

"I did, Mama, truly I did, but I just couldn't bear it. He's so pretentious. Always talking about who he knows and what he owns. And every other sentence out of his mouth begins with, 'Well, when *I* was at Harvard ...'."

Dr. Ambrose snickered at Clara's adept imitation of Edgar's excessively cultured accent. His wife gave him a withering look.

"Clara, how is it that you can take something that any other young woman would consider an attribute and turn it into a disadvantage?" said Mrs. Ambrose. "There are worse things in life than being courted by a wealthy, educated man, you know. I suggest you stop being so particular and look to your future. At your age, Helen was already engaged to George."

"I know, but ...." Clara managed to stop before she said something less than flattering about her bland brother-in-law. "Well, that was fine for Helen, but I just don't think I'm ready to get married. And if I were, it wouldn't be to Edgar Gliddon. For one thing, he's too old."

"Twenty-eight is hardly old, Clara," her mother interjected, but Clara was not to be deterred.

"And," the young woman continued, "he's not quite the social paragon you think him to be. Tonight he refused to leave my side. He didn't dance with any of the other ladies. Not even the hostess."

"Oh, my." Mrs. Ambrose frowned. "That is bad form. But, perhaps he is just so smitten with you ...."

Clara rolled her eyes.

"*Possessive* would be a more apt description. He treats me as though I'm his personal property; something to show off, like his matched set of horses. And he expects about as much conversation. Why, tonight, when the men began talking about South Carolina seceding from the Union, I started to say something and Mr. Gliddon cut me off! He patted my hand, gave me that condescending look of his, and asked if I wanted some punch."

"Well, dear," said her mother, "it's really not a young woman's place to take part in such discussions. You'd have been wise to follow Mr. Gliddon's lead in that regard."

"But, Mama, I have opinions, too!" Clara nearly stamped her foot in frustration.

"Lower your voice, Clara," said her father. "You'll wake Grandmother Blake."

Eighty-year-old Grandmother Blake's room was just off the parlor in the back of the house. Since she had come to live with them fifteen years ago, she had spent her days complaining to her son-in-law of ill-defined aches and pains, and advising all in the house on the proper conduct of their lives. Clara had no desire to add the old woman's disapproval to her mother's. She continued in a quieter voice.

"I'm so tired of all these men who think I've nothing better to do than decorate their arms, giggle at their stupid jokes, and wait around hoping they'll propose marriage. The last thing I want to do is spend my life waiting on some man and having babies. I have a brain. I want to *do* something with my life."

Clara stopped abruptly when she saw her mother stiffen. Her father's frown let her know she had, once again, gone too far.

"My life might seem small and insignificant to you, Clara," said Mrs. Ambrose, struggling to control her voice, "but I've been content to be a wife and mother. I consider it to be a woman's highest calling and I'm proud of what I've accomplished."

"I know, Mother. I'm sorry. I didn't mean …."

Mrs. Ambrose held up her hand.

"Against my better judgment, your father saw fit to send you to the Pittsburgh Female College, supposedly to improve your mind. I fear, however, it has only served to make you restless and somewhat arrogant. An education can be both a blessing and a curse for a young woman; a blessing if she uses it to enrich the life of her husband and her children; a curse if it causes her to forget her place and engage in inappropriate behavior. Behavior that will very likely cause her to end up an impoverished, lonely old maid. Perhaps you should keep that in mind the next time you turn up your nose at Edgar Gliddon. If there is a next time."

"Now, Laura," said Dr. Ambrose, "any man of worth would not be scared off by a display of intellect."

"On the contrary, Peter, a great many men of worth have been scared off," said Mrs. Ambrose. "At least three this social season. And Mr. Gliddon is hanging by a thread." She paused, searching for the right words to explain the tenuousness of Clara's situation.

"Despite your impeccable reputation, Peter, it is unusual for someone of Mr. Gliddon's social class to take such interest in the daughter of a doctor. However, Clara has been blessed with the kind of beauty that makes men willing to overlook such … obstacles. She has a wonderful opportunity here. But, she's headstrong and opinionated, and hasn't even the good sense to keep her thoughts to herself, at least until she has a ring on her finger."

"Why, Laura, I had no idea you were so devious," said her husband with a wry smile.

"Not devious, Peter, just practical. It's next to impossible for any reputable woman to make her way in this world without the support of a man. That's a fact, and all the education in the world isn't going to change it. So, unless you want your daughter to end up a spinster or some sort of social outcast, I suggest you advise her to change her behavior." With a pointed look, Mrs. Ambrose stood and walked out of the room.

"Papa, I didn't mean that the way it sounded," said Clara.

"I know," he said, setting aside his journal, "but if you truly wish to have your opinions heard, Clara, you'd best learn to choose your words more carefully." He rose and went in search of his wounded wife.

Clara's mother remained aloof and withdrawn for the next week. Her mood did not lift until Clara, overcome by guilt, accepted an invitation from Edgar Gliddon to attend the Holiday Ball at the elegant Monongahela House Hotel in downtown Pittsburgh. Evidently Edgar, unable to conceive of the possibility that any young lady might not actually revel in his company, had accepted without question the veracity of Clara's sudden headache at their last outing.

The Holiday Ball was an important society event that drew the most elite families from Pittsburgh, Allegheny City, and the surrounding towns. Mrs. Ambrose was determined Clara make a favorable impression. She personally made over Helen's elegant, blue, watermark taffeta ball gown to fit Clara's more slender figure and ensured it bared just the right amount of shoulder. She dyed two pairs of gloves to match the gown, one pair to wear and one to change into half way through the evening in case the ever-present soot of Pittsburgh sullied them. She lent Clara her ivory fan and gold necklace and, as a finishing touch, even allowed Clara to wear the ermine cape and matching muff her husband had given her the previous Christmas. The hour before the dance she spent fussing with Clara's thick hair, smoothing it into a center part, flat on top with fullness at the sides, as was the fashion. And, all the while, she drilled Clara on the proper etiquette for such a formal occasion.

A contrite Clara submitted to these preparations without complaint. She was relieved just to see her mother happy again, for the weight of her disapproval had been difficult to bear. And truly, Clara had rarely seen her mother look as happy as she did waving them off in Edgar's stylish maroon brougham on the night of the dance.

The five-story, red brick Monongahela House Hotel presided at the corner of Water Street and Smithfield Street in the city of Pittsburgh, an elegant edifice sporting a sixty-foot domed entrance, white marble floors, and balconies that overlooked the bustling wharf along the Monongahela River. Newly rebuilt after the disastrous fire of 1845 that had leveled much of the downtown, the hotel was considered to be the finest west of the Allegheny Mountains and had accommodated princes, actors, and tycoons.

On this cold Friday night after Christmas, the blazing gaslights of the Monongahela House could be seen from up and down the river, the glow piercing the thick smoke from the factories and the city's coal stoves. Carriages arrived at the front door in a constant stream and discharged men and women in fancy dress for the Holiday Ball. Guests hurried out of the winter's chill into the lobby, past gay knots of people chatting in the various parlors, and up the winding black walnut staircase to the ballroom.

Built to accommodate fifteen hundred people, the enormous ballroom was lavishly decorated for Christmas. Fresh green garlands draped with red and gold ribbons festooned every doorway and railing. Four gigantic fir trees, one in each corner, gave off a sharp pine scent that mingled with the perfumes and colognes of the guests. The multicolored spun glass and silver foil ornaments that hung from the branches reflected the glow of the gaslight fixtures along the walls and the soft light of the candles on each white linen-covered table surrounding the dance floor. Negro waiters in formal attire were stationed at intervals around the perimeter of the room and a ten-piece orchestra provided almost continuous music.

With Clara's hand on his extended arm, Edgar Gliddon, dressed impeccably in a formal black suit with tailcoat, silk cravat, and the whitest of linen shirts, entered the ballroom with his usual haughty air. The opening promenade was already in progress and smiling couples circled the dance floor in a graceful swirl of color and music. Edgar halted in the doorway.

"Damn," he muttered under his breath. "Oh, pardon me, Miss Ambrose. My failure to anticipate the jam of carriages outside has caused us to miss the Grand March."

"It's quite all right, Mr. Gliddon," said Clara. "The evening is young. There will be lots of time for dancing." She knew Edgar's irritation lay not in the fact that she had missed taking part in the Grand March, but that he had missed an opportunity to make a grand entrance, witnessed by all present.

Just then, the orchestra finished with a flourish. The dancing couples bowed and began returning to their tables, the ladies with their fans fluttering. Edgar waited and was rewarded as heads began turning to admire the handsome young couple standing at the entrance of the ballroom. As he expected, all eyes were drawn first to Clara, as his had been when he'd first spied her fidgeting next to her mother at some stifling society piano recital, and then to the man fortunate enough to be her escort. Edgar smiled. Clara could be a handful, but her beauty was such an asset he was willing to ignore her modest social standing and her outspoken ways. He felt confident that, with his continued guidance, she would learn to temper her remarks and her conduct until she became the perfect complement he expected in a woman.

Edgar held his pose a moment longer while he scanned the crowd for any persons of prominence. Failing to locate anyone of sufficient import, he guided Clara over to a gathering of his friends and acquaintances. Clara fixed a smile on her face and spent the next ten minutes struggling to remember names and family lineages. She was rescued when the violins began to play a waltz.

"Ah," said Edgar, inclining his head to the music. He placed his left arm behind his back and extended the other to Clara. "Miss Ambrose, would you do me the favor of this next dance?"

"Of course, Mr. Gliddon," she replied and placed her hand on his. She was grateful to leave behind the discussions of the weather and the latest fashions from *Godey's Ladies Book*. Besides, she loved to dance and Edgar, despite his other shortcomings, was a wonderful dancer. He escorted her to the edge of the dance floor, bowed, and took her in his arms. Deftly, they joined the stream of spinning dancers moving counter-clockwise around the floor. Edgar guided Clara with the lightest of touches, his right arm securely supporting her waist, his left arm gracefully curved with hers. Her voluminous hoop swayed to their movements, causing the blue silk to shimmer and attract admiring glances from the rest of the guests.

After the waltz, Edgar relinquished Clara to another partner for the Lancer's Quadrille. This was followed by the Galop, then another waltz, and finally, another quadrille. The music was lovely, her dance partners charming, and Clara had to admit she was enjoying herself.

Eventually, however, the physical exertion, the tightness of her stays, and the press of people caused her to feel quite warm. When the fifth dance brought them together again, Edgar noticed her flushed complexion and suggested they sit for a moment. He led her to a small table away from the dance floor. Clara sank into a chair and arranged her hoops and skirts about her carefully.

"Would you care for some punch, my dear?" inquired Edgar.

Clara gritted her teeth at the unwelcome endearment. "Yes, please."

"I'll be a moment." As he bent to kiss her gloved hand, his eyes lingered on the décolletage of her gown. Clara snapped open her fan and casually raised the fluttering shield to her bosom.

While Edgar performed his errand, Clara surveyed the room. She noted that many of Pittsburgh's social elite were in attendance, from prominent gentlemen of the railroad, coal, iron, and glass industries, with their bejeweled wives on their arms, to groups of eager young debutantes conversing in excited whispers as they discussed the relative merits of the eligible bachelors in attendance. Clara smiled and nodded to the few people she knew; mostly colleagues and patients of her father's who asked that they be remembered to him.

Suddenly, she noticed a ripple of excitement among the young women; a barely perceptible increase in the fluttering of their fans. Clara followed the direction of their gaze to discover Edgar approaching from across the dance floor. She had to admit he was handsome in an unctuous way. He was tall with a sharp profile and a carefully trimmed beard and mustache. His dark hair was slicked back with Macassar oil and he wore the very latest cut of suit, accented by a gold watch chain and fob that hung from his waistcoat pocket. But his flawless appearance demonstrated too much attention to detail for her comfort. She suspected he had spent more time in front of the mirror getting ready for the dance than she had.

"Here we are, Miss Ambrose," he said, handing her a cup of punch. "That should help."

"Thank you, Mr. Gliddon."

As Clara sipped the lemony concoction, Edgar sat drumming his fingers and gazing over her head at the crowd. Clara searched her mind for a topic of conversation.

"So, Mr. Gliddon, how is your family?"

"Prosperous. Busy. Father and Mother are currently traveling in Europe, ostensibly to purchase some original artwork. But their real purpose is to introduce my sister, Lillian, to various counts and lords, with the prospect of marriage."

"Oh, my. How does Lillian feel about that?"

Edgar gave her a puzzled look. "She's thrilled, of course."

A booming laugh erupted from a group of men in the corner of the room. Edgar brightened.

"Ah, I see Mr. Gregory from the bank is here. And Dr. Powell and young Mr. Edmundson of the steamboat line. How fortunate to find them all together. Come, Miss Ambrose, let's pay our regards."

Clara found Edgar's habit of using every social event as a means of advancing his position in society tiresome. But, mindful of her promise to her mother, she accompanied him across the floor without complaint.

As she expected, after greeting her with perfunctory politeness, the men ignored her and returned to their conversation about financial investments. Clara found it amazing the information and details men would reveal in her presence as if she were no more likely to understand or repeat them than a fly on the wall. This particular conversation, however, proved to be terminally boring.

As the four men blustered on, Clara pasted a look of polite interest on her face, but her mind and eyes kept wandering. Her gaze fell upon a trio seated on a velvet-tufted divan along the wall. She recognized the two animated young women as the Ward sisters from Allegheny City. They were perennial fixtures at the social events her mother forced her to attend. The young man sandwiched between them was unknown to her. He was ruggedly attractive with a strong, clean-shaven face and wavy brown hair, but what caught her attention was his expression. Although he smiled and nodded to each of the sisters at appropriate intervals, it was apparent to Clara that he was as desperately bored as she.

Suddenly, he looked up and caught her stare. Clara knew she should turn away, but the sudden twinkle in his brown eyes told her that he, too, recognized a kindred suffering spirit. With a hint of a smile, he nodded ever so slightly to her before the sister on his left drew him back into the conversation.

Blushing at her own brazenness, Clara ducked her head. Her discomfiture went unnoticed as the conversation around her had turned, as it always did, to a discussion of what most saw to be the inevitable war between the states.

Mr. Gregory, his fingers splayed across his ample stomach, was holding forth about the recent revelation in the press that Secretary of War John Floyd had ordered cannon and small arms, stored at the Allegheny Arsenal in nearby Lawrenceville, to be sent to forts in the south. There had been a great deal of local protest since the news broke in the *Pittsburgh Dispatch* on December 23rd, particularly in the wake of South Carolina's vote to secede from the Union on December 20th. The area newspapers were urging the populace to do whatever was necessary to thwart this affront to the Union, even to the extreme of lying down in the path of the wagons transporting the cannons to the wharf in Pittsburgh. There was much disagreement about what should be done.

As the discussion between Edgar and his companions became more heated, gentlemen gathered from around the room to listen and join in. They tried to maneuver in front of Clara, but she stubbornly clung to Edgar's side.

"How many cannons are they talking about?" asked Dr. Powell.

"More than one hundred guns. Columbiads and thirty-two pounders," said Mr. Gregory.

"Why that's almost all the cannons at the Arsenal," said Dr. Powell. "I can't believe Commander Symington's going to allow those guns to be shipped to New Orleans."

"Galveston, too," said Mr. Edmundson.

"He's got no choice. He can't disobey a direct order from the Secretary of War," said Edgar.

"He can if it's a traitorous order," countered Mr. Gregory. "Don't be an idiot, man."

Clara felt the muscles in Edgar's arm tighten, but his expression remained impassive. She experienced a twinge of pity for him at this careless public upbraiding.

"Secretary Floyd is from Virginia," continued Gregory. "He's obviously working with the secessionists so that when the war begins, the South will be armed and ready." He turned on the young steamship owner. "Edmundson. You must know the captain of the *Silver Wave*. It's moored right next to you down on the Monongahela. Can't you talk some sense into him? Tell him he simply must not transport those cannons south."

"I doubt he'd listen. Business is business, my good man," said Edmundson, folding his arms in front of him. "Nothing illegal has been done."

"Illegal, no," retorted Gregory, "treasonous, yes. The newspapers say Floyd's been trying to get munitions shipped south from arsenals all over the North."

"I heard they've been shipping out small arms, too, by railroad," said an older gentleman who had sidled up to the edge of the conversation. "Probably have been ever since Lincoln got elected in November. Why, when war breaks out we'll be fired on by guns made right here in Pittsburgh!"

"I say we go down to the wharf and make sure those cannons never get on that ship," said a small, red-faced man, addressing the crowd in general. Other voices rose in agreement.

"Better yet, let's block the gates of the Arsenal," demanded another.

Clara waited for someone to step forward with a less volatile solution, but the voices demanding immediate and forceful action grew louder.

Finally, Clara rose up on tiptoe.

"There's another way to stop it," she called out in an effort to be heard over the din.

"Miss Ambrose," hissed Edgar.

"I said, there's another way to stop the cannons," she insisted more loudly. Edgar grabbed Clara's elbow and attempted to propel her away from the heated exchange.

"Let her speak!" commanded a loud male voice.

The crowd quieted, turned, and parted to reveal the young man Clara had noticed earlier, his brown eyes now serious and locked on Edgar. He was not quite as tall as Edgar, but was broader and more strongly built.

"I said, let the lady speak," the man repeated in a more measured tone.

His challenge distracted Edgar just long enough for Clara to pull her arm free of his grip.

"Sir, the lady was just leaving," Edgar snapped, as annoyed by the young man's interference as he was by Clara's intransigence.

"On the contrary, it appears she would very much like to stay," her defender replied with a slight smile. "And I for one would like to hear what she has to say. Miss?" He nodded to Clara and waited.

A few men in the crowd nudged each other and snickered.

"Yes, let the little lady talk," called a voice from the back. "Maybe she can solve this whole secessionist problem and the country will be saved."

The crowd tittered. Even those ball attendees not part of the original discussion drew closer now, shushing each other so as to hear the exchange. Soon, the only sound was the gentle swishing of fans from the ladies gathered at the edge of the group to witness this shocking breach of etiquette.

Edgar, realizing he had been bested for the moment, decided to take advantage of this opportunity to teach Clara a lesson. With an elaborate bow, he gestured that the floor was hers, stepped back, and folded his arms.

Having suddenly been given the opportunity to voice her opinion, Clara struggled to collect her thoughts, even as she felt the color creep up from the neckline of her gown.

"You were about to say...," the young man urged, his voice not unkind.

"Yes. Well. It seems to me a reckless idea to attempt to storm the Arsenal," Clara began, her voice quavering slightly. "Or the wharf for that matter. You'd be facing trained military men who are armed and under orders to protect United States' property. People are bound to get hurt or killed."

"I see. So you think we should just step aside and let the cannons go to the secessionists?" jeered the man who had originally proposed attacking the wharf.

"No," said Clara. "I think we should use our heads to come up with a solution that will prevent both bloodshed and the shipment of the cannons south."

"And just what do you propose, *general*?" taunted another man.

The crowd chuckled.

Clara, angry now, addressed her remarks to the young man who had championed her, but in a voice all could hear.

"The order to ship the cannons came from the Secretary of War, am I right?"

"Yes," he replied.

"Who has the power to overrule such an order?"

"No one, except the president."

"Well, surely in a town such as this, with its strong political ties and many influential people, there is someone who can get President Buchanan's ear and persuade him that allowing the cannons to be shipped south would prove to be of great danger to the Union."

Her suggestion was met with a surprised silence, followed by low-level muttering.

"Hmm," mused Mr. Gregory, his brows knit in thought. "The president's cousin, Dr. J. S. Spear, lives in Lawrenceville. Perhaps we could prevail upon him to telegraph Mr. Buchanan about the depth of local feeling on this matter." Heads began to nod. "And Attorney General Stanton used to practice law here in Pittsburgh. I'm sure his colleagues in the legal profession could persuade him to speak to the president."

"Yes," said Dr. Powell, stepping in front of Clara. "Then Buchanan would have to take action, if only to silence those who call him a weak leader. Excellent idea, Gregory!"

The crowd echoed his enthusiasm. Clara watched dumbfounded as a number of the men closed ranks around Mr. Gregory. They patted him on the back and congratulated him on his brilliant plan.

"Gentlemen. Gentlemen," said Mr. Gregory. "May I suggest we continue our discussion in one of the lower salons so as not to disturb the festivities here. Ladies, if you will excuse us?"

As the self-important group of men left the ballroom, the orchestra resumed playing. The rest of the crowd drifted away, but not before many of them cast a last disapproving glance at Clara.

The young man who had spoken out for her stood shaking his head. When he saw the incredulous look on Clara's face, he gave her a rueful grin.

"Don't worry, Miss," he said, "I'm sure they're just not used to such wise words coming from so lovely a source. They'll remember it was your idea – if it doesn't work." He bowed. "If I may introduce myself; I'm Garrett Cameron of Allegheny City."

Before she could reply, Edgar stepped forward, a dark look on his face.

"Miss Ambrose, I think it's time I took you home," he said.

"I quite agree, Mr. Gliddon," snapped Clara. She turned and extended an elegant blue-gloved hand to Mr. Cameron. "Sir, I thank you for your kindness."

Mr. Cameron took her hand and bowed again. As he straightened, he gave her a look of frank admiration. Clara blushed. Then, pointedly ignoring the offer of Edgar's arm, she turned and marched out of the ballroom.

Edgar scowled at the young man before hurrying after her.

CHAPTER 2

FOR WHAT SEEMED THE HUNDREDTH time, Clara turned over in bed, yanked at her quilt, and punched the pillow. After the excitement at the ball and the angry, silent carriage ride home with Edgar, she had been unable to sleep. Those arrogant old men, she thought. How dare they appropriate her idea and dismiss her like a child. And Edgar! Rather than congratulate her on her insight, he had berated her for daring to speak at all. She lay there, playing over and over in her mind what she should have done and said to him, to all of them.

Her pleasant thoughts of revenge were interrupted by the sudden and insistent tinkling of the front door bell, followed by the heavy tread of her father descending the stairs. She lay still, listening. Muffled voices spoke briefly, then she heard her father return to his room, only to emerge minutes later and hurry back down the stairs.

Curious, Clara slipped from her bed. In her nightgown and bare feet, she tiptoed down the hall to the head of the stairs. She froze at the sound of her mother's voice coming from the study. She did not want to be drawn into a discussion of the night's events, something she had mercifully avoided earlier in the evening when she arrived home after her parents had retired.

"Who was it this time?" her mother asked, stifling a yawn. "It's two o'clock in the morning."

Clara leaned over the railing. Through the doorway of the study she could see her mother in her dressing gown in front of her father's desk, her arms wrapped around herself for warmth. Her father was packing instruments and medicines into his black bag.

"Mr. Webster's oldest son, Ethan. Mrs. Webster has come down with the catarrh."

"Again?" said her mother.

"Again. I'm taking her these powders to ease her breathing."

"I swear that woman has more ailments than anyone I've ever known. This week it's the catarrh. Last time it was salve for boils. The time before that, it was, what? Ah, yes. Tonic for her sinking spells."

Her mother shook her head. "You'd be better off just opening up a dispensary in her parlor."

"Not a bad idea, Mrs. Ambrose." Her father chuckled. "That would indeed save a great deal of time."

"And for all her illnesses, I must say I've never seen a healthier looking woman in all my days," added her mother.

"Well, sometimes appearances can be deceiving." He snapped his bag closed, walked around the desk, and kissed his wife on the cheek. "The life of a doctor's wife, eh? Don't wait up. I may be a while."

Clara scampered back down the hall. She crossed to the window of her dark bedroom and waited for her father to emerge below. After a few moments, he appeared and paused to turn up the collar of his coat against the cold. She watched him as he opened the front gate, turned left, and hurried down the sidewalk with his long, sure stride. She felt a surge of pride at his uncomplaining dedication to the sick and the poor. He was such a gentle, sincere man, so unlike the pretentious social climbers and office seekers she had met at the ball.

Clara was back in bed, almost asleep, before it occurred to her - the Websters lived in the opposite direction.

Slumped in his leather chair facing the fire, Edgar reached for the decanter of whiskey on the side table and refilled his glass. He was glad the cavernous old house was empty, but for the servants who had long since gone to bed. He was in no mood to talk to anyone. The evening had been a disaster. Not only had he been snubbed by those who mattered, those whose high opinion he had been trying so hard to cultivate, but Clara's outlandish behavior had exposed him to general ridicule.

He raised his glass and took a long sip, reveling in the slight burn at the back of his throat. Goddamn Gregory. Dismissing him like a child. He would have expected better treatment from a friend of his father's. Or, perhaps not, he realized with an audible snort.

And what could have possessed Clara? It was one thing to spout your nascent opinions to a group of society matrons, but to take on some of the most prominent people in Pittsburgh? And in such a public forum? He supposed her father was to blame for filling her young head with silly ideas and needless education. Nevertheless, Edgar would never allow her to embarrass him like that again.

And who was this idiot, Cameron?

Edgar threw back his drink, spilling a few amber drops onto his rumpled white shirtfront. The decanter clinked loudly against the rim of his glass as he filled it once more.

The odd thing was, he grudgingly admitted, what Clara had said made a lot of sense. If you wanted to avoid a war, that is. Which he didn't. Frankly, war would be good for business. The demand for iron would soar, making him a wealthy man in his own right. Then he'd be somebody. Then they'd have to listen to him. His father. Gregory. All of them.

He raised his glass. "To a long and lovely conflict."

On a dreary afternoon a few days later, Clara sat in the window seat of the upstairs hallway reading *Letters to Country Girls* by Jane Swisshelm. Clara had heard about this Pittsburgh-born champion of abolition and women's rights from her father, who had been a frequent reader of her newspaper, the *Pittsburgh Saturday Visiter*. So engrossed was she in her reading, Clara didn't hear the footsteps ascending the stairs.

"You'd best not let Mother see you with that. You know how she feels about 'that woman'."

Clara's older sister, Helen, stood over her with a knowing smile. As always, she looked as if she had just stepped out of *Godey's Lady's Book*. She wore an expensive, gray French serge visiting suit trimmed in black braid at the collar, cuffs, and hem. A matching hat was perched on her perfectly coiffed hair.

"Helen!" Clara leapt to her feet and gave her sister a hug. "I didn't know you were coming for a visit."

"Mama invited me for tea. With the weather so dreary and George always gone to his militia meetings, I think she knew I needed an outing. Honestly, the way those men carry on you'd think they wanted a war to start."

Clara heard the tension in her sister's voice. "How are you feeling?" she asked.

"As big as a house. Oh, I know there isn't much to see yet," said Helen, patting her abdomen, "but all of my clothing is getting so tight. I can't believe I still have almost five months to go. I just can't wait to hold my baby in my arms." She sighed. "Well anyway, Mama said to tell you tea is ready."

"I'll be right down."

Clara scurried to her room. With Helen looking so stylish and put together, it wouldn't do to incur their mother's disapproval by looking disheveled. As she arranged her hair before her dressing table mirror, the front doorbell rang. A friend of Mother's joining them for tea, she assumed.

"Clara. Clara, would you come here please?"

Intrigued by the quizzical tone of her mother's voice, Clara gave a last pat to her hair and hurried down the stairs. At the bottom landing she passed Mary Tierney, their cook, maid, and general housekeeper. She was wearing a black dress with a white ruffled apron and cap. Mary was thirty-three years old and had worked for the Ambrose family since emigrating from Ireland, fifteen years earlier. Never in all that time had Clara ever seen her in a uniform.

"Mary, what in the world are you wearing?" asked Clara.

"'Tis the outfit your mother picked out," hissed Mary. "She says all the *domestics* are wearin' 'em." She rolled her eyes. "I don't see why 'tis that every time your mother decides to put on airs, I'm the one who suffers."

"I think you look *lovely*," teased Clara. She jumped out of the way just in time to avoid being smacked by Mary's broom.

In the front entry, Mrs. Ambrose stood frowning at a small envelope she held in her hand.

"A servant just delivered this for you," she said. She handed the note to Clara and waited expectantly.

Clara examined the unfamiliar handwriting. It was definitely not Edgar's flamboyant script. She had not heard from him since the Holiday Ball; not surprising given the unceremonious manner in which he had deposited her on her doorstep that evening. She had been able to deflect her mother's questions about Edgar by telling her he had said he would be away for a while. In truth, Edgar had told Clara he would not call on her again until she had learned to conduct herself as a "proper lady." As Clara had no intention of doing so, she imagined Edgar would be away for a very long while, indeed.

Clara turned her back on her curious mother, pried open the envelope, and removed a single sheet of paper.

January 4, 1861

Dear Miss Ambrose:

I hope you will not think me too bold, but I inquired as to your identity after you left the dance on Friday past. I wanted to congratulate you on both the courage and good sense you displayed on that occasion in regards to the problem of preventing the movement of the cannons from the Arsenal. In case you were not aware, something very much like the plan you outlined was put into motion by the mayor of Pittsburgh and, just yesterday, the transfer of the cannons was stopped by order of President Buchanan. With cool think-

ing patriots such as you, we may yet avoid the conflict that others deem inevitable.

I pray you will allow me to call upon you in the near future to express my further regards.

Respectfully,
Garrett Cameron

Clara smiled. She would have had to be deaf not to know that the order to ship the cannon had been rescinded. The people of Pittsburgh, in their excitement at having struck the first real blow for the Union, had shot off round after round of celebratory cannon fire from the steep bluffs along the Monongahela River. The thunderous roar had reverberated for miles.

"Who is it from?" Mrs. Ambrose craned her neck for a peek at the signature.

"Just someone I met at the ball," answered Clara. She quickly slipped the note back into the envelope. "A Mr. Cameron."

"Cameron? I don't believe I know any family named Cameron. Do you, Helen?"

Helen, who had emerged from the parlor to find out what was holding up tea, shook her head.

"Is he a friend of Mr. Gliddon's?" asked Mrs. Ambrose.

"I don't think so," said Clara, suppressing a smile.

"Well, who made the introduction?"

"No one," said Clara. "He introduced himself." From behind their mother's shoulder, Helen gave Clara a warning look.

"He did?" Mrs. Ambrose frowned. "Well, who is he? Who are his people?"

"I haven't the slightest idea."

"You know nothing about the man, yet he feels it appropriate to send you a note?"

"It's just a note, Mother," said Clara. "He just wanted to pay me a compliment."

"About what?"

Clara hesitated. She knew she should keep quiet, make something up, but she just couldn't. "My political insight."

"And just how would he know anything about your *political insight?*" said Mrs. Ambrose in a tight voice.

"Well," Clara began, "the men at the ball were arguing about how to stop the Arsenal guns from being sent to the wharf, and I suggested ...."

"Oh, Clara. You didn't," cried Mrs. Ambrose, pressing her hand to her bosom. Helen turned and tiptoed back to the parlor.

"Mama, all I did was give my opinion."

"Clara, how many times have I told you, your opinions are best kept to yourself. No proper lady engages in political discussions, particularly at fancy balls. Either this gentleman ... he is at least a *gentleman*?"

"I believe so."

Mrs. Ambrose gave an exasperated sigh.

"Well, either this gentleman is woefully lacking in his knowledge of the social graces, or I fear your outspokenness has given him the impression you are a ... certain kind of woman."

"Mother!"

"Spare me your indignation, Clara. Such brazen ways are easily misinterpreted, as they obviously were." Mrs. Ambrose gestured to the envelope in Clara's hand.

"But it's just a note!" repeated Clara.

"A note to which you will not respond," said her mother in a tone that brooked no argument. "Now, we'll discuss this no further. Come in for tea." She turned and marched toward the parlor.

"Yes, Mother." Clara scowled at her mother's receding back. But when she looked down at the note in her hand, her lips curved into a smile.

"Papa, may I join you this morning?" Clara called from the porch. Her father was at the curb, checking the harness of his carriage horse in preparation for making his morning calls.

"Of course. I'd be glad to have the company."

Clara grabbed her coat and flew down the front steps. Since she had been a little girl, she had loved accompanying her father on visits to his patients. Of late, he had even begun to let her assist with some minor procedures. She had been pleased to discover that, except for some initial queasiness, she was able to withstand the sight of broken bones, blood, and infection with composure. Her participation was something they both enjoyed – and both kept quiet from her mother and grandmother, who disapproved of her "traipsing around town like a common working girl."

"What a beautiful day," Clara said as she climbed into the carriage. She declined the lap robe her father offered. "It must be almost sixty degrees."

"Yes. But these January thaws make for a lot of sick patients when the cold weather returns. I don't need that much business. Git up, Hippocrates!"

The carriage horse set off at a smart trot and, without guidance, turned left onto Butler Street to Dr. Ambrose's first call. On this beautiful morning the sidewalks were filled with people out doing their errands or just enjoying the warm spell. Almost everyone had a smile or a greeting for the well-regarded Dr. Ambrose.

Butler Street was the main thoroughfare of Lawrenceville and ran roughly parallel to the Allegheny River through the entire length of the town. Founded in 1814 by William B. Foster, father of the popular songwriter Stephen Foster, the town was named for Captain James Lawrence, the naval hero of 1812, famous for his dying declaration, "Don't give up the ship." Originally settled by the English and Scots-Irish, Lawrenceville had spent most of its early years as a quiet farming community.

By 1861, however, the face of Lawrenceville, and Pittsburgh as a whole, was changing rapidly. The increasing industrialization of America made the coal rich area around Pittsburgh, with its abundant waterways for transportation of raw materials and finished goods, an attractive location for entrepreneurs. New mills and foundries began to spring up all along the Allegheny, Monongahela, and Ohio Rivers. At the same time, a steady influx of Irish immigrants fleeing the effects of the potato famine in their homeland, as well as German immigrants seeking religious freedom, were drawn to Pittsburgh by the availability of unskilled jobs in these same mills and foundries. These immigrants settled close to their places of work. The largest German settlement was in Allegheny City on the north side of the Allegheny River, while the Irish grouped together on Creeghan's Hill between Pittsburgh and Lawrenceville, near St. Paul's Cathedral in downtown Pittsburgh, and along the Allegheny River in Lawrenceville.

Most of the middle and upper levels of Pittsburgh society were alarmed by this flood of new immigrants with their foreign tongues and religions, but Clara found them a source of endless fascination. With their strange accents, foods, and customs, they gave her a glimpse into a larger world outside of Lawrenceville; a world she longed to see.

Only a block down Butler Street, the Ambrose carriage reached the western edge of the Allegheny Arsenal. The thirty-eight acre Arsenal dominated the town of Lawrenceville. Situated just two and half miles east of Pittsburgh, this armory complex was built by the United States government in 1814 to manufacture gun carriages, horse and infantry equipment, and ammunition for the United States military. The Arsenal also served as a storage, inspection, and repair facility for the cannon and small arms made at the nearby Fort Pitt Foundry.

Butler Street bisected the Arsenal into two halves, both of which were surrounded by stone walls and guarded by uniformed soldiers at the various gates. As their carriage rattled past the castle-like main gate, Clara glimpsed soldiers and civilian workers hurrying between buildings. Groups of laughing, jostling young boys, whose small dexterous fingers were deemed ideally suited for assembling bullet cartridges, sauntered to their workstations. Wagons loaded with iron-banded wooden kegs, stamped with the name *Dupont*, rumbled toward the large laboratory buildings on the upper grounds to deliver the gunpowder needed to fill the cartridges and shells. And lined up throughout the grounds were rows and rows of cannons and stockpiles of cannonballs. The Arsenal had always employed a great many soldiers and civilians, but it was obvious from the level of current activity that that number was increasing as the threat of war loomed.

The sight of the cannons reminded Clara of the incident at the Holiday Ball and Mr. Cameron's gallant defense of her right to speak. Two weeks had passed since she had received his note and she had heard nothing further from him. She supposed she had been just a passing diversion for him; the note and promise to call, a polite gesture, quickly forgotten. She tried to brush off his silence as inconsequential, but was surprised at how disappointed she felt.

At Main Street, Dr. Ambrose turned the carriage right and stopped at a small frame house to check on the progress of a boy who had broken his arm while attempting to sled down the steep street after a snowstorm. After a short detour onto Fisk Street to treat an old man for rheumatism, they continued up the hill to the Orphans' Home near Penn Street to examine an infant who had been abandoned on the orphanage steps the week before.

As they climbed, they passed the large brick home of the Lovett family. Mr. Lovett was a successful Pittsburgh dry goods merchant who preferred to raise his family in the quieter, cleaner surroundings of Lawrenceville. On this day, they found him standing astride the furrows of the dormant vegetable garden in his side yard. Beside him, a young man in work clothes was nodding vigorously.

"Hello, Mr. Lovett," called Dr. Ambrose. "How are you this fine day?"

Mr. Lovett strolled over to the white picket fence that bordered his property. "I'm quite well, Dr. Ambrose. Taking advantage of the warm weather to go over some plans for the spring planting with my hired man. And how are you, Miss Clara?"

"Fine, thank you, Mr. Lovett." She frowned slightly. "But, where's Old Jack?"

Old Jack, really only in his late thirties, was a Negro who had worked for the Lovett family as a gardener and handyman for over ten years. Dr. Ambrose had treated him on occasion for minor illnesses and injuries. Once, when Clara was eight years old, Old Jack had whittled a little horse for her out of beech wood. She still had it somewhere.

Mr. Lovett glanced at Dr. Ambrose.

"Didn't I tell you, Clara?" said her father. "Old Jack disappeared last fall while you were still at school."

"Disappeared?"

"There was a rumor there were slave catchers in town looking for someone who fit his description," said Mr. Lovett.

"Old Jack was a runaway slave?" said Clara, incredulous.

Mr. Lovett shrugged. "Or afraid he'd be mistaken for one."

"But, that's horrible," said Clara. "This was his home. Where would he go?"

"Farther north, probably," said her father. "There are still people willing to help runaway slaves reach safety, a kind of underground railroad to freedom. Don't you worry. Old Jack was pretty smart. I'm sure he's just fine."

Mr. Lovett nodded encouragingly.

"Poor Old Jack," said Clara as they drove away a few minutes later. "It must have been awful for him, always living in fear. No one should have to live like that."

"No," agreed her father. "No one should."

When they finished their call at the Orphans' Home, Dr. Ambrose headed east on Grant Street, then turned onto St. Mary's Street for the long trek back downhill. On their right, they passed the Catholic graveyard with its stone markers and crosses. Next to it was the one-story, wood-frame Saint Mary's Catholic Church. Just the year before, a seventy-foot addition had been added to the original structure. The footprint of the building now resembled a cross.

"I can't believe how much bigger the church looks now," said Clara.

"Yes," said her father. "With so many Irish coming to the area, they needed the extra room. You know, I remember when they dug the foundation for the original church eight years ago. The Know-Nothings came at night and filled it in. But, the Irish re-dug it and set up guards with pick-axes to protect the church while building continued."

"The Know-Nothings?" said Clara.

"That's what we used to call members of the so-called *American Party*." He grimaced. "It was an entire political party made up of people who saw immigrants as a threat to what they called *real* Americans. Had quite a following for a while, including Pittsburgh's fool of a mayor, Joe Barker. They were anti-immigrant and, especially, anti-Catholic. Caused all kinds of trouble and violence. But, whenever any of them were confronted about their involvement, they'd protest they *knew nothing*. Hence the name."

"Why did they hate the Irish so?" asked Clara.

"Not just the Irish. They hated all immigrants. I guess there were just more Irish to hate. As to why they hated them?" He shrugged. "Because they were different. Because they were poor. Because they had their own language, customs, and religion. You'll find, Clara, people are often frightened by things and people that are different. And fear can quickly turn to hatred."

"I'm glad those days are over."

"My dear girl, I'm afraid they're far from over. Even today it's not safe for any Catholic man to pass by the coal yards at 28th Street alone. Mr. Burke told me that just last year, when the men of Saint Mary's wanted to attend a mission at St. Paul's Cathedral in Pittsburgh, they had to first meet at the Arsenal, then march as a group for their own safety."

"Well, that's just ridiculous," said Clara with a toss of her head. "Speaking of the Burkes, may we stop by their home today? I haven't seen Annie in such a long time."

All the holiday activities and her mother's watchful eye had prevented Clara from getting over to see her best friend. She couldn't wait to tell her about the ball, Edgar, and the elusive Mr. Cameron.

"I think we can do that," said her father. "I should check on Mr. Burke's arm, anyway. I want to make sure that burn he received at the iron mill is healing properly."

Dr. Ambrose had been treating the Burke family since they moved to Lawrenceville from New York City almost eighteen years ago, just before the fourth little Burke boy was born. Now there were seven children, four boys and three girls, the last four of whom Dr. Ambrose had delivered. The oldest daughter, Annie, was just a year younger than Clara. Over the years, the girls had become fast friends and confidantes, and Clara begged to visit whenever possible. Predictably, Clara's mother and grandmother disapproved.

"But Mama," Clara had protested one day when she was nine, "we're Irish, too. You said so."

"Scots-Irish, Clara," replied her mother. "There's a big difference."

"A big difference," sniffed her grandmother. "The Burkes are Papists. They're building a tunnel, you know. Right under the ocean. Going to try to bring the Pope over here to lord it over all of us, you understand," she added with an ominous nod.

Clara didn't understand, but after that she kept quiet about her visits to Annie. She did mention the tunnel to Mrs. Burke once, but the woman got to laughing so hard that Clara decided there was nothing to fear. Besides, Annie was her friend and that was good enough for her. Dr. Ambrose recognized the special relationship between the two girls and, in a rare display of authority, informed his wife that the girls were to be allowed to continue their friendship. Still, even after all these years, Clara and her father had an unspoken pact not to reveal the exact frequency of their visits to the Burkes.

The Burke's house was in the Irish section of Lawrenceville, on the lower part of St. Mary's Street near the Allegheny Valley Railroad Company and the factories along the river. When they pulled abreast of the house, Mrs. Burke was in the side yard hanging damp clothes on a line to dry in the sooty, chill breeze.

"Good morning, Mrs. Burke," called Dr. Ambrose. He reined in the horse and tipped his hat. "Taking advantage of the fine weather to do some laundry, I see."

"Fine weather or no, there's always laundry to do with this band of heathens," said Mrs. Burke with a wry smile. Smoothing her hair into place as best she could, she came over to the fence by the road. "And how are you, Dr. Cameron? Clara?"

"Fine, thank you," he answered for both of them. "How's Mr. Burke's arm coming along? I could take a look at it if you'd like."

"Then you'd have to be drivin' out to the mill. He went back to work yesterday. Said he's on the mend and feelin' fit as a fiddle. Good thing, too. They were about to give his job to someone else."

Dr. Ambrose frowned. He knew Mr. Burke's arm was far from healed and it was the fear of losing his job that had driven him back to work so soon. "Well, if he has any problem with it, you let me know right away."

"Thank you, Doctor."

"Mrs. Burke, is Annie at home today?" asked Clara.

Before she could answer, a petite young woman came hurrying around from the back of the house. The sleeves of her water-spattered homespun dress were pushed up, and her dark hair was a frizzy halo from hovering over a steaming laundry tub. But her blue eyes lit up at the sight of Clara and she flashed a shy, dimpled smile as she approached the carriage.

"Annie Burke, I swear you get prettier every time I see you," said Dr. Ambrose. Annie blushed as red as her soap-roughened hands.

"Papa," said Clara, "would you mind if I visited with Annie while you make your last few calls? That is, if Mrs. Burke can spare her." Both girls looked to the older woman hopefully.

Mrs. Burke put her hands on her hips. "It's precious little work I'd get out of her the rest of the day if I said 'no'."

Dr. Ambrose chuckled. "I'll be back to pick you up in, say, half an hour?"

"Thank you, Papa," said Clara. She kissed his cheek before leaping from the wagon.

To avoid the many eyes and ears in the Burke household, the two girls decided to take a stroll around the neighborhood. They linked arms and headed up the street.

"So, tell me before you burst," said Annie.

"Oh, Annie, you'll never believe what happened at the Holiday Ball."

Annie gasped in mock horror. "You finally did it. You strangled Edgar Gliddon."

"No," giggled Clara. "Not that I didn't want to."

"Pity. Go on."

"Well, we arrived at the ball and Edgar was being his usual pretentious self …."

"Wait!" said Annie. "Go back. I want to hear all the details. Tell me what you wore, what he wore. Did he pick you up in a fancy carriage with matched horses? And the ballroom. How was it decorated? Oh, and the ladies' ball gowns. Tell me about them. Don't leave anythin' out."

Clara laughed. She had forgotten how much Annie enjoyed hearing about the trappings of society events. Things that Clara no longer took notice of were like icing on an elaborate cake to Annie. Clara described as much as she could remember about that evening – the clothes, the conversation, the music, the dancing – finally ending with, "… and then I met this man." She paused for effect.

Annie raised an eyebrow. "Ah, so that's what's put the twinkle in your eye."

Clara proceeded to tell Annie about Garrett Cameron and how he had championed her right to speak at the ball.

"You spoke out in front of all those high society people?" interrupted Annie.

"I had to," said Clara. "They weren't making any sense."

"Jesus, Mary, and Joseph," said Annie, shaking her head.

"Don't worry. They didn't listen to me anyway." Clara's expression softened. "But, Mr. Cameron said I was both wise and lovely."

"Did he, now?" said Annie. "I'm going to guess Mr. Gliddon wasn't as appreciative."

"You could say that. On the carriage ride home, he told me he wouldn't call on me again until I'd learned to act like a *proper lady*."

"*Proper lady*, indeed. Good riddance, I say. He isn't near good enough for you."

"Tell that to my mother."

Annie looked at her friend, aghast. "You didn't tell her, did you?"

"No, I'm not that brave," said Clara. "But, she did find out about Mr. Cameron, because four days later he sent a note to my home."

"He didn't! What did it say?"

"He complimented me on my bravery and good sense, and said he'd liked to call on me."

"And, has he?"

"That's the problem. It's been two weeks and I've not heard another word."

"Well, there could be lots of reasons for that," said Annie. "Those society types are always travelin' about on business. Perhaps he's been away."

"Or, perhaps he found out that the woman he thought was high class is just the daughter of a small town doctor," said Clara.

"I doubt that would make a difference. It didn't discourage Edgar Gliddon or any of those other hoity-toity suitors of yours."

"No." Clara giggled. "I did that myself." Her smile faded. "It doesn't matter anyway. The whole thing's ridiculous. I don't even know anything about him."

Annie gave her friend a long look. "But, you'd like to?"

Clara shrugged.

"Well, I, for one, hope he calls," said Annie.

"Why?"

"Because I'd like to see the man who can put that expression on your face."

And for the first time since Annie could remember, her friend actually blushed.

Dr. Ambrose and Clara waved goodbye to the Burkes and headed home at a brisk trot, the horse as eager for dinner as they. Halfway down Butler Street they came upon Mr. Webster, a wholesale grocer and the husband of Dr. Ambrose's most frequent patient. He was driving towards them in a wagon piled high with wooden crates and barrels.

"Hello, Doctor. Miss Ambrose," called Mr. Webster. He reined in his team and tipped his battered hat.

"You're hard at work I see, William," said Dr. Ambrose.

"Yes, Sir. Had a special delivery to make to the wharf early this morning."

"Business is good then?"

"Too good." Mr. Webster rubbed his brow. "Expecting another order next week; a big one. I'll tell you, I'm looking forward to the day when I can get out of this line of work altogether."

Clara's father nodded. "Did your wife benefit from the cold powders I prescribed?"

Mr. Webster frowned. "My wife? Oh, yes. Yes, she did. Fixed her up good as new. Thank you, Doctor. Well, I'd best be on my way." He touched the brim of his hat. "Miss Ambrose. Nice to see you again. Give my regards to your lovely mother."

"I will," said Clara. "Good bye, Mr. Webster."

"God's speed, William," said Dr. Ambrose. Mr. Webster slapped the reins across his team's backs and rumbled away.

"Papa," said Clara, "if Mr. Webster wants to retire, why doesn't he just hand the business over to his son, Ethan? He's old enough to run it."

Dr. Ambrose smiled. "I don't think Ethan has quite the expertise or the contacts to run Mr. Webster's business just yet. And, I suspect Mr. Webster isn't really ready to retire. A man like that doesn't quit a job until it's finished."

Clara smiled. Only her father could make the humble job of a grocer sound so noble.

CHAPTER 3

AS DR. AMBROSE PREDICTED, THE cold weather returned with a vengeance during the third week of January and brought with it both snow and an unexpected invitation.

"A sleigh ride. With the Ward sisters! Oh, Clara, this is wonderful." Mrs. Ambrose practically giggled in her excitement. "I don't need to tell you that the Wards are one of the most prominent families in Allegheny City. They have that beautiful stone home on Ridge Avenue, just up the road from the Darlingtons."

As her mother prattled on, Clara stared at the folded note with *The Misses Ward* engraved on the front flap. She knew Lucinda and Marie Ward only casually, having met them at a few of the luncheons and dances her mother forced her to attend. They had exchanged only a few words, hardly enough to warrant an invitation to a sleighing party.

"See," her mother was saying, "I told you if you associated with the right people, you'd soon be admitted into their circle of friends. And who knows what kind of young men you might meet at a party such as this?"

"Hmm," said Clara as she tapped the envelope against her lip.

"Now, Clara," said mother. "You simply must go. It's important to your future. And even if you don't meet someone there, I'm sure this will lead to other invitations, and ...."

"You're right."

"Pardon me?"

"You're right," Clara repeated. "I should go. It's time I met some new people."

Mrs. Ambrose's stunned expression gave way to one of joy.

"Wonderful!" she said, clapping her hands together. "Now, we must think about what you'll wear. Oh! I know just the thing. Grandmother Ambrose's beaver-trimmed hat and coat. I think they're in a trunk in the attic. Mary. Mary!"

Mrs. Ambrose scurried off in search of the housekeeper. Clara followed behind with an enigmatic smile on her lips.

* * *

"Miss Ambrose! I'm so glad you could join us this evening." Lucinda Ward swept into the marble foyer of the Ridge Avenue home in a flurry of petticoats and fur-trimmed wool. She gave Clara a quick hug and extended her hand to Clara's father. "And Dr. Ambrose. It's been a long time."

"Yes, Miss Ward." Dr. Ambrose took her hand and bowed. "I believe the last time I saw you, you were eleven years old and quite covered with red spots."

"Father!" said Clara.

Lucinda laughed. "Don't worry, Miss Ambrose. My father delights in embarrassing me, too. He's out at the moment, but I'm sure he'd enjoy seeing you, Dr. Ambrose. Would you like to wait for him? I'm expecting him shortly."

"Thank you, Miss Ward. Perhaps another time. I have a previous appointment and I'm running a bit late. Please give him my regards."

Just then, a muscular young man with wavy brown hair descended the mahogany staircase. Clara, her suspicions confirmed, felt her pulse quicken.

"Garrett. Good. You're just in time," said Lucinda. "Dr. Ambrose, I'd like you to meet our houseguest, Mr. Garrett Cameron." Garrett stepped forward and shook Dr. Ambrose's hand. "And I believe you've already met Miss Ambrose."

"Oh?" said Clara's father.

"Just briefly, Sir," responded Garrett. "I had the pleasure of making Miss Ambrose's acquaintance at the Holiday Ball. It's nice to see you again, Miss Ambrose." He bowed politely to Clara. She responded with a curt nod.

"Mr. Cameron is my father's godson," said Lucinda. "He's staying with us while he reads law at my father's firm."

"How fortunate for you, Mr. Cameron," said Dr. Ambrose. "Mr. Ward is one of the most successful lawyers in both Allegheny City and Pittsburgh."

"Yes, Sir. I'm most fortunate," said Garrett.

"Well, I will take my leave and let you young people get on with the evening's activity," said Dr. Ambrose. "Have a good time all." With an encouraging smile only Clara could see, he exited with a bow.

Lucinda wrapped her arm through Clara's. "Well, Miss Ambrose, while we wait for the rest of our party to arrive, let me introduce you to the guests that are already here."

Lucinda steered her toward the parlor. Clara was acutely aware of Garrett following behind.

In the parlor, a number of young people were warming themselves in front of the fire. The only one Clara recognized was Lucinda's younger sister, Marie. Conversation stopped when Clara entered the room and they all turned to stare.

"Everyone," said Lucinda, "I'd like you to meet Miss Clara Ambrose of Lawrenceville. Her father, Dr. Peter Ambrose, is a friend of Father's. Miss Ambrose, this is our neighbor, Lawrence Gilbert, and our friends, Catherine Porter and James and Morgan Percy, all from Allegheny City."

James Percy came forward. "Lucinda, where have you been hiding this exquisite creature?" He bowed his dark head over Clara's hand.

"Far away from your clutches, James," teased Lucinda. "Forgive our informality, Miss Ambrose, but we've all been friends since childhood."

Garrett stepped to Clara's side. James' expression tightened ever so slightly, registering the challenge.

"Oh, Garrett, forgive me," said Lucinda. "You all remember Garrett Cameron. I think most of you met him when he visited last summer."

"Of course," said James. "So, Cameron, how goes the study of law?"

"Very well, thank you, Percy. How goes the coal business?"

"Busy and getting busier. Mr. Lincoln's election has had at least one good effect. It's increased the saber rattling between the North and the South to such a pitch that every factory is gearing up for war, which means, of course, more coal."

"Nothing like a little civil war to increase profits, eh James?" said Lawrence, resting his forearm on the fireplace mantel.

"Money is money, Lawrence," James replied, "and until war is declared – if it is declared – I shall sell to whomever is willing to buy. We are all still Americans, are we not? Even if we do not all worship at the altar of that Republican upstart, Lincoln."

"Oh, please. Not this again," said Marie as she plopped down into a chair.

"You'll have to forgive my brother," said Morgan Percy to Clara. His warm smile and open features were in sharp contrast to his brother's coiled intensity. "He's an avowed Democrat who has yet to recover from Stephen Douglas's loss in the last election."

"We could have easily defeated Lincoln," countered James, "had the southern Democrats not stormed off and thrown their support behind Breckinridge. Not to mention the votes siphoned off by Bell and his damn Constitutional Union Party. Oh, excuse me, ladies," he added and bowed in apology.

"I doubt Bell's *Old Gentlemen's Party* had a significant affect on Douglas's chances," said Lawrence. "Admit it, James. As soon as the Democrats split at the convention in Baltimore, Lincoln had it won."

"Perhaps," said James, "for all the good it will do him. Lincoln may have garnered more votes than any of the other three candidates, but he did not win a majority of the popular vote."

"Well, that's a little hard to do when most of the southern states refused to even put him on the ballot," observed Lawrence.

"Regardless," James waved away this objection, "he's a minority president with no clear mandate from the people. And his attempt to force his anti-slavery ideas on the good people of the southern states will split this country in two, you mark my words."

"Did you actually read any of Lincoln's speeches, Percy?" asked Garrett. "He only opposes the expansion of slavery into the territories. He's promised to leave it alone in those states in which it already exists. He wants to *preserve* the Union."

James snickered. "If you believe that, you're more naïve than I thought."

"James …," admonished Morgan.

"My apology, Cameron," said James with unconvincing contrition. "But, whatever Lincoln's stated position, the southern states obviously see him as a direct threat to their way of life. South Carolina, Mississippi, Florida, and Alabama have already seceded."

"And Georgia," added Lawrence.

James nodded. "And rumor has it Texas is about to join them. What's that, six states so far? Some Union."

"Why don't we wait to hear what Lincoln has to say about the situation when he gets here next month," said Garrett.

Lucinda straightened in her chair. "Lincoln is coming to Pittsburgh?"

"Yes," said Lawrence, "on his way to his inauguration. His schedule was just announced."

"How exciting," said Marie. "I've never seen a real live president before. I wonder if he's as ugly as they say."

"Will he be speaking?" asked Clara.

"Undoubtedly," said Lawrence. "People are clamoring for information on what he plans to do about the secession crisis."

"Do?" said James. "His abolitionist policies have *caused* the secession crisis."

"Surely, Mr. Percy, you're not in favor of slavery?" said Clara.

"My dear Miss Ambrose," said James, turning an indulgent smile on Clara, "I'm in favor of a peaceful resolution to this crisis. I frankly don't care about slavery one way or the other, but I hardly think it's worth dissolving the Union over. Let the southern states have their slaves and their way of life. And truly, how different is slavery from the way we treat our foreign-born workers here in the north?"

"Very different," interjected Garrett. "At least the foreign-born workers have some say over where they do and don't work. They have basic rights as human beings."

"In theory, perhaps," James responded. "But I think if you took a tour of the mills and foundries and the hovels where these people live, you'd see there's very little practical difference. In fact, the slaves may be better off. At least they have someone to care for them when they get sick or old. In the north, when our workers have ceased their usefulness, they're pretty much discarded. No, I don't think this little spat between the states has very much at all to do with human rights and everything to do with who wields the power in this country."

"I disagree," said Garrett. "Whether people realize it or not, the question of slavery is at the very heart of this dispute. And until it is eradicated, we have no right to call ourselves a country of free men."

James snorted derisively. "Good grief, Cameron. Even Lincoln doesn't go that far." He turned to Clara. "I don't know if you're aware, Miss Ambrose, but our Mr. Cameron, here, intends to build a career on righting all the wrongs of the world. Although, how he expects to make a living representing every mick, hessian, and darkie that gets caught stealing a sausage from the meat wagon, I'll never know."

Garrett took a step toward James.

"All right, you two," said Lucinda, coming between them. "This is a sleighing party, not a political debate."

"Of course, Lucinda. Forgive us," said James, but his eyes on Garrett were cold.

Just then, Stewart Oliver and his sister, Honoria, burst into the room.

"Sorry we're so late," chirped Honoria.

"Honoria just couldn't leave home until she found the exact gloves to match her hat," said Stewart, rolling his eyes. "What have we missed?"

"Oh, just the usual war talk," said Marie.

"Again? Then I'm *not* sorry we're late," said Honoria as she tucked a few stray hairs up into her fox-fur hat.

"Don't worry," said Lucinda. "The gentlemen have promised to be on their best behavior for the rest of the evening." She gave a pointed look to James and Garrett. "Now, let me introduce you both to Miss Clara Ambrose and we'll be on our way."

Reclaiming their outerwear from the butler, the laughing, chattering group tumbled outside to find three sleighs waiting: a green, six-passenger Albany sleigh and two sleek black Portland cutters. The two-seater cutters were each pulled by matched sets of bay Morgans with bells affixed to their harnesses. Two enormous gray Percherons, the very newest breed of draft horse, stood hitched to the larger sleigh. Plumes of warm air billowed from their nostrils like steam from a train engine anxious to leave the station.

"Come on!" cried Lawrence. He grabbed Lucinda's hand and hurried to one of the Portland cutters. James Percy commandeered the other and, after a moment of hesitation in which he looked from Clara to Garrett, held his hand out for Catherine to join him. The remaining six guests piled into the larger Albany sleigh, two to a seat, with Morgan Percy taking the reins. Clara found herself in the back seat with Garrett Cameron.

"May I?" he said, and began tucking a buffalo lap robe around their legs.

Before Clara could reply, James called out, "Everyone ready?" and cracked the whip over the backs of his team. They galloped off through the crisp, cold night with the other sleighs in pursuit.

Despite the fresh snow that had fallen that day, the heavily traveled streets were still bare in places, so the drivers took to the virgin fields and pastures. The sleigh runners shushed through the powder and each sharp turn kicked up a fine spray that elicited shrieks and howls from the riders. The cold wind made Clara's eyes water and rendered small talk virtually impossible, a fact for which she was grateful. She wasn't exactly sure how she had ended up sharing a lap robe with Garrett Cameron and was not at all certain she liked it. She pulled the robe up around her chin and stole a glance at him. She couldn't help but think he looked even more handsome in his winter hat and coat than he had in his formal attire; more natural, somehow. Quickly, she turned away before he caught her staring.

The party raced over the snowy fields, the smaller sleighs vying to be the first through each pasture gate. At a tight corner, the sleigh carrying James and Catherine overturned and dumped its passengers into a deep drift. The others quickly pulled to a stop and circled back.

"Are they all right?" asked Clara in alarm.

"Yes, they're fine," said Garrett. "See."

Sure enough, James and Catherine were laughing as they climbed to their feet and shook the snow from their hair and fur collars. The occupants of the other sleighs scrambled out to help them. All except Clara and Garrett.

"Couldn't have happened to a nicer fellow," observed Garrett.

"You don't like Mr. Percy much, do you?" said Clara.

"Well, I haven't known him that long, but … no. I can't say that I do. I'm afraid James Percy is a little too taken with his wealth and position in society. He operates under the mistaken assumption that he's earned it. I guess that's one of the hazards of being born with money."

"So, do you suffer from the same affliction?" asked Clara.

Garrett laughed. "Hardly." He gave her a searching look. "I take it that's important to you."

"What?"

"Money. Position."

"Not particularly." Clara turned and pretended to be engrossed in watching Morgan, James, and Lawrence right the overturned sleigh. Garrett stared at the back of her head with a baffled expression.

"Well, forgive me," he said after a moment, "but I can't think of any other reason why a woman of your obvious intelligence would endure the attentions of someone like Edgar Gliddon."

Clara whipped around to face him.

"I beg your pardon! You don't know anything about me. Or Mr. Gliddon, for that matter." The fact that he had placed her in the loathsome position of having to defend Edgar only heightened her indignation.

"I know enough to know Edgar Gliddon would never treat a woman as anything but an ornament or a temporary amusement."

"You're a fine one to talk," said Clara. "I suppose you've completely forgotten about the note you sent me after the Holiday Ball."

"I most certainly have not."

"Well, then?"

"Well, what?"

Clara looked at him with disdain. "Oh, I see. I guess it's hard to find the time to meet an obligation to a mere doctor's daughter when one is caught up in the social whirl of Ridge Avenue."

"What in the world are you talking about?" said Garrett. "You're the one who didn't have time for me."

"I beg your pardon?" said Clara.

"Three days after I sent the note, I came to your door to pay you a formal visit. Your maid informed me you weren't receiving. I left my carte de visite in hopes I might hear from you. When I didn't, I assumed you'd found out I was just a poor law student and were no longer interested."

"Mr. Cameron," said Clara in a more contrite tone, "I assure you, I had no knowledge of your visit." How odd, she thought. Mary would certainly have told her he had come to call. Unless …. Her eyes narrowed.

Garrett gave her a puzzled look. "So … you thought I never bothered to call because … and I thought …" He chuckled as the realization hit him. "Well, Miss Ambrose, it appears we've both been operating under a misunderstanding."

"Yes, it does," said Clara. They sat in silence for a moment, the atmosphere between them distinctly changed.

"But, wait a minute," said Garrett. "If you thought I'd snubbed you as not being high class enough, why did you come tonight? Surely you must have suspected I was behind the invitation."

Clara lowered her eyes. "I suspected," she said.

"Then why did you come?" he asked again.

Clara was determined not to show her hand first. "Well," she parried, "if you thought I'd snubbed you because you weren't wealthy enough, why did you invite me?"

Garrett's expression softened. "I suppose … I hoped I was wrong."

His candor disarmed her.

"So did I," she said with a shy smile.

Just then, the others returned from righting the sleigh.

"So that's how it is, eh Cameron?" said Morgan as he helped Honoria into the sleigh. "You stay here nice and warm while we do all the work."

"You seemed to have things well in hand," said Garrett.

"As do you," Morgan smirked.

Once everyone was seated, they set off again, at a slower pace this time. The flurries had stopped and the sky cleared. Morgan began singing *Silent Night* in a clear tenor complemented by the whisper of the sleigh runners and the soft tinkling of the harness bells. The other couples sang along or talked quietly. Stars twinkled overhead and the trees cast blue/black shadows on the moonlit snow. Clara thought she had never seen a more beautiful night.

"Miss Ambrose," said Garrett, "if I may ask, how did you fare with the eminent Mr. Gliddon after you left the Holiday Ball?"

"That's a rather personal question, Mr. Cameron," said Clara.

"Perhaps, but I've always thought it wise to learn as much as one can about one's adversaries."

"You consider Mr. Gliddon an adversary?"

"That's what I'm trying to determine," said Garrett. His look was both playful and intent. "In any event, I fear his first impression of me was not a favorable one."

"Nor was his last impression of me, I'm afraid," said Clara. She hastened to conceal her slip. "And, if I may ask, which of the two charming Ward sisters were you escorting to the ball that night?"

"Why, Miss Ambrose," said Garrett, "that, too, is a rather personal question. But, since you inadvertently answered mine, I will tell you. Mr. Ward was called away suddenly on business and I was enlisted to escort his daughters to the ball. I assure you, there's no romantic interest on my part in either of the young ladies. They are delightful in their own way, but rather ... traditional ... in their spheres of interest."

Clara's eyes twinkled. "You did appear a bit bored."

"Desperately," he confided, lowering his voice so as not to offend his hostesses. "Which is why I found your opinions - and your courage to express them - so refreshing."

"Then I fear you constitute a minority of one, Mr. Cameron. My comments were obviously not welcomed ... nor acknowledged."

"Nonetheless, you were proved right."

Clara cocked her head. "Mr. Cameron, either you're trying to impress me, or you're one of the most progressive-minded men I've met in a good while."

He grinned.

The sleighs left the fields and glided up and over the small drift at the side of the road onto Ridge Avenue. Up ahead they could see the blazing lights of the Ward mansion. As they pulled up in front, Garrett leaned over to Clara.

"Now that we've settled the question of our respective monetary worth, or lack thereof, would you consider allowing me to call on you?"

Any hesitation Clara might have felt in accepting his offer was dispelled by the thought of her mother's expression when Garrett showed up on their doorstep.

"Yes, Mr. Cameron. You may. Shall we say, next Sunday, about 3:00 p.m.?"

"I look forward to it, Miss Ambrose."

Dr. Ambrose hung his hat and coat on the rack in foyer. The drive home from Allegheny City always took longer than he expected. He couldn't wait to warm his icy feet by the parlor fire.

To his mild annoyance, he found Grandmother Blake already hunched near the hearth in her wheelchair, her corded hands resting on the same unidentifiable object she had been knitting for the past month. Despite the warmth of the room, she wore a wool shawl around the shoulders of her plain but expensive silk dress, both items black out of respect for her late husband. Her head was covered in an old-fashioned white cotton cap from which protruded three carefully arranged ringlets at each temple, a style that had been popular in her youth. Although she rarely ventured out of the house, Grandmother Blake was very particular about her appearance, and Dr. Ambrose marveled at the patience of his wife, who dutifully spent an hour each morning helping her mother dress and arrange her hair just the way she liked.

"Hello, Mother Blake," said Dr. Ambrose as he sank into his chair. "Are you feeling any better?"

The old woman started at the sound of his voice, then peered accusingly at him through her octagonal eyeglasses. "No," she snapped. "That medicine you gave me for my stomach upset isn't working at all."

No wonder, he thought. His mother-in-law had an incorrigible sweet tooth and had eaten almost half of the lemon cake Mary had made for dessert for dinner.

"Well, just give it time," he advised. "I think you'll find you're feeling better in a few more hours."

Grandmother Blake's dubious response was cut short when Mrs. Ambrose burst into the parlor.

"Well? How was it?" she demanded as she hurried to her husband's side.

"How was what?" said Dr. Ambrose.

"The sleighing party."

"I don't know. I left right away for a meeting at the Avery Institute."

"Oh, dear. You didn't tell the Wards where you were going, did you?"

"No, I don't believe I mentioned it. Why?"

"Why? Because not everyone feels the same way you do, Peter. Some people – good people, prominent people – might look askance at your involvement with known abolitionists and free Negroes. This is such a wonderful opportunity for Clara, being invited to join in with this particular group of young socialites. I just don't want you to do anything that might jeopardize her chances."

At the dark look on her husband's face, Mrs. Ambrose changed the subject.

"So, did you speak to Mr. Ward?"

"No," said Dr. Ambrose. "He was out when we arrived."

"Well, you didn't just leave Clara on the doorstep, did you?"

"Of course not. I took her inside and spoke to Miss Ward for a few minutes."

"Which one?"

"Lucinda, I believe."

"What did the house look like?" interrupted Grandmother Blake.

"Well, I was only in the foyer," said Dr. Ambrose, "but it was nice."

"Nice?" Mrs. Ambrose rolled her eyes.

"Were there servants? In uniform?" asked Grandmother Blake.

"I suppose. I only saw the butler."

"A butler," said Grandmother Blake, clearly impressed.

"Was Clara dressed appropriately?" asked Mrs. Ambrose. "What was Lucinda wearing?"

"I don't know," said Dr. Ambrose. "Some kind of brownish dress. With fur cuffs, I think."

His wife sighed in frustration. "Well, who else was there?"

"The only other person I saw, besides the butler, was the Ward's houseguest. Mr. Cameron, I believe his name was."

Mrs. Ambrose stopped. "Cameron?"

"Yes. I believe Clara had already met him at some dance. Apparently he's Mr. Ward's godson. He's living with them while he reads law with Mr. Ward's firm."

Dr. Ambrose stooped to remove his shoes and rested his stocking feet on the footstool before the hearth.

"Well?" said Mrs. Ambrose when he failed to speak again.

"Well, what?" her husband replied.

"That's it? That's all you were able to find out? What about his family? His background? His religion?"

"Laura, I'm a doctor, not a Pinkerton agent. And why all this interest in Mr. Cameron?"

"Well, I just want to know the kind of people with whom our daughter is associating." Mrs. Ambrose tapped her finger against her pursed lips. "It seems to me if this Mr. Cameron was someone of importance or influence, I would have heard of him by now. But, I've never heard his name mentioned at any of the teas or luncheons I've attended."

"Ah, yes. The Pittsburgh tea circuit," said Dr. Ambrose as he wiggled his toes in the warmth of the fire. "The source of all knowledge."

"Laugh if you must, but if you gather together that many women with eligible daughters, you quickly learn who's who among the young bachelors in town. I think we need to learn a little more about this Mr. Cameron before we allow him to call on Clara."

"I wasn't aware he wished to call on her."

Mrs. Ambrose hesitated. "Well ... no. I ... I just meant ... in case he did."

Dr. Ambrose's eyes narrowed. "Laura, what are you up to?"

"Nothing." She began rearranging a few knick-knacks on the mantel.

"Nothing usually means something. I suggest you just leave this whole business alone. Clara's not like Helen. If you try to orchestrate her life, she will find a way to rebel."

"Now, Peter," said Mrs. Ambrose with a patient smile, "don't you worry yourself about Clara. I know how to handle our daughter." She kissed the top of his head and left the room.

Dr. Ambrose sighed. His wife's preoccupation with Clara's marital status was exhausting, but he knew it was her way of ensuring against an uncertain future. Besides, he doubted all the intrigue and manipulation would have any effect. In the end, Clara would do whatever Clara wanted to do.

Out of the corner of his eye, he saw Grandmother Blake direct a superior smile his way.

"You never had this kind of trouble with Helen," she said before bending back over her knitting.

"No, Grandmother Blake," he said through clenched teeth, "we never had this kind of trouble with Helen." He paused. "You know, I think I could use a little something to eat. Could I interest you in a piece of lemon cake?"

The following Sunday afternoon, Garrett stood outside the front door of the Ambrose home and tried to smooth his hair in the reflection in the sidelight glass. He had already rung the bell twice and was debating whether he should try again, when the door was opened, not by the previous maid, but by Dr. Ambrose, still shrugging his way into his frock coat.

"Hello, Sir," said Garrett. "Nice to see you again. I'm here to see Miss Ambrose."

"Yes, Mr. Cameron. We've been expecting you. Excuse the dishevelment. Maid's day off, you know. Come in. Come in."

Garrett paused in the foyer.

"Let me take your coat," said Dr. Ambrose. "Clara will be down in a minute. We can wait for her here in the parlor."

Garrett followed the doctor into a cozy, book-filled room with dark cherry furniture and velvet chairs. Brass kerosene lamps glowed softly against the February gloom, and a fire curled and flared in the fireplace. A small woman in a brown striped sateen dress stood staring at the hearth. She turned and Garrett was struck by her resemblance to Clara – the same soft round face, the center-parted chestnut hair, and the wide gray-blue eyes, fringed with dark lashes. These eyes, however, lacked the innocence and openness of Clara's. These eyes were touched with sadness.

"Mrs. Ambrose, may I present Mr. Garrett Cameron."

Garrett bowed. "Good afternoon, Mrs. Ambrose."

Mrs. Ambrose nodded. She stood with hands clasped at her waist, and her face wore the same pained expression it'd had ever since Clara informed her Garrett was coming to call.

"Won't you have a seat, Mr. Cameron?" said Dr. Ambrose.

Garrett hesitated and waited for his hostess. Dr. Ambrose gestured to his wife, who reluctantly settled herself in her accustomed chair.

"So, how are the law studies going, Mr. Cameron?" asked Dr. Ambrose.

"Very well, Sir. Mr. Ward has given me a great deal of guidance and responsibility. I hope to be admitted to the bar by the end of the summer."

"Exactly how did you come to study with Mr. Ward, Mr. Cameron?" The question from the heretofore silent Mrs. Ambrose caused Garrett to jump.

"Mr. Ward is a very close friend of my father's, Madam," he replied. "They grew up together in a little town in western New York called Elmira. In fact, Mr. Ward is my godfather."

"And what sort of business is your father in?" Mrs. Ambrose continued.

"He's in the employ of Mr. Jervis Langdon of Elmira."

"I'm familiar with Mr. Langdon," said Dr. Ambrose. "Well, not personally, but by reputation. He's made his fortune in coal, lumber, and railroads, if I'm not mistaken. Seems to me I've also read his name in connection with various abolitionist groups."

Mrs. Ambrose gave her husband a cautionary look. She did not want him to stray from the true purpose of this conversation.

"And your father is an associate of this Mr. Langdon's?" Mrs. Ambrose asked hopefully.

"Yes, Ma'am," said Garrett. "My father's been doing the books for his businesses for twenty years."

"A clerk?" said Mrs. Ambrose. She blanched. "Your father's a clerk?"

"Yes, Ma'am," said Garrett with just a hint of challenge.

Mrs. Ambrose seemed to be groping. "Have you any other family?" she asked.

"No, I'm an only child. My mother passed away a few years ago."

"Oh, I'm sorry," said Mrs. Ambrose. For the first time her voice lost a little of its hard edge.

"Thank you," said Garrett. He decided to steer the conversation toward safer ground. "I understand Miss Ambrose has an older sister?"

"Yes," said Dr. Ambrose. "Helen lives just a few blocks away with her husband, Mr. George Pitcher."

"Mr. Pitcher is a banker with Mr. Mellon," Mrs. Ambrose added, stressing the word *banker*.

"And, we're expecting our first grandchild soon," said Dr. Ambrose, beaming.

"Dr. Ambrose! How indelicate." Mrs. Ambrose turned a deep shade of red.

"I apologize, Mr. Cameron. Being a doctor, I sometimes forget what is acceptable parlor conversation and what is not."

Garrett just smiled, unsure of what to say. The three of them sat in awkward silence, punctuated by the ticking of the clock. The sudden crack of a burning log made them all jump. Garrett's gaze fell upon the banner of a folded newspaper on the table next to Dr. Ambrose' chair. He seized upon it as a topic of conversation.

"Dr. Ambrose, I see you read *Frederick Douglass' Paper*.

"Yes. Are you familiar with it?"

"Very. My father started subscribing to it years ago, back when it was still called the *North Star*. It's one of the better abolitionist papers, in my humble belief. I find Mr. Douglass' opinions both informative and challenging."

"I agree," said Dr. Ambrose. He leaned forward in his chair. "And it just so happens that one of the past editors, Dr. Martin Delaney, was a colleague of mine when he practiced medicine here in Pittsburgh."

"Dr. Delaney is a Negro, is he not?"

"Yes. And one of the most dedicated doctors I've had the pleasure to know. Seven years ago, there was a cholera epidemic here in Pittsburgh. Dr. Delaney was one of the few doctors who did not flee the city. He stayed and treated the sick and dying, black and white."

"As did you, my dear," asserted Mrs. Ambrose. "But, we were discussing Mr. Cameron."

"Quite right," said Dr. Ambrose. "Mr. Cameron, may I ask, what are your views on the slavery issue?"

Mrs. Ambrose gave a small sigh of defeat.

"Well, Sir," said Garrett, "I feel very strongly that slavery is an inherently evil institution that undermines the greatness of our country. I don't see how we can call ourselves a free people, while at the same time enslaving others. I'm not sure what's the best way to go about ending it, but end it we must. And now. Not a hundred years from now." He stopped. "I'm sorry. I have a tendency to get on a bit of a soap box about this."

Dr. Ambrose smiled. "Something that will come in handy in your chosen profession."

"Hello."

They all turned to find Clara posed in the parlor doorway. She looked radiant in a full-skirted, lavender jewel-neck gown that turned her eyes a pale shade of violet. Small silver earrings sparkled at her ears and Mrs. Ambrose noted Clara had also paid particular attention to her hair.

"Good afternoon, Miss Ambrose," said Garrett, leaping to his feet.

"Good afternoon, Mr. Cameron." Clara's voice was polished, if slightly higher than normal. "I'm so glad you could come."

"It's about time you showed up, young lady," scolded her father. "Poor Mr. Cameron has been enduring our company long enough."

"On the contrary, Sir. I've enjoyed the opportunity to get to know you and Mrs. Ambrose." Garrett turned to Clara's mother. She met his smile with a stony stare.

"Well," Dr. Ambrose clapped his hands together, "Mrs. Ambrose, why don't you and I see to the tea?" He stood and held his arm out to his wife. She hesitated, looking from Clara to Garrett. Then, with a curt nod to their guest, she accompanied her husband from the room.

Garrett looked at Clara, his eyebrows raised.

"Well, Miss Ambrose. Now I understand why you didn't receive my calling card. You have a rather formidable guard around you."

"Actually, Father is a dear," said Clara. She seated herself in the chair her mother had just vacated. "But, Mother is very … particular about whom I see."

"And you. Are you particular about whom you see? Or did you accept my request to call solely because you knew it would upset your mother."

Clara had the good grace to look embarrassed. "Well, I admit, the fact that she objected was part of my motivation. But only a small part.

Frankly, I was curious about the man who stood up for me at the ball. I realized I still know very little about you."

"Well, your mother just gave me a cross-examination that would be the envy of any attorney before the bar," said Garrett, "but I can give you the short version. I'm twenty-three years old, reasonably good-looking, relatively poor, the only son of a clerk from a small town in western New York, and I've been living in Pittsburgh for six months studying law."

"Well, that explains the expression on Mother's face," said Clara with a giggle.

Just then, Mrs. Ambrose returned with the tea tray. Without a word, she set it down on the table in front of the young couple.

"Thank you, Mother," said Clara. "Would you care to join us?"

"No, thank you." Without meeting their eyes, Mrs. Ambrose left the room.

"I would say one, if not both of us, is in a great deal of trouble," Garrett said in a low voice.

"Oh, I'm sure it's me," sighed Clara. She poured a cup of tea from the silver teapot. "I seem to have a penchant for upsetting my mother – even when it's not deliberate. I fear I'm not quite the daughter she envisioned. I have a regrettable tendency to speak my mind."

"On the contrary, I find it one of your most admirable qualities."

He closed his hand around the cup she offered, but did not immediately remove it from her grasp. Clara looked up and into his eyes, and found herself drawn to what she saw there.

Back in the kitchen, Clara's mother sat furiously stirring her tea.

"You're going to break that china, Laura," her husband observed in amusement. He joined her at the table with his own cup and a cookie he had purloined from the tea service. "Now, don't blame Clara. After all, you're the one who intercepted Mr. Cameron's calling card. I warned you if you tried to keep her from seeing him, it would have the opposite effect."

"It's not that, Peter."

"Then what?" he mumbled with his mouth full of cookie.

"She's smitten."

"What?"

"She's completely smitten with this young man."

"How can you say that? She barely knows him."

"I can see it in her eyes."

"Well, what if she is?"

"Peter," she said, as if speaking to a slow child, "his father is a clerk. He has no means of his own and is living off the largess of the Wards. He's totally unsuitable. She can do so much better."

"Better than a fine young man with ambition and good morals?"

"You can starve to death on ambition and morals."

"Clara, I know many successful lawyers who do quite well. Mr. Ward, for example."

"There's no guarantee Mr. Cameron will be successful and, even if he is, it could be years before he becomes established." She shook her head. "No, I don't think it's wise for Clara to waste her time on someone with such tenuous prospects when there are so many more appropriate suitors she could be entertaining."

"But, she doesn't like any of the other suitors."

"Hardly the point," said Mrs. Ambrose. "Most people don't marry for love, you know."

"I did." He reached across the table and took her hand. "I fell in love with you the first time I saw your beautiful eyes over the top of that stack of folded sheets."

"Oh, Peter," she said, squeezing his hand. "We were unusually fortunate. We found love *and* security. My parents loved each other, too, but their marriage was filled with nothing but hardship and heartbreak. I don't want Clara to go through that."

"You mustn't worry so, Laura," he said. "Clara has a good head on her shoulders. She'll find her way."

Mrs. Ambrose's eyes filled with tears. "I just want what's best for her."

"I know, dear. But you may have to let her discover that for herself."

CHAPTER 4

IN THE DEEPENING GLOOM AND drizzle of the evening of February 14th, Clara stood among an anxious crowd at the corner of Third Avenue and Smithfield Street in Pittsburgh to await the arrival of President-elect Abraham Lincoln.

Pittsburgh and Allegheny City, just across the Allegheny River from Pittsburgh, had been in a frenzy of preparation ever since the route of Mr. Lincoln's train trip to his March 4th inauguration had been announced. Buildings and lampposts were hung with patriotic bunting and flags, a parade route planned, and speeches prepared. Local dignitaries vied for a place in the president-elect's entourage and most businesses announced they would close in honor of the visit.

On the appointed day, the Pennsylvania Dragoons, the Jackson Blues, and the Washington Infantry, all local volunteer militia groups formed during the war with Mexico, stood in full uniform at the Fort Wayne Station on Federal Street in Allegheny City. They were to escort the president-elect and his party to the Monongahela House Hotel where a specially prepared room awaited. Only the Duquesne Grays, staunch Democrats, refused to take part in the procession.

Despite a light rain, people began gathering at the station long before Mr. Lincoln's scheduled 5:20 p.m. arrival. At 5:00 p.m., the military guns along the river boomed a thunderous tribute and the crowd stirred excitedly. But the welcome was premature. An unrelated railroad accident farther up the tracks had delayed the president-elect's train. As the hours passed, the rain increased and a strong wind blew from the east. Still, the crowd continued to grow. Soon people lined the roads along the entire route from the train station to the Monongahela House Hotel, including both sides of the suspension bridge across the Allegheny River.

Clara and her father had arrived in Pittsburgh at 4:00 p.m. to stake out a prime position along the parade path. Just before 6:00 p.m., however, Dr. Ambrose was called away on a medical emergency. Clara had convinced him she would be fine alone until he got back, a decision she regretted now as, a full hour and a half later, he had still not returned.

Finally, at 8:00 p.m., the long-awaited train steamed into the station. The president-elect appeared in the doorway of the car and the damp yet enthusiastic crowd surged forward. Politely declining entreaties to speak, Lincoln hurried along the pathway cleared by the soldiers and disappeared into a waiting carriage. Other carriages filled with local officials fell into line behind those of the president-elect and his entourage. Flanked by the militia, the procession proceeded slowly across the bridge over the Allegheny River toward the waiting crowds in Pittsburgh.

Farther along the parade route, Clara shivered in the watery gaslight. Her legs felt numb from standing so long in the cold. Large raindrops fell from her umbrella onto the hem of her skirt, which was already soaked from the wet sidewalks and puddled streets. She was wondering if she should try to find a hackney cab home when a particularly strong gust of wind filled her umbrella.

"Oh, my!" she gasped as she struggled to keep it from going airborne. Suddenly, a strong, gloved hand grabbed the shaft.

"Here, now, Miss Ambrose. We can't have you flying away."

"Mr. Gliddon!" Clara's surprise at seeing Edgar was exceeded only by her shock that he had condescended to speak to her. Somehow he managed to look neither cold nor wet in his tweed overcoat and bowler, but when he touched the brim of his hat, a small stream of rainwater fell onto the pavement between them.

"What are you doing here?" Clara sputtered.

"I assume the same thing you are. Waiting to get a look at this new country-bumpkin president of ours," said Edgar. "I've just returned from a few weeks of business meetings in New York to find our little town in quite an uproar over his visit." He glanced around and frowned. "Are you alone?"

"No, I came with Father," she said. "He was called away on a case, but I expect him back at any moment."

"He shouldn't have left you here unprotected," said Edgar. "If you'll allow me, I'll wait with you until he returns."

"That's not necessary," said Clara. "Besides," she added, unable to resist a jab at his ego, "shouldn't you be at the Monongahela House with the other dignitaries?"

"I'm afraid when it comes to greeting the new President of the United States, my name gets pushed pretty far down the list," replied Edgar. He brushed a few raindrops from the shoulder of his coat. "That will change, however. All in good time."

Same old Edgar, thought Clara. If there was anything he believed in, it was his ability to get what he wanted. Well, there was one thing he could not have.

"I must say, Sir, I'm surprised you even deigned to speak to me," she said with what she thought was obvious sarcasm.

"Well, Miss Ambrose, I'll admit I was upset with you at our last meeting ...."

"*You* were upset ...." Clara began. He held up his hand.

"... but, given your youth and inexperience, I'm willing to leave your unfortunate faux pas in the past. Besides, how could I stay angry with one who looks so exquisitely charming, even in the rain."

Clara gaped at him. "Of all the .... "

Her impending tirade was cut off by the roar of the crowd announcing Lincoln's approach.

"Here he comes! Here he comes!" people began to shout. Their words were punctuated by the advancing tromp of marching feet and the high trilling of fifes.

Clara craned her neck to look down the street. She could just make out the lines of militia and the carriages approaching through the gas-lit darkness. People cheered and waved sodden handkerchiefs and small flags as the entourage passed and continued down Smithfield Street to the even larger throng waiting outside the hotel. Clara saw her brother-in-law, George, marching with the Jackson Independent Blues and thought she glimpsed the president-elect in the window of one of the carriages. But in the rain and gloom, she couldn't be sure.

"Well, that was certainly anti-climactic," sniffed Edgar as the crowd began to disperse, either towards their homes or closer to the Monongahela House for a possible second look at the new president. He turned to Clara. "Miss Ambrose, may I escort you home?"

"No, thank you," she said curtly. "I'll just wait here for Father."

"Come now. It may be quite a while before he's able to come for you. I doubt he would want you standing here alone on the dark streets until all hours."

"Really, Mr. Gliddon," said Clara, more forcefully, "I'll be fine."

"Nonsense." Edgar reached for her arm. "I'll have my man bring the carriage around."

"That won't be necessary," said a familiar voice.

They both turned to find Garrett Cameron standing behind them. His expression was genial, but his wide-legged stance was vaguely threatening.

"Mr. Cameron?" said Clara.

"Good evening, Miss Ambrose." Garrett tipped his hat. "And Mr. Gliddon, isn't it? I believe we met at the Holiday Ball."

"Did we?" said Edgar.

Garrett ignored the affront and turned to Clara.

"Miss Ambrose," he said, "your father wants you to hurry home before you catch a chill. I have his carriage waiting over on Wood Street."

"Really?" Edgar looked at Clara accusingly. "Well, Miss Ambrose, since you've obviously made other … arrangements, I'll bid you good night." Without a word to Garrett, he turned on his heel and stalked off into the night.

"Pleasant fellow," said Garrett. He offered his arm to Clara. "Shall we?"

Clara handed him her umbrella and placed her hand on his arm.

"How ever did you find me?" she asked as Garrett guided her around the people and standing water remaining on the sidewalks.

"I ran into your father on his way to visit a patient. He told me you'd come down to see the president-elect together, but he'd had to leave. He was worried about you down here alone, but couldn't leave his patient. So, I offered to find you and escort you home."

"You know, Mr. Cameron," said Clara, "I think Mr. Gliddon got the impression you and I had planned this little rendezvous."

"Did he?" said Garrett. "Imagine that." He paused. "I must admit, I *was* a little surprised to find you in the company of the eminent Mr. Gliddon."

Clara sneaked a peek at Garrett's face, but it was too dark to read his expression.

"No more surprised than I. He just appeared out of nowhere."

"Perhaps I arrived at an inconvenient moment?"

"Oh, no," said Clara, "your timing was perfect. I was just about to beat him senseless with my umbrella."

Garrett chuckled. "I would have enjoyed watching that."

When they arrived at the carriage, he helped her up into the passenger seat.

"So, did you get to see Mr. Lincoln?" he asked once they were on their way.

"I'm not sure. I think I saw him in the window of the carriage, but it was so dark."

"Well, if you'd like another opportunity to see him, he's scheduled to give a speech from the balcony of the hotel tomorrow morning."

"Yes, I know. I'm coming back to hear him," said Clara. "I'm curious to hear what he has to say about the proposed tariff as it relates to the local iron industry, as well as his views on the current crisis between the states."

Garrett laughed.

"What's so funny?" asked Clara.

"Miss Ambrose, you are a most unusual woman."

Clara spent the rest of the dark carriage ride back to Lawrenceville trying to figure out if she had been insulted or complimented.

Very early the next morning, Clara and her father returned to Pittsburgh for the president's address. Helen had wanted to join them, but the weather was still cold and drizzly, and Mrs. Ambrose forbad it "in her condition."

Dr. Ambrose managed to secure a prime location directly across Smithfield Street from the Monongahela House Hotel on the stoop of a building that provided both a good view of the president's balcony and partial protection from the rain that continued to fall.

By 7:30 a.m., umbrellas filled the streets around the hotel and, by the time Mr. Lincoln appeared at 8:00 a.m., a crowd of some 10,000 people roared its welcome.

Clara could see the president-elect towering over the local dignitaries clustered around him on the balcony. With his long angular face and deep-set eyes, she thought him not so bad looking; certainly not as hideous as the newspaper cartoons portrayed him.

After a brief introduction by the mayor of Pittsburgh, Mr. Lincoln began to speak. His lawyer-trained voice was sonorous, and his manner calm and relaxed. He even joked with the crowd in a good-humored way. He spent the majority of his speech addressing the pending tariff vote, something which would affect the ability of the people of Pittsburgh to receive a fair price for their products. His treatment of the looming crisis between the states was brief and intended to cool the hotheads in the crowd. He referred to the threat of secession as an "imaginary crisis," one that could be avoided through diplomacy.

After fifteen minutes, he thanked the crowd for their attention, bowed, and left to catch the train for his next stop.

"Well, what did you think?" asked Dr. Ambrose as he and Clara waited for the crowd to thin.

"He certainly seems an intelligent, well-spoken man," said Clara, "but I can't help but feel he's minimizing the threat of the seceding states to the Union."

"Hello, Dr. Ambrose. Miss Ambrose." Garrett Cameron stood on the sidewalk at the foot of the stoop.

"Well, hello, Mr. Cameron," said Dr. Ambrose. "I see you wanted another glimpse of Mr. Lincoln, too."

"Yes. It's not every day we get to see a real live president here in Pittsburgh."

"Let me thank you again for rescuing my daughter last night. I'm afraid my profession has a tendency to interfere with my family obligations."

"It was my pleasure, Sir. I appreciate you trusting me with so precious a charge." Clara lowered her eyes under Garrett's gaze.

"So, what did you think of Mr. Lincoln?" asked Dr. Ambrose.

"A fine orator," said Garrett. "So fine one could almost believe what he says about the secession crisis being imaginary, were it not for the fact that, five days ago, the southern states officially declared themselves the Confederate States of America."

"And elected former Secretary of War, Jefferson Davis, as their president," added Dr. Ambrose, nodding gravely.

"I suspect Mr. Lincoln is just trying to keep the lid on the kettle until he can get to Washington and see what's really going on," said Garrett.

"I don't envy him," said Dr. Ambrose. "Tempers are running high on both sides. The abolitionists are anxious to use this conflict as a way to finally end slavery and the southern states rights activists see it as an opportunity to break free of the federal government, once and for all. I'm afraid there may be no way out of this situation short of war." He shook his head slowly. "Well, enough of that talk. Can we offer you a ride anywhere, Mr. Cameron?"

"No, thank you, Sir. I have business at the courthouse."

"Perhaps another time."

"I look forward to it. Good day. Good day, Miss Ambrose." Garrett touched the brim of his hat and strode away.

"You were unusually quiet," commented Dr. Ambrose as he and Clara walked to their carriage.

"I was just trying to comport myself in the manner Mother would have wanted," Clara replied.

Dr. Ambrose gave her a dubious look. "Well, I must say Mr. Cameron seems like a fine young man. Intelligent. Respectful. And he has the most uncanny ability to locate you in large crowds."

"Oh, Father!" admonished Clara.

Edgar sat at his desk in the top floor office of Gliddon Irons Works on Rebecca Street in Allegheny City and stared out the window at the rain-pocked waters of the Allegheny River. The gray of the day matched his mood. Despite the work that had piled up during his trip to New York, he was finding it hard to concentrate. His reaction to seeing Clara on the street yesterday had caught him off guard. He thought he had successfully put her out his mind. He had barely thought of her at all while he was gone; four, five times, at most. But, seeing her again …. He couldn't explain it, the attraction she held for him. It wasn't merely her beauty, which, granted, was arresting. He knew a lot of beautiful women. But there was something about her….

"Sir. The mail."

Edgar jumped. It was positively unnerving the way his father's old secretary glided soundlessly about the offices of Gliddon Ironworks. He would fire the pinched little man if he could, but Mr. Peterson had been in his father's employ for over twenty-five years and his knowledge was invaluable. Besides, he knew where all the skeletons were hidden.

"Leave it on the desk, Peterson," snapped Edgar. "And close the door."

Once the man had gone, Edgar began rifling through the accumulated correspondence. He stopped when he reached a thin envelope with a European postmark.

Well, that didn't take long, he thought. He picked up a silver letter opener, slit open the flap, and extracted a single sheet of paper. The accusatory script leapt from the page in bold strokes.

February 2, 1861

Edgar,

It has come to my attention that your behavior of late has been the cause of some comment among the better circles of Pittsburgh society. I speak, of course, of the incident at the Holiday Ball.

When I passed the day-to-day operation of Gliddon Iron works on to you, I stressed the importance of establishing your own reputation within the business community. Pivotal to this process is the acquisition of a suitable spouse. I should not have to remind you that your choice of a wife must be beyond reproach, as must the selection of those young ladies under consideration for the title. From what I understand, this doctor's daughter possesses neither the proper breeding nor the necessary social graces. It is time you stop acting the irresponsible roué and choose an appropriate young lady who, by her lineage and conduct, will serve as the perfect complement to a man in your position. If you must occasionally give vent to a young man's natural urges, I suggest you do so discreetly at one of the many establishments intended for that purpose.

In any event, there can be no excuse for exposing the family name or the company's reputation to the salacious whispers of others. I must insist you rectify your behavior and look to your future and that of this family.

Sincerely,
Charles Whittington Gliddon

For a brief moment, Edgar was once again that little boy trembling beneath the disapproval of his emotionally distant father; a father who signed his letters to his son in the same way he signed his business contracts. But Edgar quickly quashed the hurt with the soothing balm of his anger.

How dare his father send pronouncements from on high, speaking to him as if he were a dullard to be ordered about. He would see whomever he wished, whenever he wished. And the attack on Clara's character was wholly unfair. She might be outspoken, but her virtue was unquestioned. What upset him the most, however, was the realization of just how much his father's opinions had influenced his own, down to his very choice of words.

Edgar walked to the window and stood with his hands clasped behind him.

Was that truly what he wanted – a "perfect complement"? He had thought so. It was certainly what so many of his class deemed appropriate: an arranged marriage for appearances; a series of mistresses for one's physical or emotional needs. But, his father's cold words had ripped away the lush trappings that concealed the cage of society's expectations. Edgar had glimpsed his future and was filled with revulsion. Could he actually bear to marry someone purely for the status she would lend? Someone like his own over-pedigreed mother, a cowering shadow whose enfeebled love for her only son could not withstand the force of her husband's dictatorial rule? Having endured a loveless childhood, did he truly want a loveless marriage, as well?

Suddenly, Edgar knew what he wanted. Not a wife who was a mere asset or adornment, nor someone who would cater unquestioningly to his every whim. He wanted someone who could be a true partner; someone intellectually worthy, with both beauty and spirit. He wanted someone like … Clara.

Seeing Clara again had rekindled Edgar's interest; the prohibitions in his father's letter had fanned that interest into a blaze. If Edgar wanted Clara, he would have her; his father, society – and Garrett Cameron – be damned.

Edgar crumpled the letter into a ball, turned, and tossed it into the trash bin.

"Clara." Mary Tierney stuck her head into Clara's bedroom. "It's that darlin' Mr. Cameron, come to call. He's waitin' for you down in the parlor."

Clara tossed aside her book and hurried to the dressing table mirror.

"He's become quite the regular visitor, hasn't he now?" said Mary.

"Don't you start with me, Mary. I have enough trouble dealing with Mother."

"You'll have no trouble with me over the likes of Mr. Cameron. In fact, if I was a wee bit younger, I might take a fancy to him meself." Mary winked and left the room.

While Clara hastened to get ready, Garrett and Dr. Ambrose chatted amiably in the parlor. In the two months since Garrett had been calling on Clara, he and Dr. Ambrose had formed a friendly bond. Mrs. Ambrose always seemed to be otherwise occupied during his visits.

"And what do you two have planned for today?" said Dr. Ambrose.

"With your permission, Sir, I thought I'd take Miss Ambrose for a walk around the Arsenal wall. It's such a beautiful spring afternoon; it seems a shame to stay indoors."

"Quite right. April days like this are far too rare not to be enjoyed."

Just then, Clara glided into the room. She was wearing her newest spring dress, the one with the bell sleeves and the large pastel floral pattern. The expression on Garrett's face made her happy her mother had insisted she buy the expensive fabric.

"Hello, Mr. Cameron," she said.

"Hello, Miss Ambrose."

They stood gazing at each other until Dr. Ambrose cleared his throat.

"Yes. Well," said Garrett, "Miss Ambrose, would you care to accompany me on a little stroll?"

"I'd be delighted. Just let me fetch my bonnet and shawl. Goodbye, Papa," she said as she kissed her father on the cheek. I'll be back before supper."

"Good bye, you two. Enjoy yourselves."

As soon as the door closed, Mrs. Ambrose emerged from the kitchen. She hurried to the parlor window and drew aside the curtain.

"Just look at that," she clucked as the young couple hurried off down the sidewalk. "He doesn't even own a carriage to take her around in."

Dr. Ambrose came and stood behind her at the window. "From the look on her face, I don't think she minds."

He smiled as he watched Clara and Garrett disappear, but Mrs. Ambrose' face was as dark as the clouds over the Pittsburgh mills.

Lost in conversation, Garrett and Clara walked along Butler Street to the southwestern edge of the Arsenal grounds, turned right, and began the slow climb up Pike Street. A stroll around the eight-foot stone walls of the Arsenal was a popular promenade for the people of Lawrenceville, and there were many couples out enjoying the warm weather. Some, like them, were in various stages of courtship; others pushed baby carriages while older children scurried about their feet. In the heat of summer, mothers frequently aired their babies beneath the shade of the majestic oak and hickory trees that stretched their limbs from behind the Arsenal walls. On this early spring day, however, only soft green fuzz showed on the tips of the branches overhead.

About half way up the hill, Garrett and Clara passed the First Presbyterian Church across the street on the right. Clara smiled and waved to a black-clothed clergyman who was just climbing down from his carriage. The minister cast a critical look at Garrett before nodding stiffly and disappearing into the church.

"I see you have friends in high places," said Garrett.

"Reverend Lea's a long-time friend of the family," explained Clara. "He baptized me in that very church." She cocked her head. "Are you a religious man, Mr. Cameron?"

"God fearing, yes. Religious, no. In my experience, most religions espouse love while practicing exclusion and condemnation. I take no issue with those who choose to follow a particular religious doctrine," Garrett hastened to soften the effect of his words, "I just never found one that made any sense to me."

Clara was more surprised than shocked. To be honest, she had never given religion much thought. Church was just something one went to on Sundays because one's family went or, to be honest, to show off a particularly fetching gown or hat. The thought of actually choosing one's religion based on one's beliefs, rather than the other way around, had never occurred to her.

While Clara digested this particular bit of spiritual treason, they continued their walk up the hill. In the houses on either side of the church property, the warm weather had brought on a flurry of spring cleaning. Women beat rugs over porch railings or leaned out of second stories to wash windows clean of winter grime. In the front lawn of one house, a young woman knelt to clear away the winter debris from her flower garden while her infant child slept in a basket at her feet.

"How is your sister feeling?" asked Garrett. "From what your father told me, the baby must be due fairly soon."

"Oh, she's fine. She tends to get a bit dramatic at times, like she's the only woman in the world who's ever had a baby."

"I assume all first-time mothers feel that way."

"I suppose. But she has Mother and George waiting on her hand and foot, even though Father says she's as healthy as a horse," Clara giggled. "Helen hates it when he says that."

"I can imagine."

"You know, I have to confess," said Clara, "I never thought too much of George. He was always a little too rigid and, well, boring for my taste. But he certainly has proved himself a devoted father-to-be."

"Yes, people can surprise you, sometimes," agreed Garrett.

Suddenly, Clara cried out, "Oh, look!"

She picked up her skirts and trotted across Pike Street to where a large bush bordered the walkway leading to a house. With a wistful smile, she fingered the small green leaves that were beginning to sprout from the woody stems.

"Lilacs. I just love lilacs. My mother and I planted one in our back yard when I was six years old. It's huge now. And every May it has the most wonderful pale purple blossoms."

"That's it," said Garrett, snapping his fingers. "I've always caught a hint of fragrance when I'm around you. I couldn't place it until now."

"It's lilac water," confirmed Clara.

Garrett took a step closer to her. She could feel his presence behind her as if he had pressed up against her.

"I smell it in my dreams," he said in a low voice.

Clara, no stranger to compliments from men, found herself quite unsettled.

"Did you know they live forever?" she ventured.

"Who does?" said Garrett absently, distracted by the curve of her neck.

"Not who. What." She turned to face him. "The lilacs."

Garrett raised an eyebrow.

"No, truly," she said. "Long after we're gone, this lilac bush will live on and produce beautiful flowers, year after year. Then, even when it does die, if you burn the wood, you can still smell the perfume in the smoke. So, in a way, lilacs live forever. That's why they're said to symbolize eternal love."

"How beautiful," he said. His eyes told her he was not referring to the flowers. Flustered, Clara re-crossed the street to the Arsenal sidewalk. Garrett fell into step beside her.

As they rounded the top of the Arsenal grounds along Penn Street, they passed a young couple headed in the opposite direction. The man was dressed in the uniform of a United States soldier, most likely stationed at the Allegheny Arsenal; the woman, young and petite, clung to his arm. They were deep in conversation and from the look on their faces, not a happy one.

"Do you think it will happen?" said Clara when they were out of earshot. "The war."

"Yes," said Garrett. "Absent a miracle, I'm afraid I do."

"So does my father. He's very concerned. You know, he fought in the war with Mexico. But, he never talks about it."

"You father has dedicated his life to healing people. Witnessing the killing and dying that goes on during a war must've been particularly hard on him."

"If there is a war, will you go?"

"Of course, if my country needs me."

"I should like to be able to go."

Garrett chuckled. "The rebels would have no choice but to surrender if they came upon you in the ranks."

"No, I'm serious," said Clara. "I wish there was something I could do. Be a soldier or a nurse. Something. Anything." She sighed. "Being a woman is so limiting."

"Well, I wouldn't worry," said Garrett. "If war comes, I'm sure there will be many things we'll all be called upon to do that will test our limits. Still, I pray we can avoid war all together."

"Of course, you're right," said Clara, chastened. She looked over at him. "Are you always this level-headed?"

"Frankly, I find it quite difficult to be level-headed around you."

Clara hid her pleased expression beneath the brim of her bonnet.

They continued on through the bright April sunshine and turned left on Covington Street to head back down the hill. In the yard of the Orphan's Home, four little girls were playing tag. Their Irish accents were plain as they called to each other.

"I'd love for you to meet Miss Burke sometime," said Clara. "She's my dearest friend. I've told her about you."

"Oh? And what did you tell her?"

"Only that you are … amusing," she teased.

"Amusing, eh?" said Garrett. "This Miss Burke. Is she a classmate of yours from the Pittsburgh Female College?"

"No. I've known her since I was little. My father's treated her family for years. I used to stay and play with her when he went on his calls. She lives on the other side of St. Mary's Street, below Butler."

"Isn't that the Irish district?" he said in surprise.

"Yes, it is," said Clara, immediately on guard. "Miss Burke is Irish. Is that a problem?"

"Not for me. But I assume your mother had something to say about it."

"Yes, indeed. She didn't mind so much when I was little, but now she thinks that *the people who matter* will look down on me for having her as my friend."

"And what do you think?"

"I think people who look down on other people because of race or religion, or money, are no better than ..." She stopped as two matronly women going in the opposite direction cast her disapproving looks. "I'm sorry," she said, "I didn't mean to get so carried away."

"You feel things very strongly, don't you, Miss Ambrose?" said Garrett.

"Too strongly, I suppose. But, it's just that there's so much ... injustice in the world. I can't bear to sit by and do nothing."

"Still, you must get weary trying to right all the wrongs by yourself."

"You're mocking me," accused Clara.

"No, I assure you, I'm not," said Garrett. "I admire your passion and your willingness to act upon it. I am, by nature, more cautious, more deliberate. And, as a lawyer, I'm being trained to look at all sides of an issue, weigh all the evidence, anticipate all the possible outcomes. It can be fairly immobilizing. I wish I had your fervor."

"And I wish I had your self control," said Clara.

"Perhaps we could learn from each other."

Clara looked up at him, and saw the earnestness behind the smile.

"Perhaps we could," she replied.

When they returned to the house on Allen Street, Garrett paused on the front stoop.

"May I call on you again next Sunday?" he said.

"I'd like that," Clara replied.

Garrett bowed and kissed her gloved hand. She felt the heat right through the cloth.

"Good afternoon, Miss Ambrose."

"Good afternoon, Mr. Cameron."

Clara slipped into the house and closed the door. Leaning against it, she sighed. Garrett Cameron. Had there ever been a more perfect name?

"Clara? Come in here, please."

Clara stiffened, but dutifully followed her mother's voice into the parlor. She found her mother seated with her hands folded and lips tight. Her father, oblivious, smiled at Clara briefly and returned to his book.

"I'll come straight to the point," said Mrs. Ambrose. "Clara, I don't think you should continue to encourage this young man."

Dr. Ambrose looked up in surprise. "Laura, I thought we'd agreed ...."

"Peter, I cannot sit idly by and watch our daughter ruin her life."

"What are you talking about?" said Clara.

"I'm talking about Mr. Cameron," replied her mother. "You must stop seeing him."

"But, why?"

"Because he's not the type of man with whom you could have a successful marriage."

"How can you say that? You hardly know him."

"I know enough. He comes from very modest means and he's practically penniless."

"Now, perhaps," said Clara, "but he's reading to be a lawyer. Besides, I don't care if he has money or not."

Her mother's smile had pain behind it.

"You say that now because you're young and you've never known anything but warmth and security. But, once you found yourself living in some mean hovel with a hungry baby and another on the way, you'd quickly learn just how important money is. All the fine things you've enjoyed, all the advantages we've given you, would be out of reach for you and your children." She shook her head. "Clara, you wouldn't be happy."

"Happy? You don't care if I'm happy!" said Clara, her voice rising. "You just want me to marry into a wealthy family so you can boast to all your friends."

"Clara!" said her father.

"That's not true, Clara," her mother said quietly.

"It *is* true!" insisted Clara. "Garrett Cameron is a wonderful man, but just because he hasn't any money, you dismiss him. Well, I care about him. He's smart and he's kind, and he's worked his way up from practically nothing."

"Yes, and nothing is what you'll end up with if you marry him," said her mother.

Clara opened and closed her mouth like a fish drowning in air. Then, giving a small cry, she ran from the room.

After a few minutes, her father knocked on her bedroom door.

"Clara?" He peeked in to find Clara sobbing into her pillow. He sat down next to her on the bed, but before he could say a word, she was off.

"Oh, Papa. How can she say those things? She doesn't care at all about how I feel."

"Now, Clara, your mother just wants to be sure you're taken care of."

"No. She just wants to use my marriage as her entrée into high society."

"You're wrong, Clara," he said in a stern voice. "You're very wrong, and I won't have you saying such things about your mother. Sit up and listen to me."

Clara raised herself to a sitting position and angrily wiped at her swollen eyes.

"I never told you girls this – your mother asked me not to – but I think you need to understand why she acts the way she does.

"Your mother hasn't had an easy life. When she was twelve years old, her father's apothecary shop was destroyed in a fire. Her family lost everything – the shop, their home over the shop, all their belongings. They went from having a comfortable life to having nothing. Without the money to rebuild, they had to move to a little shack down by the river. Her father, Grandfather Blake, took a job as a common laborer in one of the local mills, a job for which he was ill-suited, physically. Within two years, he was dead.

"Grandmother Blake took in laundry to try to make ends meet and your mother worked right alongside her. Many were the nights she went to bed hungry and exhausted from long days of washing and ironing. Still, when I first saw her delivering clean linens to the Hand Hospital where I worked, I thought she was the prettiest thing I'd ever seen. But so fragile and lost. Not until we'd been married for some time, and she got used to being safe and secure, did she lose that haunted look.

"So, if she seems a bit preoccupied with you making what she calls a 'successful marriage,' I assure you, she has only your best interests at heart."

"I never knew ...." said Clara.

"No. Nor will you ever let on that I told you. But I couldn't have you continue to judge her so harshly. You have a bright mind, Clara, and a strong will. It's time you developed some compassion, too."

He rose to leave and paused at the door.

"About Mr. Cameron. Just give your mother some time."

"Thank you, Papa," she said. But she didn't see how anyone or anything could ever change her mother's mind.

CHAPTER 5

WAR COMMENCED!
SURRENDER DEMANDED! ATTACK ON FORT SUMTER!

THE COPIES OF THE APRIL 13, 1861 morning edition of the *Pittsburgh Gazette* were snatched out of the newsboy's hands as fast as he could raise them. Garrett, passing through Market Square that Saturday morning, managed to grab one of the last ones. He stepped away from the gathering crowd and leaned against the brick wall of the Market House to read the fateful news.

At 4:30 a.m. on Friday, April 12th, Confederate State troops had fired on the Federal garrison at Fort Sumter in Charleston, South Carolina. Details from the initial telegraphed report were sketchy, but the import was clear. The South had struck its first blow for independence.

When Garrett looked up, life as he had known it had already changed. All around the square, people were rushing past on foot, on horseback, and in carriages. Flags appeared from nowhere and the air was filled with cheering and shouting as the building emotion of the past months was released in a patriotic frenzy. Men and women, alike, were publicly proclaiming their outrage at the Rebel attack and their intention to punish the South for this affront to the Union.

All that day, the people of Pittsburgh and the nation waited for news of Fort Sumter's fate. The telegraph soon tapped out the answer. After withstanding the Rebel bombardment for thirty-two hours, the outgunned, out-manned Union forces surrendered at 2:30 p.m. on Saturday, April 13th. Although there was no loss of life in this initial encounter and no formal declaration had yet been made, everyone knew there was no going back. The war had begun.

Following services on Sunday morning, April 14th, Clara paced outside the First Presbyterian Church. She had remained behind on the pretense of spending some additional time in prayer, and though her mother had given her a strange look, she merely cautioned Clara not to be late for Sunday dinner. Much of the congregation lingered in the churchyard in little pockets of worry, the war talk hanging over them all like a dark cloud amid the spring sunshine.

"Clara!"

Annie Burke appeared at the end of the church walkway. She had come straight from Mass at St. Mary's, as evidenced by the fact that she was wearing her best cotton print dress, lace shawl, and ribbon-trimmed bonnet. Clara rushed to meet her and the girls embraced. Arm in arm, they headed down Pike Street, away from the eyes and ears of the other parishioners.

"Oh, Annie. I'm so glad you got my note. I've wanted to talk to you ever since we heard the news. Can you believe it? Attacked by our own countrymen!"

"I know. 'Tis war, for sure," said Annie. "Me ma is beside herself. She has a brother in New Orleans, and she fears he'll be fightin' on the side of the Rebels."

"I never knew that." Clara hesitated. "Does he ... does he own slaves?"

"Sweet Jesus, no. Uncle Liam doesn't believe any man has the right to own another. But he doesn't like to be told what he can and can't do, either. By man or government."

"Your poor mother."

Annie nodded. "That's not the half of it. As soon as they heard about Fort Sumter, all four of me older brothers started talkin' about how they were goin' to sign up and lick the Southerners, all by themselves. You'd think they was headed off to a carnival, the way they was carryin' on."

"I know. Every boy and man I know is talking about volunteering."

Their conversation was momentarily interrupted by the rumble of an approaching U.S. Army supply wagon. Such wagons were a common sight around the Arsenal, but today the speed of the horses seemed particularly urgent; the faces of the soldiers driving, especially grim. Clara and Annie watched as it disappeared through the Pike Street gate.

"Well," said Annie as the dust settled, "everyone says the war can't last very long. A few months at best. The North is just too strong."

"I wish I could go," said Clara. "I'd sign up in a minute."

Annie laughed. "I believe you would."

"I would," Clara insisted. "But, I'll probably be left at home to knit socks with all the old women."

"I hope not," said Annie. "You're a terrible knitter." They both chuckled. "So," she continued, "is your young man goin'?"

"I've not spoken to him yet," said Clara. "But, he told me not long ago he'd fight if the Union was threatened."

"Yes, well, it certainly seems to be threatened now," said Annie.

When they reached Butler Street, the girls parted, but not before one last hug, an embrace made more poignant by the sudden uncertainty of their futures.

* * *

About an hour later, Helen and George arrived for their weekly Sunday dinner at the Ambrose home. But when Mrs. Ambrose greeted them at the door, her eldest daughter collapsed into her arms in a cloud of crinoline and lace.

"Mother, tell him no!" Helen sobbed. "Tell him he can't leave me now!"

George stood behind her on the stoop with a somber look on his face.

"Good heavens!" said her mother. With a questioning glance at George, she put her arm around her eldest daughter and guided her toward the parlor. "Sh, now, Helen. Calm yourself. This isn't good for the baby."

"Good for the baby?! Leaving me here alone isn't good for the baby," whimpered Helen. George followed without a word.

Dr. Ambrose and Clara, who had been playing cards, got to their feet as the unhappy couple entered the room. The ruckus even awakened Grandmother Blake from her nap in front of the fire.

"Here, now. What's happened?" said Dr. Ambrose. He helped his wife ease their pregnant daughter onto the divan. Helen sagged onto her mother's shoulder while her father knelt to take her pulse.

"The Jackson Independent Blues are going to volunteer their services to the Union army just as soon as President Lincoln puts out the call," said George quietly. "And I'm going with them."

In the silence that followed, all that could be heard was Helen's pitiful sobs.

"Now?" said Mrs. Ambrose, lifting her head from tending to her daughter. "With Helen so close to her confinement? Surely there are plenty of other men who can take your place."

"I'm sure there are, Mother Ambrose," said George, "but I will not have another man take on what should be my responsibility. I would be shirking my duty if I did not remain with my unit and fight to defend the Union."

"And what about your duty to Helen? And the baby?" said his mother-in-law.

George's pale face colored, but his tone was resolute. "I agree the timing couldn't have been worse, but many of the men have families and obligations that would justify their choosing to step aside and let someone go in their stead. But at this time of crisis, duty to country must take precedence. If I'm not willing to fight to preserve the country I love, what assurance for the future can I offer Helen and my child? No, I could not live with myself if I refused the call."

Dr. Ambrose rose to his feet. "I'm sure this was a difficult decision for you, George, but times like these require sacrifices. Of all of us," he added with a pointed look at Helen and his wife. He reached out and shook George's hand. "I applaud your patriotism. Rest assured we'll look after Helen and the baby."

"Thank you, Sir. I was hoping you'd say that."

Mrs. Ambrose said nothing, but hugged the now sniffling Helen even tighter.

"Now," said Dr. Ambrose, "I believe dinner is waiting. George and Helen, when you're ready, please join us. Grandmother Blake, may I escort you into the dining room?" Dr. Ambrose grasped the back of his mother-in-law's wheelchair. He paused. "Mrs. Ambrose? Clara?"

With a nod, Mrs. Ambrose gently eased Helen from her shoulder, patted her hand, and followed her husband. Clara, too, did as she was told. But as she passed George, she paused and gave his arm a squeeze.

Who would have thought George would be the one to make the first sacrifice of the war, thought Clara as she followed her parents out of the room. Garrett was right. Sometimes people did surprise you.

As expected, Washington's reaction to the attack on Fort Sumter was swift. On the 15th of April, President Lincoln sent out the call for 75,000 volunteers to join the Federal army for a three-month tour of duty in defense of the Union. The response was immediate. Through-out the North, many more than the number requested volunteered their services.

Pennsylvania quickly filled its quota of sixteen regiments – totaling almost 14,000 volunteers – with men already in militia units. But many more clamored to serve, enough for thirty more regiments. In small towns all over the state, these eager men formed themselves into vol-unteer companies and flocked to Pittsburgh, Harrisburg, and Philadel-phia in hopes of being among the next recruits accepted into Federal service. There was general agreement the war would not last very long and the men did not want to miss out on this great adventure of their young lives.

On the afternoon of the 16th of April, Garrett paced the parlor of the Ambrose home and silently rehearsed the speech he had prepared. When Clara entered the room, he faced her and took a deep breath.

"So," she said, "you've volunteered to fight."

"How did you know?" sputtered Garrett.

Clara smiled. "Because it's what I'd do, if I could." She motioned for him to join her on the divan.

"I've signed on with a company called the Pittsburgh Rifles," said Garrett. "A first-rate company, all handpicked men. Unfortunately, Pennsylvania has filled its quota of regiments with men already in militia companies, like the Negley Guards and the Pennsylvania Zouaves."

"I know. My brother-in-law, George, is going with the Jackson Blues."

"Is he?" said Garrett with a touch of envy. "Good for him. But, there are so many more who want to serve."

"Yes. I've seen them on the streets," said Clara. "And more seem to be arriving from the countryside every hour."

"Well, rumor has it they'll be forming up all the extra volunteers into a state reserves corps soon," said Garrett, excitement creeping into his voice, "and the Rifles intend to be one of the first companies accepted into it. We're already raising money for guns and uniforms so that when the call comes we'll be ready."

So, thought Clara, Garrett, too, had been touched by the war fever. She tried to mirror his enthusiasm, but Garrett saw the apprehension in her eyes.

"What's wrong?" he asked.

"Nothing," said Clara. "I'm very proud of you. It's just that …." She looked away. "Everything's happening so fast."

Seeing her reaction, Garrett softened his rhetoric. "Yes, it is," he said. "So fast, in fact, the war will probably be over before I get anywhere near the fighting."

"Would that upset you?" she asked.

Garrett reached out and took her hand. "What I want is for this war to be over quickly, with the Union preserved; a Union of free men. Then we all can return to our lives. And to the people we love."

Clara looked up at his face, so earnest and determined.

"With men like you on our side," she said, "we cannot fail."

Not all the men of Pittsburgh were willing or eager to march off to war. Some viewed the outbreak of hostilities not as an opportunity to defend their country, but as a chance to line their own pockets. Believing, as most did, that the war would be over in a few months, they rushed to make as much profit as they could from the mobilization of the civilian population. The immediacy of the crisis caused the government to abandon its usual lengthy procedure of soliciting bids for the various goods needed to equip, clothe, and feed the army, and large contracts were awarded with little or no knowledge of the vendor's reputation. While many of these vendors were reputable businessmen, a significant number were fraudulent and provided inferior goods at inflated prices. Before long, many of the three-month volunteers found the shoes they had been issued fell apart within a few wearings, as did uniforms made of a cheap material called *shoddy*. This left the soldiers ill-clad, and contributed a new word, meaning inferior product, to the lexicon.

But, the big money was in the production of the coal and iron used to make the cannons, muskets, and rifles of war, and in the manufacture of the rails for the railroads that would transport troops and supplies to the various battlefronts. Government war contracts provided mill and foundry owners with the opportunity to make huge fortunes, and men like Edgar Gliddon and James Percy made shrewd use of their pre-war contacts to win lucrative contracts from unscrupulous members of the military and government.

As volunteers all over the country rushed to recruiting stations, soldiers already in the nation's service hurried to Washington to protect the capital. Their presence, however, was not universally welcome. On the 19th of April, less than a week after the surrender of Fort Sumter, the first blood was shed.

Clara was in the kitchen helping Mary slice a ham for dinner when Dr. Ambrose stormed in with the news.

"Well, it's started," he said, flinging the Saturday morning edition of the *Pittsburgh Gazette* onto the table. The headlines read, *Troops Attacked by Secessionists. BATTLE IN BALTIMORE.*

"Oh, no," said Clara.

"Oh, yes." Her father pointed accusingly at the paper. "It says right there that soldiers of the 27th Pennsylvania and the 6th Massachusetts were attacked by a crowd when they tried to march through Baltimore to switch trains for Washington."

"Was anyone hurt?" asked Clara. She wiped her hands on her apron and reached for the paper.

"Four soldiers and twelve civilians were killed, and many more injured. They say some of the Massachusetts boys fired into the crowd after they were pelted with bricks and stones."

"Jesus, Mary, and Joseph," said Mary. She made the sign of the cross, the knife still in her hand.

"At least the 6th Massachusetts had guns to defend themselves," said Dr. Ambrose. "Apparently, the Pennsylvania boys were so eager to get to Washington they boarded the train in Philadelphia unarmed and still dressed in civilian clothes. When they reached Baltimore, the mob attacked them as soon as they got out of the railroad car. The local officials finally managed to get the brigade back on the train, but refused to let them continue through the city. They had to return to Philadelphia." He shook his head. "A fairly humiliating ending to such a brave response."

"I knew many Marylanders were pro-southern, but I had no idea they would go so far as to attack our troops," said Clara. Suddenly, her eyes widened. "Oh, Papa. What about George? He'll be leaving for Washington soon with the Jackson Blues."

"I wouldn't worry, Clara. The army won't let itself be caught unprepared like that again. And Washington won't tolerate that kind of threat so close to the capital."

Dr. Ambrose's analysis of the situation proved correct. Although secessionists attempted to prevent additional Union troops from reaching Washington by destroying the railroad bridges leading into Baltimore from Philadelphia and Harrisburg, subsequent northern regiments quickly rerouted through Annapolis. They repaired and relaid the tracks and bridges as they went, and arrived in Washington on April 25th. Less than a month later, martial law was declared in Baltimore. Federal troops occupied the city for the remainder of the war.

On April 24, 1861, the first of the three-month men from Allegheny County – the 3rd, 5th, and 7th Pennsylvania Infantry Regiments – prepared to leave Pittsburgh. A heavy rain prevented the review of the troops that had been planned for the Commons in Allegheny City, so the men slogged their way through the mud, across the Allegheny River by way of the Hand Street Bridge, directly to the Pennsylvania Railroad Depot on Grant Street in Pittsburgh. There, three trains, totaling thirty-three cars, waited to take them to Union army camps in Harrisburg, York, and Philadelphia.

Despite the weather, a large crowd lined the streets to bid the boys farewell. They began to cheer as the measured tramp of thousands of feet and the high sweet sound of the fifes playing *The Old 1812 Quickstep* announced the approach of the Union soldiers. Flags held high, flanked by officers on horseback they came, resplendent, if slightly damp, in their militia uniforms, muskets over their shoulders, the burnished barrels catching what light broke through the smoke and rain-laden skies. These young men, who only weeks before had been clerks, farmers, coal miners, lawyers, draymen, glassmakers, boat builders, and students, now joined together in a credible display of an army. Caught up in the excitement, people called out to soldiers they knew, or to no one in particular.

"Go get 'em, boys!"

"Huzzah for the Union!"

Flag-waving children sat on their father's shoulders, women smiled through their tears, and young men watched with envy as on and on the soldiers came, shoulder to shoulder, filled with the patriotic spirit of their great mission. There seemed no doubt that these brave young men would win a quick victory for the Union.

Standing on the sidewalk of Liberty Avenue with her parents, Clara, too, cheered and applauded.

"Aren't they splendid, Papa?" She turned to her father and was stunned to find his face somber and his eyes bright with tears.

"Papa, what is it?" said Clara.

Mrs. Ambrose placed a questioning hand on her husband's arm.

"All those young boys," he said. He shook his head slowly. "Those brave, innocent boys. They have no idea. No idea at all." He sighed and patted his wife's hand. "Come. Let's go home."

As Clara followed her parents through the crowd, she turned and watched with a new eye as line after uniformed line of young men marched away and out of sight.

At the end of April, the 12th Pennsylvania Infantry, including Company A, the Jackson Independent Blues, received orders to leave for the front. A cold spring rain fell once more and Helen, too pregnant and much too distraught to follow her husband to the station, remained at her parents' house in Lawrenceville in the care of her mother. At the last moment, Dr. Ambrose was called out on a medical emergency. This left Clara as the sole member of the Ambrose family to see George off to war.

Standing beside the hissing train, Clara handed George the gifts the family had made for him: extra socks from Grandmother Blake, a sturdy cotton shirt from Mrs. Ambrose, some home-baked bread and cookies from Mary, and a *housewife* from Dr. Ambrose – a sewing kit that, from his own military experience, he assured George would come in handy. Nodding his thanks, George stashed each gift in his knapsack.

"12th Pennsylvania! Board the train!" shouted a lieutenant. The screeching of the train whistle underscored his order and all up and down the train platform sergeants bellowed to their respective companies to get aboard.

"Wait, George," shouted Clara over the din. "There's one more thing. From me." She handed him a small book.

"A bible?" he said.

Clara shrugged. "I thought it might help you ... pass the time."

"Why, thank you, Clara," said George. "It's a most thoughtful gift." He leaned down and gave his surprised sister-in-law a kiss on the cheek. "Goodbye now," he yelled over the insistent train whistle. "Write me as soon as the baby's born. And tell Helen ...." He hesitated, embarrassed.

Clara smiled. "I will."

George nodded, turned, and ran to join his regiment, already aboard the moving train.

All up and down the cars, soldiers hung out of windows and doorways. They called, waved, and craned their necks to get a last glimpse of loved ones, for no one knew how long. Standing on the platform, Clara blinked back tears as she watched the train disappear.

"Allow me, Miss Ambrose." Edgar Gliddon appeared at her elbow and proffered a linen handkerchief.

Goodness! thought Clara. The man is forever sneaking up on me. Still, it was comforting to see a familiar face, even his. She waved away the handkerchief. "No, thank you. I'm fine."

"Seeing someone off, were you?" he said.

"Yes. My brother-in-law, George Pitcher. He's with the 12th Pennsylvania."

"His leaving must be difficult for your sister ... in her condition."

How indelicate for Edgar to allude to her sister's pregnancy, thought Clara. But she supposed social mores were often the first casualties of war.

"Yes, but he felt duty bound. We're all quite proud of him."

Edgar cocked an eyebrow. "Indeed." He tucked the handkerchief back in his pocket. "Well, may I walk you to your carriage ... or have you another escort lurking about?" He made an exaggerated show of scanning the crowd.

Clara pursed her lips. "No, I came alone."

"Do you think that advisable, with all the riff-raff in town?" Edgar asked with real concern.

"Circumstances prevented the rest of the family from coming to the station. Besides, I'm perfectly capable of driving a carriage by myself."

"I'm sure you are," he said. "Still ...." He offered his arm. After a moment's hesitation, Clara placed her hand on his.

"And what brings you down to the station, Mr. Gliddon?" asked Clara as they made their way from the crowded depot to the street. "Are you saying goodbye to someone, too?"

"No. Actually, I was meeting with some railroad and government officials in the depot office. With all these troops and supplies rushing to the front, there's a tremendous need for iron rails for additional track. I intend for Gliddon Iron Works to be one of the major suppliers."

"I see," said Clara. "Business as usual."

"Hardly *as usual*, but business, indeed."

"Have you no intention of joining the fighting yourself then?"

Edgar gestured to the bustling street filled with carriages, wagons, civilians, and would-be soldiers.

"As you can see, the city is filled with men eager for a chance to enlist, more than they can use. I feel I can do more to help the war effort by using my expertise in the manufacturing area."

"How admirable of you," said Clara. "And how lucrative."

"Come now, Miss Ambrose," said Edgar, "there are many ways to provide service to our country. Some of us will fight on the front lines and some of us behind the scenes."

"And yet, those on the front lines risk injury and death, while ... what exactly is it you risk, Mr. Gliddon?"

By this time, they had reached Clara's carriage. She shunned Edgar's offer of assistance and climbed up into the driver's seat by herself. Edgar smirked. Those delicate features concealed a sharp mind and an even sharper tongue. This was going to be a challenge. But, he did enjoy a challenge.

"At the moment, I risk being late for another appointment. Good day, Miss Ambrose," he said, tipping his hat. "Always a pleasure."

He sauntered off down the sidewalk as yet another regiment of troops marched up the street in the opposite direction, bound for the trains that would take them to war.

The spectacle of soldiers marching through the streets soon became commonplace in Pittsburgh, Allegheny City, and Lawrenceville. Every day, drums rolled and martial bands played as more and more volunteers from western Pennsylvania arrived, alone or in company strength, some in uniform, most without, ready to offer their services to the Union. Recruiting offices popped up on every corner and had little difficulty filling the ranks of new companies. But, with the Federal quotas already filled, these new companies had nowhere to go.

Suspecting these men might be needed in the conflict ahead, and cognizant of the three hundred miles of Pennsylvania's territory that bordered the slave states of Virginia and Maryland, the governor of Pennsylvania, Andrew G. Curtin, called for the legislature of the Commonwealth to meet in extra session, scheduled for April 30, 1861, to vote on the establishment of a Pennsylvania Reserve Corps.

In the meantime, the local Pittsburgh Citizens' Committee of Defense, which was organized just after the attack on Fort Sumter to provide support and direction for the local war effort, decided something needed to be done with the crush of volunteers crowding Pittsburgh's streets, hotels, and saloons. Headed by prominent Pittsburgh Judge William Wilkins, the Committee persuaded Governor Curtin to establish a military camp on the site of the old Allegheny Fairgrounds, approximately two miles northeast of Pittsburgh. Here the troops would be sheltered and trained while they awaited the formal decision of the state legislature.

On Saturday, April 27th, the Pittsburgh Rifles learned they were one of only six companies from Allegheny County included among the first companies ordered to report to the fairgrounds the following Monday. That night, the men of the Pittsburgh Rifles met in the Lyons Building on Fifth Street and officially elected a captain. Prominent citizens with connections to the company provided them with new breech loading Sharps rifles. All that was left was to say goodbye to family and friends.

At 11:30 a.m. the next day, Garrett knocked on the door of the Ambrose home. Mary ushered him into the parlor where an unusually somber Dr. Ambrose stood gazing into the fire.

"Good morning, Sir," said Garrett. "I apologize for calling so close to Sunday services."

"No need, Mr. Cameron. I assume you're here to see Clara."

Before Garrett could answer, Clara hurried into the room. The two young people stared at each other with their hearts in their eyes. With a nod to his daughter, Dr. Ambrose left them alone.

"Well, we just got word," said Garrett. "I'm to report tomorrow."

"Tomorrow?!" said Clara. "Where?"

"The fairgrounds. They've established a camp there for all the volunteers waiting to be called up for service. Named it Camp Wilkins, after the judge. If I pass my medical examination, I'll be stationed there with my company until they decide where to send us."

Clara walked over to the hearth, picked up a poker, and made a show of pushing around the coals. "How long will that be?" she asked.

He shrugged. "That depends on the war. Could be weeks, could be months." When she didn't respond, Garrett added, "On the brighter side, it's a much shorter trip from the fairgrounds to Lawrenceville than it is from Allegheny City. And I promise I'll come to see you every time I get leave."

"Then this isn't really goodbye," said Clara.

"No. Not yet."

He joined her in front of the fire. The two of them watched the flames in silence.

"It doesn't seem real, does it?" he said after a moment. "It's like some big Independence Day celebration with bands playing and soldiers marching. But, we're at war with our countrymen. Our own brothers." He turned to her. "You know I'd never leave you but for my duty to my country."

"I know," said Clara. She looked into his eyes. "It's part of the reason I care for you so very much."

Despite her best efforts, her composure began to crumble. Garrett gathered her in his arms, unmindful of who might see. He could feel her trembling. He bent his head to hers and kissed her tenderly. She did not hesitate, but returned his kiss, her lips soft and warm against his. After a long moment, he forced himself to pull away. Clara remained with her head back and eyes closed.

"Oh, Mr. Cameron," she breathed.

"Under the circumstances, perhaps you should call me 'Garrett'."

Clara opened her eyes to find him grinning down at her.

Embarrassed, she ducked her head. "Yes, I guess that would be more appropriate."

"And may I call you 'Clara'?" he asked. He lifted her chin. "For I confess, I've thought of you as my own sweet Clara for some time now."

In answer, Clara rose on tiptoes and kissed him again. He responded, less gently than before and, sliding his hand to the small of her back, drew her toward him. For a moment, the world and all its problems disappeared.

This time, she pulled away first. Resting her cheek on his chest, she listened to the rapid beating of his heart. "Oh, Garrett," she sighed, "what's to become of us?"

"Listen," he said as he stroked her hair, "there's a good chance this war will be over before I even get into action. You saw those boys from the 7th Pennsylvania the other day. They'll make quick work of those Rebels. You'll see. Then we'll have all the time in the world."

Clara nodded without conviction. They held each other tight, never wanting to let go.

All over the country, North and South, the scene was repeated as young men and boys enlisted in the service of their country. Mothers wept and fathers saw their sons off through bright eyes. Wives, often with babes in arms, bravely bid their husbands goodbye.

The pulse of the country quickened as the two sides prepared to meet in battle. And hardly a life in the land would escape the conflict untouched.

CHAPTER 6

ON MONDAY MORNING, MAY 6TH, 1861, Garrett and the rest of the one hundred and three men and officers of the Pittsburgh Rifles marched through the streets of Pittsburgh to the entrance of the newly designated Camp Wilkins. The site of the former fairgrounds, the camp was bounded by Penn Street on the north, Clymer and Wilson Streets on the west and east, respectively, and the Pennsylvania Railroad tracks at the base of Herron Hill, to the south.

The opening of the camp had been delayed until May 2nd to allow the new commanding officer additional time to turn the wooden livestock pens, sheds, and exhibit buildings into makeshift barracks, commissaries, and administrative offices for the sixteen volunteer companies – approximately 1,200 men – who would be the first to call the converted fairgrounds home. The Pittsburgh Rifles were the last of this group to report, having waited until the arrival of the uniforms promised them by a group of wealthy local citizens. Now uniformed, armed, and eager to begin their training, they formed behind a brass band and paraded to the gates of the camp.

As soon as they entered the grounds, the men were directed to report to the medical officer for a physical examination. Garrett lined up with the rest of his company outside a wooden building that had most recently served as the venue for floral exhibits.

"Next!"

The line shuffled forward as the volunteers waited to be seen by a cadre of doctors assigned the task of determining their fitness for service in the Union army. Men of every shape, size, and age, anxious to be accepted, subjected themselves to all manner of probing. They complied with commands to jump, squat, bend over, and open their mouths. Garrett waited his turn, sandwiched between a portly gentleman in his thirties and a thin boy who couldn't have been more than seventeen years old.

The doctor at the head of their line was a squat little man with an oversized mustache that blended into a full thick beard. He alternated between barking commands at the hapless recruits and making notations at a desk stacked high with papers. At the moment, he was reaching up to thump the chest of a tall, emaciated volunteer who was attempting, unsuccessfully, to suppress a persistent, deep cough.

"Notice you have a cough there," said the doctor as he felt the man's neck and peered into his eyes.

"Just getting over a slight cold. Be right as rain in a day or two. Ready to fight."

"Show me your teeth."

The tall man made a tobacco-stained grimace.

"Hmm," grunted the doctor. He gave the man one last head to toe perusal, then made a mark on the paper in front of him.

"You pass. Take this paper and report to the officer outside. Next!"

The line stuttered forward.

"Uncle Sam don't seem too particular who he lets into this army," muttered a man in line behind Garrett. "That scarecrow don't look like he'd last through a day's march, much less a campaign."

"Next!"

"What's with checking the teeth?" asked the skinny boy as they inched forward again. "Is he trying to tell his age?"

"Naw," replied the first man. "They just wanna make sure you got enough good teeth to bite off the end of a cartridge paper so's you can load your rifle. No teeth, no bullet." The man squinted at the boy. "Say, ain't you a little young to be signing up?"

"Hell, no," said the boy, pulling himself up to his full height. "I turned eighteen my last birthday."

"Uh huh," replied the man.

"Next!"

Garrett stepped up to the desk and waited while the doctor scribbled on a paper in front of him.

"Name," snapped the doctor without raising his head.

"Garrett Cameron."

"Age."

"Twenty-three."

"Open your mouth."

Garrett stood with his mouth hanging open. Finally, the doctor glanced up, made a mark in his notes, and handed a sheet of paper to Garrett.

"You pass. Take this outside."

"Is that it?" asked Garrett in surprise.

"You appear to be a strong healthy young man," said the doctor. "Is there some reason I shouldn't pass you?"

"No."

"Then I suggest you move on. I've got at least thirty more men to examine today and you're slowing me down. Next!"

When all the men of the Pittsburgh Rifles had been examined and deemed fit or unfit for service, the assistant quartermaster, wearing sergeant's chevrons, led them down a dusty street to their barracks, an old wooden shed Garrett was pretty sure had served as a cow barn at the fair the previous summer. As the Rifles walked down the dirt and straw covered aisle, Garrett saw that many of the stalls and pens were already occupied by men looking uniformly bewildered at what was to be their first billet.

The sergeant stopped and directed the new men to peel off, four to a stall.

"Come on, come on. We haven't got all day," he barked.

Garrett paused in the opening of the nearest stall. A lean, twenty-something young man with a dark mustache and neatly trimmed goatee sat on the ground with his back against the rough plank wall. Garrett remembered seeing the man at the company meeting the previous Saturday. He had been regaling a group of volunteers with his humorous stories.

At the hesitant look on Garrett's face, the man grinned.

"Welcome to the Monongahela House Hotel," he said and spread his arms theatrically. "Pull up some straw and have a seat."

"Thanks," said Garrett. He set his knapsack on the ground and sat down.

"As you can see," said the man, "no expense has been spared in seeing to the comfort of the brave defenders of the Union." He put out his hand. "Name's Rawlin McMahon. Rawlie. From Pittsburgh."

Garrett shook the man's hand. "Garrett Cameron. Allegheny City." Glancing up, Garrett spied a bird's nest balanced in the rafters directly over his head. "I must say, this place isn't quite what I expected."

"I understand the food's delightful, too," said Rawlie. "Shit!" He shifted to one side and pulled a rusty nail out from under the seat of his pants. "My first battle wound." He tossed the offending nail into a corner. "So, what do you do for a living?"

"I'm reading to be a lawyer," said Garrett. "You?"

"I'm a clerk at Graff, Bennett and Company, the rolling mill. Seems most of the fellows I've met in the Rifles are pretty well educated: businessmen, students, even a steamboat captain. I just hope some of them can shoot."

"Well, I guess we'll find out pretty soon," said Garrett. Suddenly tired from the tension and excitement of the morning, he stretched out on the straw and rested his head on his knapsack.

"Enjoy the leg room while you can," said Rawlie. "Word is once we're settled in, they'll be bringing in more companies. We'll be stacked up in here like cordwood."

As if on cue, two more men appeared at the opening to the stall. One was a clean-shaven man in his mid-thirties with a steady gaze and a large, oft-broken nose. He had a homemade wooden fife tucked into his belt. The other recruit was a very tall gangly boy with just a hint of a dark beard fringing his angular jaw.

"Good God, it's Abe Lincoln himself," cracked Rawlie. The boy turned crimson.

"Sergeant said we're to set up in here," said the older man.

"There must be some mistake," said the boy. "There hardly seems room."

"No mistake," said Rawlie. "They're putting four of us in every stall. The cows had it better."

The older man set down his bag. "I'm Frank Ford," he said. "And this long tall drink of water is Joe Frye."

"Where're you two from?" asked Garrett.

"Birmingham, other side of the Monongahela," said Frank. "I was a foreman at Fahnstock, Albree and Company glass works. This spot taken?" He pointed to the pile of straw next to where Garrett had been lying.

"Help yourself," said Garrett.

Frank lay down and placed his hat over his face.

"What about you, Abe?" said Rawlie.

"Joe," corrected the boy. "I'm a student at Duff's Mercantile College."

"How old are you?" asked Garrett.

"Eighteen. Almost," said Joe, somewhat defensively.

"Shit. I got underdrawers older than you," said Rawlie.

A bugle call interrupted any further conversation.

"What's that?" asked Joe.

"That would be the call to dinner," said Frank, rising stiffly to his elbows. At the others' quizzical looks, he explained, "I was in the army for a short stint during the Mexican War."

The four stallmates joined the stream of men heading in the direction of the former Mechanics Hall, a large building now designated as the commissary. A sergeant stood outside the entrance and shouted orders at the men.

"You will be divided within your company into messes of six men each. Get to know each other. These are your new best friends. Fall in! Tallest to smallest."

The sergeant grouped Garrett, Rawlie, Joe, and Frank with the two men behind them – a twitchy young recruit with a reddish mustache and a prodigious set of sideburns and a grizzle-bearded man of at least forty. The older man's dour expression was made even more menacing by a diagonal scar that extended from his forehead to his jaw.

Each of the men was issued a tin plate, knife, fork, two spoons, and a tin cup. In single file they shuffled forward to receive their rations, which consisted of a hard biscuit called hard tack, salt pork, beans, coffee, and sugar. Staring in dismay at the food on his plate, Garrett followed his new messmates to a spot beneath the shade of one of the few trees on the fairgrounds.

"Well, I guess we ought to introduce ourselves," said Frank when they were all seated. "I'm Frank Ford, from Birmingham. Garrett Cameron, here, is from Allegheny City. Rawlie McMahon and Joe Frye, both from Pittsburgh. Glassmaker, would-be lawyer, clerk, student," he said pointing to each in turn.

"I'm Caleb Layton," said the younger, red-haired man. "I'm a camera operator from Pittsburgh. Well, an assistant to one anyway. And this is Leonard Studer."

The older man took a sip of coffee and nodded.

"And what do you do for a living?" asked Rawlie.

"Whatever needs doin'," drawled Leonard without looking up from his plate.

Rawlie smirked. "Been doin' that long?"

"Long enough," Leonard replied.

Rawlie refused to let go. "Nice scar you got there. Souvenir from an angry husband?"

Leonard raised his head and his piercing blue eyes fixed Rawlie from beneath shaggy brows. "Naw. Got it from asking one too many questions."

Rawlie held up his hands in surrender and turned back to his food.

"Say, do they really expect us to eat this stuff?" asked Caleb. He held up the piece of salt pork and sniffed it.

"This is pretty standard fare in the field," said Frank. He dipped his hard bread into his coffee. "But, I'm sure once we get a company cook, things will improve."

"I dare say the kind ladies of Pittsburgh will also provide us with a few nice treats as soon as they learn of our plight," said Rawlie. "And I intend to inform them as soon as possible."

After taking a few tentative bites, Garrett set down his plate.

"You gonna finish that?" asked Joe.

"No. Go ahead." Garrett watched in amazement as the young man devoured his leftovers.

"I noticed we seem to be one of the few companies here with uniforms or guns," said Caleb. "Any word on when the rest of them get outfitted?"

"Nobody seems to know," said Rawlie. "All the officers will say is 'soon'."

"So, what do we do in the meantime?" asked Joe.

Frank looked at him and smiled.

"We drill."

And drill they did. Each and every day the men of Camp Wilkins rose at 5:00 a.m. for reveille and roll call. From then on their day consisted of drill and instruction, interrupted only by meals and short periods of rest. The recruits were taught how to salute, how to stand, how to march, and how to turn and move as one. There were drum and bugle calls to learn as well: calls for reveille, breakfast call, sick call, drill, dinner, retreat, assembly of the guard, tattoo, and taps. Each call had to be learned and obeyed quickly. The harangues of the officers rang through the camp as they sought to impose discipline on the bumbling, inexperienced volunteers. When tattoo sounded at 9:30 p.m., many of the men fell into bed and were already asleep when lights out sounded at 10 p.m.

In reality, many of the officers were as green as the recruits. Officers were elected by the men of their company, and positions often were awarded without regard to prior military experience. Many an officer was chosen on the basis of popularity, political influence, or simply because the man had organized the unit. Although some men rose to the challenge and learned to lead on the job, in the early days of the war many companies found themselves in dangerous situations due to inexperienced or ineffectual leadership. But, even those companies with experienced leadership encountered difficulties as the recruits, used to independence and democratic participation, initially balked at the dictatorial rigidity of military rules.

Little by little, however, the men began to master the rudiments of soldiering. They learned to *March by the Flank*, *By Company into Line*, and to execute various wheeling movements. They drilled until the dust swirled high into the air and what little grass was left around the camp was ground into the dirt. This constant marching, along with revolving guard duty, the lack of uniforms and guns, and the monotonous food at what the men had sardonically dubbed *The Camp Wilkins Café*, quickly made the men proficient at another important soldierly skill – complaining.

There was some relief from the drudgery of camp life, however. Not long after the first companies entered Camp Wilkins, sutlers' tents sprang up around the perimeter like desert flowers after a rain. These independent vendors filled the soldiers' needs for tobacco, dry goods, and liquor, and offered a wider variety of foods to supplement the bland fare available from the commissary.

The men spent their limited free time on various sports and leisure activities, such as pitching quoits (a game similar to horseshoes, played with iron rings), holding boxing matches, playing cards, reading, or writing letters.

One of the most popular diversions, however, was the afternoon dress parade. The commander had ordered the camp be opened to the public between the hours of 3:00 p.m. and 6:00 p.m. so that those who wished could watch the regimental drill and parade. The presence of an army camp was a novelty for the people of Pittsburgh, and each day a large crowd turned out. Some had loved ones in the ranks, but others came just to enjoy the spectacle of the massed force of men. The troops looked forward to this pageant as much as the visitors, for afterwards they were allowed to mingle with the crowd, who showered the soldiers with homemade baked goods and praise.

As soon as she learned about the public dress parades, Clara pleaded to be allowed to attend.

"I don't see why not," said Dr. Ambrose.

"Peter," admonished Mrs. Ambrose, "I hardly think it's appropriate for our daughter to be seen lurking around an army camp."

"But, Mama," said Clara, "everyone goes. Marie Ward told me that she, Lucinda, and all of the young society ladies take food and home-made items to the soldiers as often as they can. It's considered quite patriotic."

Dr. Ambrose cast a knowing look at Clara, but she maintained her innocent expression.

"Really?" Mrs. Ambrose frowned. "Well … in that case …. But no more than once a week. And only when your father can serve as an escort."

"But Papa's been so busy lately with all the people in town," said Clara. "What if he's called away?"

"On those occasions, I think Mary would be an acceptable chaperone," said Dr. Ambrose. Mrs. Ambrose started to protest. "If her duties allow," he amended.

Clara suppressed a triumphant smile when her mother agreed to this arrangement without further argument.

* * *

Although the opening of Camp Wilkins had temporarily reduced the numbers of soldiers crowding the streets of Pittsburgh, the Pennsylvania State Legislature was slow to admit more units to the camp. In the meantime, Pittsburgh had become a major terminus for Federal troops heading to Washington or to the western Department of the Ohio, as well as a gathering spot for volunteers from all over the western part of the state who were hoping to be accepted into Federal or Reserve service. A constant stream of these recruits arrived daily, by steamboat, train, wagon, and on foot, most of them with nowhere to go and all of them needing to be housed, fed, clothed, and entertained. Within weeks of the opening of Camp Wilkins, the hotels, restaurants, and inns were once more filled to bursting, as were the theaters, saloons, and brothels.

The populace watched with a mixture of pride and dismay as these eager volunteers poured into Pittsburgh and strained not only the city's physical resources, but its social boundaries. To be sure, the prostitutes were doing an unprecedented business, but even the respectable women of Pittsburgh found themselves engaged in activities heretofore thought improper. With so many of their own men off to enlist, more and more women were seen driving their own carriages, conducting business alone, or walking the streets unescorted. The young women of the city had never seen so many handsome, eligible young men, and many a flirtatious glance and conversation were exchanged that would have been thought scandalous only months earlier. The immediacy and headiness of the war had loosed the moral stays of society, and the effects were already evident on the streets of Pittsburgh.

The yellow, horse-drawn Citizens Street Passenger Railway car, the one with the picture of the white swan painted upon it, rattled to a stop at the corner of Sixth Street and Penn Street in Pittsburgh. Annie paid her fare to the conductor and teetered down the aisle to an empty seat midway back. She had been up and out early to deliver some sheet music from Father Andrew Gibbs, the pastor of St. Mary's Church in Lawrenceville, to the choir director of St. Paul's Cathedral on Fifth Street in Pittsburgh for use in a special Mass to be said for the departing soldiers. The nature of the errand required she dress in her best and most confining clothes, and just the four-block walk from the cathedral to the streetcar in her stays and petticoats left her feeling flushed and breathless. She tugged surreptitiously at the bodice of her dress and wondered how Clara could bear to wear such oppressive clothes every day.

As the omnibus headed northeast on Penn Street toward Lawrenceville, Annie closed her eyes. So much was happening so quickly these days. Her four older brothers had joined an infantry company stationed at Camp Wilkins, and her mother was worried sick they would be called up for Federal service at any moment. Annie was more concerned about the loss of their boat builders' wages, not that the no-accounts had taken that into consideration when they enlisted. Now it fell to her to find some paying job to help the family meet the financial shortfall. That meant her dream of furthering her education with the nuns at St. Mary's would have to be put on hold indefinitely. She wished she could talk to Clara about it. She wondered if she dared risk Mrs. Ambrose's chilly disapproval to pay her friend a visit on the way home.

"Excuse me, Miss. Is this seat taken?"

Annie opened her eyes to find a large, rough-looking man in a worn suit looming over her. His leer revealed yellowed teeth and Annie detected the sour smell of alcohol on his breath. Pittsburgh was filled with such toughs these days, come to join the army or to make money off its proximity.

"Yes, 'tis," she snapped, and turned her head toward the window.

"Ah, so you're a little Mick, are ya?" The man plopped down onto the seat next to her. "Just spent a lovely evening on Virgin Alley with one of your kind," he slurred. He leaned in close. "Wish I'd known you was around though. Great improvement over the homely little strumpet I was with."

Annie was trying to decide whether to slap the man or scream, when a large hand grabbed the drunk by the shoulder and jerked him from the seat.

"I believe the lady told you this seat was taken." A young man in uniform stood in the aisle with the drunk firmly in his grip.

"Hey! Get off!" protested the man.

"Get off? Well, why didn't you say so?" The soldier spun the man around and pinned his arms behind his back. "Conductor, this gentleman would like to get off."

The conductor, who had witnessed the exchange, reined the horses to a halt in mid-block. Annie's rescuer propelled the drunk down the aisle and sent him airborne out the doorway of the car. The man landed in an indignant heap on the street. With a nod to the conductor, the soldier straightened his sack coat and made his way back down the aisle to Annie.

"May I, Miss?" he gestured to the seat beside her.

Annie nodded and moved her skirts aside.

"Are you all right?" the soldier asked quietly as the omnibus lurched into motion.

"Yes," replied Annie in a shaky voice. "Thank you, Sir. I don't know what I'd have done if you'd not come along."

"Have you no escort?"

Annie smiled. "I'm afraid that sort of custom is not practiced in my part of the city."

"Well, it's obviously needed for someone as attractive as you," the man replied without artifice. Annie blushed. "Regardless, I'm sorry you were subjected to such treatment. I'm afraid the presence of the army has drawn all sorts of people to Pittsburgh."

She nodded, embarrassed yet relieved to have the protection of this handsome young man.

The car reached the end of the line at Clymer Street at the western edge of Camp Wilkins. As the passengers began exiting the car, the soldier turned to her once more.

"Have you far to go?" he asked. "I could escort you the rest of the way if it would ease your mind."

"No, thank you, Sir. It's kind you are to offer, but I've just a few blocks more."

"You're sure?"

Annie nodded.

"Then I'll bid you good day, Miss." The man rose and bowed to her before hopping off the streetcar.

The eyes of every female passenger on the car watched the broad-shouldered soldier stride down Penn Street, turn, and disappear through the camp gate. Lost in thoughts of her chivalrous rescuer, Annie alighted from the car and strolled through the streets of Lawrenceville. She was at her own doorstep before she realized she had forgotten to stop and see Clara.

On the second Saturday after the Pittsburgh Rifles arrived at Camp Wilkins, Dr. Ambrose agreed to take Clara to the afternoon's scheduled dress parade. Clara fidgeted all through dinner and leapt up from the table as soon as she was excused.

"Honestly," said Mrs. Ambrose as her younger daughter bolted from the dining room to change her clothes, "you'd think she hadn't seen him in a year rather than just a few weeks."

Dr. Ambrose reached for his wife's hand. "I remember that feeling. In fact, I still feel that way."

"Oh, Peter," scolded Mrs. Ambrose.

Upstairs, Clara was staring in dismay at the dresses in her armoire. This would be the first time she had seen Garrett since he had enlisted, and she wanted to look her best. She tried on four different outfits before deciding on the blue and white linen dress with the full, curtained skirt. She arranged her dark hair into a loose bun at the nape of her neck and pinned a blue flowered hat to her head at a jaunty angle. Finally, she tied a white ribbon bearing a cameo around her neck and pulled on her white cotton gloves.

"Well," she remarked to her reflection in her dressing table mirror, "if that doesn't make him take notice, nothing will."

She glided down the stairs and into the parlor. Her mother was at her writing desk.

"I'm ready," Clara announced, making a quick twirl. "Where's Father?"

Her mother looked up from her correspondence.

"Oh, Clara, I'm so sorry, but your father was called away on an emergency. He hoped to be back by now, but it appears he was detained longer than expected."

Clara's face fell. "But … but, the dress parade starts in half an hour."

"I know it's disappointing, dear, but it can't be helped. People rarely get sick at convenient times."

"What about Mary? Father said she could chaperone in his place."

"*If* her duties allowed," said her mother. "But, I'm afraid she has far too much to do today."

Clara cast about desperately for a solution. "Mother," she said, biting her lip, "do you think you could come with me?"

"I'm afraid that's not possible, Clara." Mrs. Ambrose gestured helplessly to her desk. "As you can see, I have all of this correspondence to attend to, as well as the week's meals to plan." She shook her head. "I'm sorry, dear."

As her mother bent back to her writing, Clara's eyes filled with tears of frustration. She understood now. There would always be too many duties for Mary; her mother would always be too busy. Her mother had never intended for Clara to visit the camp at all. Oh, how could she be so cruel?

Just then, Mary entered the parlor.

"All right," she said as she pinned her straw hat to her head, "let's be goin'."

"Going where?" said Mrs. Ambrose.

"To the army camp," said Mary. "Dr. Ambrose said if he wasn't back by half past two, I was to take Clara, meself."

"Oh, Mary!" exclaimed Clara.

"That's very kind of you, Mary," her mother interrupted, "but I'm afraid it just isn't possible. You have far too many tasks to complete before the end of the day. For instance, the windows need to be washed …."

"Done."

" … and the linens changed."

"I changed all the beds this morning."

"Really?" Mrs. Ambrose raised a skeptical eyebrow.

Mary nodded. "Even hung the quilts out to air, it bein' such a nice day and all."

Mrs. Ambrose pressed her lips into a thin line. "Well, you simply cannot leave before the marketing is done."

"I went to the market while the linens were dryin'. Stopped at the butcher, too. Found a lovely chicken. It's all seasoned and ready to slip into the oven for supper with some fresh vegetables tucked all 'round. And I made the doctor's favorite pie while I was doin' the bakin' for the soldiers." She nodded to the two cloth-covered baskets on her arm.

"My, my," said Mrs. Ambrose, "you've been uncommonly productive today, Mary."

"It's the weather, Ma'am," said Mary. "It's invigoratin'."

"So, may I go, Mother?" asked Clara.

Mrs. Ambrose glowered at Mary. "Yes," she said through clenched teeth, "you may go."

"Thank you, Mother," said Clara. "And, thank *you*, Mary." She gave the housekeeper a quick hug.

"Watch me hat! Watch me hat," said Mary, grabbing her bonnet to keep it from falling.

Mrs. Ambrose turned back to her desk and jabbed at her inkwell.

"Mary, you are a life saver," said Clara once they were outside.

"Well, you can thank you father. He knew how much you were lookin' forward to this visit, so he gave me a little advance notice just in case he got called away."

"But, how did you manage to get all that work done?"

"I was what you might call particularly motivated," said Mary. "I've me own boyo over to the camp; one o' the cooks, from me own County Mayo. Besides, it was worth it just to see the look on your mother's face – like she'd sucked an entire tree full of lemons."

Clara giggled.

As the two women, baskets in hand, strolled along Butler Street in the late spring sunshine, they marveled that even here, in little Lawrenceville, the streets were filled with soldiers.

"Well, would you look at that," said Mary. Across the street was a beaming young woman with a soldier on each arm. "It's Emma Norris. Homely as a mud fence, God help her. And now look at her. Paradin' down the street like the Queen of England."

"Sh!" warned Clara. "She'll hear you."

"I tell you," Mary continued, unchecked, "this war was the best thing that ever happened to the spinsters of Lawrenceville. Meself included," she added with a chuckle.

As the two women reached the outskirts of Camp Wilkins, a Citizens Passenger Car from Pittsburgh pulled up and discharged its load of gaily dressed visitors. Mary and Clara joined the crowd as it funneled through the main gate.

"Glory be!" said Mary. "The whole town must be here."

In fact, almost six thousand people had turned out to see the dress parade, everyone from mill workers to bank executives, and their families. Clara recognized some of her father's patients and colleagues, a few schoolmates, a couple of judges and politicians, and some of the daughters of the women in her mother's tea group.

"Here's a good spot," said Mary. She and Clara staked out a position near the reviewing stand from which to watch the troops. And not a moment too soon, for the edges of the parade grounds were quickly filling up, with even more spectators finding seats on the hillside near the Pennsylvania Railroad tracks. Anxiously, Clara scanned the crowd.

"There she is," she cried after a few moments. "Annie!" Clara waved excitedly. "Annie! Over here."

Annie Burke hurried toward them as quickly as the two large baskets in her arms would permit.

"I was afraid you might not find us in this crowd," said Clara as she hugged her friend. "Good heavens. What do you have in those baskets?"

"Spice cakes," Annie replied. She pulled back a checkered cloth to reveal the still warm confections. "Ma wanted me to bring some for me brothers and I made a few extra to sell. I've a little business sellin' cakes and bread to the soldiers. Now that me brothers are in the army, Ma and Da can use the extra income."

"Annie, you are so clever," said Clara.

Any further discussion was cut off by the sound of a bugle and drums announcing the start of the dress parade. Lines of men marched by columns across the dirt-packed parade grounds, formerly the infield of the fairground's racetrack. Despite the hodgepodge of clothing owing to the lack of uniforms, the men made a credible enough display to elicit enthusiastic applause for the few simple maneuvers they performed.

As Clara searched the ranks for Garrett, her gaze passed over a group of top-hatted dignitaries in the reviewing stand. Suddenly, she spied Edgar Gliddon among them. He was staring directly at her. Quickly, she turned away.

"Clara. What's wrong?" asked Annie, noticing her high color.

"Edgar Gliddon's here," Clara whispered.

"Where?" Annie craned her neck for a glimpse.

"Don't look! I don't want him to know I saw him."

When the dress parade ended and the men were dismissed from the ranks, the crowd began to disperse, some to return home, others to mingle with the soldiers on the parade ground.

"Come," Clara said to Annie. "I can't wait for you to meet Garrett … Mr. Cameron."

"Now remember," said Mary, "meet me at the front gate at 5:30 p.m. No later. Your mother will have me head if I'm not back in time to make the supper." She bustled off in search of her cook.

Clara and Annie walked down onto the parade ground in search of Garrett and Annie's brothers. Many of the men had lingered to talk to friends and family, and quite a number of heads turned as the two attractive young women – one tall and willowy, the other shapely and petite – passed through the crowd.

Suddenly, Edgar appeared before them.

"Ah, Miss Ambrose," he said, bowing. "I thought I saw you in the audience. I was afraid I might have missed you. Did you enjoy all the pageantry?"

Clara forced a smile. "Yes, Mr. Gliddon. I thought the soldiers performed splendidly."

"Did you?" he said. "I thought they looked quite raw – mismatched uniforms, little weaponry, and inexperienced leadership. But then I assume that's why some of the local military leaders and committee members asked me to attend."

"Why, Mr. Gliddon," said Clara, "are you planning to volunteer?"

Edgar laughed aloud. "Hardly." He suddenly noticed the young woman standing by Clara's side. "I beg your pardon. Miss Ambrose, would you be kind enough to introduce me to your lovely companion?"

"Of course," said Clara. "Miss Burke, may I present Mr. Edgar Gliddon."

Edgar raised an eyebrow at the name. His suspicions were confirmed the moment Annie spoke.

"How do you do, Mr. Gliddon," she said in her soft brogue.

Edgar's congenial expression evaporated. With a dismissive glance he turned back to Clara.

"So, Miss Ambrose. Exactly what brought you to Camp Wilkins today, other than your undying admiration for our defenders of the Union?"

"Miss Ambrose and me are visitin' me brothers," blurted Annie before Clara could answer. "Gabriel, Liam, Daniel, and Francis. They've all signed up to fight in the war, all four of them, glory be to God. It's just that proud of them, I am." Clara stared at Annie wide-eyed as she rambled on in an exaggerated brogue. "And seein' as how soldierin' is such a difficult life, I brought them these lovely spice cakes. Made them meself from me ma's recipe from the ol' country. Had the priest pray over them to give them special healin' powers. Guaranteed to scare away bullets. Wouldja be wantin' one, Mr. Gliddon?"

Annie pulled a cake out of her basket and thrust it at Edgar. He stepped back as if fearing contamination.

"No. No, thank you," he said. With a wary, sidelong look at Annie, he addressed Clara once more. "Miss Ambrose, I'm afraid I've other dignitaries I simply must speak to before they leave. I'll look forward to conversing with you at a time when you're not so ... encumbered." He tipped his hat and hurried away.

Clara turned to Annie. "What in the world has come over you?"

Annie's feigned sweet expression turned sour. "He's even worse than you said. The nerve of the man! What business is it of his who you came to see today? And did you see the way he looked at me when he realized I was Irish? He immediately assumed I was ignorant and common." She gave a wry smile. "So, I just thought I'd live up – or should I say, down – to his expectations. Besides," she added with a giggle, "I ran him off, did I not?"

Clara looked at her with a mixture of amusement and admiration. "You did indeed."

"Miss Ambrose!" Garrett strode across the parade ground. He couldn't believe how lovely Clara looked standing there in her blue dress, like a piece of the sky had fallen to earth. He desperately wanted to kiss her lips, but settled for kissing her hand. The look in her eyes assured him his feelings were returned.

"Oh," said Clara, suddenly remembering her manners. "Mr. Cameron. May I present my dearest friend ...."

"Well, hello again," said Garrett.

"It's you," sputtered Annie.

"You two have met?" said Clara.

"Yes," said Garrett. "Well, not formally. We met on the omnibus last week."

"He was the one I told you about," said Annie. "The soldier who came to me rescue."

Clara gave Garrett a grateful look. "Why am I not surprised," she said. "Well, Mr. Cameron, may I formally introduce you to Miss Annie Burke."

Garrett bowed over Annie's hand. She blushed to the tips of her ears.

"Miss Ambrose speaks very highly of you, Miss Burke."

"Does she now?" said Annie. "That's very nice of her. And you. I mean, to help me out the way you did." Her color deepened. "Well, I'll be goin'. I've to get these cakes to me brothers. 'Tis lovely to meet you again, Mr. Cameron. Goodbye. Goodbye, Clara."

Annie scurried off, her baskets cutting a wide swath through the crowd.

"Was it something I said?" asked Garrett, chuckling.

"No," said Clara. "Believe me, she's not always that tongue-tied. I think she was just surprised you turned out to be her rescuer. Should I be jealous?" she teased.

"Desperately, if it will keep that look in your eyes," said Garrett. "Come. Walk with me." He took her basket and offered his arm to lead her away from the appreciative eyes of his fellow soldiers. "Do you have any idea how much I've missed you?" he asked in a husky voice. "How much I looked forward to seeing you today?"

"Yes, because I feel the same way," she answered. "This has been the longest two weeks of my life. Tell me everything. Do they work you too hard? Do you have enough to eat?"

Garrett shrugged. "The food is bland, the drilling is monotonous, and we've had no word on when to expect uniforms or guns for the rest of the men. Other than that ....."

"Sounds pretty dismal," said Clara.

"On the bright side, they've outfitted our stalls with raised planks for us to sleep on, so no more sleeping on the ground."

"You're sleeping on wooden planks?"

"Well, we cover them with straw. It's not so bad." Clara looked unconvinced. "The men in my company, and in my mess in particular, are a good bunch of fellows. And our officers are experienced; something that can't be said of some of the other companies' officers. That's going to be very important when we get into the fight … if we ever do." The frustration crept into Garrett's voice. He banished it with a smile. "So, tell me what's going on in the outside world."

"Well, every day more volunteers are arriving from all over the state," said Clara. "And for every soldier, ten other people appear intent on selling him something. It's a great time to be a shop owner or an innkeeper. Or a saloon keeper. Mother says she doesn't feel safe on the streets anymore with all the riff-raff about. That's part of the reason she insists on my having a chaperone if I wish to come see you."

"I hate to admit it, but she's probably right," said Garrett. "But, how is it you were able to come alone today? Not that I'm complaining, mind you."

"Father made Mother agree to let Mary act as my chaperone whenever he can't." She giggled. "I'm afraid she's not a very good one."

"I always knew I liked her," said Garrett. "How is your father, by the way?"

"Actually, I'm a little worried about him," Clara confided. "He's incredibly busy, what with all the new people in town, soldiers and civilians, and all of them needing a doctor. But beyond that, he seems so, I don't know, distant lately."

"Have you tried talking to him about it?"

"I tried once. He just patted my hand and said everything was fine. But I know him. There's something troubling him."

"Be patient. I'm sure he'll tell you when he's ready."

Clara gave him a grateful smile. "Oh Garrett. I always feel better after I've talked with you."

"I'm glad," said Garrett, "but I must confess there are other things I'd like to do with you than talk."

He pulled her behind the corner of a building and took her into his arms.

Annie stood at the end of a long line of sutlers' tents with one basket over her arm and the other one empty at her feet. It had taken no time at all to sell the majority of her spice cakes. Her brothers had spread the word among their comrades who had, in turn, spread the word of the comeliness of the vendor. Annie was just happy to be kept busy, for every time there was a lull, she relived her embarrassment.

She still couldn't believe the handsome streetcar soldier of her fantasy had turned out to be Clara's Mr. Cameron. And what a stuttering fool she had made of herself when they were introduced. Now, as the crowds around the sutlers' tents dwindled, she struggled with another unpleasant emotion: jealousy. It wasn't that Annie had designs on Garrett, specifically. But she did envy Clara the thrill of a young woman with a handsome young man in her thrall.

Annie supposed that, despite their great friendship, she had always been a little jealous of Clara; a little bit in awe – of her beauty, her clothes, her education, and the apparent ease of her life. But what she most envied about Clara was her view of the world.

Clara believed in a world where good triumphed over evil; a world in which distinctions based on race, religion, ethnicity, or wealth had no meaning. Annie lived in the real world; a world of prejudice and poverty, of drunken fathers out of work and mothers with too many mouths to feed, of good people broken by the day-to-day struggle to survive. Annie recognized the naiveté of Clara's position and attributed it, in part, to Clara's sheltered upbringing. But there was more to it than that. Clara was, at heart, an optimist with an irrepressible belief in the ultimate goodness of those around her. And, despite all the evidence to the contrary, she made Annie want to believe it, too.

"Miss?"

Annie looked up into the soft brown eyes of a very tall soldier. She realized he must have been standing there for some time.

"Yes?"

"The cakes?" stammered the young man. "I was wondering if I might buy two?"

"Yes. Of course, of course." Annie fumbled in her basket. "That'd be four cents, please."

He counted out the coins and placed them in Annie's outstretched hand.

"You're Daniel Burke's sister, aren't you?"

"I am. You know Daniel?"

He nodded. "He's in a different company, but he beats me regularly in the camp-wide foot races."

Annie lowered her head to hide her smirk. She didn't doubt it. Daniel was known for his speed, and the soldier before her was a great stork of a man. It would take him a mile just to get his legs unfurled. "He is a fast one."

The silence stretched between them.

"I'm Joe," the soldier blurted suddenly. "Joe Frye."

Annie looked up at him again. He was nice looking in an unfinished way; one of those young men whose looks would find him in maturity, a maturity he was obviously trying to hasten with a determined fringe of beard. He blushed under her scrutiny and his shyness touched her heart.

"Pleased to meet you, Mr. Frye," she said.

They both turned at the sound of a bugle call.

"That's the call to supper." His tone was apologetic. Placing his cap on his head, he paused. "Will you ... will you be coming back? To sell the cakes, I mean?"

Annie hesitated. "Perhaps. As long as there's a demand."

"Oh, there will be." His grin started small and broadened. "I'll see to it." He touched the brim of his cap. "Good day, Miss Burke."

"Well!" huffed Annie, hands on hips, as she watched him trot away. "Perhaps not so shy after all."

But, suddenly she felt a little less envious of Clara.

CHAPTER 7

ON THE 20TH OF MAY, Clara and Mary were in the kitchen baking yet more loaves of bread for the soldiers when they heard a loud thump overhead.

"Mama!" came Helen's insistent voice. Clara and Mary exchanged looks.

As the baby's birth neared, Dr. Ambrose had confined Helen to bed rest. Bored with spending her days reading and napping, she kept Mrs. Ambrose, Clara, and Mary running up and down the stairs to tend to her every need. At the moment, Mrs. Ambrose was out of the house on social calls.

"I'll go," said Clara with a sigh. "Her Highness probably just wants the window opened again."

"I just closed it for her not ten minutes ago," said Mary. She shook her head as she brushed an egg wash over her lineup of loaves.

Clara trudged up the stairs to her sister's room and opened the door.

"Helen, Mother's not here. What do you …." The words stuck in her throat. Helen lay on the floor, her face contorted in pain. The lower half of her nightgown was soaked in fluid and blood.

"Oh, my God!" Clara rushed to her sister's side. "Mary!" she shouted. "Mary!"

Within moments, Mary burst into the room. "Jesus, Mary, and Joseph!"

"Quick," ordered Clara. "Help me get her onto the bed."

The two women struggled to lift Helen's limp body.

"I'll see to her," said Mary. "Go find Dr. Ambrose."

Clara raced down the stairs, threw open the front door, and nearly collided with her father, who had just stepped onto the stoop.

"Papa! Oh, thank God," she gasped. "The baby's coming, and something's very wrong."

"Where's your mother?" said her father, already on his way up the stairs.

"Out on visits."

"Find her," he said, and disappeared into Helen's room.

Clara located her mother at the third house she checked. The two of them rushed home to find Mary coming out of Helen's room, her arms filled with soiled towels.

"How is she?" asked Mrs. Ambrose.

"The baby's turned wrong, bless its little soul," said Mary in a hushed voice.

"Clara, you wait here," said Mrs. Ambrose. She entered the room and closed the door behind her.

Clara paced the hall for what seemed like hours. She flinched every time she heard Helen moan or scream. Mary ran in and out, fetching things for Dr. Ambrose while mumbling the rosary under her breath. Whenever Clara asked what was going on, she would just shake her head. As time went on, Helen's cries became weaker. Clara didn't see how her fragile sister could possibly withstand the ordeal much longer. Suddenly, she heard a baby cry. She had almost forgotten about the baby in her worry over Helen. Was it a boy or a girl? And how was Helen? She pressed her ear to the door and listened to the rustling and murmuring from within. The baby had stopped crying. Was that good or bad? wondered Clara. And why was there now no sound at all from Helen?

Just when Clara thought she would go crazy, her mother opened the door. Looking weary but relieved, she smiled.

"Would you like to come in and say hello to your new nephew?"

"It's a boy?" said Clara.

Mrs. Ambrose nodded happily.

Clara peeked in the doorway. Her father, with his shirtsleeves rolled up to his elbows, was packing up his instruments while Mary gathered up the bloody sheets. Helen, looking pale and small, lay in the freshly made bed. In the crook of her arm, a little bundle mewed softly. As Clara tiptoed to the bedside, Helen's eyes fluttered open. Her smile, though exhausted, was radiant.

"Well, what do you think?" she asked, her voice weak and raspy.

Clara pulled back the corner of the baby blanket and peered at the tiny red-faced infant, asleep with one perfect little hand under his chin.

"Oh, Helen. He's beautiful," whispered Clara. Her father and mother came up behind her.

"Caused his mother quite a time," said Dr. Ambrose as he beamed down at his daughter and his new grandson. "He wanted to come into the world his own way. I warned you, Helen. Boys are stubborn."

"Just like his father," said Helen with a flicker of a grin.

"Do you know what you're going to name him?" asked Clara.

Helen nodded. "George and I talked about it before he left. We're naming him after his daddy's company. Jackson Blues Pitcher." She glowed with pride.

Clara's eyes widened. "Oh. What a unique name," she managed.

Her father placed his arm around Clara's shoulders. "Come. Let's let these two get some sleep."

"I'm going to stay for a little while," said Mrs. Ambrose. She settled into the rocking chair beside the bed. Dr. Ambrose kissed the top of her head.

"All right, Grandmother."

Mrs. Ambrose smiled.

"Really, Papa," said Clara as they stepped into the hallway and closed the door behind them, "are they both going to be all right?"

"Yes, Clara," said her father. "It was a little touch and go with Helen for a while, but she should be fine now." He sighed. "We have a lot to be thankful for."

"Yes," said Clara, "not the least of which is that George didn't end up joining the Zouave Cadets."

"Sh, Clara! She'll hear you," said her father. But he chuckled the whole way down to the kitchen where Mary poured them both a much-needed cup of tea.

A few days later, Dr. Ambrose drove Clara into Pittsburgh to pick up some items for the baby. Mrs. Ambrose remained behind, unwilling to trust the care of both Helen and little Jackson to Mary, much to the housekeeper's indignation.

Clara scoured the Market House for cloth, soft yarn, buttons, and various colored threads to be used in making baby clothes and blankets. Dr. Ambrose spent his time visiting a few of the recruiting stations and talking with the officers about the medical situation in the newly-expanded Union army. Afterward, Clara and her father treated themselves to supper at the St. Charles Hotel and lingered over coffee to discuss the war news. By the time they headed back to Lawrenceville, the sun had already dropped below the line of trees high atop Coal Hill across the Monongahela River.

As their carriage traveled along Penn Street past Camp Wilkins, Clara could hear the bugles and the faint barking of officers directing the troops in the assembly of the guard. She peered through the fading light to see if she could spot Garrett among the assembled men, but, if he was there, he was indistinguishable from the rest of the dusty brown recruits. Her disappointment was not lost on Dr. Ambrose.

"How's Mr. Cameron doing, Clara?" he asked.

"All right, I guess. He's getting frustrated though. There's still no word on uniforms or guns for the rest of the men. And they've heard nothing as to when or if they'll be called up, or when they'll receive their pay. And, every day more men arrive, with no place to put them."

"Sounds like typical army life," said her father. He patted her hand. "Don't worry. I get the feeling your Mr. Cameron can handle himself pretty well."

"I hope so, Papa," said Clara.

They had just passed the main gate of the camp when a familiar wagon drew near, headed in the opposite direction.

"Hello, Dr. Ambrose. Miss Ambrose." Mr. Webster tipped his hat as he pulled up alongside them.

"Hello, Mr. Webster," said Clara. "You're working late tonight."

"Yes, indeed. No rest for the wicked. I've got to get down to the wharf before 9:00 p.m. Got a keelboat shoving off that's waiting for this load of molasses." With a jerk of his head, he indicated the barrels that filled the back of his wagon.

"Where's it headed?" asked Dr. Ambrose.

"Down the Ohio to the Quakers at New Brighton," said Mr. Webster.

Dr. Ambrose nodded.

Just then, a small noise came from the back of the wagon; a slight cough, a muffled stirring, barely audible over the traffic in the street. Dr. Ambrose and Mr. Webster exchanged a quick look.

"Well, I'd best be off. Don't want to keep the boat captain waiting."

"Goodbye, Mr. Webster. Take care," said Dr. Ambrose.

The two wagons drew away from each other and Clara turned her head for a last look back at Camp Wilkins. As her gaze passed over the bed of Mr. Webster's wagon, she was startled to see a dark eye peering at her from a hole in one of the barrels. It was there and gone in an instant.

Clara gasped and grabbed her father's arm.

"Papa!" she said in a low voice. "There's someone ... or something hiding in the back of Mr. Webster's wagon."

"I'm sure you're mistaken," he replied without even turning his head.

"No! I saw something. I'm certain of it." Clara began to turn once more.

"Clara!" snapped her father. "Face forward."

She gaped at him in surprise.

"I did not see anything," he repeated. "And neither did you."

"But ...."

"Listen to me carefully," he said. "Forget what you saw or think you saw. A great many good people could be hurt by letting our imaginations and our tongues run wild." He looked at her, his eyes solemn. "Do you understand?"

And suddenly, she did. The late night calls; all the medicines for Mrs. Webster, despite her apparent robust health; Mr. Lovett's knowing smile; her father's unusual interest in the destination of a load of molasses.

"Yes, Papa." She reached over and gave his hand a squeeze. "But, aren't you taking an awful risk?"

"Sometimes you have to do what's right, regardless of the risk," he answered.

Clara linked her arm through his and rested her head on his shoulder. She had always loved her father, but she was only now beginning to realize just how truly good and courageous a man he was.

At the start of morning drill, Garrett stood with the rest of the Pittsburgh Rifles on the parade grounds at Camp Wilkins. As they waited, formed in company at shoulder arms, Garrett was acutely aware of the wail of steamboat whistles on the Allegheny River a few blocks behind him, and the nearby chugging of the locomotive on the Pennsylvania Railroad tracks to his front. They were familiar sounds, sounds that reminded him of his life *before*.

"Company! Right face!" came the command.

The company pivoted and was now facing southwest toward Pittsburgh. Through the ever-present smog, Garrett could identify the spires of the First Reformed Presbyterian Church, Trinity Church, and the twin spires of St. Paul's Cathedral jutting up from the skyline of the city some two miles distant. He was struck by the unreal nature of his situation. How odd it was, in this familiar place, to suddenly find himself a soldier, his every move regimented and prescribed, drilling and training to meet other soldiers on the field of battle.

"Forward! March!"

The men stepped off, coming to four abreast, marching shoulder to shoulder. Rawlie and Caleb were on either side of Garrett in the rank, Joe behind him in the file, and Frank and Leonard on either side of Joe.

"By files, right! March!"

The company turned in the direction of the river. Above the buildings and factories that blocked his view of the water, Garrett could see Troy Hill rising up on the far side marking the eastern most edge of Allegheny City. Barely a month ago, he had roamed the streets and hills of that shaded place at will. He had watched the river below as it flowed toward its meeting with the Monongahela and contemplated what the future might bring. Now his free time was restricted to a two-hour pass, once a week, and his future was in the hands of others.

"By files, right! March!"

Now they were facing northeast toward Lawrenceville. Down the narrow streets to his left, just beyond the foundries and iron works that crowded the shore, Garrett caught glimpses of the Allegheny River and of Herr's Island, sitting like a ship in the middle of the current. But his thoughts were on a red brick house, less than a mile away, where a girl waited for him; a beautiful, headstrong, witty girl with whom he was pretty sure he was in love. He should be spending this lovely May day with her, listening to her laugh, and watching the soft contours of her face as she told him of her hopes and dreams.

"By files, right! March!"

Once again, the entire company pivoted on its heel. As they made this last turn of their rectangular march, Garrett's gaze came to rest on the Western Pennsylvania Hospital situated on the hill just beyond the Pennsylvania Railroad tracks at the southern edge of the camp. At the base of the four-story brick building, to the left of the main door, he noticed a bit of color, just the slightest tinge of pale purple amid soft green. He smiled.

The doorbell jangled a third time.

"Mary? Mary! Where is that girl?" In exasperation, Mrs. Ambrose put down her pen and rose from her desk. Muttering about the worthlessness of servants, she opened the front door. "What in the world?"

An enormous bouquet of purple lilacs filled the doorway. They spilled from a glass vase at the bottom of which appeared two legs.

"Delivery for Miss Clara Ambrose," said a muffled voice from behind the flowers.

"Oh, my. Come in, come in." Mrs. Ambrose stepped aside as the deliveryman maneuvered the flowers into the foyer.

"Where shall I put them, Ma'am?" he asked.

"In the parlor, please," said Mrs. Ambrose. She motioned to her right. How exciting, she thought. Such an extravagant display. Who could they be from?

Clara appeared at the top of the stairs.

"What's all this?" she asked.

"I don't know," twittered her mother, "but they're for you."

The deliveryman emerged from the parlor. He tipped his hat to the ladies and turned to leave.

"Wait," said Mrs. Ambrose. "Is there a card?"

"No card, Ma'am," he said. "My instructions were to deliver the flowers and the young lady would understand. Good day."

In the parlor, Clara stared in amazement at the profusion of lilacs. Her mother joined her, a knowing expression on her face.

"Oh, Clara. I'll just bet they're from Mr. Gliddon. I'd heard he was back in town. This is just the sort of extravagant thing he'd do."

"No, they're not from Mr. Gliddon," said Clara with a certainty that caused her mother's face to fall.

"Well then, who?" Mrs. Ambrose's eyes narrowed. "Don't tell me they're from that Mr. Cameron. He couldn't possibly afford such a display."

Clara reached out and touched one of the velvety petals.

"Yes, I do believe they're from Mr. Cameron," she said with a widening smile.

Her mother pursed her lips. "I should have known. How inappropriate. Does he really suppose he can win you over with such a gaudy show?" She sniffed. "Oh, my. The scent is so overpowering it's giving me a headache." She pressed her handkerchief to her nose. "Mary! Come help Clara remove these flowers."

Her impatient tone drew the attention of Grandmother Blake in her room off the parlor.

"Good heavens!" exclaimed the old woman as she rolled her chair into the room. "Who died?"

"No one died, Mother," snapped Mrs. Ambrose. Without further explanation, she stalked off in search of the housekeeper.

As her mother's voice faded away, Clara cupped a bunch of the flowers in her hands and buried her nose in the fragrant blooms. Her mother was right. The flowers were an extravagant gesture, and not one Garrett could really afford. Which made it all the more wonderful. She was touched by the fact that he had remembered how much she loved lilacs. She wondered, did he also remember their meaning?

"I just love the smell of lilacs," purred Grandmother Blake.

"So do I, Grandmother," said Clara. "So do I."

Rawlie returned from leave one night to find Garrett, Caleb, and Joe playing cards in the aisle of the shed. They sat on empty hardtack crates and used an overturned barrel as a table. Frank leaned against the wall of one of the stalls and played a plaintive tune on his fife while Leonard, seated on another crate over to the side, dug at his thumbnail with a small knife.

"Ah, gentlemen, gentlemen," said Rawlie, "here you sit, wasting your time, while I'm out providing for our well-being." With great ceremony, he produced six, light brown eggs from the pocket of his coat and placed them on the barrel.

"Where'd you get those, Rawlie?" asked Joe.

"A generous chicken donated them to the cause of preserving the Union."

Frank stopped mid-song. "You mean you stole 'em from some poor farmer," he said.

"'Stole' is such an ugly word," said Rawlie. "Besides, I'm sure the man would not begrudge a decent fried egg to the men defending our country's flag."

Leonard grunted and continued with his personal hygiene efforts.

"So that's where you've been all night," said Garrett as he discarded. "Plundering the local chickens?"

"Actually, I was plundering the girls over at Mrs. Black's on Third Street." Rawlie chuckled when Joe, as expected, turned bright red. "You boys should have come with me. The ladies were very entertaining tonight."

"You're becoming quite a frequent customer over there," observed Caleb.

"Well, the girls are particularly free with their favors, seeing as how I'm a lonely soldier heading off to war."

Frank snickered. "You're about the most un-lonely soldier I've ever met. Aren't you afraid you'll get the clap?"

Joe sank behind the protective fan of his playing cards.

"Nah. Mrs. Black runs a clean house. Her girls are all well cared for. And well paid, I might add." Rawlie cast a critical eye on young Joe. "Say, Joe, you ought to come with me some time. I'll bet you could use a little education in the female department."

"Joe's already got his eye on a girl," said Caleb, pleased to be in possession of this inside information. "He's been hanging around that pretty little Irish lass who sells the spice cakes outside camp."

"I have not," said Joe.

"Oh, no?" said Caleb. "You've bought a cake from her every day for the last two weeks."

Garrett kept his eyes on his cards. He and Clara had made a pact not to interfere in the budding romance between Annie and his lanky messmate.

"I just have a craving for sweets, is all," said Joe.

"Which brings us back to the subject of Mrs. Black's," said Rawlie. "What about you, Garrett? Can I interest you in some female companionship?"

"I'll pass," said Garrett.

"Oh, I forgot. You already have a young lady. By the way, who is that beauty I see you talking to after drill, now and again?"

"Not anyone I'd mention in the same conversation as Mrs. Black's girls," said Garrett without looking up from his hand.

"Sorry. Didn't mean anything by it," said Rawlie.

"All right. I call. What've you got?" said Caleb.

Garrett splayed his cards on top of the barrel. "Full house."

"Aw, geez!" Joe threw his cards down in disgust.

"Cameron, you're the luckiest son of a bitch I've ever known," said Caleb.

"And that'll do it for me. Good night, gentlemen." Garrett went into the stall and stretched out on his straw-covered plank. He pulled his cap over his face to signal his desire to be left alone.

From the dark interior of his hat, Garrett let his mind drift to Clara. She was not someone he wanted to discuss with the randy Rawlie. She was the bright light in all of his thoughts, the one he thought about when he awoke in the morning and when he went to bed at night. Still, the intimations of Rawlie's sexual escapades made his longing for her even more acute, and he found it very difficult to fall asleep.

By the end of May, there were over twenty companies at Camp Wilkins, totaling approximately two thousand men. With that many men in so small a place, conditions were rapidly deteriorating. The parade grounds and company streets were muddy quagmires when it rained, dust clouds when it was dry. The barracks were overcrowded and the sanitation facilities inadequate. Many sickened from the nutritionally deficient food, the poor sanitation, and the close proximity of so many men.

Morale was also breaking down. The thirteen dollars a month in pay the men had been promised had not yet arrived, and no one seemed to know when or if it would. But, most galling was the fact that the State of Pennsylvania had not yet provided the promised uniforms, guns, ammunition, or accoutrements.

When this situation became known to the people of Pittsburgh, they responded immediately. Prominent citizens and benefactors adopted whole companies and provided them with uniforms and/or weapons. Donations of blankets, pillows, shirts, underclothes, and even shoes flowed into the camp. The ladies of the area joined together in small groups to bake, sew, and knit items needed by the troops, and held fundraisers to purchase the rest. These efforts were greatly appreciated by the soldiers, who often formally thanked their benefactors in the local newspapers.

Despite these efforts, however, many of the men were still inadequately supplied. They continued to drill with sticks and poles, and they grumbled about when, if ever, they might actually receive their weapons.

It seemed the long wait was over when, in early June, a number of wagons loaded with guns rumbled through the gates of Camp Wilkins to wild cheering from the men. Upon examination, however, the guns were found to be old flintlocks and muskets of such inferior quality they were likely to blow up the first time they were fired. The guns were locked away in headquarters and never distributed. The men's morale plummeted once more.

"Fine army we're going to be," said Rawlie." What do they want us to do, throw rocks at the Rebels?"

A few days later, however, the men of Camp Wilkins received some welcome news. Sixteen companies, including the Pittsburgh Rifles, were being transferred to the newly established Camp Wright, located near Hulton Station, twelve miles farther up the Allegheny River.

"Do you think it'll be better there?" asked Joe one night after tattoo.

"Any place would be better than here," said Caleb.

Only Garrett seemed to have mixed emotions about the move. Although he, too, was anxious to leave the squalor of Camp Wilkins, he knew it would be more difficult for Clara to visit him at Camp Wright. Still, the move might mean they were closer to being taken into the Federal army, closer to getting into the fight. The prospect filled him with both excitement and trepidation.

CHAPTER 8

"PETER, THEY CAN'T FORCE YOU to go!" Mrs. Ambrose gripped the carved mahogany bedstead as she watched her husband take a few last personal items from the dresser drawer and place them in a small valise on the bed.

"They're not forcing me, Laura," replied her husband. He stuffed another clean shirt into his case. "I volunteered to go. They need all the doctors and surgeons they can get, particularly ones with prior military experience. I know what these young soldiers are going to be facing. I couldn't live with myself if I didn't go."

"But, must you go right now?"

"It's as good a time as any. Helen is on the mend and baby Jackson is thriving. Besides, Clara and Mary are both here to help you. And my friends in the military tell me the 27th Pennsylvania Infantry Regiment needs another surgeon right away."

"The 27th Pennsylvania?" Mrs. Ambrose searched her memory. "Wasn't that the regiment that was attacked in the riot in Baltimore?"

"Yes. They've regrouped and reorganized, and are now on their way back to Washington to be attached to General McDowell's Army of Northeast Virginia. I'm to report to Washington to be sworn into Federal service and join them as soon as possible."

"But, Peter," said Mrs. Ambrose with a quavering voice, "how am I going to get along without you?"

"Laura, you're going to be fine. I've taken care of everything. Mr. Jenkins from next door has promised to look in on you, and I've made arrangements with Mr. Hendrickson down at the bank to pay whatever bills you may have from our account. And you can always reach me through regimental headquarters if there's an emergency. All indications are this rebellion will be put down quickly. I shouldn't think I'd be gone for more than a few months. The war will certainly be over by Christmas. And with Helen and the baby, you'll be so busy the time will fly. And I promise to write you as often as I can."

"But, what if you're hurt, or …." She couldn't finish the sentence.

Dr. Ambrose paused in his packing. "Laura. Come here." Moving his valise aside, he sat down on the bed and drew her down beside him. "Nothing is going to happen to me. I'll probably be assigned to one of the general hospitals far away from the actual fighting. I'll be quite safe, I assure you. And so will you." He put his arm around her trembling shoulders.

After a few moments, Dr. Ambrose emerged from the bedroom alone, his valise in one hand, his doctor's bag in the other. As he descended the stairs, Clara waited by the front door with his hat in her hand.

"Papa?"

"Yes, Clara."

Clara looked up into her father's face and saw the lines of care there as if for the first time. This was not a young man eager to rush to the glory of battle, but a dedicated doctor motivated by his own experience with the horrors of an earlier war to assuage, in whatever small degree, the pain and suffering of those called to fight this one.

"I just wanted you to know how very proud I am of you." Her voice caught and she flew into his arms, her tears dampening his coat. He hugged her and kissed the top of her head.

"Clara, listen to me. I need you to be strong while I'm gone, for the sake of your mother, your grandmother, and your sister. You've always been the practical one in the family, and they're going to lean on you." He held her gently by the shoulders and looked into her eyes. "Now, you must promise to write to me and let me know what's happening here at home. The real situation. No sugar coating or hysterics."

"I will, Papa. I promise," she sniffed.

"That's my girl, my steady rock." He took the hat from her and settled it on his head. Striding to the door, he paused with his hand on the doorknob.

"With any luck, I'll be back before young Mr. Cameron gets up the courage to ask you to marry him."

"Father!"

He smiled and winked. Then he was gone.

In both the North and the South, the departure of the men for the war initiated great change in the lives of the women left behind. Mrs. Ambrose found herself in the unaccustomed role of handling all of the family's monetary affairs. She also dealt with the tradesmen when the roof leaked, ordered coal for the stove, and settled accounts at the butcher, the blacksmith, the grocer, and the clothier. Clara was surprised and impressed by her mother's ability to handle these unaccustomed duties.

Helen, in addition to caring for her baby, assumed the majority of Grandmother Blake's care. Fortunately, she exhibited her mother's patience in dealing with the finicky old woman.

Grateful her father had taught her how to harness and care for their carriage horse, Clara became the family driver. She drove her mother on her daily errands and appointments, and soon became quite adept at maneuvering through streets crowded with carriages, wagons, and soldiers. With so many men off to war, it was no longer unusual or frowned upon to see an unescorted woman out walking or driving by herself. Clara enjoyed the freedom this allowed, and occasionally took advantage of the situation to visit Annie, either at home or at the little confectionary stand she had set up amid the sutlers outside Camp Wilkins.

As promised, their neighbor, Mr. Jenkins, was quick to attend to any little things that needed to be fixed around the house. But, he had his own family to care for, and Mrs. Ambrose hated to bother him too often. More and more, as time passed, she and Clara were the ones to fix a broken chair leg or un-stick a window.

The Ambrose ladies also did whatever they could to support their men in the field. They joined with a group of local women to sew shirts, knit socks, roll bandages, and assemble food packages, not only for their loved ones, but for the constant stream of soldiers who came through Pittsburgh on their way to unknown battlefields in both the eastern and western theaters of the war. From the grateful looks on the faces of the recipients, they knew their efforts were appreciated.

Still, as Clara sat among the chatting, knitting women in yet another parlor, she sometimes had the overwhelming urge to scream.

Outside Camp Wilkins, Annie stood beneath a crude canvas awning in a long line of sutlers' tents and rearranged the spice cakes on the table she had made by placing a plank of wood atop two barrels. Since the announcement that a portion of the camp's population was being reassigned to the new Camp Wright, business had been slow as the soldiers prepared for the move. She had sold only three cakes all morning and her feet hurt from standing on the hard ground. She was contemplating packing up early when a familiar lanky figure approached. Her heart took a little leap.

"Miss Burke," said Joe. He swept the cap from his head and made an awkward bow. Annie noticed he had shaved his fringe of a beard. Rather than make him look younger, she thought it gave his face a more handsome, earnest look.

"Private Frye," said Annie, smiling. "The usual?"

"Yes, please."

Annie wrapped two cakes in brown paper and handed them to Joe. Their fingers touched briefly as he tendered the coins. Annie felt her color rise.

"Thank you." Joe stood fidgeting for a moment. "Miss Burke, I don't know if you've heard, but we're being moved up river to the new camp."

Annie hid her dismay beneath down turned lashes. "I didn't know your company had been chosen to go."

Joe nodded. "Tomorrow morning. So, I just wanted to let you know... well, I'm sorry, really sorry, I won't be able to come by any-more. For the cakes."

Annie smoothed and re-smoothed some of the remaining brown paper. "Well, now," she said after a moment. "Camp Wright's not so very far away. If that's where a good part of the soldiers are goin', I may just have to look into relocatin' me business."

Joe brightened. "Really? That would be wonderful. 'Cause I'd really miss y..., your baking. All the fellas would." He placed his cap on his head, almost dropping one of the cakes in the process. "Well, I guess I'd better be going." He gave her a lopsided grin. "Good day, Miss Burke."

Annie smiled as she watched him bounce back to the barracks.

On June 8, 1861, the men of the Pittsburgh Rifles filed into their newly constructed barrack at Camp Wright. The seventy-five by eigh-teen foot wooden building was designed to hold an entire company of approximately 110 men, and was divided into apartments for the sol-diers; apartments that smelled of freshly milled pine rather than the stale manure and animal sweat that had permeated their billet at Camp Wilkins.

"Not too bad," said Rawlie as he tossed his knapsack onto a wooden bunk.

"Yeah," said Joe. "This place is a thousand times better than Camp Wilkins."

Camp Wright was situated on a broad field of green grass just behind and above the buildings of the Hulton Train Station, a stop on the Allegheny Valley Railroad line that ran along the Allegheny River. The ground sloped upwards from the sparkling river for about three hun-dred yards and was surrounded by thick forest on three sides. An orchard was located in the center and the camp received fresh, clean water from two springs, one on either side of the camp.

The barracks, as well as the wedge or "A" tents that provided tem-porary housing for those companies whose permanent barracks were still under construction, were set out in rows in the orchard. The parade ground was across the railroad tracks in a large hayfield down near the river approximately a half mile from the camp proper. A spacious kitchen and hospital were being built to service the troops, but already food was more plentiful than it had been at Camp Wilkins. Once the ever-enterprising sutlers arrived outside of camp to peddle additional wares, there was little the men lacked in the way of comfort.

As the summer days heated up, the men enjoyed bathing in the river, despite the slick of oil that floated on the waters. Just two years before, the nation's first oil well was drilled upstream in Titusville, Pennsylvania. The oil not collected in barrels at Titusville was swept away by Oil Creek into the Allegheny, where it bobbed in iridescent globules on the surface of the water. This made things difficult for men attempting to wash their shirts in the river, for no matter how much soap they used, the shirts were well-oiled by the time they were through. Still, each evening would find over a thousand men splashing in the water or scattered along the riverbank, where they enjoyed the breeze while they talked or wrote letters. Compared to what they had left behind, Camp Wright was a vacation spot for the soldiers.

But, there was no vacation from guard duty, drill, or training. Each morning at 8:00 a.m., the guard was set for a twenty-four hour duty, divided into three shifts. Each shift stood two hours alternately throughout the day for the entire twenty-four hours. Those not on guard duty or ordered to help build the remaining company barracks were engaged in daily squad, company, and regimental drills. And there was always the interminable waiting – for uniforms, guns, and news as to when they might go to war.

As Garrett feared, the move to Camp Wright made it harder for Clara to visit, but not because of any difficulty with transportation. On the contrary, the Allegheny Valley Railroad, responding to the desire of the public to visit their sons and loved ones at their new location, quickly instituted a special train service. Seven trains made the trip to and from Camp Wright daily. The problem was, as always, Clara's mother. Now that Garrett was assigned to a camp almost twelve miles from Lawrenceville, Mrs. Ambrose absolutely forbad Clara from traveling such a distance without a male escort.

Although Mrs. Ambrose thought her problem with Garrett had been neatly solved by the military, Clara was not so easily deterred. She discovered that Dr. Russell, a close colleague of her father's, had a son stationed at Camp Wright. A few well-placed hints and lovesick sighs elicited an offer from the older man to serve as her escort. Faced with so trusted and reliable a chaperone, Mrs. Ambrose felt duty bound to honor the wishes of her absent husband and allow Clara to visit the camp on those occasions Dr. Russell could accompany her.

Unfortunately for Clara and Garrett, Dr. Russell's practice prevented him from visiting the camp every week, and Garrett's short leaves left them little time to be together. After much scheming, however, Clara and Annie devised a way to send messages back and forth between the pining couple. Following breakfast on the agreed upon day, Clara would offer to take Jackson for a walk around the Arsenal walls. Annie would meet her on the Covington Street side of the Arsenal, take the letter and package Clara had hidden in the baby carriage, and board the train for Camp Wright at the Lawrenceville station. Her return trip would bring a message from Garrett to Clara, to be delivered during the week at a *chance* meeting of the two girls at the market.

Eluding the watchful eye of Mrs. Ambrose was all very clandestine and exciting, and the girls felt like war spies. But still, the days stretched endlessly for Clara on those weeks when she couldn't see Garrett. Hungry for news of him and his company, she scoured the daily papers, since there was almost always a paragraph or two on happenings at Camp Wright. And she wondered – if she felt this way now, how would she feel when he was separated from her by hundreds of miles and facing enemy guns?

"Mr. Cameron. Mr. Cameron!"

Turning in the direction of the voice, Garrett found Annie standing at the camp gate with a basket and a package in her arms.

"Why, Miss Burke. What are you doing here? I thought Clara ... Miss Ambrose, was coming with Dr. Russell today." His disappointment was plain as he searched the small crowd of visitors behind her.

"She couldn't come. Dr. Russell had an emergency." Garrett looked so forlorn, Annie was almost tempted to reach out and pat his arm. "She asked me to tell you how sorry she was, and that she'd try to come next week. And, she asked me to give you this."

Annie handed Garrett a small bundle wrapped in brown paper. As he examined the package, Annie started to fidget.

"Mr. Cameron. I was wonderin' ...." She held out a basket covered with a red checked cloth. "Would you be givin' this to ... your messmates for me? They're just some cakes and things left over at the end of the day."

"Why, of course, Miss Burke," said Garrett, suppressing a smile. "But, why don't you deliver it yourself? I believe some of the boys might be at the barracks right now."

"Oh, no," said Annie. "No. I wouldn't want to be a bother. If you could just deliver it for me, that'd be grand."

"Of course." Garrett took the basket from her hand.

"Well, I'll be goin', then," she said.

"But you just got here. Can't you stay and visit for a while?"

Annie's surprise turned quickly to discomfiture. "Sure'n I wish I could," she said, slowly backing away, "but I've things to deliver to me brothers. And I promised me ma I'd be back to help with the supper."

"Miss Burke. Wait." Garrett closed the gap between them. "Miss Burke, I just wanted to say how much I appreciate all you've done for Miss Ambrose – and for me – acting as our messenger. You've been a good friend. To both of us. And I thank you from the bottom of my heart." He made a deep, sincere bow. When he raised his head, he was surprised to find Annie staring at him, all trace of bashfulness gone.

"Mr. Cameron," she said in a voice that shook only slightly. "I've somethin' to say to you. Clara is me closest friend in the world, as close to me as me own sister. And I'd do anything for her. But, you should know that for all her sophisticated ways, she's truly an innocent. She's never been hurt or disappointed by the people she loves and trusts. If you truly wish to thank me, you'll honor her and do nothin' that might cause her pain."

Garrett considered the five feet of determination standing before him.

"You need not worry about the depth of my regard or my feelings for Miss Ambrose," he said solemnly. "Were it not for the war ...." He stopped. "I promise you, Miss Burke, I will honor her all the days of my life."

Annie weighed the sincerity of his pledge. Satisfied, she nodded. "Then I'll say good day to you, Mr. Cameron." Her shy smiled returned. "And thank you for deliverin' the basket." She made a small curtsy and hurried away.

Garrett stood and watched her go. He had never seen this side of Annie, her fierce loyalty to her friend. What a curious little thing she was; a strange blend of timidity and strength. Suddenly, he felt better knowing Annie would be here with Clara when he left. It was reassuring to know that someone would be watching over the woman he loved, someone who cared about her as much as he.

That same Saturday afternoon, Clara emerged from the dressmaker's shop on Diamond Street in downtown Pittsburgh with a bundle under her arm. Helen had decided to treat herself to a new dress, something

Clara saw as an extravagance considering their uncertain financial future. But, their mother felt that if it would help Helen cope with the stress of being a new mother with an absent husband, it was worth the expense. Eager to get out of the house for even a few minutes, Clara had offered to pick up the fabric samples.

Turning left toward Market Street, Clara negotiated the crowded sidewalk with difficulty. The streets were so much more congested since the war, and it was difficult to prevent her hoop skirt from being bumped and stepped upon. The crush of people only served to further dampen her mood, already foul since she had been unable to visit Garrett as she planned.

Suddenly, she saw a familiar figure approaching. She turned away quickly and pretended to be engrossed in examining the contents of a shop window.

"Good morning, Miss Ambrose," said Edgar, tipping his hat. "In the market for a new saxhorn, I see?"

Clara realized with chagrin that she had stopped in front of a music shop displaying the latest in brass instruments.

"Yes, Mr. Gliddon," said Clara. "It's never too late to take up a new pursuit."

"Indeed," said Edgar with an amused look. "Well, if you're out shopping, perhaps you'd like some company."

"Actually, I've completed my errands and am on my way to catch the passenger car for home."

"Then, by all means, let me help you with your package."

Before she could protest, Edgar slid the bundle from beneath her arm. Not wanting to make a scene in the middle of the crowded sidewalk, Clara resisted the urge to grab it back. She placed her hand on the arm he offered and set off at a brisk pace so as to end their stroll as soon as possible. But, as they entered the busy streets surrounding the Market House, she found she was grateful to have someone guide her through the crush of carriages, carts, and shoppers.

"Our quiet little hamlet certainly has changed, has it not?" said Edgar as he steered Clara around a rowdy crowd at a vendor's stall that was doing a brisk business selling obscene playing cards.

"Yes, it has," said Clara. "And not all for the good, I'm afraid." She gave a withering glance to a rough-looking man who was openly ogling her.

"All the more reason for you to take care with whom you associate," said Edgar.

Clara smiled. "Don't worry, Mr. Gliddon. I think my reputation will survive my being seen with you."

"I'm serious, Miss Ambrose," said Edgar. "In fact, I've been meaning to talk to you about your choice of companions ever since I saw you at Camp Wilkins with that Miss Burke. Surely, she's not really a friend of yours?"

"She most certainly is," said Clara. "I've known her since I was a child."

"Well then, I'd say it's high time you put aside the things of child-hood," said Edgar. "I'm telling you this for your own good. You must give some thought to appearances. A creature like that is not a proper companion for a young woman of your social status."

Clara pulled her arm away and turned to face him. "What an incred-ibly unkind thing to say."

"The truth is often unkind," he replied, "but it is the truth nonethe-less. If you ever hope to rise in society, you must surround yourself with the right kind of people."

"I assume by 'the right kind of people' you mean people who build their wealth on the backs of the very people they disdain."

Edgar chuckled. "Miss Ambrose, sometimes I forget just how young you are."

Just then, two men headed in the opposite direction stopped abreast of them. One of them was in uniform. Both looked vaguely familiar to Clara.

"Well, Edgar Gliddon," said the man in civilian attire. "How unex-pected to find you out and about."

"I leave the office on occasion, Percy," said Edgar. He turned to the soldier and looked him up and down. "Well, Morgan, James here told me you'd decided to join our gallant fighting men, but he neglected to tell me you'd reached the rank of lieutenant."

"Not surprising," said Morgan with a sidelong glance at his brother. "James considers my volunteering to be the utmost folly."

"Gentlemen," said Edgar, "may I present …."

"Miss Ambrose, isn't it?" said Morgan with a smile. "How nice to see you again."

"And you, Lieutenant Percy," said Clara. "Mr. Percy," she added with a nod to James.

"You know each other?" said Edgar.

"Yes," said James. "We met at a sleighing party at Lucinda Ward's home last February."

"Really?" said Edgar. "And here I thought you devoted all your time to your coal business."

"I still recall your beautiful a cappella rendition of *Silent Night* on that occasion, Lieutenant Percy," Clara said to Morgan.

"You flatter me, Miss Ambrose," said Morgan. "But, I, too, remember that innocent night quite fondly, particularly in light of the present crisis. Say, do you remember a young man named Garrett Cameron? He was part of our group that evening."

"Yes," said Clara, coloring ever so slightly.

"He's in my company."

"You're with the Pittsburgh Rifles?" she said in surprise.

"Why, yes. How did you know?"

"Mr. Cameron and I have ... stayed in touch."

"A most fortunate man," said Morgan.

Only James noticed the scowl that passed over Edgar's face.

"Would you give him my regards?" said Clara.

"Of course," said Morgan.

"Forgive me, Miss Ambrose," interrupted Edgar, "but if you wish to catch the omnibus ...."

"Oh, I'm sorry," said Morgan. "We didn't mean to keep you. We'd best be off anyway. We're dining with our parents before I have to report back to camp. Good day, Miss Ambrose." He touched the brim of his hat. "Nice to see you again, Gliddon."

James bowed to Clara and, with a knowing smirk directed at Edgar, strode off after his brother.

"How do you know the Percy brothers?" asked Clara as she and Edgar continued toward their destination. Her conversation with Morgan Percy had caused her to forget her anger at Edgar.

"I do a lot of business with the older brother, James," said Edgar. "His company provides most of the coal for my rolling mill. A shrewd business mind, that one. Morgan, however, is another story."

"Morgan Percy seems a very kind man," said Clara. "And a patriotic one."

"Another boy playing at soldier," sniffed Edgar.

"Hardly a boy if he's been chosen to be an officer by the men of his company."

"Ah, yes. Men like Mr. Cameron. I'd wondered what had happened to him."

"Mr. Cameron volunteered immediately after Fort Sumter was fired upon," she said, unable to keep the pride from her voice.

"Well, I feel safer already," said Edgar.

Clara, her ill humor returned, glared at him.

"So," Edgar continued, "you and Mr. Cameron have 'stayed in touch.' Really, Miss Ambrose. I'd have thought you'd have tired of that particular little dalliance by now."

Clara bristled. "I assure you, Sir, I do not dally."

"Nor do I, Miss Ambrose," said Edgar with a pointed look.

By now they had reached the intersection of 6th Street and Penn Street where the Citizen's Passenger Railroad car was just approaching. Edgar signaled the car to stop, helped Clara up onto the step, and handed her her package. She fairly snatched it out of his hand.

"Good day, Miss Ambrose," he said with a slight bow. "I hope to see you again soon."

"Not if I can help it, Sir," she snapped, and turned on her heel.

Edgar's courteous expression changed to a frown as he watched the railcar clatter down the street. The news that Cameron was still interested in Clara – and she in him – complicated things. He would have to be more cautious. Too strong a hand might drive her straight into Cameron's arms. He would have to come up with a new tack to win Clara over. But win her, he would.

True to his word, Dr. Ambrose wrote to his family almost every day. He was attached as a medical surgeon to the 27th Pennsylvania Regiment encamped on the Kalorama Heights overlooking Washington. While the regiment drilled in the June humidity and heat, Dr. Ambrose – now Major Ambrose, the rank accorded all army surgeons – spent the majority of his time dealing with cases of measles, diarrhea, and stomach complaints. In his letters, he lightheartedly complained of the food and the greenness of the soldiers. More serious was his criticism of some of his fellow surgeons, many of whom had very little medical training, but rather had acquired their position through the intervention of well-placed political figures. *I wonder*, he wrote, *if these same politicians would be so free with their patronage should these barbers and bloodletters be operating on their own sons.*

The medical situation in the Union army in the summer of 1861 was chaotic at best. Although no large scale battles had yet been fought, the Medical Department was already having difficulty dealing with the increasing numbers of men contracting malaria in the swamp-like conditions around the steamy capital. There were also numerous cases of measles, mumps, chronic diarrhea, and other illnesses resulting from the exposure of soldiers from more isolated rural areas to such large numbers of people. As far as preparing for battle casualties, there was as yet no system in place for evacuating the wounded, and many of the surgeons appointed to the volunteer regiments had little or no medical training in how to treat the injured, on or off the battlefield. The Medical Department was woefully unprepared and quickly becoming overwhelmed.

Fortunately, a movement arose among the civilian population to remedy this situation. Driven primarily by the various ladies aid societies that had formed throughout the country, and modeled on the British Sanitary Commission that operated during the Crimean War, the United States Sanitary Commission was formed in the early spring of 1861. The members of the Commission pushed for reforms within the medical branch of the army that would lead to better hygiene, better nutrition, and more efficient organization. Despite initial resistance, the Union doctors soon came to welcome the Commission's suggestions and, most particularly, its supplies.

In response to Dr. Ambrose's letters, the ladies aid group the Ambrose women had joined kept a steady stream of medical supplies and food packages flowing directly to him in Washington. Mrs. Ambrose took comfort in the fact that her husband remained in the capital city, safe from any incursions by the Confederate army.

On a beautiful Friday afternoon in mid-July, Lieutenant Morgan Percy granted Garrett a special four-hour leave. Garrett took the Allegheny Valley Rail Train to the Lawrenceville station, and practically ran the mile and a quarter to Clara's house. As he waited for someone to answer the door, he smiled in anticipation of her reaction.

"I'm comin', I'm comin'," said a muffled voice. Mary opened the door and gasped. "Jesus, Mary, and …."

Garrett put his finger to his lips.

"Would you just look at you," she whispered, a broad smile on her face. "You're a gorgeous sight, you are. Come in. Come in." She closed the door behind him. "Miss Clara will be so surprised. And, you're in luck. Herself is out for the entire afternoon. Now, wait right here." Mary giggled as she disappeared toward the back of the house.

"He is?" he heard Clara exclaim a moment later. She burst from the kitchen and rushed to the front door. At the entryway, she froze. There stood Garrett in a new gray uniform trimmed with a single row of shiny brass buttons down the front, his forage cap under his arm, and a proud smile on his face.

"Well, what do you think?" he asked as he pulled the sack coat smooth.

"You got your new uniform," managed Clara.

"Yes," said Garrett. "Isn't it splendid? They were finally issued to the whole camp this week. And a trainload of guns arrived at Hulton Station on the 15th. They're not much, mostly old converted flintlocks, but at least now all the men are armed. We look like a real fighting unit. And the Pittsburgh Rifles have received their official designation." He replaced his cap and stood at attention. "You're looking at Private Garrett Cameron, Company A of the 9th Pennsylvania Reserves regiment." He saluted smartly. "Hey, what's the matter?"

Clara's lips trembled. "It's just that you look … like a real soldier."

He gave her a puzzled smile. "Well, that was the idea, wasn't it?"

She nodded unconvincingly. He hurried to her.

"Oh, Clara. I'm sorry. I guess I didn't think about how this would affect you. It's just that we've waited for so long. Now, at last, I feel like I'm a real part of this army, ready to fight. You understand."

"Of course I do." She wiped at her eyes. "It was just a bit of a shock, that's all." She stepped back, looked him up and down, and forced a small smile. "You do look wonderful, you know."

He grinned. "Don't I?"

"Come. Sit with me," she said. "I want to hear everything."

Garrett followed her into the empty parlor. Clara hesitated, then slid the pocket doors closed behind them. She turned to find him standing directly in front of her.

"My mother's not …."

"I know…" said Garrett. He swept her into his arms.

The two kissed as if they might never get another chance, eagerly, passionately. They reveled in the taste, touch, and smell of each other, overcome by a sudden desperate physical longing. Garrett's hands slid down to Clara's waist and he pulled her even closer. Neither could decide whether to fight it or give in. Finally, Clara pushed away.

"Garrett," she gasped, "I've never been a woman to swoon, but if you don't stop right now, I fear I will." She wobbled over to the divan.

Garrett ran his fingers through his hair. "You're right. I'm sorry. You're right." He paced to the empty fireplace and back. Suddenly, he looked down and frowned. "Besides, I think you wrinkled my uniform."

Clara laughed. "Oh, Garrett," she said, relieved – and disappointed – to be back on safe ground. She motioned for him to join her on the divan.

"Why didn't you tell me you were coming?" she asked. "I might have been out and missed you."

"They didn't allow my leave until the last minute. Besides, I wanted to surprise you."

"Well, you certainly did that." Clara's expression turned serious. "The fact that you've been issued uniforms, does that mean you're closer to being sent to fight?"

"I hope so. I mean," he added hastily, "if I have to go, I want to get on with it, not spend my days in endless drilling."

"I understand," said Clara. "If I was in your position, I'd be eager to get into the fight, too. Despite the danger, I'd much prefer going off to war than being left behind to wait and wonder."

"I'm not so sure you're not in danger here," said Garrett.

Clara scoffed. "What possible danger could there be in Lawrenceville?"

Garrett shifted uncomfortably. "I wasn't going to say anything. I have no real right. But … Lieutenant Percy mentioned he saw you on the street the other day." He paused. "He said you were with Edgar Gliddon."

Clara rolled her eyes. "Yes. I was out on an errand and he followed me to the passenger car like a stray puppy."

"I don't like that man being anywhere near you."

"Why, Garrett. I do believe you're jealous."

"I'm serious, Clara. I don't trust him. He has a questionable character and a lot of powerful friends. And it appears he's never quite gotten over his infatuation with you."

"Garrett, believe me, the last thing in the world you have to worry about is Edgar Gliddon. There's nothing he could ever do that would make me the least bit interested in him." Clara's gaze softened. "My heart is already spoken for."

Garrett drew her to him, gently this time. The kiss they exchanged was long and deep.

"Oh, Clara," he murmured, "I miss you so much already, just being here in camp. How will I endure it when we're separated by so many miles?"

Clara's eyes filled with tears. She straightened and placed her hand on his heart. "But, we won't be separated. Not really. I'll be with you. Here. If you're ever lonely or scared, just listen to your heart and I'll be there."

Garrett covered her hand with his.

"Clara Ambrose. I love you."

Clara looked into his eyes and saw something much deeper than passion or longing. She knew in that moment her soul had found its mate.

"I love you, too, Garrett. And I always will."

* * *

The following week, Annie stood under the awning of the shoe-maker's shop on Wood Street and stared out at the steady drizzle.

"And me without me umbrella," she muttered. Pulling her shawl over her head, she hugged the package she carried close to her body and dashed across the slippery cobblestone street. She leapt the puddle at the curb and crashed right into the brass-buttoned chest of a Union soldier on the opposite sidewalk.

"Oh!" she cried as she dropped her package. The man reached out to steady her.

"I'm very sorry, Miss. I didn't see you ... Miss Burke?"

Annie peered out from beneath her dripping shawl. "Mr. Cameron?"

"Fancy running into you." Garrett chuckled. "I see the rain caught you unaware, as well."

"I'm afraid so."

He bent to pick up her package. "Say, since we're both half drowned, perhaps you'd like to join me for a cup of coffee? There's a restaurant down the street where we could wait out the rain."

Automatically, Annie opened her mouth to decline. Then she stopped. Why not? she thought. She had spent most of the day doing errands for her family. And she hadn't done anything but cook and clean and wash for so long. Why not, indeed?

"Yes, Mr. Cameron," she said, surprising them both, "I think I'd enjoy that."

The warmth of the restaurant felt good after the dampness outside. They hung their wet things on the coat rack and were shown to a table by the window that provided a nice vantage point from which to watch people scurry in and out of the puddles.

"What has you out on this miserable day?" asked Garrett as the waiter poured two billowing cups of coffee.

"Me da was having some special shoes made for me brothers. Said the ones the army gave them weren't worth the leather they were made out of, if, indeed, it was leather." Garrett nodded. "What about you?" said Annie. "Are you desertin' already?"

She smiled and a dimple appeared in her cheek. The rain had caused her dark hair to curl, and it framed her face in a way that made her blue eyes even bluer. Garrett suddenly realized that, so besotted was he by Clara's classical beauty, he had never really taken the time to notice that Annie Burke was a very pretty young lady.

"I had a little errand to do myself. We finally got paid, so ... may I show you?" He pulled a small package from the pocket of his coat and handed it to her. She unwrapped the brown paper to find an ambrotype of him looking handsome, solemn, and determined in the full gray uniform of the 9th Pennsylvania Reserves.

"I had it done at Boyd's Gallery on 5th Street. He's supposed to be very good, but I don't know." He looked at the picture and frowned. "Do you think Miss Ambrose will like it?"

Annie smiled. Men could be so silly. "I do, indeed."

"I wanted her to have something to remember me by when we're called up."

Annie's expression fell. "Is that to happen soon?"

He shrugged. "We hear rumors every day. I don't believe any one of them, but the sheer number of them is increasing."

Annie sipped her coffee. "Do you think it will last long? The war, I mean."

Garrett paused before answering. He knew Annie's brothers were in the Reserves and, of course, there was Joe. He didn't want to frighten her. But as she sat there waiting for his reply, he saw in her eyes a quiet courage that encouraged him to speak freely.

"Yes, I do. I think Northerners underestimate the determination of the South. And I think the Southerners underestimate the loyalty of our people to the idea of Union. Despite our differences, we're all Americans. Stubborn and determined. Yes, I fear the fight will be a long one."

Annie sighed. "Then we'll just have to do what we have to do for as long as we have to do it."

"You don't seem afraid," said Garrett.

"Oh, I am," she said. "I've heard enough of me da's stories of the troubles in Ireland to know when men get to fightin' over a country, there'll be blood and killin' beyond anyone's imaginin'. But I also know that sometimes you have to fight for what's right."

"You sound like Clara."

"Oh, no," said Annie. "That one's out to save the world. I'm just tryin' to protect me own little corner of it." Her face darkened. "But, it appears this is a fight none of us can avoid." She glanced out the window. "Ah, look. The rain has stopped."

Sure enough, the pedestrians had lowered their umbrellas and were picking their way through the water and slop.

"I'd best be goin'," said Annie. "Me ma will wonder what happened to me."

"And I'm supposed to meet the boys over at Trimble's Varieties." He stopped, embarrassed.

Annie smiled. "It's all right, Mr. Cameron. I've a father and four brothers. I'd not be shocked by the idea of you goin' to a minstrel theater."

"And you won't …."

"No, I won't be mentionin' it to Clara either."

Garrett gave her a grateful smile. He paid the bill and insisted on escorting Annie to Penn Street to catch the passenger car.

"You know, Miss Burke," he said as they strolled along, "Private Frye asked after you the other day."

"Private Frye? And which one is he now?"

Garrett chuckled. Annie was not beyond being coy. He knew she and Joe had shared a glass of lemonade the day of the Independence Day celebration at the camp. A major step for them both.

"Tall. Young. Buys an awful lot of spice cakes."

A smile tugged at the corner of Annie's mouth. "Ah, yes. I think I remember him."

"May I give him your regards?" asked Garrett as the streetcar approached.

"If you like," said Annie. Garrett helped her up onto the car. "Good-bye, Mr. Cameron. And thank you for the coffee."

"It was my pleasure. Oh, and Miss Burke? Please don't tell Miss Ambrose about the ambrotype. I want it to be a surprise."

"Sure'n haven't I kept your secrets all this time?" said Annie. "You can depend on me, Mr. Cameron."

The streetcar pulled away and Garrett headed down Penn Street for his rendezvous at Trimble's. As he walked, he puzzled over Annie and Joe's snail-like courtship. At the pace they were going, they would be in their dotage before they got around to making their true intentions known. Perhaps he should say something to Joe to spur him along.

"Mr. Cameron!"

A fancy black carriage piped in green with the letter *G* on the door splashed over to the side of the curb. Edgar Gliddon leaned out the window and motioned to Garrett with the leather riding crop he held in his hand.

"You're just the man I want to talk to," said Edgar.

"Oh?" said Garrett. "Concerning?"

"Concerning a mutual friend of ours. A Miss Ambrose."

Garrett stood pokerfaced while he waited for Edgar to continue.

"As you may know," said Edgar, "Dr. Ambrose has enlisted in the service of the Union, as has Miss Ambrose's brother-in-law, Mr. Pitcher, leaving Miss Ambrose, her mother, grandmother and sister unprotected in Lawrenceville. Given that you yourself could be called up at any moment, I just wanted to ease your mind by letting you know that while you're off risking your life to keep the Union safe from

Rebels and slave owners, I will be here at home watching over Miss Ambrose. As a friend of the family, of course."

Garrett stepped to the side of the carriage. Edgar did not flinch, but his grip on the riding crop tightened.

"See here, Gliddon," said Garrett. "Miss Ambrose has made it clear to you that she neither desires nor appreciates your attentions."

"Come now, Cameron," said Edgar, flicking a piece of mud from the side of the carriage. "Even someone as inexperienced with the ladies as yourself must know they frequently say the opposite of what they mean."

"Not Miss Ambrose. She is very clear about her preferences." Garrett leaned in close. "And she prefers me."

"Really? Well that should be of great comfort to you during those long nights around the campfire. But, for your sake, I do hope it doesn't take too long for this little spat to play itself out. It's been my experience that women tend to prefer the daily attentions of a live man over a … fading memory." Edgar's smile was filled with malice. He thumped twice on the roof of the carriage with the head of the crop. "Good day, Mr. Cameron," he said as the driver clucked to the horses. "And good luck."

With fists clenched, Garrett watched the carriage depart. He knew Edgar was just trying to provoke him, to make him doubt Clara's devotion to him. But, there was truth in Edgar's calculated words. Once Garrett was called up to duty, he could indeed be gone for a very long time … perhaps, forever. It was just this uncertainty that prevented him from proposing to Clara, as much as he longed to do so. He didn't think it fair to bind her to a man who might never return. Still, she had pledged her heart to him, as solemn as a vow, and he believed her.

However, he couldn't help but feel he was marching off to war while leaving a significant enemy to operate unchecked behind his own lines.

On July 22nd, the Pittsburgh newspapers carried the shocking news of the Union army's defeat in a battle the previous day near a little creek called Bull Run, located just twenty-five miles southwest of Washington near Manassas, Virginia. The news of the rout alarmed and sobered the people of the North. How could it have happened? Who was this General Jackson who the papers described as having *stood like a stone wall* and turned the tide for the Confederates? How could these Rebels have defeated their splendid army? The people clamored for answers even as they tried to reconcile themselves to the fact that the war might be longer and more difficult than they had imagined.

The fiasco at Bull Run was alarming on a more personal level to the members of the Ambrose family. Mercifully, George's unit had not taken part in the battle, but they knew from newspaper reports that the 27th Pennsylvania had most definitely been involved. Anxiously, they awaited word from Dr. Ambrose.

The official Union response to the Confederate victory at Bull Run was immediate. As its streets filled with wounded, frightened, retreating soldiers, Washington sent out an urgent call for 500,000 additional troops to serve for three years. Within a few days, they requested 500,000 more. Most of the original three-month men re-enlisted immediately, but many more were needed.

On July 22, 1861, the Pennsylvania Reserves, including the newly-minted Private Garrett Cameron, received orders to leave immediately for Washington to be sworn into Federal service.

CHAPTER 9

IN THE EARLY MORNING HOURS of July 23, 1861, Camp Wright was a frenzy of activity as the Pennsylvania Reserves prepared to leave for the special trains that would take them first to Harrisburg, then Washington. The soldiers hurriedly packed up their belongings, bedrolls, and tents, while officers shouted orders over the sound of drums and bugles.

The 9th Pennsylvania Reserves regiment, including Company A, the Pittsburgh Rifles, was scheduled to leave at 8:00 a.m. from the Pennsylvania Railroad Station. Mothers, fathers, wives, children, and sweethearts rushed to the depot to say farewell to their loved ones, off to war at last. Amid the noise and confusion on the station platform, Clara and Garrett tried to summon the courage to say goodbye.

"… and try not to worry about your father," said Garrett over the din. "The doctors are kept well back from the actual fighting. It's probably just the confusion around the battle that's making it difficult for him to reach you."

Clara nodded rapidly.

Garrett's messmate, Frank, trotted by and tipped his hat to Clara. "Come on, Garrett. We gotta go."

"I'll be right there." Garrett looked at Clara. "I've got to leave," he said, making no move to do so.

"I know," said Clara. Her voice quavered ever so slightly. "Before you do, I have something for you." She reached into her reticule, pulled out a small leatherette case, and handed it to Garrett. He opened it to find an ambrotype of her dressed in a blue ball gown. She was standing with one arm draped over the back of a chair and was staring at the camera with a clear direct gaze.

"It's the dress you wore to the Holiday Ball," he said.

"Yes," she said, pleased he recognized it. "I wanted you to remember how I looked the first time you saw me."

"I've never forgotten," he said. "I'll keep it with me always." He slipped the image into his pocket. "I have something for you, too."

He reached into his knapsack and pulled out a small folded piece of cloth. Clara unwrapped the fabric to reveal a filigree gold locket on a chain.

"Oh, Garrett. It's beautiful."

"Open it," he urged.

Clara removed her glove and pried open the oval locket. On one side was a cropped ambrotype of him, the one he had taken right after he received his Pennsylvania Reserves uniform; on the other, a small sprig of dried lilac. She caught a slight whiff of its fragrance. She looked up at him questioningly.

"You once told me that lilacs never die," he said in a husky voice. "I wanted you to remember, every time you look at this locket, that neither will my love for you."

Clara closed the locket with trembling fingers. Without a word, she handed it to Garrett, turned around, and lifted her hair. He drew the chain around her throat, fastened the clasp, and kissed the downy nape of her neck. When Clara turned back to him, her eyes were bright.

"I shall never take it off," she whispered, and pressed her hand to the locket where it rested just below the notch of her throat.

The bugle blared assembly.

"I really have to go," said Garrett. He gripped Clara's hands tightly. She tried to smile, but her lips trembled. Finally, with a small sob, she threw her arms around his neck and buried her face in his chest.

"Oh, Clara. My beautiful Clara," said Garrett. He held her tight and inhaled the fragrance of her hair. "No one in the history of the world has ever loved anyone the way I love you. You'll be in my thoughts every day and every night." He raised her damp face to his and kissed her with such tenderness she thought her heart would break.

When at last they pulled apart, she placed her hand on his heart and stared deep into his eyes.

"Garrett Cameron, I love you. Promise me you'll come back."

He placed his hand over hers.

"I promise," he said.

Garrett took her hand from his chest and, closing his eyes, kissed the soft flesh of her palm. Then he turned and walked away.

Five days after Garrett's regiment left for Washington, the long-awaited letter arrived from Dr. Ambrose. Clara, Helen, and Grandmother Blake gathered around Mrs. Ambrose as she read the news.

July 24th, 1861

> *My dearest loved ones,*
> *Please forgive me for not writing sooner, but the reasons were good ones, as I will explain.*

As you have probably heard by now, there has been a great battle with disastrous results for our army. As I write this in my tent, it has been three days since what they are calling the Battle of Bull Run took place. We thought we had the Rebels on the run, but it was they who got the best of us in the end, driving us nearly to the outskirts of Washington in a mad panic. It was a pitiful sight: officers deserting their men; soldiers running, dropping their weapons; civilians, who'd come to view the battle as one might go to see a play, fleeing for their lives, their picnic baskets forgotten and trampled by our own retreating troops. And the wounded; the poor pitiful wounded. We doctors did what we could for them, but often the wagons that were intended to convey them to the safety of our lines were commandeered by their cowardly comrades who sought any means possible to escape the battlefield. The poor souls lay in the hot sun of the open fields and cried out for treatment that for many came too late. The army has learned a costly lesson – the Rebels have come to fight, and I fear it will not be the quick war we all hoped for.

I, myself, am well, though somewhat exhausted after operating almost non-stop for two and a half days. But I know without a doubt that my presence here has already made a humble difference to some. I pray you will forgive my absence from you, something made bearable for me only by the knowledge of how very much I am needed here.

I must post this letter now and catch a few hours of sleep. My love to you all. I remain,

Your devoted husband and father

"Thank heaven he's all right," said Helen as she rocked her baby in her arms. "But, how dreadful about our soldiers. I can't believe they actually ran from the Rebels."

"It's a good thing Father was there to help care for the wounded," said Clara. "As much as I miss him, I guess he was right to go."

Their mother sat in silence, staring into the fire.

With the war escalating, Clara's desire to do something to help the Union cause intensified. She desperately wanted to volunteer as a nurse and use the skills learned at her father's side. And why not? she thought. Things were running smoothly at home. Surely the needs of wounded soldiers superseded her father's request that she remain behind. But when she raised the issue after supper one night, her mother was adamant.

"Absolutely not, Clara. I forbid it."

"But, Mama. I can help. I know I can. I've learned a lot from all the years of accompanying Papa on his calls. And I read in the paper that Miss Dorthea Dix, the Superintendent of Army nurses, has sent out a call for female volunteer nurses."

"I saw that advertisement," said Mary as she placed the silver coffee service on the table. "Miss Dix specifically requested plain women over the age of thirty. I'm afraid you don't qualify on either count, darlin'."

"That's hardly the issue," snapped Mrs. Ambrose. "And don't you have something to attend to in the kitchen, Mary?" As the housekeeper stomped off, Mrs. Ambrose turned back to her daughter. "Clara, nursing is no job for a woman. You have no idea the type of … *duties* you'd be expected to perform. It's indecent."

"It needs to be done by someone," said Clara.

"Not by you," replied her mother. "Besides, you're needed here. You know Grandmother Blake needs constant care, and Helen has her hands full with the baby." She shook her head. "No. It's just not possible."

Mrs. Ambrose reached for the coffee pot and the sight of her face in the glare of the lamplight halted Clara's protest. There were tense lines around Mrs. Ambrose's mouth and eyes, and her skin seemed stretched taut over her cheekbones. Clara watched as her mother sipped her coffee and noted how the cup rattled ever so slightly as she lowered it to the saucer. With sudden clarity, Clara realized her mother wasn't pleading on behalf of Grandmother Blake or Helen or the baby. She was pleading for herself.

"All right, Mother," Clara said softly.

Mrs. Ambrose reached out and patted Clara's arm.

"I know it's hard to wait and wonder. I'm afraid it's a woman's lot. The best we can do is keep busy. And pray."

"George?" Helen stared in disbelief at the uniformed soldier standing at the front door in the August heat. "George!" She flew into her husband's arms.

Hearing her cry, the rest of the household hurried to the entry to find the couple locked in an ardent embrace. Clara, Mrs. Ambrose, and Mary exchanged amused glances while they waited for the lovers to separate. Finally, Mrs. Ambrose cleared her throat.

"Welcome back, George," she said as the couple, flushed and embarrassed, pried themselves apart. "My, don't you look wonderful!"

And indeed, he did. Gone was the softness that had blurred his features, replaced by a thin muscularity, and his pale complexion above the thick beard was now tanned by the sun.

"I'm sure it's just the uniform, Mother Ambrose," said George, but he was clearly pleased.

"Mr. Pitcher," said Mary, "there's someone else here who would like to say hello." She stepped forward and placed three-month-old Jackson in his father's arms.

"Oh, my," murmured George as he stared down at his son. The baby gurgled and flailed his little arms in the vicinity of George's nose.

"What do you think?" said Helen.

"He's so tiny."

"Tiny!" scoffed Mary. "He's a great bear of a child, he is. Does nothin' but eat, cry, and ... well. He keeps us all goin', I'll tell ye that."

George looked from the child to his wife. His eyes filled with tears. "Thank you," he whispered. Helen's smile was radiant.

"Here, now," said Mrs. Ambrose as she reached for the baby, "give him to me. You two need a little time to get reacquainted. I'll call you when supper is ready."

Too eager to even blush at her mother's implication, Helen linked her arm through George's and led him up the stairs.

Clara followed Mary and her mother to the kitchen. She was happy for Helen, but the return of her sister's husband made Clara's longing for Garrett even more acute. As she helped Mary prepare the meal, Clara tried not to think of the reunion taking place in the bedroom over her head.

Suddenly, a happy thought came to her. Now that George was back, there would be someone here to look after the household, someone to relieve her mother of the emotional and financial burden of caring for the family. George's return meant Clara would be free of her promise to her father. She began to hum as she sliced the bread for supper.

To celebrate George's homecoming, Mrs. Ambrose instructed Mary to set the table with the best linen, china, and silver. Clara cut some fresh flowers from the garden and arranged them as a centerpiece between the two matching candelabras. Mary labored all afternoon on the meal, and beamed with pride as she served a tender beef roast surrounded by potatoes and green beans, a large boat of gravy, steamed potatoes, fresh tomatoes, fresh-baked bread with dairy butter and honey, and a sweet custard for dessert. The women watched with a mixture of delight and shock as George devoured the meal and sopped up every drop of the gravy with a hunk of soft bread. As Mary served the coffee, they leaned in to hear of George's adventures.

"There's not much to tell really," he said as he added extra cream to his third cup of coffee. "After a few weeks at Camp Curtin in Harrisburg, we were sent to guard the Northern Central Railroad track between the Pennsylvania line and Baltimore against saboteurs. Never saw a Rebel. Never even fired a shot." He took a loud slurp of his coffee.

"George!" admonished Helen softly.

"That's because no one dared challenge you," said Clara, ignoring his social gaffe.

"Perhaps. But I joined up to fight, not play nursemaid to some railroad."

"I'm sure your service, while uneventful, thank heaven, was important to the defense of our nation," said Mrs. Ambrose.

"But there's still much to be done," said George. "Bull Run showed us the Rebels mean to fight. This war could go on for a long time unless we are unwavering in our commitment to put down this rebellion. We must strike a blow for the Union that will show the South they cannot prevail."

"That's true. That's true," nodded Grandmother Blake.

Clara's eyes widened at this tough talk from her brother-in-law. More than his looks and manners had been hardened in his three months with the army.

"Well, Lincoln's call for more men should show them we mean business," said Clara.

"Yes," said George. "And now, with General McClellan replacing General McDowell as commander of the army, we'll have a well-trained, well-equipped force, ready and eager to fight. There'll be no more Bull Runs. Our soldiers will take the fight to the Rebels. And I plan to be with them."

Helen stopped with her cup halfway to her mouth. "What do you mean? Your enlistment is over."

George avoided her eyes while he dabbed at his mouth with his napkin. "I've decided to re-enlist with one of the new three-year regiments. I've been accepted into Company B of the 46th Pennsylvania Infantry."

None of the women said a word, afraid to even move. Helen placed her cup on its saucer with deliberate care.

"When did you make this decision?" she said, her mouth a thin line.

"The boys in the Jackson Blues have been talking about it for some time," said George. "Most of them are re-enlisting."

"I see," said Helen. "And when would you be leaving?"

"I'm to report to Camp Curtin in two weeks," said George.

Helen stared at him blankly. Then she rose from her place. "Excuse me, please," she murmured, and hurried from the room.

"Helen. Helen!" George raced after his wife.

Clara, Mrs. Ambrose, and Grandmother Blake exchanged looks. They were crestfallen for Helen, and for themselves. Shaking her head, Mary cleared the dessert plates.

"Oh, my," said Mrs. Ambrose. "I wished he'd told her in private. Prepared her somehow. Prepared us all."

"Yes," said Clara as she watched her own dreams of freedom evaporate.

The relationship between Helen and her husband was strained for the remainder of his visit. At the end of the month, Helen accompanied him to the train station for his trip to Harrisburg. When she returned, she retired to her room for the rest of the afternoon. Clara was at a loss as to how to comfort her.

"Give her time," counseled Mrs. Ambrose. "Just give her time." For she knew all too well that platitudes about duty and country would not shorten the days of waiting, lessen the worry and fear, nor warm an empty bed.

CHAPTER 10

"DAMN IT, GARRETT. THOSE REBS are shooting at us again."

Rawlie's voice, coming from behind a nearby tree, sounded more irritated than frightened. Garrett peered through the drizzle at the shadowy forms on the Virginia side of the Great Falls of the Potomac River, raised his rifle, and fired off an answering shot in their general direction.

"It's like shooting at ghosts," said Garrett as he crouched behind a large boulder to reload. "I don't think either side has hit anyone all week."

"That's just fine with me," said Rawlie. "If I die, I want it to be in a grand and glorious battle, not picked off behind a tree like some mangy squirrel."

Off to the right, Joe craned his neck over the top of a rotting oak stump.

"Joe, get your goddamn head down!" barked Rawlie. "You're gonna draw their fire."

No further shots came, however, and gradually the birdcalls and other forest noises returned, adding melody to the ever-present undertone of the cascading river.

Garrett rested the muzzle of his rifle in a depression in the boulder in front of him. The rain that had started after midnight had turned to a fine mist, but water droplets continued to fall from the leaves of the trees and the brim of his forage cap onto his rubber poncho. The air smelled of damp vegetation, wet wool, and wood smoke from the regiment's campfires. His stomach growled, but there was not much to look forward to in that regard. While on picket duty, the men existed on what were called *marching rations*, consisting of hardtack and salted pork or beef. Garrett found he was beginning to dream about soft bread, fresh snap peas, and fruit. To take his mind off his stomach, he let his thoughts drift back over the events of the past five weeks.

It seemed a lifetime since he'd waved goodbye to Clara on the train platform in Pittsburgh. On the trip east to Harrisburg, the trains bearing the 9th Pennsylvania Reserves regiment had stopped at numerous little towns to pick up more volunteers. At each station the people of Pennsylvania greeted them with cheers, band music, and baskets filled with food. The heady send-off kept spirits high, despite the heartbreak of leaving home and loved ones.

When they reached Camp Curtin in Harrisburg, the men felt the full magnitude of the call to arms. Thousands of recruits from all over the state, from large cities and small hamlets, dressed in every conceivable uniform or still in civilian clothes, were gathered at this stepping-off place. The 9th Pennsylvania was assigned a staging area, outfitted with haversacks and other necessary equipment and provisions, and told to get some sleep.

The next day, July 24, 1861, the 9th Pennsylvania boarded open railroad cars for the trip to Baltimore. The festive mood of the troops sobered as they crossed the Pennsylvania line into the slave state of Maryland. Determined to avoid a repeat of the riots that greeted the 6th Massachusetts and the 27th Pennsylvania in Baltimore in April, the men readied their guns and ammunition. Garrett rubbed his hand along the stock of his Sharps rifle. He was thankful the Pittsburgh benefactors of Company A had seen fit to provide the men with such fine guns. Observing his gesture, a private in Company C, the Iron City Guards, snickered.

"At least you got something to shoot with if there's trouble," he said. "These old muskets we got are just as likely to blow up in our faces as the secessioners'."

As they approached the outskirts of the city, the men peered out of the railcars. On this occasion, however, the Baltimoreans greeted the imposing body of armed, uniformed men with nothing worse than sullen expressions and glares. The Pennsylvania Reserves marched across town from the Bolton Depot to the Camden Depot without incident and boarded the train for Washington. They arrived in the capital the next morning and set up camp within sight of the Washington Monument and the Capitol Dome, both edifices still under construction, much like the fledgling nation they represented.

On the 28th of July, 1861, the 9th Pennsylvania Reserves regiment was formally mustered into United State service and received the official Federal designation of the 38th Pennsylvania Volunteer Infantry. Most of the men, however, continued to refer to themselves by their Reserves designation.

After a week of drilling and training, the entire regiment was ordered to march to Tennallytown, Maryland, approximately six miles northwest of the capital. A general camp of rendezvous had been established there for the thirteen infantry regiments, the one cavalry regiment, and the one artillery regiment that made up the entire body of the Pennsylvania Reserves. They were placed under the command of General

George McCall, a Pennsylvanian, and officially designated as a division within the new Army of the Potomac, known as McCall's Division.

Upon their arrival at Tenallytown, the men of the Pennsylvania Reserves were issued tents. Some of the companies received Sibley tents – large bell-shaped structures resembling Indian tipis that could house a dozen men or more. Garrett's company was issued the smaller wedge or *A* frame tents. Sweating beneath the August sun, Garrett and his messmates had stared in dismay at the pile of canvas and poles dumped at their feet by the quartermaster wagon.

"How the hell do you put this thing together?" asked Joe.

"Nothing to it," said Frank. "You boys just follow my lead."

The *A* frame tent consisted of a piece of canvas stretched over a horizontal ridge pole, supported on each end by two upright posts. The canvas was staked to the ground on either side and had folding flaps on the ends that could be opened or closed, depending on the weather. The roof sloped down on either side from the ridge pole so that only in the center could the average size recruit stand erect. These *A* frames were normally intended to house four men, but with the large number of soldiers in camp, the orders were to assign six men to each tent.

Under Frank's direction, Garrett and the rest of the mess laid out the canvas and set the poles. A few false starts and one partial collapse later, they had completed the task.

"There. Fit for a king," pronounced Frank.

Caleb poked his head inside. The floor space of the tent was only about seven feet square, barely large enough to fit the six of them and their belongings. "There's not much room in here," he remarked.

"You get used to it," said Frank. "Of course, you gotta sleep like spoons at night."

"Next to old Leonard?" said Rawlie. "See here, I'm willing to fight for my country, but that's asking too much!"

Leonard glared at him amid the others' laughter.

Tennallytown became a small tent city with its own layout and order. Each regiment had its assigned area. Within that area, each company was grouped together with a street running between their tents. The color line was in the front of the camp, perpendicular to the company streets; the officers' quarters were in the rear, parallel to the color line. The baggage trains were behind the officers' tents.

Once the shelters were erected, the Pennsylvania Reserves settled into a routine of camp and picket duties. This included guarding the Chain Bridge over the Potomac River, a mile and a half away, the route deemed most likely for a Rebel assault. When not on guard duty, the men took turns on construction details assigned to fortify and build new forts to add to the growing ring of defenses protecting Washington.

Each of the thirteen infantry regiments of the Pennsylvania Reserves also performed a ten-day tour of picket duty in the wild, rocky country around the Great Falls of the Potomac, about fifteen miles northwest of Tenallytown. For most of the regiments, this proved to be a fairly uneventful assignment patrolling the Maryland side of the river, the monotony relieved only by the occasional ineffectual exchange of gunfire with the enemy pickets guarding the Virginia side.

In the early morning of September 4th, however, while the 7th Pennsylvania Reserves regiment stood its turn at duty, the Union picket station was fired on by long-range rifled Confederate artillery, which had been wheeled into position, undetected, on the opposite shore. The attack was broken off before the Union could bring its own rifled artillery up from Tenallytown and no one was seriously injured. The incident, however, escalated the tension between the opposing armies.

Garrett and the 9th Pennsylvania Reserves were the very next regiment assigned to picket duty at the Great Falls following the attack. But, in the past week they had done little more than trade insults and sporadic rifle fire with the Rebels across the river.

Garrett shifted his weight. His legs were stiff from standing so long in the dampness. Again he tried to peer through the gray mist for any sign of movement on the opposite shore, but the rocks and pines seemed deserted. Off to his right and left, he could see the other men of Company A resting on their guns. Today, as on so many days, it appeared all they were guarding against was boredom.

Garrett's mind wandered to what Clara might be doing. Was it raining now in Lawrenceville, too? Did she look out and wonder how he was? She was always in his thoughts and he knew he was in hers. Her letters came with each mail, sometimes three and four at a time. They were full of stories intended to cheer him; stories of little Jackson, who, since the fame of Stonewall Jackson at the Battle of Bull Run, had been hastily re-dubbed, 'J.B.'; of Annie, whose spice cakes had become somewhat famous with the recruits crowding into Pittsburgh; and of Grandmother Blake, who seemed determined to knit a pair of misshapen socks for every soldier in the Union army.

In each letter, Clara also expressed her frustration that she couldn't do more to help with the war effort. He had chuckled when he read about her telling her mother she wanted to be a nurse. He knew such a thing would be unthinkable to Mrs. Ambrose. But then, many previously unthinkable things had happened since the war began. Six months ago he could not have foreseen that today he would be walking a post in the rain somewhere in northern Virginia, a target for his southern countrymen. Fighting a wave of homesickness, Garrett pressed his hand to his coat where the case containing Clara's picture lay in an inside pocket next to his heart.

Suddenly, Garrett heard a rustling behind him. He whirled around to find a small squad of men approaching through the drizzle.

"Who comes there?" he demanded, rifle raised.

"Relief," came the reply.

"Halt!" said Garrett. "Advance, Corporal, with the countersign."

A corporal emerged from the gloom. Garrett recognized Corporal Mulhern from Company B.

"Trimble's Variety," said Mulhern.

Grinning, Garrett lowered his rifle.

"You're relieved," said the corporal. "Private Weis, take over this man's post."

Garrett nodded to his replacement and fell into line with the rest of the squad. They marched to the next picket post, and the next, until all the men of Garrett's company had been relieved. Then, with their minds on a warm fire and a hot cup of coffee, the damp, tired squad followed the corporal back to the picket station.

As soon as they reached their tent, Garrett and his messmates got a fire going beneath the canvas overhang. Leonard put on a pot of coffee, and Frank and Joe began heating up some of their beef ration. Caleb removed his wet socks, draped them over a stick, and held them over the flames to dry.

Garrett shrugged out of his rubber poncho and retrieved his tin cup from inside the tent. Reaching around Caleb's socks, he poured himself a cup of coffee. He settled onto the log-turned-bench next to Caleb, took a piece of hardtack from his haversack, and attempted to take a bite.

"Geez," Garrett exclaimed, grabbing his jaw. "How do they expect you to eat this stuff? I nearly broke my tooth."

"Try crumbling it in your coffee," said Frank. "Softens it right up."

Garrett did as the older soldier suggested. Suddenly, the surface of his coffee was alive with thin, squirming bugs.

"What the hell is that?" cried Garrett.

Leonard glanced over at Garrett's cup with mild interest.

"Shit, that's just boll weevils from the hardtack. They don't much like hot coffee."

Garrett threw the contents of his cup onto the ground in disgust.

"Here now," said Leonard. "No need to be wastin' good coffee. Just skim them crawlies off the top. They don't affect the taste none." As if to demonstrate, Leonard picked a particularly large weevil out of his own cup and tossed it into the fire. He watched it sizzle before taking another big draft on his coffee.

"I don't mind the worms half as much as these goddamn graybacks," said Rawlie as he joined them at the fire. He scratched at his head. "One of these mornings, we're going to wake up to find the whole camp has been carried off by lice."

"I hope they take the commissary first," said Frank. He threw a half-eaten piece of beef back onto his plate in disgust. "That meat's so salty I'm getting blisters on my tongue."

"If you're not going to eat it, I'll take it," said Joe.

"Boy, you'll eat anything, won't you?" said Rawlie.

"Aw, it isn't so bad," said Joe. "You just gotta swallow it quick." He took the leathery meat Frank handed him and downed it in two gulps.

Rawlie shook his head. "And there goes another fine cavalry mount."

Joe looked at him in dismay. "You're just kidding, right? It's not really horsemeat."

Caleb nickered softly.

"Of course not," Garrett assured him. "They ran out of horsemeat last week. That's probably mule."

"Or dog," Frank suggested.

"Aw, geez." Joe leapt to his feet and hurried off in the direction of the sinks. Even Leonard cracked a smile.

"Maybe we shouldn't tease him so much," said Caleb with a chuckle.

"What else would we do for fun?" said Rawlie. "Besides, he's better off than the rest of us. If he can eat that stuff and survive, he can survive anything."

On the 16th of September, the 9th Pennsylvania gladly relinquished picket duty to the 11th Pennsylvania and began the long march back to Tennallytown. They could smell the smoke from the campfires long before they could see the camp itself. Rounding a last wooded bend in the road, the panorama of the main Pennsylvania Reserves camp spread out before them.

Thousands of white canvas tents were laid out in orderly rows; each regiment in its own section; each company within the regiment with its own street. The wagons of the baggage trains were parked behind the tents and hundreds of cavalry horses grazed around the perimeter. In fields and open areas, officers shouted orders to uniformed men at drill. Supply and munitions wagons rumbled through the company streets while officers and their aides hurried to and fro on missions of unknown importance. In front of their tents, soldiers not on duty cooked over small fires, wrote letters, played cards, read, or talked. All was systematic and precise, a fitting testament to the organizational skills of the new Commander of the Army of the Potomac, General George B. McClellan.

After the shocking defeat at the Battle of Bull Run, Lincoln had appointed General McClellan to replace the hapless General McDowell as commander of the eastern branch of the Union army. McClellan's talent for training and equipping an army was reflected in the increased discipline and order now exhibited by the men under his command. The Army of the Potomac was being honed into a true fighting force with a renewed sense of pride, and the military appearance of the Reserves camp at Tennallytown reflected this new confidence. In response, the men of the 9th Pennsylvania straightened their ranks and quickened their step as they entered the camp proper.

As the Pittsburgh Rifles passed by the company streets of the 8th Pennsylvania Reserves regiment, a soldier Garrett had befriended at Camp Wright called to him from his tent.

"Hey, Cameron. You boys missed all the excitement."

"What excitement?" said Garrett.

"The flag presentation ceremony," said the man as he fell into step beside Garrett. "Six days ago. The President, General McClellan, Secretary of War Cameron, and a whole bunch of top hats from Washington were here. Ladies, too. Came out to watch Governor Curtin hand out the new regimental flags. The entire Corps turned out for dress parade. The bands played and there were speeches. And when Governor Curtin arrived, the artillery fired off one hell of a salute."

"Sorry we missed it," said Garrett.

"Wait 'til you see the flags. They're impressive."

The 9th Pennsylvania saw the new colors that very afternoon. As the bands played, the Reserves marched in brigade strength. As usual, each regiment carried its state colors – a gold-fringed flag consisting of the standard thirteen red and white stripes with a blue canton containing the State Seal of Pennsylvania surrounded by thirty-four stars representing all the states in the Union. But now, in addition, each regiment's color guard carried its own new regimental banner – a yellow-fringed flag of blue silk with the coat of arms of the State of Pennsylvania in the center surrounded by thirteen gold stars.

When the regiments came to *Parade Rest* to await the receipt of orders, Garrett stared up at the regimental flag fluttering in the breeze. Emblazoned on two red ribbons above and below the coat of arms were the words: *9th Pennsylvania Reserves Regiment, 38th Pennsylvania Volunteers.* He felt a surge of pride. He wondered when they would get the opportunity to prove themselves in battle. He hoped the day would come soon.

Clara closed the door of the apothecary shop and hurried down Butler Street toward home. Helen's baby had contracted a case of the sniffles and Mrs. Ambrose had sent Clara off to find one of the few doctors left in town she trusted to treat him. The doctor had been out on calls, however, and Clara could do no more than leave a message for him to come by the house as soon as he returned. In the meantime, she had gone to the chemist's to obtain the tonic her father used to give the sick babies at the Orphans' Home. She hoped it would soothe little J.B. – as well as her worried sister and mother – until the doctor could arrive.

Despite the sunshine that peeked through the ever-present clouds of smog, the September wind was cool and Clara pulled her shawl tighter around her shoulders. As she passed the Allegheny Arsenal grounds, the sight of the soldiers standing guard at the gates made her think of Garrett. Virginia should be warmer than Lawrenceville, she reasoned. Still, she worried. Was he cold? Did he have enough to eat? Was he lonely? Although she had just written Garrett a letter that morning, she decided to write him another as soon as she got home.

"Miss Ambrose!"

Clara turned to find Edgar Gliddon exiting the gate of the lower Arsenal. She had not forgotten his disparaging remarks about both Annie and Garrett on the occasion of their last meeting. Jutting her chin, she kept walking. But, with his long stride, Edgar soon overtook her.

"Miss Ambrose," he said again. "Please, I need to speak with you."

"I'm sorry," she said coolly, "I'm in a hurry."

"So I gathered. Is everything all right?"

"Everything's fine."

"May I offer you a ride then?" Edgar gestured back to his shiny maroon brougham waiting at the curb in front of the Arsenal. The thought of being trapped in a closed carriage with Edgar made Clara distinctly uncomfortable.

"No, thank you," she said. "I'm practically home."

"Well, then please let me escort you," he said. "It would give me the chance to apologize."

Clara stopped. "You? Want to apologize?"

"Yes." He swept the hat from his head. "For my behavior the last time we met. I fear some of my comments may have been misconstrued."

"Nothing was misconstrued," Clara snapped. "You were quite clear – and insulting."

"For which I am most repentant," said Edgar. "You must understand, Miss Ambrose, my remarks, however misguided, were motivated by my concern for you and your reputation. I realize now, however, that I was wrong to question your choice in companions. You are a grown woman and capable of making your own decisions."

Clara looked at him suspiciously. "To what do we owe this drastic change in attitude?"

"The war, I suppose," he said solemnly. "It has exposed many of our social prejudices to be just that – narrow-minded bigotry and intolerance. You were well ahead of me in that regard, I fear. And, the recent loss of life suffered by our army has underscored the folly of wasting what time we have on this earth on petty concerns."

"I hope you believe that to be true," said Clara, unconvinced.

"Oh, I do," said Edgar. "I most certainly do. So, once again, I hope you will accept my apology. I would hate for my careless words to harm our ... special friendship."

Clara felt a shiver of revulsion. Still, he seemed sincere.

"I accept your apology, Mr. Gliddon," she said.

"Thank you, Miss Ambrose. You have no idea how much that means to me."

Avoiding his earnest gaze, Clara resumed walking.

"So, what brought you out to the Arsenal today?" she asked, eager to move the subject to less personal ground.

"I was meeting with Commander Symington to inform him of the status of his most recent order. Gliddon Iron Works is providing the specialty iron for the various accoutrements the Arsenal makes for the army – latches for the ammunition boxes, rings and buckles for the harnesses for the artillery horses – small things like that."

"Seems a rather routine subject to require the attention of the president of Gliddon Iron Works," said Clara.

Edgar couldn't help but smile. He had, in fact, been laying the groundwork for what he hoped would be a much more lucrative Federal contract in the future. Clara's innate understanding of the politics of business was most uncommon in a woman. And it only added to her allure.

"I like to keep a close watch on everything having to do with my interests," he replied.

Just then, they reached the Ambrose house. Seeing it through Edgar's eyes, Clara was suddenly and painfully aware that the iron fence was in need of paint, the shutter that had come loose the previous week was still hanging askew, and the grass of the little front yard, usually so neatly trimmed, was overgrown and weedy.

"How are you and your family faring, now that all the men are in the army?" asked Edgar. There was genuine concern in his voice.

"We're managing just fine," said Clara. "Father left us well provided."

"I'm sure he did," Edgar replied. "Still, I'd be happy to look in on you from time to time."

"I assure you, that won't be necessary," said Clara. She searched her mind for some witty comment, some exiting remark that would make him understand she resented his attempts to insinuate himself into her life.

Suddenly, Helen burst from the house.

"Clara! Clara!" she cried as she threw open the gate. Her face was streaked with tears and long strands of hair had escaped her crocheted net.

"Helen! What's the matter?" said Clara.

"It's the baby," she wailed. "He's much worse. His fever's risen, and he just cries and cries. Where's the doctor?"

"He was out on rounds. I had to leave a note."

"Oh, no!" said Helen. "What are we going to do?"

"Try to stay calm, Helen. I'm sure the doctor will come as quickly as he can." Clara reached into her bag and pulled out a small brown bottle. "In the meantime, I brought this tonic. Father always used it for sick babies. Maybe it will help." She took Helen's elbow and propelled her toward the house. Suddenly remembering Edgar, she glanced over her shoulder, but he was no longer on the sidewalk. Probably scared off by the thought of a sick child, she thought with disdain.

Clara could hear the baby's pitiful wails the minute she opened the front door. She hurried up the stairs to the nursery where she found her mother pacing with the child on her shoulder.

"Oh, Clara," said Mrs. Ambrose over the baby's cries. "Thank heaven you're back. Where's the doctor?"

"Out on calls. I left a note."

Mrs. Ambrose said nothing, but Clara could see the panic in her eyes. In the doorway, Helen whimpered.

"Here," said Clara, reaching out her hands, "let me take him." As she cradled the baby in her arms, she could feel the heat radiating from his little body. She knew the tonic would be worthless in a situation like this. She tried to remember how her father treated fever cases in young children.

"Helen. Quick. We need some ice." Clara laid J.B. down in his crib and began stripping him of his blanket and clothes.

"Clara! What are you doing?" asked Helen as the baby's howls increased. "He'll catch cold."

"We have to cool him down or he'll go into convulsions. It's all right. I've watched Father do this a hundred times. Now, run get some ice. Hurry!"

Helen was gone in a flash. Mrs. Ambrose stepped to Clara's side.

"Do you know what you're doing, Clara?" she said.

"I only know this is what Father would do with the little babies at the Orphans' Home. He said it's important to keep the fever from getting too high for too long, or the baby could ...." She stopped.

"The baby could what?" demanded Mrs. Ambrose.

Clara glanced at the doorway. "The baby could suffer damage to his brain," she said quietly.

Mrs. Ambrose went pale and nodded.

In a few minutes, Helen returned with a pail of ice. Clara instructed her sister to shave the ice into small pieces, which she and her mother wrapped in clean nappies. Gently they tucked the ice-filled cloths around J.B.'s naked body. His wailing cries raised an octave as the cold cloths touched his skin and the women crooned to soothe him.

Suddenly, there was a firm rapping on the open bedroom door. A distinguished looking gentleman with a neatly trimmed gray beard stood in the doorway. He wore an expensive, well-cut suit and carried a black bag.

"Excuse me," he said over the baby's cries. "I rang the bell, but for obvious reasons, no one heard me. I'm Doctor Todd, Mr. Gliddon's personal physician. He said you might be in need of my services."

"Oh, thank God," said Mrs. Ambrose. "Yes, Doctor. Please come in."

Doctor Todd leaned over J.B.'s crib. "Now, what seems to be the matter, little man?" He looked into the baby's eyes and ears, and pressed his ear to the baby's chest. Nodding, he looked up at the three women. "I'll need a few moments. If you could step outside please. Except for the mother."

Clara and Mrs. Ambrose retreated to the hallway and closed the door.

"How did Mr. Gliddon know to send a doctor?" whispered Mrs. Ambrose.

"I ran into him on the street this morning," said Clara. "He was escorting me home when Helen came out to tell me the baby had taken a turn for the worse. He must have gone immediately to summon his own doctor."

"What a wonderfully thoughtful thing to do," said Mrs. Ambrose.

"Yes," Clara agreed grudgingly, "it was."

They were having tea in the kitchen when Doctor Todd came down the stairs with a much calmer Helen.

"Master Pitcher is going to be just fine," he said. "He has a bit of an ear infection. I've given him some drops to ease the pain and swelling. He should be completely recovered in a few days."

"Oh, thank heaven," said Mrs. Ambrose. "With his high fever, we were so afraid it was something much worse."

The doctor nodded. "A fever like that can be indicative of many things, some of them quite serious. And the fever can be dangerous in and of itself. You were wise to use the ice packs."

Mrs. Ambrose cast a grateful look at Clara. "What do we owe you, Doctor Todd?" she asked.

He put up his hand. "It's all been taken care of. Besides, I consider it an honor to serve the family of Dr. Ambrose. I'm a great admirer of your husband and his work within the community."

"You're most gracious, Sir," said Mrs. Ambrose.

"Well, I'll be off then," he said. "Mrs. Pitcher, just remember to put those drops in the child's ears three times a day. And send for me if you have any more problems."

"Thank you, Doctor," said Helen.

"I'll see you out," said Mrs. Ambrose.

As their mother left with the doctor, Helen slumped in her chair. "What a day. I was so worried. I don't know what we'd have done had it not been for Mr. Gliddon."

Clara sipped her tea in silence.

While she waited for the secretary to announce her presence, Clara stood in the outer office of Gliddon Iron Works and stared out the window at the skyline of Pittsburgh across the river. She hoped Edgar was available to see her. It had taken all of her determination to make this call. The sooner it was over, the better.

She looked past her reflection to the factory buildings below. The grimy brick structures hugged the shoreline of the Allegheny River, which was thick with barge and steamboat traffic. Heavy dark clouds rose from the factory smokestacks and crept downriver to blend with the airborne detritus of the other factories, mills, and furnaces that circled the city like a necklace of glowing embers.

She had an inkling of what went on inside those blackened brick walls at the base of those belching stacks. Once, when she and Annie were nine and eight, respectively, Mrs. Burke had sent them to the mill to deliver Mr. Burke's forgotten lunch pail. As they waited for the foreman to come take the tin pail from them, they had peered through the partially open door to find a scene out of one of Reverend Lea's hellfire sermons. Dark, sweat-covered men, their faces ghoulishly illuminated in the flash and glare of the furnaces, maneuvered giant ladles of liquid iron about the factory floor, like muscled midwives guiding molten streams of living metal into molds and shapes and life.

No wonder Edgar is so caught up with power, Clara thought. Who wouldn't be when each day was spent harnessing and directing the very elements of nature itself.

The door to the inner office opened.

"Why, Miss Ambrose," said Edgar with a broad smile. "What an unexpected pleasure."

"Hello, Mr. Gliddon," said Clara.

"That will be all, Mr. Peterson," Edgar snapped at his secretary. The little man had been staring open-mouthed at the beautiful young woman beneath the veiled bonnet, her presence such a welcome change from the stodgy, cigar-smoking men who usually frequented the office. He quickly returned to his desk and began shuffling papers.

"Won't you come in?" Edgar gestured to the door of his office.

Clara entered the room, a large mahogany affair filled with expensive furniture and what appeared to be Italian landscape paintings in gilt frames. Edgar closed the door behind them, but made a point of leaving it slightly ajar. He escorted Clara to one of the tufted armchairs that faced the massive leather-topped desk on which piles of paper were arranged in meticulous order. Hanging on the wall behind the desk, an oversized portrait of an older man, who could only be Edgar's father, stared down with a look of dyspeptic disapproval.

Edgar circled to the other side of the desk, leaned back in his brown high-backed chair, and smiled at Clara over laced fingers.

"Now, to what do I owe the pleasure of your visit?"

"I came to thank you for your kindness in sending your doctor to treat my sister's baby," she said.

"Your mother and your sister each sent lovely notes expressing their gratitude, but I'm honored to be graced with a personal visit from you, as well. I trust the little one is all right?"

"Yes, just an ear infection, thank heaven. But it could have been much worse. Dr. Todd's presence greatly alleviated everyone's fears."

"I was glad to be able to help. The doctor told me you were quite composed under the pressure of the situation. My compliments."

"Well, I've had the benefit of assisting my father with some of his patients over the years."

He smirked. "Why am I not surprised?"

Ignoring his jibe, Clara opened her reticule. "I must insist, however, that we pay for Dr. Todd's services."

Edgar put up his hand. "That's really not necessary, Miss Ambrose. I was happy to do it. Besides, Dr. Todd is on retainer with my family. I assure you, he's well compensated, whether he does favors for me or not."

"Well ...." Clara hesitated. She hated to be beholden to Edgar, but what he said made perfect sense. And the Ambrose family's finances were increasingly precarious these days. Neither her father nor George had received their army pay as of yet, and the family's savings were dwindling at an alarming rate. She pulled the string of her purse closed. "Thank you, Mr. Gliddon. That's very kind of you." She took a deep breath. "Actually, there's a second reason for my visit today. I ... I wanted to apologize to you for my behavior."

"Oh?" said Edgar, taken aback by this rare moment of contrition on her part.

"Yes. I'm afraid I've been unfair to you over the past few months, regarding your service to the Union. In questioning your motives, I may have been a bit ... quick to judge."

Edgar hid his amusement as she struggled with her apology.

"I realize industries such as yours are essential to the war effort," she continued, "and I should not have assumed you are driven by monetary concerns rather than patriotism. Your recent kindness to my sister is proof that you are capable of great generosity. I shall try to remember that in the future."

Edgar found her naiveté almost touching. "Thank you, Miss Ambrose," he said. "Though I labor behind the scenes, it's good to be appreciated for my efforts. Especially by you."

Clara managed a noncommittal smile. Her unpleasant mission completed, she stood and extended her hand. "Well, thank you again, Mr. Gliddon."

"You're most welcome," he replied. He held her hand for just a second too long.

As he watched the young woman scurry through the outer office, Mr. Peterson could only wonder what she might have said to put that grin on Mr. Gliddon's flinty face.

CHAPTER 11

WHILE HER MOTHER STIRRED A large pot of porridge on the stove, Clara sat at the kitchen table and perused the October 3, 1861 edition of *The Daily Pittsburgh Gazette*. Helen had taken the baby out for some fresh air, and Grandmother Blake had fallen asleep in her wheelchair at the table. Enjoying this rare moment of calm, Clara and her mother had fallen into a companionable silence.

Suddenly, an article caught Clara's eye.

"Mother! Listen to this!"

Grandmother Blake stirred. Clara lowered her voice as she read.

> *Considerable excitement existed in Lawrenceville during Wednesday, in consequence of the discharge of two hundred boys in the United States Arsenal in making cartridges, etc. It would appear that during the past few months, matches have been found no less than three times, in rooms where these boys were employed, and extravagant rumors have been circulated in regard to attempts to blow up the magazine, etc. Some of the people residing near the Arsenal were so apprehensive under the excitement of these rumors, that they feared to lay down at night, lest they be blown to fragment before morning.*

"Had you heard anything about this?" asked Clara.

"Not a word," said Mrs. Ambrose. "Good heavens. Commander Symington should keep a better eye on those garrison boys."

"It appears he's done more than that," said Clara. She continued reading aloud.

> *The first and second scare passed off without any other notice than the gossip of the village and a "sensation' item in one of the newspapers. The third discovery of matches, however, if we are correctly informed, has induced commander of the Arsenal, Major Symington to discharge all of the boys heretofore employed in the place, numbering about two hundred. As the work which these lads were engaged is indispensable under existing conditions, their places are being filled by girls as rapidly as possible. What benefit is likely to result from this change we are at a loss to determine, and there are persons at the village who pronounce the act a wanton display of arbitrary poser. So many boys, thrown out of work at the*

approach of winter, must cause no little provocation, although it will be a measure lessened by the opportunity afforded to the girls, however, questionable the change may be in a moral and social point of view.

"Do you know what this means?" said Clara.

"Yes," said Mrs. Ambrose as she removed the pot from the heat. "It means the whole world has lost its sense of decency."

"No, Mother, it means I could get a job at the Arsenal."

Mrs. Ambrose scoffed. "I hardly think so, Clara."

"Why not? It's good, honest work. And it could help the Union win the war. It says here that it pays fifty cents a day. If I worked a full six-day week ... let's see ... that's twelve dollars a month!"

"Clara, I forbid it."

"But, Mother," said Clara, quietly, "we need the money."

Mrs. Ambrose hesitated for the barest of moments. "Not so badly that we need to sacrifice your good name. No daughter of mine is going to parade around in front of a bunch of soldiers and engage in manual labor."

"But, lots of girls are working now."

"Working class girls and immigrants. Not you," said her mother. "I know money is tight, but we can make ends meet if we're frugal. Your father's pay should be coming through any day now. And George's, as well. They said it might occasionally get delayed." She shook her head. "No, we're going to be just fine."

She continued stirring the porridge more vigorously now. Clara sighed and let the subject drop.

Shivering in the cold of the early October morning, Garrett squatted as best he could over the freshly dug sink. It was his third trip since reveille. Like most of the camp, he was suffering from diarrhea – the *Virginia Quickstep* the older soldiers called it – brought on by poor diet and proximity to others who were sick. There wasn't much to be done about it. The rations were what they were – salt pork, bread, and coffee, with vegetables and fruits being hard, if not impossible, to get on any regular basis – and it was difficult to avoid contact with those who were sick. At least half the men seemed to be suffering from some type of illness at any one time. At sick call each morning, the surgeon would routinely prescribe quinine or blue pills of mercury and chalk, regardless of the complaint. But the men were reluctant to avail themselves of even these questionable remedies. A trip to the surgeon's tent was thought by many to be the last trip you would ever take.

Garrett considered himself lucky to just be battling a case of loose bowels. Almost six hundred soldiers in the Pennsylvania Reserves division were stricken with various illnesses. The 6th Pennsylvania had been hit particularly hard, with one hundred and sixteen men, including some of the officers, down with typhoid fever contracted while first camped on the swampy land around Washington. Just last week, they had buried another two men. An outbreak of measles was also working its way through the ranks. Garrett noted that, for whatever reason, most of the city boys seemed to be faring better against this illness than those from the country. He'd had measles as a child, and so had avoided this deadly outbreak when it swept through the 9th Pennsylvania.

Having finished his business, Garrett stood to button his trousers. At least the cooler weather kept the stink from the sinks down, he thought with a wry grin. He swore the enemy would smell the Union army coming before it could see them. But then, he guessed the Rebs didn't smell any better.

As Garrett tramped back to his tent, a light rain began to fall. The dampness seemed to seep into his very bones. He turned up the collar of his thin jacket and quickened his pace. Over near the cavalry tents, the horses were tethered to a rope suspended between two trees. They dozed on three legs, their heads down, coats darkening with rain. The regiment's streets were almost deserted. Now that drill was over, no one was out that didn't have to be. The people back home would be surprised to know how much of waging war was made up of this, thought Garrett – just sitting around waiting. It seemed that the soldiers of the Union army spent most of their time killing nothing but time. Like the rest of the men, he wondered when, if ever, they would actually get to fight.

Clara huddled beneath a lap robe in her carriage outside the post office at the corner of Fifth Street and Smithfield in Pittsburgh. Her mother had gone into the building to check, yet again, if Dr. Ambrose had sent a letter, hopefully one containing his army pay. Three weeks had passed without a letter – three months without any pay – and both their worry and their financial problems were increasing accordingly.

As she sat shivering, Clara saw Edgar Gliddon, looking prosperous and warm in a fur-trimmed woolen coat, hat, and leather gloves, emerge from the City Hall building next door. When he turned and started down Smithfield Street in the direction of her carriage, she sank further down into the robe.

Since her visit to his office to apologize, Edgar had been a frequent caller at the Ambrose home, to the delight of everyone in the household but Clara. She had tried mightily to keep her promise to try to view Edgar's actions in a positive light, but every self-aggrandizing word out of his mouth had only served to convince her that her initial assessment of him had been correct. His brand of patriotism was much more about riches than risk. As her family did not share her opinion, Clara had decided the best course of action was to have as little contact with him as possible. Accordingly, she breathed a sigh of relief when he crossed the street and headed down the opposite sidewalk.

Moments later, Mrs. Ambrose came hurrying out of the post office, a letter clutched in her hand.

"Well, we've heard from your father," she panted. "He's safe, thank God. But there's still no money." Gathering her skirts, she climbed up into the carriage. "I can't imagine what's holding up his pay. How does the government expect people to live? Oh! Mr. Gliddon!"

Clara whipped around to find Edgar standing on the street side of the carriage.

"Please forgive me, Mrs. Ambrose," said Edgar, doffing his hat. "I didn't mean to startle you. I saw you from across the street and thought I'd come over and pay my respects. Hello, Miss Ambrose." He smiled warmly at Clara. She nodded.

"There's nothing to forgive, Mr. Gliddon," said Mrs. Ambrose in her best society matron voice. "It's always a pleasure to see you. We've missed your company of late."

"Yes, I'm afraid I was detained in Washington longer than I had hoped."

"I trust it was a successful trip for you," said Mrs. Ambrose.

"Well, yes. Yes, it was," said Edgar. "Gliddon Iron Works has just been awarded a government contract to provide a large portion of the iron rails needed to expand the railroads to transport our troops – should they ever decide to leave the safety of the capital."

"How wonderful," said Mrs. Ambrose. The slight to the Union soldiers was lost on her, but Clara scowled at Edgar.

"Yes, I'm honored to do my part for the war effort," said Edgar. "But, I do regret the demands of business have prevented me from calling on you and your family as often as I would like."

"You needn't feel obligated to check on us, Mr. Gliddon," snapped Clara.

"Oh, but it's an obligation I enjoy."

"And we enjoy your company." Mrs. Ambrose shot Clara a sharp look. "Please feel free to call on us at anytime."

"You are most gracious," said Edgar. "Now, if you will excuse me, I have an appointment. Mrs. Ambrose. Miss Ambrose." He touched the brim of his hat and strode away.

Mrs. Ambrose placed her hand on Clara's arm.

"Oh, dear. Do you think he heard what I said about your father's pay?"

"No, Mama," Clara lied. "I don't think he heard."

"Good." Mrs. Ambrose tucked the lap robe around her legs. "I would hate to have our temporary financial problems jeopardize your prospects."

Clara slapped the reins smartly against the back of the startled carriage horse. Honestly, she thought as they bounced over the cobblestones. Even in the midst of war, some things never change.

"Mama, how can you remain so enamored of Mr. Gliddon?" said Clara. "Didn't you hear the way he disparaged the courage of our troops?"

"I'm sure he didn't mean it that way," said Mrs. Ambrose. "And I do wish you'd stop finding fault in everything he says and does." She clutched the carriage canopy support as they careened around a corner. "Slow down, Clara! You're driving too fast."

"Mother, I've tried to give him the benefit of the doubt. I really have. But, the man is manipulative and opportunistic," said Clara.

"How can you say that?" said Mrs. Ambrose. "Mr. Gliddon's behavior toward you and this family has been nothing short of chivalrous. He's obviously taken with you and wants only to come to your rescue, despite the disgraceful way you treat him."

Clara slowed the horse to let a column of soldiers pass by. "I don't need rescuing."

"We may all need rescuing if your father's pay doesn't come through soon," said her mother. "And I for one feel safer knowing there's at least someone we can go to for help." She pulled the scarf tighter around her neck.

Clara, noting her mother's pale complexion, closed her mouth and urged the horse into a brisk trot once more.

In early October, McCall's Pennsylvania Reserves division received orders to leave Tennallytown and move to a more permanent camp near Langley, Virginia. On October 9, 1861, they began their march, entering Virginia by way of the heavily guarded Chain Bridge.

The Chain Bridge was actually a long wooden truss bridge atop stone pillars, but it retained the name of its predecessor, a chain truss bridge that, nine years earlier, had collapsed into the waters of the Potomac. The current bridge resembled a long, rectangular garden arbor with heavy wooden cross beams overhead and to each side.

As the leading ranks of the Pennsylvania Reserves approached the bridge, Garrett felt a prickle of excitement and fear. With each step, they were leaving the relative safety of the Maryland side of the river and entering enemy territory. His apprehension was heightened by the presence of a small battery positioned at the entrance of the bridge with its field guns trained on the Virginia side. Garrett knew that a larger Union battery atop the Maryland heights behind them also watched their progress. He wondered who and how many were watching them from the Virginia side?

In line of march, the 9th Pennsylvania stepped onto the bridge. The sound of their tramping feet was muffled by the dirt and sand mixture atop the wooden plank flooring. Garrett glanced over the side at the roiling, rock strewn waters of the Potomac River, then up ahead at the wooded hills and bluffs of Virginia that loomed ever closer.

"Well, Clara," he whispered, patting the pocket of his jacket where he kept her picture, "here we go."

Six miles later, the Reserves halted at their new encampment, Camp Pierpoint. Situated on the extreme right of the line of the Army of the Potomac, Camp Pierpoint was just thirty miles from the Confederate army's encampment at Centerville, Virginia. Rebel raiders and foragers were frequently sighted in the area. Accordingly, the atmosphere was more urgent than it had been at Tennalyville. Schools for officers were established, drilling increased, and discipline was more rigid.

At Camp Pierpoint, the Reserves were organized into three brigades. The 9th Pennsylvania was placed in the Third Brigade under Brigadier General Edward O. C. Ord.

"Anybody know anything about him?" asked Joe as he plunked down by the fire that evening and tugged at his boots.

"West Point, I heard," said Frank.

"Hope he knows how to fight," said Caleb.

"Been fightin' Seminoles down South," said Leonard from behind his coffee cup. "He knows how to fight."

Garrett warded off Rawlie's predictable query with a why-bother shake of his head.

Not long after they arrived, the men of the 9th finally received the regulation Federal uniform consisting of a blue cap with a black-tarred visor, a dark blue sack coat, and light blue trousers. This uniform had become the standard for the entire army so as to avoid the deadly confusion that had occurred at the Battle of Bull Run when different units, both Confederate and Union, mistakenly fired upon their own men because of the hodgepodge of uniform colors on both sides.

As each day passed, the weather grew progressively colder with temperatures inching toward freezing at night. In mid-October, the men awoke to find a silvery frost clinging to the leaves, grass, and the exterior of their tents. This only served to increase the grumbling over the fact that their allotment of overcoats had not yet arrived from the commissary.

Finally, in early November, a line of supply wagons rumbled into Camp Pierpoint with the long-promised shipment. The men crowded around the wagons in the biting wind.

"Hallelujah," said Garrett as he grabbed one of the folded bundles from the supply sergeant. He slipped his arms into the sleeves of the light blue, woolen great coat, buttoned up the front, and smoothed the attached shoulder cape. "Ah," he sighed. "I can't remember the last time I was warm, really warm."

"Hey, Leonard," said Rawlie. "Aren't you going to try on your new hat?" Rawlie was already sporting one of the new wide-brimmed black Hardee hats that had been handed out with the coats.

Leonard shook his head. "That big thing's just beggin' to be shot off. I'll just keep my old forage cap."

"Aw, damn." The mild oath, coming from young Joe, sounded more plaintive than angry. The men turned to find him staring down in dismay at his new coat. The hem, which came to mid-calf on most of the men, barely covered Joe's knees, and the sleeves left a long expanse of bony white wrist showing below the cuff.

"I guess the army didn't count on soldiers your size," said Garrett, trying not to laugh.

"You know, Joe," said Rawlie, "the 11th Pennsylvania's got that really short lieutenant. Maybe you two can work out some kind of arrangement where you can have the parts of the coat he's not using."

"Very funny," said Joe. "You're not the one who's going to be freezing on picket duty. Damn. I'm going to see if they've got anything bigger." As he trudged back to the quartermaster sergeant, a light snow began to swirl around their heads.

That evening at supper, Garrett sat wrapped in his great coat in front of the campfire. Balancing his knapsack on his knees as a writing surface, he pulled out the half-finished letter he had been penning to

Clara. He was almost down to his last sheet of writing paper and reminded himself he would need to go back to the sutler soon to get more. He licked the nib of his pen, and began to write.

> *Sometimes, as the light recedes at the very edge of the day and the last notes of the bugle fade, I sit in front of my tent and look out over the vast canvas city of this great army. A kind of calm descends with the twilight. The men gather around their campfires, and the scent of wood smoke, coffee, and frying fatback drifts on the cool night air. The sound of low voices and quiet laughter ebbs and swells, and often you can hear a fiddle or fife being played, or voices blended in song. At such times, I feel a kinship to these men I've never felt before, and a sense of pride to be joined with them in the service of my country. Were it not for the grim task ahead of us, or the fact that my being here means I must be separated from you, I feel as if I could contentedly remain in their company for the rest of my life.*
>
> *But, morning will come with reveille, its barked orders and endless drilling. The petty squabbles and complaining will resume and this euphoria of kinship will recede before the boredom, inanity, and stink of a soldier's life. But, beneath it all, the bond remains. I feel sure it will carry us through this conflict in good stead.*
>
> *It may seem an odd thing, but I am almost looking forward to battle. When you train as long and hard as we have, you want to get into the fight and have it done.*
>
> *Word has reached us of a disastrous defeat for our boys a few weeks ago at a place called Balls Bluff, not far up river from where I sit. The men say the attack was ill-conceived – straight up a bluff into the mouth of enemy cannon. More than 800 Union men were lost, some drowning in the river as they attempted to flee. The news from out west is no better. Yet, here we sit, day after day. The question on every man's lips is when will we fight? When?*

The entire Union was asking the same question. While initially the North cheered McClellans' skill at turning the disorganized Federal army into a well-drilled, well-provisioned force, as the weeks turned into months with still no movement against the Confederates, the cry for action became louder. Each day, telegraphed messages from Washington urged McClellan to make some kind of move and the Northern newspapers wondered aloud when the Union army would retaliate for the July defeat at Bull Run.

Now, as winter approached with no definitive action being taken against the Rebels, many began to question McClellan's willingness to actually lead the army into battle. The North wanted a victory, and wanted it soon.

CHAPTER 12

AS THE COLD WEATHER SETTLED into the Virginia country-side in November of 1861, the Union and Confederate armies remained thirty miles apart. Each side regularly sent out foraging and scouting parties, but no major offensive was planned. Both pro-Union and pro-Confederate citizens lived in this disputed territory, and rumors as to the activities and whereabouts of both armies swirled through the towns and the opposing army camps.

Garrett and the men of the Pittsburgh Rifles had their first near encounter with the enemy in mid-November. Along with four other companies of the 9th Pennsylvania Reserves regiment, they were assigned to check out a rumor that the Rebels were advancing their line closer to that of the Army of the Potomac. They ventured out, only to find the Rebel position unchanged. Upon returning to camp, however, they discovered they had been shadowed by Confederate cavalry for much of the way back.

"Damn! I can't believe we missed our first real chance at the Rebs," said Caleb as they discussed the news around the campfire that night.

"Doesn't sound like they were lookin' for a fight," said Frank. "Just keepin' an eye on us. Like we were on them."

"We've been in this army for nearly seven months and we've still never been in a battle," said Joe. "I don't know how we expect to defeat the Confederates if we don't ever actually fight them."

"There'll be plenty of fighting," said Leonard. "You can be sure of that. Enjoy the quiet while you can."

"You talkin' from experience, Leonard?" probed Rawlie.

Leonard took a sip of coffee. "Just talkin' common sense."

The two armies continued to harass each other through the rest of November and early December. A few sympathizers were arrested and a few minor skirmishes broke out. But still, no major battles were joined.

On the 19th of December, General McCall received a reliable report that a large force of enemy cavalry, accompanied by a Rebel wagon train, was foraging in the vicinity of the town of Dranesville, Virginia, just twelve miles from Camp Pierpoint. General McCall was determined the Rebels not be allowed to roam the countryside at will. After consulting with General McClellan, McCall ordered the entire Pennsylvania Reserves division to be ready to march at daybreak.

At 6:00 a.m. on the 20th of December, the Pennsylvania Reserves, including Garrett and the rest of the Pittsburgh Rifles, stood at attention in front of their tents. The plumes from their breath rose in the cold clear air as they waited for their orders. Each man had been instructed to carry a full forty rounds in his cartridge box and a day's worth of rations in his haversack, a sure sign they were about to see action.

The Pittsburgh Rifles and another company of sharpshooters – Company E of the 13th Pennsylvania, known as the Bucktails for the deer tails they wore affixed to their hats – were to be deployed as skirmishers on this expedition to Dranesville. The Third Brigade, which included the 9th Pennsylvania Reserves, was to lead the advance, followed at intervals by the First and Second Brigades.

At the order to *Form Skirmish Lines*, the Pittsburgh Rifles and the Bucktails spread out on either side of the Leesburg/Washington Turnpike and began moving west. All eyes and ears were alert for first contact with the Confederates. Behind the skirmishers came the Third Brigade's cavalry, followed by the artillery, with the infantry bringing up the rear.

With his rifle at the ready, Garrett picked his way through the brittle brown fields and the occasional wood lots that bordered the road. The frost from the silvery grasses dampened the bottoms of his trousers, and the coffee he had downed that morning sloshed and rolled in his stomach. He was conscious of his comrades spread out around him, their heads swiveling as they gripped their rifles, pushing forward toward what they all hoped would be their first real meeting with the enemy.

Just east of the village of Dranesville, the Leesburg/Washington Turnpike met the Leesburg/Alexandria Turnpike atop a high hill, known as Drane Hill. There, the two roads converged to form the Leesburg Pike, which ran through Dranesville and eventually led northwest to Leesburg, Virginia. From Drane Hill, this road dipped down into a valley, then climbed a smaller hill on which sat the town of Dranesville, its church clearly visible in a grove of large oaks. This smaller hilltop looked west over a vista of open farmland and scattered woods. South of the town was a heavily wooded area cut by two more roads that eventually met and headed southwest toward Centreville.

Concealed in and around Dranesville was a Confederate brigade under the command of cavalry officer, General J. E. B. Stuart, assigned to provide protection for their forage wagons. General Stuart was known in both the North and South, not only for his bold actions at

Bull Run, but for his flamboyant dress, which included a wide-brimmed hat trimmed with a large feather, a red-lined gray coat, and high black cavalry boots that came over the knee. Stuart's brigade consisted of two squadrons of cavalry totaling approximately 150 men, the four pieces of Cutt's Battery, and 1600 infantry troops divided between four regiments: the 1st Kentucky, the 6th Carolina, the 10th Alabama, and the 11th Virginia.

Garrett and the other Union skirmishers approached the village cautiously. Despite the cold, Garrett felt a trickle of sweat run down the center of his back. His eyes swept the sheds, buildings, and windows of the town for signs of the enemy. He braced for the crack of the first shot, but the Confederate cavalry pickets had vacated the town and, in fact, could be seen galloping along the Leesburg Pike to the northwest.

The lead columns of the Pennsylvania Reserves reached Dranesville just after noon. With the rest of the Third Brigade strung out behind him, General Ord, accompanied by his aides and officers, reined his horse to a halt atop the second, smaller hill.

"Lieutenant," barked the general. The adjutant hurried to the general's side. "Instruct Captain Easton that I wish him to deploy his artillery on this hill near the church."

"Yes, Sir." The officer saluted and galloped off in search of the artillery captain.

General Ord raised his field glasses and continued to monitor the movement of the enemy pickets.

"Strange," he muttered to himself. The fleeing Rebels had stopped, turned, and now appeared to be watching the approach of the Federal army. "I don't like this. I don't like this at all. They would not be so bold were there not a larger Confederate force nearby."

The general turned in his saddle and searched the surrounding countryside. His eye was immediately drawn to the higher Drane Hill, some six hundred yards to his rear at the intersection of the two turnpikes. The strategic importance of that hill became immediately clear. Not waiting for a messenger, the general galloped over to the battery that was unlimbering its guns near the church.

"Captain Easton!" shouted General Ord as he reined his horse to a halt. The artillery captain turned and saluted. "Remove your battery from this hillside with all deliberate speed and proceed at once to set up on that larger hill behind us. We must control the high ground before the Rebels do. I will instruct the other batteries to set up alongside you."

"Yes, Sir."

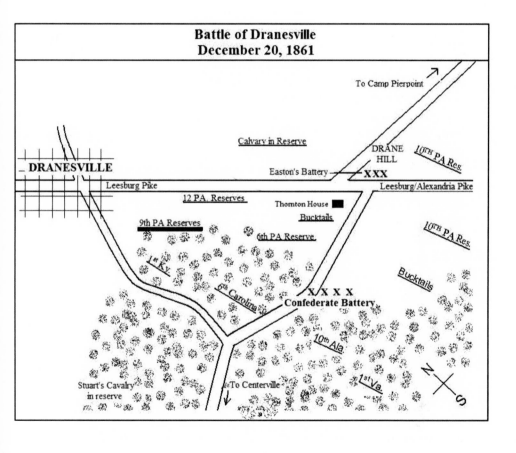

**Battle of Dranesville
December 20, 1861**

To Camp Pierpoint

Calvary in Reserve

DRANE
HILL

10ᵀᴴ PA Res.

Easton's Battery

XXX

DRANESVILLE

Leesburg Pike

Leesburg/Alexandria Pike

12 PA. Reserves

Thornton House

9th PA Reserves

Bucktails

6th PA Reserve.

10ᵀᴴ PA Res.

1ˢᵗ Ky.

Bucktails

6ᵗʰ Carolina

X X X X
Confederate Battery

10ᵗʰ Ala.

Stuart's Cavalry
in reserve

To Centerville

1ˢᵗ Va.

N

S

Immediately, the artillery horses were put back into the traces, and the cannons and limbers were soon careening to the crest of Drane Hill.

General Ord's intuition was correct. Confederate General Stuart was at that very moment marching his four regiments through the woods on either side of the Centreville Road in an effort to cut behind the Union troops and gain the advantage of Drane Hill. But Easton's mad dash successfully placed the Union artillery atop the hill first.

Having lost the race to gain the high ground, Stuart set up his battery in a slight depression along the Centreville road south of town. At about 2:00 p.m., he began firing upon the Federal artillery and the gathering Yankee infantry. The dip in the terrain offered the Rebel guns some protection, but also made it necessary to aim the barrels of the guns at a sharp angle to clear the elevation. As a result, despite heavy firing, the majority of their rounds sailed up and over the heads of the approaching Federals.

Captain Easton, on the other hand, trained his cannons on the smoke rising from the Confederate battery. Within three shots, he completely destroyed one of the enemy's guns. The caisson exploded in a brilliant burst of fire. When the smoke cleared, wounded and dying men and horses lay about their disabled cannon.

As this artillery duel continued, the regiments on both sides of the fight began to form in line of battle. The Pittsburgh Rifles and the Bucktails, out in front on the skirmish line, were recalled to join their regiments. This they did at the trot as stray shots burst around them and artillery shells screamed over their heads.

Jogging back to the 9th Pennsylvania's place in line, Garrett tried to control the surge of adrenaline racing through his veins. This was it. They were to fight, at last. Up ahead to his right, he could see the other three regiments of the Third Brigade coming into line; solid ranks of men in blue with arms at *Right Shoulder, Shift*; each with its regimental flag snapping in the wind. For a moment, he was struck by the pageantry of thousands of uniformed men, marching in formation as they had been trained. Only this time, it was not a drill.

Suddenly, an enemy shell struck just off to Garrett's right. He was pelted with dirt, his ears rang, and his nose filled with the caustic smell of gunpowder. Wide-eyed, he fought off the urge to throw down his gun and hurtle back to the relative safety of his regiment.

As Garrett and the other skirmishers approached the Union lines, they came abreast of General Ord and his aides, who were surveying the gathering battle lines from horseback just in front of the Federal troops. The men paused briefly to salute their commander.

"Come down on them, boys, like the wild cat in the mountain," urged the general, returning their salutes as they streamed by.

The two batteries, Union and Rebel, were at the approximate center of their respective lines of battle. On either side of the Centreville Road, where the ill-fated Confederate battery had set up, the ground was heavily wooded. Stuart divided his four regiments, two on either side of this road, and ordered them to march north through the woods to engage the Union troops. So dense was the undergrowth in this area that in the midst of moving to their assigned positions, two of the Rebel regiments mistook each other for the enemy and opened fire. Men lay dying before the mistake was discovered.

On Drane Hill, just to the right of Easton's battery, a brick house, known as the Thornton House, became a haven for some of the sharp-shooting Bucktails. From the vantage point of the house's doors and windows they were able to inflict considerable damage on the advancing Rebel ranks.

To the right of the Bucktails, on the extreme right of the Federal line, the 9th Pennsylvania Reserves regiment took up its position and waited for the order to enter the thick pine forest on the west side of the Centreville Road. Garrett and the rest of Company A hurried into place on the far right of their regiment's line.

"Battalion!" shouted the 9th's colonel as he raised his sword in the air. "Shoulder arms! Forward! March!"

The 9th Pennsylvania stepped off in two lines and entered the dense woods. The pungent smell of pine mixed with the acrid smoke drifting from the batteries. The men struggled to keep their lines as tree limbs snapped in their faces and the thick underbrush pulled at their legs.

After advancing a couple of hundred yards, they suddenly saw troops approaching to the front and right of them, their exact identity obscured by the trees and thick brushwood.

"Are they ours or Rebs?" said Rawlie at Garrett's elbow.

"I don't know," Garrett replied in a low voice.

"Well, I don't want to shoot our own men," said Joe, in line next to Rawlie.

The same dilemma of identification confronted the officers.

"9th Reserves! Halt!" commanded the colonel. The order echoed down the line from company to company. The ragged lines halted and the men dressed their ranks as they peered nervously into the dense growth.

"Captain," barked the colonel. An officer hurried to his side. "Can you identify those men?"

"I'm not sure, Colonel, but I think they might be the Bucktails."

Just then, a voice called out from the brush up ahead.

"Don't fire on us!"

"Are you the Bucktails?" shouted a soldier from the far side of the 9th Pennsylvania's line.

"Yes," shouted the voice in reply. "We are the Bucktails. Don't fire."

Joe turned to Garrett. "Good thing we checked," he said.

Suddenly, a volley of musket fire erupted from the underbrush. In the flash and smoke, a number of the Pennsylvania boys crumpled to the ground. The unit ahead was not the Bucktails, but the men of the 1st Kentucky, a Confederate regiment.

"They're Rebs!" yelled Garrett. He dropped to one knee and took aim.

Joe stood frozen in place.

"Get down!" Rawlie yanked Joe to the ground by his elbow.

"Fire at will!" bellowed the 9th's colonel as he thrust his sword in the direction of the Rebel lines.

The 9th Pennsylvania began returning fire as quickly as possible. The air filled with the crackle of rifle fire and the shouts and screams of the men. Minie balls whizzed by in both directions. The bullets made sharp thwacking noises when they hit a tree, more muffled sounds when they found a softer target. Again and again, Garrett reloaded his rifle and aimed at the shadowy forms that flitted through the smoke and trees up ahead.

The Rebels soon gave way and the 9th Pennsylvania pursued them deeper into the woods. As the men in blue advanced, they stepped over and around Rebel bodies. The number of dead and wounded attested to the deadliness of the Union fire.

Meanwhile, in the center of the battlefield, with almost his entire battery disabled, Confederate General Stuart was making a last bold attempt to gain control of the field. He ordered his two regiments on the east side of the Centreville Road to charge on the Thornton House, near the center of the Union line, in hopes of driving the Federals from their commanding position. In order to do this, however, the Confederate troops had to cross a large area of open field. They quickly became targets for the Bucktails in the house, the Union artillery on Drane Hill, and the other Union infantry regiments on that side of the road.

In light of this withering fire, and having learned of the approach of the other two Pennsylvania brigades, Stuart withdrew his regiments.

Confident that his forage wagons had returned safely to the Confederate lines, he retreated and carried his disabled cannon off by hand. The Federals did not pursue.

As the Union soldiers watched what was left of the enemy abandon the field, they cheered and waved their hats and regimental flags.

The victory did not come without cost, however. In a battle lasting less than two hours, seven Union soldiers lay dead on the field; sixty-one more were wounded. The Confederate casualties were estimated to be close to two hundred. Though not a tremendous loss in numbers, these were the first battle deaths experienced by the men of the Pennsylvania Reserves, and their joy at their victory was tempered by the sight of their comrades who had fallen.

Garrett leaned on his rifle and watched four members of the Pittsburgh Rifles carry one of their own badly wounded men off the field. Garrett's relief at having acquitted himself well in this, his first battle, turned to sorrow at the loss of this comrade with whom he had lived, drilled, and marched for the past eight months. And, Garrett realized with growing shame, beneath his sorrow was a feeling of intense gratitude that it wasn't him.

Chastened and exhausted, Garrett shouldered his rifle and rejoined the remaining men of his company.

The news of the Union success at the Battle of Dranesville reached the Northern newspapers just before Christmas. Although not a large or particularly significant battle when viewed in light of the massive conflicts to come, the victory at Dranesville received great play in the Northern press as the first bit of good news for the Union since the disaster at Bull Run. Pennsylvania, in particular, cheered the brave performance of their Pennsylvania Reserves Corps.

Knowing any letter from Garrett would lag the official reports by days or even weeks, Clara rushed to the newspaper office to read the broadsides containing the list of casualties. She ran her finger down the alphabetical list of killed and wounded, and gave a small cry of relief when his name was not there.

"Is he all right?" asked a quiet voice at her elbow. Clara turned to find Annie standing there.

"Oh, Annie," said Clara, reaching for her friend's hand. "Yes. He's all right. He's not listed."

"Glory be to God," said Annie. She made the Sign of the Cross.

Suddenly, Clara realized she had been so worried about Garrett that she had not thought to look for Annie's brothers' names on the list.

"Annie. Your brothers?"

Annie smiled. "They're fine, too. In fact, accordin' to the paper, their regiment was held in reserve. Never even got into the fight, which I'm sure they'll see as a great injustice."

Clara hesitated. "And Private Frye?"

Annie blushed. "It appears he was unharmed, as well."

They hugged each other in relief. Suddenly, they heard a wailing cry. They turned in time to see an older woman collapse in the arms of her equally stricken husband.

"Come. Let's go," said Clara. The two girls hurried down the street, away from the mixed scene of relief and despair.

"This is so hard," said Clara as they walked along. "The waiting, not knowing."

Annie nodded. "Very hard, indeed. Have you heard from your father?"

"He writes frequently, but the letters come in bunches, so sometimes we won't hear from him for a week or two. It's very wearing on Mother."

"Me ma and da are havin' a hard time of it, as well. The house seems so empty without the boys, and me brothers are not much for writin'. Still, they do try to send home their pay when they receive it, but that's hit and miss."

"I know what you mean," said Clara. "Father was sure our savings, along with his army pay, would stand us in good stead. But he's been gone seven months and has only been paid once. It's the same story with my brother-in-law, George. And with Helen and the baby living with us now, money is getting tight.

"Then you might be interested in a bit of news I have," said Annie. "Come the first of the year, I'll be joinin' the workers at the Arsenal. Makin' bullet cartridges. It's good money. And, they're lookin' for more workers. If you were to get a job there too, we could help our families and spend every day together. It'd be fun. And you'd be doin' somethin' to help win the war, like you said you wanted."

Clara shook her head. "I already asked. Mother forbad it. She thinks it would be 'unseemly' for me to work at the Arsenal." She caught herself. "Oh, Annie. You know I don't feel that way."

"It doesn't matter," said Annie, jutting her chin. "I'm not too proud to do what needs to be done for me family. And for our boys in the army." At the repentant look on Clara's face, she softened. "Still, it would've been fun to do it together."

"Yes, it would," agreed Clara.

* * *

Not long after the Battle of Dranesville, the Pennsylvania Reserves were ordered to set up permanent winter quarters at Camp Pierpoint. Since the location was damp and muddy, the various companies within each regiment took turns draining and grading the area to make it more habitable. The soldiers put extra effort into making their own personal quarters as comfortable as possible. To the dismay of the local farmers, they swarmed over the Virginia countryside like termites. The men cut down trees and tore apart abandoned and not-so-abandoned buildings to obtain the materials needed to build the more substantial shelters that would be their homes for the next few months. Garrett and his messmates were determined not to be left wanting.

"Garrett! Garrett! Lend us a hand."

Garrett looked up from his digging to find Rawlie and Caleb staggering toward him through the frozen mud. They were carrying a large stack of weathered beams bristling with rusty nails. Joe followed just behind them with a load of bricks in his arms. Garrett threw down his shovel and seized the end of one of the beams.

"Where'd you get all this?" he said.

"We found an old barn, two hills over," said Caleb. "Grabbed these just before the boys from the 8th Pennsylvania showed up."

"Yeah, and I got these." Joe displayed the bricks with a proud grin. "Ought to make a pretty good chimney, don't you think?"

The messmates dumped their scavenged materials on the ground in front of their *A* frame tents where Frank, Leonard, and Garrett had already begun digging a shallow rectangle in the hard ground. Frank, based on his prior military experience, had assured them a shelter sunk partially below ground would stay much warmer in the winter cold. Leonard took the first shift guarding their cache of wood and bricks while the other five manned the shovels.

"Jeez, Joe," grumbled Rawlie as he hit another rock, "we wouldn't have to dig this thing so deep if you weren't so damn tall."

"Aw, quit your griping," said Frank. "We'll all appreciate the extra head room when it's finished."

Once they had the floor of the shelter dug down about two feet deep, they began setting the walls. They positioned the boards, one atop the other, leaving space for a door, until the height from the floor to the top of the walls was nearly six feet. The gaps and chinks between the logs were filled with a sticky mud mixture. Then, using long lengths of saplings cut from the nearby woods, they raised the rafters and gables, which they covered with their canvas tent to form a ceiling. One gable end they filled with shorter pieces of the wood, the other end with an old rubberized poncho. When finished, even 6'3" Joe could stand upright comfortably in the center of the cabin. For a share of the men's coffee and sugar rations, a mason from Company D was persuaded to come in and build a respectable fireplace out of the purloined bricks and some additional stones the men had gathered. On top of the chimney, to improve the draft, they placed a mud-lined pork barrel obtained from the commissary.

They labored hard on the inside of the hut, as well. They split logs to lay down a rough floor. Pieces of these same logs were used to make the frames for the bunk beds. Barrel staves were nailed to the frames as a bottom support for the *mattress* – a thick layer of pine needles, topped with an army blanket. They hammered pegs into the walls to hang their belongings and made chairs from sawn off stumps. Leonard demonstrated a flair for carpentry by fashioning a serviceable table out of an empty hardtack case mounted on legs made of sturdy saplings.

"Where'd you learn to do that?" asked Rawlie.

Leonard spit a stream of tobacco juice onto the ground near Rawlie's feet. "Harvard," he said.

Rawlie looked at Garrett and rolled his eyes.

When all was finished, the men stood in the middle of the company street to survey the completed structure.

"It's the best damn shelter in the regiment," pronounced Frank.

"Wait. It needs one more thing." Rawlie disappeared behind the hut and returned with a three-foot long piece of board. He proceeded to nail it to the center post of the front gable. *Monongahela House Hotel* it read in white painted script.

"Perfect," said Garrett. "Now, shall we retire to the bar for brandy and cigars?"

On Christmas Eve, 1861, Clara stood alone in the parlor and hung strings of popped corn and dried fruit on the small fir tree on the table in the front window. Decorating the tree was usually a family event filled with laughter and singing. This year, no one else seemed to have the heart for it.

At the end of November, in an effort to cut expenses, Mrs. Ambrose had to let Mary Tierney go. Clara missed Mary's steady presence and sharp wit, not to mention the way she kept the house running. Mary had been like a second, less disapproving mother to her, and her leaving left a hole in Clara's heart.

Most glaring, of course, was the absence of the men. The previous Christmas, Father and George had joined in the festivities, but this year they were celebrating the Lord's birth in army camps far away. Clara hoped her father, brother-in-law, and Garrett had received the Christmas boxes the Ambrose women had sent by Adams Express. Each box contained a mix of tasty treats, reading material, and useful items like woolen socks, scarves, and gloves. Mr. Webster had stopped by in early December with a bottle of brandy for her father. Clara had added it to his box, secreted in a tin marked *"peanuts"* to avoid discovery by any thirsty soldiers handling the brigade mail. She hoped before he shared it with his patients, her father would enjoy a little of it himself.

Among the items in Garrett's box, Clara had included a lilac-scented letter filled with her longing for him. Garrett's absence had made Clara realize that, though she had been alone before in her life, this was the first time she had ever felt truly lonely.

She sighed and reached for another string of dried fruit.

Christmas day dawned cold and bleak. The Ambrose women trooped off to church and valiantly joined the congregation in singing the old Christmas hymns. But the dearth of male voices was painfully evident, and the tunes sounded thin and forced.

When they returned home, Clara, Helen, Mrs. Ambrose, and Grandmother Blake dutifully went through the motions of the holiday. They sat in the parlor and exchanged modest gifts that reflected their increasingly precarious financial situation. Little J.B. gurgled happily amid the colorful paper and ribbons, and provided the only real bright spot in the day.

"Well, I guess it's time for the meal," said Mrs. Ambrose, rising from her chair.

"I'll set the table," said Helen.

They were all busy in the kitchen when the front door bell chimed.

"Who could that be?" said Mrs. Ambrose.

"I'll go see," said Clara. Wiping her hands on her apron, she traipsed down the hallway and opened the door. On the stoop stood Edgar Gliddon, dressed in a gray cutaway coat, black and gray striped silk waistcoat, and top hat. He was holding an enormous basket wrapped in white netting and tied with a red satin bow.

"Happy Christmas, Miss Ambrose," he said with a broad grin.

"Mr. Gliddon! What are you doing here?" blurted Clara.

"Clara! Is that any way to greet a guest?" scolded Mrs. Ambrose as she hurried up behind her daughter. She gave Edgar her sweetest smile. "Do come in, Mr. Gliddon. And a Happy Christmas to you, as well."

"I hope I'm not interrupting your festivities," he said. "I just wanted to bring you ladies a little holiday cheer."

"How kind of you," said Mrs. Ambrose. "Clara, why don't you go to the kitchen and tell Helen that Mr. Gliddon is here." She stared pointedly at Clara's apron. Before Clara could respond, Helen entered the foyer with J.B. on her hip.

"Why, Mr. Gliddon," said Helen, "what a pleasant surprise."

"Good morning, Mrs. Pitcher," said Edgar. "And how is the little man?" He leaned his face close to the baby, who promptly reached out and smacked him on the nose. Clara bit her lip to keep from laughing.

"J.B., no!" cried Helen. "Oh, dear! I'm so sorry, Mr. Gliddon."

"No harm done," said Edgar. Checking his nose for injury, he forced a smile. "I love a spirited child."

"Would you like to set your basket down?" suggested Mrs. Ambrose.

"Yes. It is a bit heavy." Edgar followed her into the parlor and placed the basket on the tea table. With great ceremony, he bowed to Grandmother Blake who had just wheeled in from the kitchen. The smile she gave him was positively coquettish.

"Well, Mrs. Ambrose," he said, gesturing toward the basket, "perhaps you would like to do the honors?"

"May I?" she twittered. She undid the bow and peeled away the white netting to reveal a treasure trove of fancy pastries and cakes, wrapped packages for each of the ladies, and a wooden train for J.B. The gifts were chosen with an exquisite sense of taste – expensive, but not so expensive as to cross the lines of propriety.

"Oh, Mr. Gliddon. You're too kind. I don't know what to say," said Helen. She inhaled the scent of the lemon soaps he had given her while J.B. contentedly gummed the toy caboose.

"Truly, Mr. Gliddon," said Mrs. Ambrose as she cupped a delicate glass bird in her hand, "you've brought some unexpected joy into a somber Christmas. How can we ever thank you?"

"On the contrary, I should thank you," said Edgar. "My own family is in New York and it eases my loneliness to share a bit of this Christmas day with all of you."

"Yes," said Mrs. Ambrose, nodding sympathetically. "We know how difficult it is to be without loved ones on Christmas."

His parents were likely off enjoying the New York social scene, thought Clara. One could hardly equate that with the pain of separation felt for loved ones at war.

"Don't you agree, Clara?" Mrs. Ambrose was staring at Clara with an expectant smile on her face.

"I'm sorry?" said Clara.

"I was saying, Mr. Gliddon should join us for Christmas breakfast. Don't you agree?"

"Yes, of course," said Clara without enthusiasm.

"I'd be delighted," said Edgar. There was just the barest hint of triumph in his voice.

At breakfast, Clara watched with grudging admiration as Edgar worked his charm on the Ambrose women. He allowed Mrs. Ambrose and Helen to fuss over him, and responded with just the right amount of flattery, sincerity, and humor. Even Grandmother Blake enjoyed his company; so much, in fact, she didn't once complain about the food.

Following coffee in the parlor, Helen excused herself to put J.B. to bed for his nap. Mrs. Ambrose suggested Grandmother Blake retire, as well. She wheeled the protesting old woman to her room off the parlor and left Clara and Edgar alone.

Refusing to squirm under Edgar's steady gaze, Clara sipped her coffee.

"The color becomes you," he said finally. He nodded toward the green silk scarf he had given her as a gift. "As I knew it would."

"Really, Mr. Gliddon, you're much too generous," said Clara.

"Oh, the scarf was just for your mother and sister to see." He reached into his pocket and pulled out a long velvet case. "This is for you." He placed the box on the table in front of her and smiled in anticipation of her response.

Clara stared at the box. She knew she should refuse the gift outright, but her curiosity got the better of her. She opened the box to find a beautiful bracelet of braided rose gold arranged on a bed of white silk. From the center of the bracelet hung a small medallion engraved with the letter *C*.

"Mr. Gliddon," said Clara after a moment of stunned silence, "I can't accept this."

"Of course you can," said Edgar. "I had it made just for you."

She closed the box and set it back on the table. "No," she said. "It's too extravagant, too … personal. Such a gift would indicate there is something more between us than there is."

Edgar leaned forward. "There can be, you know."

Clara met his eyes. "No," she replied evenly. "There cannot. I have pledged my heart to another."

The corner of Edgar's mouth curled slightly. "I suppose we are talking about Private Cameron. Miss Ambrose, I realize it's not unusual for someone of your youth and gender, prone as you are by nature to emotional vagaries, to be temporarily attracted to the drama and excitement of … how shall I put it … an inappropriate liaison. Fortunately, such adolescent fantasies are soon outgrown."

"Mr. Gliddon, I am not a child," said Clara.

"Then do not behave as one," he snapped. "You cannot seriously believe your future lies with that penniless soldier."

"My future lies where I say it does," said Clara.

Edgar smiled. "Very well, Miss Ambrose. I am a patient man. Play out your little charade with the gallant Mr. Cameron. But, you will do well to remember that I am not a man to take 'no' for an answer, in business or in my personal life. When I want something, I get it. No matter how long it takes."

Edgar stood and slipped the jewelry box back into his coat pocket.

"One day soon, Miss Ambrose, you will let go of your romantic notions. I will hold onto this until then. Happy Christmas," he said with a bow.

As he left the parlor, the door to Grandmother Blake's room closed with a soft click.

CHAPTER 13

JANUARY OF 1862 BROUGHT SNOW and cold to Virginia. Except for meals, drill, and picket duty, the men of Camp Pierpoint spent most of their time in the relative warmth of their log huts and shelters.

"Hey, fellas," said Caleb, looking up from an old newspaper his family had sent him. "We're heroes. It says right here in the *Pittsburgh Dispatch* that our fight at Dranesville was 'the first Federal victory south of the Potomac.' The whole country's singing the praises of the Pennsylvania Reserves."

"As well they should," said Rawlie. He spat on the toe of his leather brogan and buffed it with a piece of cloth.

Garrett was rereading his latest letter from Clara. She, too, had written of the continued public reaction to what was being called *The Battle of Dranesville*, and the morale boost it had given the people of the North. But more important to him was the other information in her letter.

> *I've some sad news to report. One of Annie's brothers, Daniel, contracted an illness when he arrived at the camps outside Washington. He didn't want to worry the family, so he swore his brothers to secrecy. We just got word he died on Christmas day. Mrs. Burke is beside herself with grief. Annie is stoic, but I know she's heartbroken. Sometimes we here at home forget that the battlefield is not the only place our soldiers face danger.*
>
> *We've not heard from Father since Christmas. Mother is very worried. I've tried to reassure her by telling her the mails are unpredictable, but I confess, I'm worried, too. Still, I'm sure by the time you get this, we'll have received a letter from him.*
>
> *Annie is working at the Arsenal. I've been after Mother again to let me work there, too, but she still refuses. It's so frustrating. Perhaps, if rising prices force her to give up her afternoon tea, she may yet weaken.*

His reading was interrupted by the sound of bugles calling the regiment to fall in for dress parade. The men grabbed their coats and scrambled through the doorway. Blinking in the gray light of the winter day, they assembled by company and marched to the parade grounds to join the rest of the regiment behind the color line. As they stood shivering in ranks, the colonel of the 9th Pennsylvania handed the regiment's state flag to his adjutant who, in turn, handed it to the color bearer. The color bearer raised the banner high.

"Well, I'll be damned," whispered Rawlie.

The state colors of the 9th Pennsylvania Reserves regiment now carried the words, *Dranesville, December 20, 1861*, emblazoned in gold letters across one of the stripes.

The colonel stood before the regiment with his hands behind his back. The only sound was the snapping of the flag in the wind.

"Gentlemen," he began, "as you can see, our battle flag has just been returned to us from Washington. It now bears the proud record of our victory at the Battle of Dranesville; a commemoration of your valiant service in that action. Let us never forget the courage exhibited by those who fought in that battle and the ultimate sacrifice made by those who fell. It is my fervent hope and belief that we shall continue to build upon this record and bring continued honor to the name of the 9th Pennsylvania Reserves regiment."

"Huzzah! Huzzah!" cheered the men without prompting.

Garrett squinted up at the flag and felt a pride swell in his chest; a pride in his regiment, his company, and himself. They had struck their first blow for the Union. They had been tested and not found wanting.

Once dress parade was over, the men hurried through the frozen company streets to return to the warmth of their cabins and tents.

"Before we're through, I'll bet our regiment will have more battles to its credit than any other regiment in the whole army," boasted Caleb.

"That's an honor I'd just as soon not have," said Leonard.

"Come on, Leonard," said Caleb. "Don't you want the 9th to be famous?"

"I'm not here to get famous. I'm just here to win a war. Soon as that's done, I'm going home. Right now, I'm going to go take a shit." Leonard shuffled off in the direction of the sinks.

"God, he takes the fun out of everything," said Caleb.

Frank gave Caleb a measured look. "You seem to forget, we lost sixty-eight Union soldiers in that battle, killed and wounded; twenty-two of them from our own regiment. Not much fun in that."

Caleb fell silent.

Garrett lagged a little behind the rest of his messmates. He had gone to war, his heart filled with patriotic fervor, to preserve the country he loved. Now, however, with the addition of those gold letters on the regiment's flag, he realized his purpose had shifted. He was no longer fighting just for the lofty ideals of Union and freedom, but for the very lives of the men around him. And, just as important, for the memory of those men who had fallen. With the shedding of that first blood, the war had become personal.

Garrett took a last look over the hodge-podge of dwellings that sheltered the men of the 9th Pennsylvania and followed his fellow soldiers into the warmth of the cabin.

As the workers from the Allegheny Arsenal exited the large main gate leading from the upper grounds, Annie paused beneath the stone archway to raise the hood of her wool cloak. She didn't really mind the cold, however. She was too excited at having received her first week's pay. Three whole dollars. It was more money than she had ever earned in one week. With her three surviving brothers in the army and the three girls still at home, that would go a long way toward putting food on the family table. And perhaps it would ease her parents' financial burden, if not their grief, just a little.

There had been a few anxious moments during the past week. Each day, Annie endured the curious looks of the soldiers and male civilian workers as she scurried up the hill to the small laboratory building to begin a long day of rolling bullet cartridges. Mr. Geary, the foreman of the room to which she had been assigned, had not been terribly pleased at the prospect of supervising girls and barked his instructions as she struggled to learn the process of filling, pinching, and bundling the cartridges. But, as the days passed and she and the rest of the girls proved more dexterous, less disruptive, and more amenable to instruction than the recently fired boys, his disposition improved. When they met their quota, she actually saw him smile.

Although the work was exacting and monotonous, Annie was grateful to have it. Not only did it enable her to help her family and benefit the war effort, it also filled the time. Since the men had gone off to war, Annie and Clara had each taken on more duties for their respective families, which resulted in fewer opportunities to be together. Annie missed her friend. She grieved for her brother. And, she missed the charmingly awkward attentions of Joe Frye. The war had interrupted their nascent romance, but he sent her sweet, rambling letters from wherever he was stationed, which she carefully answered. And she hadn't forgotten her secret promise to him. Perhaps, when the war was over ….

Annie's thoughts were interrupted when she saw a man wearing a velvet-collared Chesterfield topcoat and a fur hat emerge from the gate to the lower Arsenal grounds across the street. He paused to pull on his gloves and, although she hadn't seen him since the day he snubbed her at the dress parade at Camp Wilkins, something in his haughty demeanor made her realize it was Edgar Gliddon. She scowled. She knew the man continued to press his unwelcome attentions on Clara and, as the Ambrose family's economic situation worsened, the pressure on Clara to make a "smart match" increased accordingly. Annie wanted to take Edgar Gliddon and Mrs. Ambrose and shake them both.

Suddenly, Edgar looked up and caught her eye. A look of mutual recognition and loathing passed between them. Then Annie put her nose in the air, turned on her heel, and strutted down Butler Street toward home.

Clara clutched the collar of her coat as the drafty Citizens Passenger Railway car rattled its way northeast along Penn Street. A freezing wind blew off the Allegheny River and heavy gray clouds, mixed with the smoke and soot from the mills, blocked whatever feeble warmth the February sun might have provided. Looking out the frosty window, down a side street to the river, she glimpsed Herrs Island. Legend had it George Washington once spent a night on that island after falling off a raft into the icy river on a day such as this. If so, Clara wondered how he had survived the chill to go on to become president.

Clara was returning home from the Market House in downtown Pittsburgh where she had gone in hopes of striking a better deal than she could get at the grocers in Lawrenceville. But the high inflation that accompanied the war was driving up prices everywhere, and the basket on her arm was distressingly light.

At the end of January, the family had finally received a letter from Dr. Ambrose in which he assured them of his safety. The letter had also included three hundred and twenty dollars, almost an entire two months' pay. This money was immediately applied to outstanding bills due the butcher, the grocer, and the coal man. Despite this welcome influx of cash, however, and the many cost saving methods the family employed, it was becoming harder and harder to make ends meet. Just this morning, Clara's mother had confided that the savings Dr. Ambrose was so sure would sustain them until his return were running out. When they were gone, Clara was not sure what they would do. Her mood was as bleak as the weather.

The streetcar rumbled toward the edge of the Allegheny Fairgrounds, the former site of Camp Wilkins. Once the Pennsylvania quota for troops was filled, the camp had been closed in December of 1861, only a few months after the last troops left for the seat of war. In

January of 1862, Camp Wright also closed, and the property, lumber, stoves, and everything else left behind were sold at auction. Gone were the drilling, cursing, laughing soldiers, off to distant battlefields. Looking out over the empty fairgrounds, it was almost as if they had never existed. Clara brought her hand to the locket around her neck. But, it was real. He was real. And he would return to her. He promised. He would return.

A cold steady rain pummeled the troops of the Pennsylvania Reserves as they slogged west toward Centreville. Garrett hunched beneath his rubber poncho, but couldn't prevent the icy drops from seeping beneath his collar and soaking the neck of his great coat. The roads were ankle deep or deeper in mud churned up by marching feet, and it took all his concentration to keep his balance.

Since March 15th, the 9th Pennsylvania had been on the move, from Camp Pierpoint to Falls Church, then Alexandria, and now on to Centreville. Still, despite the foul weather, Garrett, like the rest of his regiment, was excited to be heading off after the Confederates at last.

All winter, waiting for orders at Camp Pierpoint, the men had grumbled and chafed at newspaper reports chiding McClellan and the Army of the Potomac for their failure to retaliate in any definitive way for the Rebel army's actions at Bull Run. The headline, *All Quiet Along the Potomac*, picked up by a number of the northern newspapers, had become a national taunt and shame.

"I guess they've forgotten about Dranesville," groused Caleb as the men huddled in their cabins against the February cold.

"I think people were expecting a major offensive of some kind," said Garrett. "A move by the whole army."

"Well then, why doesn't McClellan do something?" said Caleb. "We could practically spit from here to Centreville. One good fight and we could clear out the whole lot of 'em."

"Nobody knows for sure how many of them there are," said Frank. "The newspapers say McClellan's tryin' to make sure we have enough men and ammunition to win the day. He doesn't want another Bull Run."

"Besides, do you really want to go trompin' around in this weather?" asked Rawlie. "The mud's hip high out there."

"Anything beats sittin' here freezin' our balls off," said Caleb.

The long-awaited order came down in early March. Having learned that the main Rebel force at Centreville had suddenly abandoned its camp and was headed south, McClellan ordered the Union First Corps, to which the Pennsylvania Reserves were now attached, to head off in pursuit. The 9th Pennsylvania hurriedly broke camp and set out, rendezvousing along the way with other Pennsylvania Reserves units, all determined to catch and punish the Rebels for their bravado.

As the Union troops approached the abandoned Rebel fortifications near Centreville, however, it became obvious from the size and the extent of the defenses that the Confederate forces had been much less formidable than McClellan had claimed. In fact, only about 48,000 Confederate troops – slightly more than half the number estimated by McClellan – had been encamped at Centreville.

"Shit. Look at that," said Rawlie as they marched past the Rebel breastworks.

There on the earthen wall sat some of the vaunted Confederate *artillery* that had so paralyzed McClellan. As the men drew closer, they could see the fearsome guns trained on Washington were really just large wooden logs, shaped like cannons and painted black to fool the Union intelligence gatherers.

Leonard spat on the ground. "Quaker guns," he said. At the puzzled look on Garrett's face, he explained, "Fakes. They won't shoot."

"You mean this is what we've been guarding against?" said Caleb.

"God, this is embarrassing," said Frank, shaking his head.

The regiments marched on through the intermittent rain toward the main Rebel supply depot at the railhead at Manassas Junction, seven miles to the south. They could smell the depot long before they reached it.

In his haste to leave before his movement was detected by the Union troops, the commander of the Confederate Army of Northern Virginia, General Joseph Johnston, had ordered all supplies and equipment that could not be readily transported be burned or destroyed so as to deny their use to the Union army. The men of the First Corps gaped in amazement at the acres of ruined materials, ordinance, burned out rail cars, and wagons that lay broken and scattered in the wake of the retreating army.

When, at last, the weary Federals reached the deserted Rebel quarters near the old Manassas battlefield, General McDowell called an extended halt in order to consult with his superiors over the next course of action. Released from the ranks, the men quickly appropriated the vacated cabins and huts. They were glad to have more substantial shelter against the cold wind swirling through the streets of the abandoned camp.

Garrett ducked his head into the nearest cabin. It was constructed of rough-hewn logs chinked with mud, and had a split-log floor and a chimney made of stones. The roof had a few holes, but he figured he and the boys could fix that in no time. The rest of his messmates soon joined him.

"Well, the Rebs left us quite a cozy little house," said Frank. "A little fixin' up here and there, a little furniture, and we'll be snug as a bug in a rug."

"Look here." Caleb picked up what was left of an old shoe, the laces missing and the sole completely gone. "The Rebs skedaddled right out of their shoes."

"Gonna be a mighty cold walk back to Richmond," said Rawlie.

The men set to work. With the addition of some mud plaster, handmade shingles, and some rough furniture, they made the cabin a passable place in which to wait; wait for the spring campaigning weather to begin; wait for orders to move elsewhere; just wait.

A few days later, after morning drill, Rawlie suggested they ask the captain for permission to visit the nearby Bull Run battlefield. Leonard and Frank declined to come.

"I've seen plenty of battlefields," said Frank. Leonard just shook his head.

Garrett, Caleb, Joe, and Rawlie showed their passes to the pickets stationed at the edge of camp and began walking north. They passed Henry House Hill, where the ruins of the stone house stood as testament to the intensity of the past July's artillery fire. Off to the east they could see the stone bridge over Bull Run Creek that had provided one of the few escape routes for the retreating Union troops. The four men climbed open rolling hills, interspersed with woods, to the site of the fiercest fighting. The winter-brown fields and pastures that had seen the first real bloodshed of the war looked smaller, somehow, than the stories made them sound; less grand a place to die than Garrett had imagined. The men stopped at the crest of a hill while a cold wind whipped across the bleached, keening grasses.

"Oh, my God. Look," said Joe.

Scattered about the open fields were small mounds of what appeared to be dirt, rocks, and rags. In horror, the men realized they were actually the partially unearthed bodies of the dead from the previous July. Time, weather, and rooting pigs had exposed the skeletal remains of those who had been too hastily buried. Pale skulls were visible, and here and there a bony hand reached to the heavens for aid.

"You think they're ours, or theirs?" whispered Caleb.

"Does it matter?" said Garrett.

The four men returned to camp in silence.

Clara awoke in her bedroom with her heart pounding. Her skin was damp with perspiration despite the frigid March night. She didn't remember the specifics of the dream that had upset her, but its lingering effects made it impossible for her to remain in bed. Pulling back the covers, she grabbed her dressing gown and tip-toed down the hallway to the window seat overlooking Allen Street.

For so many years she had retreated to this, her favorite spot, to read, think, and dream. From this cushioned perch she had watched her father leave each day to visit his patients. Later, it was here she had waited for Garrett to take her walking. Now, everything was changed. Her country was at war and the two men she loved most in the world were who-knows-where on faraway fields of battle. She took some measure of comfort in the fact that her father was away from the fighting in the relative safety of a general hospital. But Garrett was on the front lines. The thought of him being wounded – or worse – froze her heart. Yet all she could do was sit and wait.

Clara had taken to pacing the house of late, her restlessness seeking some outlet, and these sleepless nights were becoming more frequent. She wanted to do something for the Union beyond knitting socks and rolling bandages. At the same time, she knew how much she was needed here at home. Her mother could not carry the responsibility of Grandmother, Helen, and the baby, alone. And her father's parting words rang in her ears. She felt trapped by the responsibility – and guilty about feeling trapped. She wanted to scream from the frustration of it. Instead, she rested her head on her knees. The moonlight caught the single tear that slipped down her cheek.

As the days turned into weeks, the 9th Pennsylvania Reserves and the rest of McDowell's First Corps remained at Manassas and awaited orders. During this time, the men were still required to drill and pull guard duty. But, they also took advantage of the delay to pay long overdue attention to some housekeeping and hygiene concerns. They mended and washed their clothing and darned their socks. They frequented the barber to get beards trimmed and teeth pulled. The braver or more desperate ones reported to the surgeon's tent to have boils lanced and blisters bandaged.

What free time they had, the men filled with favorite diversions. Out of knapsacks came cards, dice, and checkers. A couple of men from Company E were fairly accomplished singers and musicians, and would entertain the rest of the men with minstrel tunes or heartbreaking songs of home. The ever-present sutlers tents sprang up almost as soon as the wheels stopped turning on the regiments' wagons. Beyond them appeared the tents of the camp-followers – laundresses, photographers, escaped slaves, referred to as *contrabands*, and prostitutes – all offering their services to the men in blue.

While the Pennsylvania Reserves were billeted in Manassas, a young Negro boy, not more than thirteen years of age, entered the camp. He was small and thin, with skin as dark as Garrett had ever seen. He said his name was Canary and that he had run away from a plantation not far to the west to help "Mr. Linkum's army" fight the Rebels.

A lieutenant from Company F of the 9th Pennsylvania Reserves quickly took the boy on as his personal servant. Canary could be seen cleaning the man's boots, mending his clothes, and cooking his food. True to his name, he sang while he did his tasks in a high clear tenor that seemed to know no upward boundary of range. He became quite a favorite of the men, a kind of camp mascot, and always complied with their requests to sing – old Negro spirituals, minstrel songs, and newer camp songs the soldiers would teach him. Canary was unfailingly polite and subservient, but his dark eyes missed nothing that happened around the camp. This enabled him, for the most part, to avoid trouble. But still, there were some soldiers who took every opportunity to tease and torment him, secure in his unwillingness or inability to fight back.

One afternoon, when a warm breeze hinted of the coming spring, Garrett sat reading outside his tent in the Virginia sunshine. Suddenly, a shadow passed over the page. He looked up to find Canary standing there with his head bowed.

"Excuse me, Suh," he said without raising his eyes.

"Yes, Canary. What is it?"

"I's just wonderin' … I sees you, lots a times, readin' books ' n' such. So, I's wonderin' … if'n I was to do things for you, like shine your shoes or cook special for you – could you, maybe, learn me how to read?" The entire time he spoke, he kept his eyes on the ground.

Garrett knew it was against the law in the South to teach slaves how to read, a crime punishable by flogging – or worse. He was sure Canary knew it, too.

"Yes, Canary," said Garrett. "I think I could do that. And teach you to write a little, too, if you'd like. But you'd have to be willing to work hard."

Canary looked up and the determination shone from his eyes. "Oh, yes, Suh. I's used to hard work." A rare smile lit his face. "But this be the fust time I gets to work at sumpin' just for me."

Following their conversation, Canary showed up at Garrett's hut almost every afternoon after chores. Most of the other soldiers looked askance at Garrett's efforts to teach the young contraband to read and write. Rawlie took to calling Garrett, "Professor." But Garrett found he looked forward to his time with Canary. He reported on his progress in his letters to Clara.

> *Canary plays dumb when he's around most people, but he's as smart as a whip. When we sit down to read, he's like a sponge, always asking questions, always eager to learn. I remember how I couldn't wait to get out of school. It's fairly humbling to see this boy thirst for that which I took for granted.*
>
> *Quite a few contrabands have attached themselves to the army, sometimes with entire families in tow. They usually end up doing work for one of the officers – cooking, washing, mending, and the like – usually unpaid. It pains me to see the way some of the men treat them. But they work without complaint, perhaps because even this is better than what they knew. Still, there is in them an indomitable spirit, an unfailing hope in the future. If we succeed in freeing these people – as we must – there will be great changes ahead for us all.*

Garrett decided not to tell Clara about the other people who trailed after the Union army. *Ladies of the evening* followed along in their own wagons, and many of the soldiers were eager to spend their infrequent pay on this welcome diversion. Some of the generals saw these camp followers as detrimental to the discipline of the army and discouraged their presence. Others seemed indifferent or turned a blind eye. Not surprisingly, many of the soldiers who frequented the tents and wagons of these prostitutes developed venereal diseases, which they brought back to their unsuspecting wives and sweethearts at war's end.

On a windy afternoon at the end of March, the long overdue mail wagon arrived. The men of the Union First Corps crowded around it in hopes of receiving a letter, package, or newspaper; proof they had not been forgotten by the folks back home.

"Cameron!"

"Here!"

The sergeant tossed Garrett a battered brown package wrapped in twine. Like a dog with a bone, he tucked it under his arm and trotted back to the cabin to open it in private.

Clara had sent him a small treasure trove of goodies, things he had requested in his letters and some small luxuries she thought he might like. Best of all was a letter. He held it to his nose and swore he caught the faint smell of her perfume. Leaning closer to the fire, he opened the letter and began to read.

March 3, 1862

Dearest Garrett,

I hope this letter finds you well. As I write, a cold rain is beating against my window, and I can only pray you are somewhere safe and warm. To that end, I have included extra socks – a little lumpy in the toes, as I knitted them myself – and a warm flannel shirt (Don't worry. Helen made the shirt.). I've also included a shirt that Annie made for Joe, extra long in the arms and body, along with a note from her to him. See that he gets them, will you? As far as I can tell, the two of them have been corresponding fairly regularly. Annie doesn't say much about it, but seems pleased with Joe's attention. Perhaps we've unwittingly made a match between them. Time will tell.

The family is well, but missing our men. Of necessity, we've all become proficient at skills we'd never imagined doing before. In a way, it's strangely empowering, although I can't say I'll be sorry to hand the chore of cleaning the stable back to Father when he returns.

And me? Mine is a life lived holding my breath. Nine months you've been gone, and each day I pray for your safe return so my heart can start beating again. My pride in your sacrifice struggles with my fear for your safety. Yet, I feel so selfish in light of the sacrifice of others. Please take care of yourself, Garrett. I pray each day the Lord will bring you safely home to me.

All my love,
Clara

P.S. Do you miss me, too?

Oh, Clara, he thought as he stared into the fire. The pain of missing her was a physical thing, clawing at his heart. He almost preferred long days spent marching or the single-mindedness of battle, for it helped him forget, if only for a little while, the pain of her absence. He longed for the day he could be with her again, hold her in his arms and kiss her soft lips. On that day, he would ask her to marry him. Until then, all he could do was his duty.

The blanket at the doorway of the cabin was pulled aside and a dim light flooded the room. Rawlie entered holding a letter and a copy of *Harper's Weekly Newspaper* he had purchased from a vendor who frequented the camp. The rest of the messmates filed in behind him. Joe was the only one without something from the mail wagon.

"Ah, another package from the beautiful Miss Ambrose, I see," said Rawlie, glancing at the bounty on the table. "You will share with your dear old friends, won't you, Garrett?"

"Don't I always?" Garrett picked up a bar of soap and flipped it to Rawlie. "I think this was meant for you."

"You're too kind." Rawlie pocketed the soap and sat by the fire to read his letter. Caleb was already there, his red head bent over an old *Pittsburgh Dispatch* sent to him by his father.

"Caleb," said Garrett. He tossed him a small bag. "Here's some lemon drops for your sweet tooth. Leonard, a tin of your favorite chewing tobacco. And, Frank, this salve is for your sore feet."

"The woman's an angel," said Frank as he reached for the jar of ointment.

Joe looked at Garrett expectantly. To save on the money it cost to send items by Adams Express, Clara and Annie sometimes combined their gifts in one package. But, Garrett had returned to reading his own letter. With silence descending on the cabin, Joe finally picked up an old dime novel and fanned the pages listlessly.

"Oh, Joe," said Garrett with a twinkle in his eye, "I almost forgot. These are for you." Joe pounced on the note and the folded shirt he proffered.

"Is Miss Ambrose writing to young Joe now?" asked Rawlie.

"No," said Joe, unable to conceal a grin. "These are from Miss Burke."

"The Irish lass from Camp Wilkins? Joe, Joe," said Rawie with a shake of his head. "I know Garrett, here, is a lost cause, but I thought you had better sense. Don't you know women are nothing but trouble?"

"Don't go tainting the boy's mind," said Frank. "If you find women to be trouble it's because of the type of women you keep company with."

"You know, Rawlie," said Caleb, "those women you've been visiting in those wagons at the edge of camp are the same ones that were keeping company with the Rebs not so long ago. Your prick's gonna end up with a southern drawl."

Leonard gave a hearty guffaw.

Rawlie smiled. "If so, it was worth it just to get a chuckle out of old Leonard."

"Haven't you ever been in love, Rawlie?" asked Joe.

A flash of pain crossed Rawlie's face. He gazed into the fire for a long moment before replying. "Yes," he said in a low voice. "In fact, I have. Once. And I don't expect I'll ever find that kind of love again."

The rest of the mess exchanged surprised looks over his bowed head.

"Gee, Rawlie," said Joe, "I didn't know. I'm sorry."

"It's all right," said Rawlie, waving away his apology. "It's just ... once you care for someone the way I did, you never quite get over it." He stared down at his shoes. "It's hard for me to talk about ... but there's a song that pretty much says how I feel." He raised his head. "Frank, you probably know this one. It's by our own Stephen Foster. Maybe you could give me a little accompaniment."

Moved by Rawlie's unusual show of emotion, Frank nodded. He took the fife from his belt, raised it to his lips, and waited for Rawlie to begin. Rawlie took a deep breath and began to sing in a low, plaintive voice. After a few lines, Frank, holding back a smile, picked up the melody.

The morn of life is past,
And evening comes at last;
It brings me a dream of a once happy day,
Of merry forms I've seen
Upon the village green,
Sporting with my old dog Tray.

Leonard snickered and Garrett shook his head. Joe, still puzzled, frowned as Rawlie, with his voice gathering strength, slid into the chorus. The rest of the Pittsburgh boys joined in.

Old dog Tray's ever faithful,
Grief cannot drive him away,
He's gentle, he is kind:
I'll never, never find
A better friend than old dog Tray.

"Aw, shit, Rawlie. You're singin' about a dog," Joe said in disgust. "I should've known."

"Still probably better lookin' than most of the women he's been with," said Caleb.

"I am highly offended," said Rawlie. "I cannot argue the point, but still, I am highly offended."

When the laughter died down, Joe looked over at Garrett.

"You gonna ask Miss Ambrose to marry you, Garrett?" he asked.

"If she'll have me," Garrett replied.

"Now, Garrett," said Rawlie. "Why would you want to go and do a thing like that? Don't get me wrong. Your Miss Ambrose is a real lady, and a beautiful one at that." He nodded toward Clara's picture propped open next to Garrett's bunk. "But marriage can be a very constricting life for a man, if you get my meaning. Don't be too hasty to do something you might regret."

"The only regret I have is that I didn't marry her before I left Pittsburgh," said Garrett.

"Why didn't you?" asked Joe.

Garrett shrugged. "It didn't seem fair to bind her to me when there was no way of knowing if I'd be coming back."

"Well, you'd just better hope one of those stay-at-home dandies hasn't turned her head," said Rawlie.

"I'm not worried about that," said Garrett. "I trust Miss Ambrose completely."

Still, it took him a long time to fall asleep that night.

CHAPTER 14

WHILE THE UNION FIRST CORPS waited for orders at Manassas, the rest of the country, North and South, was horrified by the news coming out of western Tennessee. On April 6th and 7th, 1862, a tremendous battle was fought around the small Shiloh Methodist Church near the town of Pittsburg Landing on the banks of the Tennessee River. During the two days of fighting, the barely victorious Union troops suffered over 13,000 casualties; the Confederates, almost 11,000. Such numbers had been unthinkable at the beginning of the war.

In the wake of this battle, Secretary of War Edwin Stanton requested the chief quartermaster in Pittsburgh, Pennsylvania, to arrange for steamboats to help transport the wounded from the battlefield.

Two ships were chartered to make the trip down the Ohio to the Tennessee River and were outfitted with cots and mattresses. Doctors and nurses, male and female, volunteered to staff these ships and provide desperately needed care to the wounded soldiers that were still waiting, days after the battle, in horrific conditions on overcrowded, understaffed hospital barges alongside Pittsburg Landing.

The people of Pittsburgh rallied to the cause. They donated bandages, food, sheets, blankets, pillows, towels, nightshirts, and slippers – anything that might contribute to the comfort of the wounded.

Clara begged her mother to allow her to join this expedition as a nurse, to no avail. So she turned her efforts to working with their ladies aid group to provide as many of the necessary supplies as possible before the relief ships steamed for Tennessee.

Clara brought her carriage to a halt in front of the warehouse of Graff, Bennett and Company on Water Street alongside the Monongahela Wharf. Her horse tossed its head in alarm at the noise and clatter of the dockside. Carriages and heavy drays rumbled back and forth over the cobblestone street. Longshoremen cursed and cracked their whips over the backs of horse and mule teams pulling wagons up and down the slope from the street to the long row of steamboats lining the wharf. Whistles blew and men shouted orders as civilians, soldiers, and goods filed on and off the gangplanks, while steady river traffic streamed by on the Monongahela River behind them.

"Easy, Hippocrates," said Clara. She patted the old gelding's neck and tied him to an iron post at the side of the warehouse. Looking around for someone to help her, she spied a workman pushing a small cart loaded with boxes.

"Excuse me, Sir."

"Ya, Miss," he said as he doffed his cap.

"I have some supplies here for the hospital ships going to the Shiloh battlefield. I understand this is the collection point?"

"Ya, Miss. I be back to unload dem for you right avay."

As he disappeared into the darkness of the warehouse, Clara turned to watch the bustle of activity around her. Anchored at the wharf just down from the warehouse, the two ships chartered for the relief expedition, the *J. W. Hailman* and the *Marengo*, were already being loaded with supplies provided for the soldiers by the people of Pittsburgh.

"Here ve go, Miss," said the workman, returning with an empty cart. He removed the boxes of carefully packed bandages, socks, and nightshirts from Clara's carriage. Her ladies aid group had labored long days and nights to have everything ready in time for the relief mission, and Clara was pleased to note the efforts of their small group almost filled the pushcart.

"Thank you, Sir," she said when he finished.

"No. Tank *you*, Miss," he replied. "I haf a son mit de 74th Pennsylvania. Makes me feel gut to know dat if he ver injured people vould take care of him like dis. I don't know vhat de soldiers vould do mitout you kind ladies."

"On the contrary, Sir," said Clara. "What would we ladies do without the sacrifices of our soldiers? And their families?"

The man touched the brim of his cap and wheeled the loaded cart into the warehouse.

Clara untied her horse and climbed into the carriage; no easy feat in her hoop skirt. She still had three packages – one each for her father, George, and Garrett – to mail at the post office before her errands were finished. She guided Hippocrates away from the curb and set off, the crowding on the wharf precluding anything faster than a walk.

As she rounded the corner by the Monongahela House Hotel onto Smithfield Street, she saw a familiar carriage at the curb. She had not spoken to Edgar since she had rejected his gift at Christmas, but his smug words on that occasion still made her angry.

No sooner had the thought entered her mind than she saw him standing outside the front door of the hotel. He was chatting with a familiar looking gentleman in a top hat. She realized it was James Percy. The two of them gave off an air of money and arrogance, two young men on the brink of turning impressive fortunes into unheard of wealth. She turned her head away and attempted to hide beneath the brim of her bonnet.

Suddenly, a heavily loaded dray came careening down the street toward Clara's carriage. The huge draft horses lunged in harness, and sent mud and flecks of frothy sweat into the air. Pedestrians and carriages hurried out of its path, the men cursing the reckless driver. As the heavy wagon bore down upon them, Clara's horse shied and gave a frightened whinny.

"Easy, boy. Easy." Clara sawed at the reins in an attempt to control the fractious animal. The horse reared and bolted to the side, slamming Clara hard against the interior of the buggy. As the dray roared past, Clara's wild-eyed horse dragged the carriage part way up onto the crowded sidewalk. Some men were able to grab his bridle and stop him before the buggy overturned.

"Are you all right, Miss?" asked one of the men.

Clara pushed herself up to a sitting position, and gave a yelp as a sharp pain shot through her shoulder. Suddenly, two strong arms scooped her out of her seat and deposited her onto the safety of the sidewalk.

"Miss Ambrose! Are you hurt?" asked Edgar, peering into her face. "Shall I summon a doctor?"

"No, no. I'm all right," said Clara. She winced as she rubbed her shoulder. "Just a bit bruised."

"Damn fool driver," Edgar muttered as he glanced down the street after the offending dray. "He could have killed you."

"Fortunately, I'm a little tougher than I appear," said Clara. She began to straighten her disheveled clothing. The trembling of her hands did not escape Edgar's notice.

"Come with me," he said firmly.

"But, Hippocrates …," she began.

"The horse will be fine. You there," Edgar commanded a man in the crowd. "Tie this animal to the hitching post." He turned back to Clara. "And you," he said in a softer tone, "will kindly accompany me inside the hotel."

Clara, more shaken than she liked to admit, nodded and took the arm he offered.

As Edgar escorted her to one of the side parlors, the feel of her body leaning against his for support stirred unaccustomed feelings within him. Not just the usual lust. He felt protective; needed. And it felt good.

"Please. You should sit for a moment," said Edgar. Clara gratefully sank down onto one of the upholstered couches.

"A cup of hot tea and a glass of whiskey," Edgar ordered the Negro waiter who had hurried to his side. "And be quick about it."

The waiter returned almost immediately and placed the two drinks on the small table in front of the couch. Clara leaned forward to take the tea.

"Wait," said Edgar. He poured a generous dose of whiskey into her cup.

"Mr. Gliddon, I don't believe in taking spirits," said Clara.

"This is purely for medicinal purposes, Miss Ambrose. Now drink."

Clara took a few sips of the doctored tea and felt a slow warmth spread through her limbs. After a few more sips, she could feel herself relaxing.

"There," said Edgar. "Your color looks better now. And I believe your soul is still intact." Clara couldn't help but smile.

"Yes. I do feel better. Thank you, Mr. Gliddon."

"You gave me quite a scare," scolded Edgar. "I've never approved of young ladies driving themselves about in carriages, but it's particularly dangerous these days with the large numbers of vehicles crowding the streets."

"It was an accident, Mr. Gliddon. It could have happened to anyone, male or female."

"But it happened to you," said Edgar. Clara was surprised to hear real concern in his voice.

"I'm fine, Mr. Gliddon. Truly," she assured him. "Thank you for coming to my rescue." She smiled. "You were quite gallant."

"You have a way of bringing out my better nature," he replied. He gave Clara a look of such unguarded sincerity, she was left momentarily speechless.

"Well," she said, rising to her feet, "it's time for me to be on my way. Thank you again for your assistance. And for the ... tea."

Edgar stood. "Surely you don't intend to drive yourself home after this?"

"Of course," she said as she pulled on her driving gloves. "The great crisis is past. I am perfectly capable of driving myself back to Lawrenceville."

"Under normal circumstances, perhaps," said Edgar, "but you've had quite an unsettling experience this afternoon. You know," he said, lowering his voice, "it's not a sign of weakness to accept the help of others."

Clara felt her resolve falter. After all these months, how lovely it would be to let someone else be in charge; to shift the burden to stronger shoulders, if only for a little while. She fought off the temptation with a shake of her head.

"Thank you, but no," she said.

"Nonsense," said Edgar. "I'll take you in my carriage and have my man bring yours along."

"Mr. Gliddon," Clara fought to control her temper, "as I've told you before, I am not a child. Please do not treat me as one."

A wry smile crept over Edgar's face. "Well, I can see you are definitely feeling more yourself. May I at least walk you to your carriage?"

"Yes," Clara relented. "You may."

As Edgar stood on the sidewalk and watched Clara's carriage pull away, James Percy came and stood by his elbow.

"A remarkable young woman," said James. "She appears to be as brave as she is beautiful. And," he added with a smirk, "she seems to be one of the few women of our acquaintance who is able to resist your charms."

"Ah, but my dear Mr. Percy, a little resistance makes the eventual victory that much sweeter."

"Perhaps," said James. "But, I think you may have met your match in this one, Gliddon."

"I may have, indeed," said Edgar thoughtfully. He smiled and slapped James on the back. "Come. Let's finish our discussion."

As the warmer temperatures of April began to break winter's hold, McDowell's First Corps received orders to abandon their camp near Manassas Junction and march south once more. Although Garrett and his comrades were eager to be advancing toward the Confederate capital of Richmond, they did not relish the frequent rains, muddy roads, or the prospect of attempting to cross the numerous spring-swollen rivers in the midst of hostile Rebel territory. Putting his shoulder to the wheel of yet another artillery caisson mired to the wheel hubs in sticky Virginia clay, Garrett began to miss the boredom and fetid cabin air of winter camp.

Ten days and 40 miles later, exhausted and convinced they would never be truly dry again, the men of the 9th Pennsylvania halted at the town of Falmouth, Virginia, on the east bank of the Rappahannock River. There they spent a welcome three weeks resting while they regrouped with the other divisions of the First Corps who continued to stagger in.

* * *

"Hey, lookee what I got."

Waving a rumpled newspaper in the air, Joe strode down Company A's main street at the Reserves' bivouac near Falmouth. His messmates, who were lounging outside their tent enjoying a brief respite from drilling and guard duty, looked up in interest. Joe handed the paper to Frank.

"*The New York Times*," said Frank. He glanced at the April 22nd date. "And only a week old."

"You'll never guess where I got it," said Joe with a sly grin.

"Sutler's wagon, I assume," said Garrett.

"Nope," said Joe. "Some of the boys on picket duty down by the river traded some coffee to the Reb pickets on the other side for it. Said they used a little handmade toy sailboat to send it across."

"Messed up war when the Rebs can get the Northern papers before we do," said Rawlie.

"Well, I'll be damned," said Frank who had been carefully studying the front page. "It appears McClellan is finally on the move. He's landed at the old Revolutionary War fort at Yorktown and has it under siege."

"Where's Yorktown?" asked Caleb.

"About twenty miles below Richmond, at the end of the Peninsula," said Frank.

"How'd the army get way down there?" said Caleb.

"McClellan probably walked across the water," said Rawlie.

In fact, while the 9th Pennsylvania and the rest of the Union First Corps had been doggedly chasing General Johnston's Rebel army overland from northern Virginia southward toward Richmond, Union General McClellan had put into motion an audacious plan to swing around and attack Richmond from the south.

The bulk of the Army of the Potomac was transported by boat down the Potomac River to the Chesapeake Bay and landed below Richmond at the base of the peninsula formed by the York and James Rivers. From there, the army would march north to the Confederate capital. Soon to become known as the Peninsula Campaign, it was the largest American waterborne invasion attempted to that date and involved 400 ships and barges transporting more than 100,000 men, 300 cannon, 25,000 horses, mules, and cattle, and tons of equipment.

"If Mac's comin' up from the south and we're pressing down on Richmond from the north, we ought to be able to catch those Johnny Rebs between shit and sweat," said Caleb slapping his thigh.

"Do you think this really could be it?" asked Joe. "The beginning of the end?"

"Lotta miles to travel; lotta men to kill before this is over," said Leonard.

"Still, it's been almost a year," said Joe. "Sure would be nice to head home."

No one said anything, but six Union soldiers allowed themselves a few quiet moments to think about what could be.

Clara opened the cast iron oven door and peered at the dark, mis-shapen lump.

"Oh, no!" she cried. Grabbing the hot pan, she sent it clattering onto the kitchen table. She stood there, hands on hips, and glared at the smoking results of her morning's efforts.

Just then, Mrs. Ambrose breezed into the kitchen.

"Hello, Clara. How's the ... oh, my," she exclaimed when she spied the blackened, lopsided loaf. "Well, never mind, dear." She patted Clara's arm. "I'm sure with a little butter, it will be just delicious."

Clara raised an eyebrow. "My, you're in a good mood."

"Yes, I am," replied her mother as she removed her straw bonnet. "It's a beautiful spring day, the war news is good, and you'll never guess who I ran into on Market Street this morning."

"Who?"

"Edgar Gliddon."

"Oh." Clara kept her tone neutral. The sooner her mother moved on from this subject, the better.

"Actually, he approached me. Broke off his conversation with some important looking Union officers just to come over and inquire how we were getting along. Such a thoughtful man. And patriotic. You know, he provides an enormous amount of iron for the Union railroads."

"Not for free, Mother."

"Well, of course not. But I hardly think money is his motivation, given the wealth he has already."

"Money is always Edgar's motivation, Mother. Money and power." She hesitated. "Doesn't it bother you at all that he stays home while George and Father are off doing the actual fighting?"

"Not everyone can be on the battlefield, Clara," said Mrs. Ambrose. "Actually, Mr. Gliddon confided to me his personal desire to don a uniform. But, he felt his talents are best used producing the metals that will help us win the war. He's a true hero in his own way."

"That's not exactly the word I'd use," said Clara.

"Well," said Mrs. Ambrose with a twinkle in her eyes, "perhaps you can discuss that with him on Sunday. I've invited him to speak to our ladies aid group meeting."

"Oh, Mother, you didn't!"

"I most certainly did. And I'm going to invite ladies from some of the other relief organizations to attend, as well. Mr. Gliddon is an influential member of the Committee of Public Safety, and he was quite receptive to the idea. He agreed it makes sense to combine all of the separate little relief groups operating in and around Pittsburgh into one large entity that can more efficiently provide for the needs of our soldiers. I thought the ladies would be very interested in hearing how they could become part of that effort."

"And that's the only reason you invited him here?" said Clara.

"Of course," Mrs. Ambrose replied. "Why else?"

Clara looked askance at her mother. "Well, I'm afraid I shall be otherwise engaged on that day."

"You most certainly will not," said Mrs. Ambrose. "You will be here to help me host, and you will treat Mr. Gliddon with the respect and cordiality due a guest in our home. Frankly, I was surprised he accepted my invitation after the shameful way you've treated him in the past. And after all the kind things he's done for us."

"What's shameful is the way you keep trying to throw me at him."

"Really, Clara," sniffed Mrs. Ambrose, "I don't know which is worse – your ego or your manners."

On Sunday afternoon, the Ambrose's parlor was filled to bursting with women. Additional chairs had to be brought in from adjoining rooms to accommodate the large number of eligible daughters who had suddenly decided to accompany their mothers to hear Mr. Gliddon speak, and the high color on many of their rapt faces could not entirely be attributed to the warmth of the May afternoon.

Clara watched the proceedings from the entrance to the parlor. Edgar had greeted her upon arriving, but was immediately pulled away by other ladies clamoring to make his acquaintance. It was with some difficulty that Mrs. Ambrose finally called the meeting to order.

Following a glowing introduction by Mrs. Ambrose, Edgar gave a brief description of the purposes and good works of the local Subsistence Committee. He likened it to the newly created United States Sanitary Commission, which provided food, medical supplies, and nutritional advice to the Union army. When he finished, he asked that a spokeswoman from each of the small groups explain their work.

One by one, the women described their efforts to provide food, clothing, blankets, bandages, and medicines to the various soldiers who came through Pittsburgh, as well as those already in the field. The duplication of labor was obvious, and the women were excited about the possibility of having the local Subsistence Committee coordinate their efforts.

When all were finished, Edgar rose to his feet.

"Ladies, I am awed and humbled by the patriotism and dedication exhibited by you on behalf of our brave soldiers. Already, and at great personal sacrifice, you have provided untold encouragement and comfort to those warriors who carry the banner of our proud Union. I will return to the Committee on Public Safety and wholeheartedly promote your inclusion in the Subsistence Committee so that it may oversee and direct your efforts to better achieve your objectives. And, as a humble demonstration of my admiration for you, I promise to pledge the sum of five hundred dollars to that committee to be used to further your meritorious work."

A chorus of *ohs* burst from the ladies in attendance. Thirty pairs of gloved hands broke into muffled applause and radiant faces beamed at their handsome benefactor. The women leapt to their feet and their hoops skirts gently collided as they crowded around Edgar to thank him for his generosity.

Clara took refuge in the kitchen from this unabashed show of adoration. She was in the midst of preparing the tea tray when she felt someone come up behind her.

"So, this is where you're hiding," Edgar murmured in her ear. Clara jumped and whirled around.

"Mr. Gliddon! You startled me," said Clara. "And I'm not hiding. I just came in to get the tea." She began arranging the cups on the tray.

Edgar frowned. "Miss Ambrose, it pains me to see you and your family struggling so."

"Mr. Gliddon, as I've told you before, we're doing just fine."

"Oh? And is that why you've taken over the maid's duties?"

Clara bristled. "Whatever *duties* I take on are of no concern to you."

"On the contrary, everything you do is of concern to me." Edgar took a step closer. "I did have another reason for coming here today, aside from my involvement in the Subsistence Committee."

"Oh?" said Clara, fighting to keep the sarcasm out of her voice.

"Miss Ambrose, you cannot be unaware of my feelings toward you. And, at our last encounter, I thought I detected a certain … softening on your part toward me as well."

Clara saw in Edgar's eyes the same surprising tenderness she had glimpsed when he rescued her from her carriage accident. Not wanting to wound him unduly, she chose her words carefully.

"Mr. Gliddon, you've been a friend in need to me and my family on a number of occasions, and I am truly grateful. But, I'm afraid you may have mistaken gratitude for ... something more."

"Perhaps," he said. "Even so, I know many successful unions that have been built on less."

Taken aback, Clara struggled for a reply.

"If by union, Mr. Gliddon, you mean marriage, I believe love to be an essential requirement."

He smiled. "And love may yet grow. But, these are difficult times, Miss Ambrose. One must be realistic. This war may last a long while yet, and there's no telling when or, forgive me, *if* your father or brother-in-law will return. If you were to become my wife, I could see to it that your family is taken care of, no matter what happens. It would ease your mother's mind, as well as her burden, tremendously." He wrinkled his nose. "And you would not be reduced to doing menial jobs around the house."

"You overestimate my distaste for domestic work, Mr. Gliddon," said Clara. She turned back to the tea tray.

Suddenly, Edgar grabbed her by the wrist, his face thunderous. Just as quickly, he released her.

"Do not make light of my offer, Miss Ambrose," he said, regaining his composure. "I'm talking about your future. Our future."

Shaken, Clara gave him a wary look. "You and I have no future, Mr. Gliddon." Without realizing it, her hand went to the locket at her throat. The gesture was not lost on Edgar. His eyes hardened.

"I see," he said. He leaned against the kitchen table and folded his arms. "Tell me, have you heard from the valiant Private Cameron lately?"

"Yes," said Clara. "He writes often. His regiment is with McDowell's army, somewhere near Falmouth, Virginia."

"Well, if they are, they won't be for long," said Edgar.

"What do you mean?" said Clara. "What have you heard?"

"I'm afraid there have been a few changes in the fortunes of our army, of late. I assume you're aware of Stonewall Jackson's recent successes in the Shenandoah Valley?"

Clara nodded. As George's regiment was thought to be involved, Helen had been following the newspaper reports closely. The news had not been good. So far, in battle after battle, Stonewall's 17,000 man *foot cavalry* had out maneuvered and defeated Union forces twice its size.

"Well, as you might imagine," continued Edgar, "official Washington is completely panicked, fearing the Rebs will soon be marching down Constitution Avenue. So, they've recalled the majority of McDowell's forces from Falmouth to increase the defenses around the Capital."

"Then Private Cameron is on his way back to Washington?" said Clara. Despite the threat that necessitated the return of his regiment, she was buoyed by the fact that Garrett would be moving closer to home.

"I'm afraid not," said Edgar. Relishing the distress it would cause her, he meted out his information morsel by morsel. "You see, Lincoln had originally promised to send three divisions to reinforce McClellan's Army of the Potomac down below Richmond. Seems our boys in blue are meeting with a bit of resistance on their way up the Peninsula. I should expect there will be a major battle soon. You can be sure the Confederates won't give up Richmond without a fight."

"What does that have to do with Private Cameron?" demanded Clara.

"Well, apparently, despite the threat posed by Old Stonewall, Lincoln couldn't completely renege on his promise of aid to McClellan. So he's still sending one division to the Peninsula. My sources tell me it's the Pennsylvania Reserves."

At the stricken expression on Clara's face, Edgar feigned a look of concern. "Oh, I shouldn't worry about Private Cameron. He seems an incredibly lucky man." He stared pointedly at the locket, then slowly raised his eyes to hers. "Still, one wonders just how long such good luck can hold."

"I have to get these things in to the ladies," said Clara. She picked up the tray and moved to leave. Edgar blocked her way.

"Spurn me now if you wish, Miss Ambrose," he said in a low voice. "But, there will come a day when you will need my help; will beg me for it. And I assure you, it will not come cheap."

"Mr. Gliddon," said Clara, "unless you'd like to wear this hot tea on your expensive trousers, I suggest you let me pass."

Their eyes locked in challenge. Then, with a curt bow, Edgar stepped to one side.

Only through sheer force of will did Clara manage to keep the cups from rattling as she left the kitchen.

* * *

By the last week of May, 1862, the Army of the Potomac, meeting minimal resistance, had fought its way up the Peninsula to within seven miles of Richmond. McClellan massed his army around the eastern and northeastern side of the Confederate capital in an arc straddling a tributary of the James River known as the Chickahominy River. His intent was to capture Richmond by siege and artillery bombardment. To this end, he had set up his base of supplies at the town of White House Landing, approximately twenty miles east of the city. McClellan positioned the larger part of his army to the north of the Chickahominy, both to protect his supply base at White House landing and, as yet unaware that Lincoln had changed his mind about sending reinforcements, to be ready to meet up with McDowell's troops when they marched down from Falmouth. This left just two corps – less than 30,000 men – south of the river.

The heavy rains of April and May had turned the normally shallow, slow-moving Chickahominy into a nearly impassable torrent that flooded the surrounding land and washed out most of the bridges along its length. This natural impediment made it difficult for the two parts of McClellan's divided army to support each other in case of attack. This fact was not lost on Confederate General Johnston, who had now reached the outskirts of Richmond with the major portion of the Rebel army. Johnston decided to take advantage of the numerical disparity between McClellan's separated forces, as well as the protection provided by the flooded Chickahominy, to attack the southern, weaker wing of the Army of the Potomac.

On May 31st, Johnston's 42,000 Confederate troops advanced on the Union flank near the village of Seven Pines, seven miles east of Richmond. They successfully drove the Federals from their positions, only to be forced to yield much of the ground the very next day when determined Union reinforcements, braving rickety footbridges over the rushing Chickahominy, arrived to reinforce the outnumbered Union troops near the railroad station at Fair Oaks.

Although neither side could declare a clear victory in this confused battle, it did yield one important result, one that would greatly affect the course of the rest of the war. General Johnston was wounded in the first day's fighting and carried from the field. To replace him, Confederate President Jefferson Davis chose his own personal military advisor: General Robert E. Lee.

Clara placed the last bit of coal in the stove and kicked the door closed with her foot. She had only a few minutes to get the upstairs beds changed before Grandmother Blake would be clamoring for her breakfast. She wiped her hands on her apron and grabbed the folded stack of linens she had brought in from the clothesline earlier that morning. As she headed for the stairs, she caught sight of her reflection in the front hall mirror. Her face was flushed from the heat of the stove and she had a streak of black soot over one cheekbone.

"My, Miss Ambrose," she said, tucking a stray lock of hair back into her headscarf, "you certainly look stylish this morning. If only the Ridge Avenue crowd could see you now."

The front door opened and closed with a soft click. Clara turned to find her mother standing motionless in the front hall. Her face was drained of color.

"Mother? What is it?"

Mrs. Ambrose looked at her with red-rimmed eyes. "I've just come from the newspaper office. The casualty lists are in."

Clara froze. "Not Father."

Mrs. Ambrose shook her head. "It's George," she whispered. Her eyes flicked towards Helen's room at the top of the stairs. "He's ... he's been killed."

"Oh, Mama," said Clara, bringing her hand to her mouth. "When? How?"

"On the 25th of May, in fighting near Winchester, Virginia. That's all it said." Mrs. Ambrose untied her bonnet as if the effort was almost more than she could manage. She slumped into the chair next to the front hall table. "Oh, what am I going to tell my poor Helen?"

Just then, they heard stuttering steps in the upstairs hall.

"No, no, no, you little scamp. Come back here."

One-year-old J.B. appeared near the top of the stairs, his chubby legs churning. Helen followed in close pursuit. She scooped him up in her arms and blew on his bare belly, which caused him to squeal in delight. Placing the child on her hip, she descended the stairs. But her happy smile faded when she saw the expressions on the faces of her mother and sister.

"What's wrong?"

Mrs. Ambrose stood. "Helen, we've had some bad news," she began. "Clara, why don't you take J.B. for a moment?"

"No." Helen clutched the baby tighter as Clara reached out her arms. "Just tell me."

"It's George," said Mrs. Ambrose, her voice beginning to break. "I've just come from the newspaper office. His name is on the casualty list."

Helen's face tightened. "Has he been wounded?"

"Helen," said Mrs. Ambrose, "George has been killed."

"No," she said, shaking her head in a dismissive way. "No. I just got a letter from him. He's fine. There's been some mistake."

Mrs. Ambrose put her hand on Helen's arm. "I spoke to an officer down at the train depot. He said there's been a lot of fighting in the Shenandoah Valley. George's regiment was heavily involved. I'm afraid it's not a mistake."

Helen stared at her mother for a long moment while her son giggled and played with the ribbon on the collar of her dress. "I have to get J.B. his breakfast," she announced finally. She turned and headed for the kitchen.

"Mother, should I …." Clara began. Her mother shook her head.

"Let me go to her," said Mrs. Ambrose. With a sigh, she followed her older daughter down the hallway.

The Ambrose women donned the official black dresses and veils of mourning, draped the lower windows of the house in black cloth, and placed a black wreath on the door. Since George's body could not yet be retrieved from the battlefield, a memorial service was held at the Ambrose home. Flowers and candles filled the parlor, and a melaino-type portrait of George in his uniform, taken the previous August before he reenlisted, was displayed on a wooden stand. Friends of the family gathered and the Reverend Lea from the First Presbyterian Church said a few words. But, without the body, Clara thought it all seemed empty and surreal.

The long afternoon was spent greeting George's acquaintances and business associates who had come to pay their respects. Edgar made a brief appearance, which Mrs. Ambrose, at least, seemed to find of some comfort. However, Clara smiled for the only time that day when she saw Annie making her way through the mourners.

"I'm so sorry," said Annie as she embraced Clara.

"Thank you, Annie," said Clara. "And thank you for coming." She knew it could not have been easy for Annie to brave Mrs. Ambrose and this bastion of Presbyterianism to be there.

"It was the least I could do after you came to the funeral Mass for our Daniel," said Annie. She sighed. "We used to get together for happy occasions. Now it's funerals. So many funerals." She squeezed Clara's hand. "How's Helen?"

Clara shrugged. "She's going through the motions, but she hasn't cried or spoken of George since she heard the news."

Annie nodded. "Probably the shock of it. And so soon after havin' the baby."

Clara's eyes filled with tears. "It's all so tragic," she said. "I miss the way things were before." She smiled sadly. "I miss *you*. How is work at the Arsenal?"

"Fine," said Annie. "A bit monotonous, but good pay. Any chance you'll be joinin' me?"

Clara shook her head. "Mother's still dead set against it."

"Well, maybe it's for the best," said Annie. She glanced across the room to where Helen and Mrs. Ambrose sat on the divan, their tea gone cold in the cups on the table in front of them. "She and your sister will be needin' you around more than ever now."

"Yes," said Clara. She took as deep a breath as her corset would allow. "I suppose they will."

In the days following the funeral, Helen remained in her room. She divided her time between embroidering a little dress for J.B. and sleeping for hours on end. As a new widow, it was deemed socially permissible for her to leave the house to visit close relatives or go to church, but she had no interest in doing either.

At the end of June, a package arrived containing George's personal affects. Included was a letter from his colonel praising him for his service. Helen refused to look at any of it. Mrs. Ambrose packed everything away in a box for safekeeping for J.B.

Clara grew increasingly worried about her sister's refusal to face the fact of her husband's death.

"Leave her be, Clara," said her mother. "She'll accept it when she's strong enough. People mourn in their own way, in their own time. All we can do is be here for her."

The running of the house now fell almost entirely to Mrs. Ambrose and Clara. They divided the chores as best they could, while at the same time caring for the physical and emotional needs of Helen, J.B., and Grandmother Blake. Grandmother Blake was becoming more critical and demanding with age, and there were times Clara wanted to bite the old woman's head off. But, Mrs. Ambrose was unfailingly patient and kind with her mother.

Falling exhausted into bed each night, Clara marveled at her mother's stamina. But she worried about her, too. Not only was Mrs. Ambrose broken-hearted for her eldest daughter, she was also increasingly concerned about her own husband. They had not received a letter from Dr. Ambrose since early June, more than three weeks ago. Clara watched her mother grow thinner and thinner from anxiety and worry. She realized the fearful look she saw in her mother's eyes was the one her father had described when relaying the tragedies of her mother's youth. And there didn't seem to be anything Clara could do to make things better.

CHAPTER 15

GARRETT LEANED ON THE RAILING of the steamer, *Georgia*, as it made its way up the York River and watched the shoreline of tidewater Virginia slide past. He could smell the mud of the marshes and the salt air from the nearby ocean. Birds of types he had never seen before flew among the reeds at the water's edge. Large cranes with twig-like legs observed the soldiers' passing from the shallow water, then took flight slowly and deliberately, their giant wings beating the air with rowers' strokes, their legs trailing behind them. Behind and ahead, Garrett could see other ships of the makeshift armada – steamboats, sailing vessels, and barges – each with it cargo of talking, laughing men in blue leaning over the rails and spitting streams of tobacco into the murky water.

Since boarding the ship with his regiment at Aquia Creek on the upper Potomac on June 10th, 1862, Garrett had been overcome with a feeling of powerlessness unlike anything he had ever known. Accustomed to being in control, he felt swept away, not just by the current, but by a series of events and decisions over which he had no say. His first glimpse of the vastness of the upper Chesapeake Bay, the closest he had ever been to the ocean, only served to reinforce this sense of his own insignificance. The war was taking him farther and farther from Clara, and with each day that passed, the odds against him returning to her seemed to increase. This sense of unease was reinforced by the presence of a large number of embalmers of the dead who were accompanying the armada in expectation of numerous casualties in the coming battles.

Joe came up beside Garrett and leaned on the railing.

"Feeling any better?" asked Garrett. Joe had spent most of the trip through the choppy waters of the bay with his complexion a pale shade of green.

"Yeah, some," he answered, "but I may never eat again."

Suddenly, a group of Negroes appeared along the left bank of the river. The men wore large straw hats; the women bright red, blue, and yellow bandanas. They were singing and dancing in excitement at the sight of the flotilla of Union troops headed north through Virginia. This jubilant reception had occurred more than once along the trip upriver, and while many of the soldiers laughed at the slaves' antics, Garrett felt buoyed by their obvious joy in seeing the Federal troops.

The Union army's success in the war would not only preserve the Union, but quite possibly mean their freedom.

"You ever know any Negroes, Garrett?" said Joe.

"A few," said Garrett. "Canary, of course. And, back in Elmira, the caretaker of the cemetery was a Negro."

"I never have," said Joe. "Never even seen any as dark as the Negroes they have down here." He hesitated. "Some of the boys are saying that's what this fight's really about. Freeing the Negroes. They say if that happens, they'll be living right next to us, taking our jobs, maybe even voting. I'm not so sure I'd like that."

Garrett shrugged. "It's not whether we'd like it; it's whether it's right. The way I see it, it comes down to one question: Do you believe Negroes are real people and not some inferior race like the Southerners say? If you do, then they should have the same rights and opportunities as you and me."

"But a lot of the boys say they're not real people. At least, not like us. They say they're more like smart monkeys."

Garrett snorted. "That'd still make 'em smarter than most of the fellas you've been talkin' to. Have you ever heard Frederick Douglass talk, or read any of his writings?" Joe shook his head. "You do that. Listen to one of his speeches or read one of his essays. Then tell me whether you think he's just a 'smart monkey.'"

Joe looked dubious. "I still don't think I'd want 'em living next to me."

"To be truthful, I don't know how I'd feel about that, either," said Garrett. "But I do know we can't go on the way we have been, keeping an entire race of people in slavery for our own benefit. It's just morally wrong."

"Yeah, but I can't help but feel if you free them, all hell's gonna break loose."

"Maybe," said Garrett. "But then, they've already been living in hell for quite some time."

Joe made no reply, but continued to watch the dancing slaves until they slipped out of sight behind the river bend.

Following the stand-off at the Battle of Seven Pines/Fair Oaks, Union General McClellan hurried to strengthen the southern wing of his army. He transferred the bulk of his troops, some 70,000 men, south of the Chickahominy River to take up positions in front of Richmond. This left just the 18,000 man Fifth Corps, under General Fitz-John Porter, north of the Chickahominy to protect the supply base at White

House Landing. Despite the fact that Stonewall Jackson's successes in the Shenandoah Valley Campaign had drawn away most of the reinforcements expected from McDowell's First Corps, McClellan felt the imminent arrival of the additional 9,500 men of McCall's Pennsylvania Reserves division, added to the Fifth Corps, would provide sufficient manpower to protect the Union base from enemy attack.

Garrett paused at the top of the gangplank and gaped at the beehive of activity that was White House Landing. A forest of smokestacks, masts, and sails swayed above the boats, barges, flatboats, and sloops that crowded the docks. The river bank was stacked high with crates, barrels, bales, and boxes containing tons of rations, equipment, and ammunition, with thousands of tons more waiting to be off-loaded from boats at the wharf or anchored in the river. Some of the boats even carried locomotives, boxcars, or flatcars intended to transport supplies by way of the Richmond and York River Railroad. The railroad trestle bridge, destroyed by the Rebels and rebuilt by the Union troops, could be seen just beyond the chaos of the docks.

Just back from the wharf, a canvas tent city extending at least a half mile inland had sprung up to house and feed the soldiers, and to serve as offices for the government and commissary officials who were ostensibly in charge of this massive supply depot.

Beyond the tents, a huge area was set aside as a wagon park, another as an artillery park filled with long rows of cannons, mortars, shot and shell, and yet another as a storage area for the mountains of baled forage needed to feed the herds of horses and mules. The air smelled of river mud, wood smoke, animals, and sweat and reverberated with the shriek of steamboat whistles, shouted orders, drum beats, bugle calls, marching feet, teamsters cursing and cracking their whips, the clang of blacksmiths' forges, and the cries of sutlers hawking their wares. Into this roiling pot staggered the ship-weary soldiers of the Pennsylvania Reserves division.

"Keep moving, keep moving," bellowed a sergeant. Garrett teetered down the wooden plank to join his company, gathered to one side at the edge of the wharf.

Young Joe stood near the bottom of the gangplank, his feet splayed awkwardly.

"How come it still feels like we're moving?" he said.

"'Cause you're still on the water," said Leonard. He spat a stream of thick tobacco onto the boards beneath their feet. The gooey mass quickly disappeared between the cracks. Garrett realized they were standing on a platform made by laying wooden planks over barges and canal boats. These floating docks stretched across the shallows of the Pamunkey River so that the supplies, animals, and people needed to keep the Army of the Potomac running could be transported to shore from the boats anchored in the deeper channels of the river.

"Company A! Fall in!" shouted an officer. The Pittsburgh Rifles hurried into line with the rest of the regiment. "Right face. Forward. March!"

The makeshift dock swayed as the men of the 9th Pennsylvania Reserves regiment marched toward shore and gratefully stepped onto dry land for the first time in more than two days. They tramped through the crowded streets of the landing on a path that paralleled the rail line, the same route taken by the other Pennsylvania Reserve units that had arrived before them.

"Where're we going, anyway?" asked Rawlie as they slogged through the mud.

"The colonel said we're being assigned to General Porter's Fifth Corps," said Garrett.

"Porter. What's he like?" asked Caleb.

"Same as all of them," said Leonard. "Shiny buttons. No brass."

"Good God. I think Leonard told a joke!" said Rawlie.

"Nah, that's just the heat getting to you," said Frank.

Farther back from the river, the 9th Pennsylvania came upon a section of relatively empty, large walled tents. These were the hospital tents, set up and ready to deal with the expected casualties from this great push on Richmond. The sheer number of tents quickly dampened the talking and joking among the men.

Beyond the hospital tents were the sutlers' tents advertising a variety of goods. A thin man dressed in a bedraggled suit and a tall top hat began pushing handbills into the soldiers' hands as they passed by.

"Gentlemen! Gentlemen! Please, take one of these," he said with a toothy smile. "And tell your friends," he called after them as they marched away.

"Aw, shit," said Caleb. He threw the paper on the ground.

"What is it?" asked Garrett.

"Embalmers."

"Bunch of ghouls," muttered Frank.

Over the next few days, the thirteen regiments of McCall's Pennsylvania Reserves division were reunited. Then, as a body, they marched in relatively easy stages to the eastern outskirts of the town of Mechanicsville, which was located on an area of high ground on the north side of the Chickahominy River, approximately six miles northeast of Richmond.

The Reserves set up camp behind a swampy tributary of the Chickahominy known as Beaver Dam Creek, which ran east and southeast of the town. From this base camp, rotating regiments of pickets were sent out to occupy Mechanicsville and to guard along the river, lest the Rebels attempt to seize the high ground for their artillery. The Union guards reported being able to hear the voices of the Rebel pickets across the swollen water.

Returning to camp after their regiment's three-day turn on picket duty, Garrett and the men of Company A were heating up a supper of coffee and beans when Thaddeus Minter, a private from Company H, came limping along the pathway between the tents. His face was a study in pain and concentration.

"Here comes the biggest beat in the Union army," said Frank under his breath.

"Hey, Thaddeus. What's with the leg?" called Rawlie.

"Think I twisted an ankle," Minter replied with a grimace. "Hurts like hell."

"Seen the surgeon?" said Rawlie.

"On my way now. I just hope he doesn't put me on sick call."

"Yeah," said Rawlie. "That'd be a shame."

Minter waved and hobbled off into the darkness.

"Must be a big fight comin'," said Frank.

"Why do you say that?" said Joe.

"'Cause every time it looks like we're going to meet the Rebs, Private Minter comes down with some sort of ailment. He spends more time in the surgeon's tent than the surgeon."

Just then, Caleb came trotting back from the sinks, his eyes wide.

"Say, fellas," he said, "I just ran into a soldier from the 5th Pennsylvania. His regiment's stationed over in the town, and he said if you stand on the rooftops, you can actually see the spires of Richmond not more that five or six miles away."

"Five or six miles." Joe whistled. "We could be there by the end of the week."

"They're not going to give up Richmond without a hell of a fight," said Frank.

"Come on, Frank," said Rawlie. "You saw the men and provisions at White House Landing. There's no way the Rebs can match us in manpower or ordinance. They'd be fools to keep fighting."

"Maybe," said Frank.

"What do you think, Leonard?" Garrett turned to the taciturn old soldier who sat cleaning his teeth with a small twig.

"I think there's no tellin' what a man will do when he's fightin' for his home and family."

"Still," said Caleb, brushing away the old man's pessimism, "I say we'll be raising the Stars and Stripes over Richmond by Independence Day. We could be home by the end of the summer!"

Garrett said nothing, afraid to let himself even hope it could be true.

As the main body of McClellan's army gathered in front of Richmond, the outnumbered Rebels, under the leadership of their new commanding general, General Robert E. Lee, went on the offensive. McClellan's decision to leave just Porter's Fifth Corps north of the Chickahominy to guard White House Landing had been discovered by General J. E. B. Stuart's cavalry in a daring four-day reconnaissance ride around McClellan's forces from June 12th to the 15th. The details of his intrepid ride were trumpeted in the Richmond papers, which also made much of his flamboyant dress and boasting style.

"Goddamn peacock," said Caleb when word of Stuart's ride filtered down to the rank and file. "Makin' us look like fools. I'd love to get just one shot at that dandy."

"I'd love to find just one Union cavalry officer with his guts," said Frank.

Based on the information provided by Stuart, Lee began to plan an immediate attack on the northern, weaker wing of McClellan's army. Lee decided to pull three divisions of the Rebel army from the defense of Richmond and send them in a frontal assault against Porter's Fifth Corps. Relying on McClellan's chronic overestimation of the size of the enemy forces arrayed against him, Lee bet that McClellan would be unwilling to risk pulling his larger southern force from Richmond to come to Porter's aid. At the same time, Lee would secretly bring Stonewall Jackson's army down from the Shenandoah Valley to attack Porter's right flank. This would result in a total force of 60,000 Confederates against the 30,000 Union troops stationed north of the Chickahominy.

After conferring with his generals, Lee set the attack for June 26th near the town of Mechanicsville.

The bold plan might have worked had Jackson's vaunted foot cavalry exhibited their customary speed in making their way south from the Shenandoah Valley. But, Jackson's force failed to arrive at the appointed time on the morning of the 26th. By late afternoon, Confederate General

A. P. Hill, who had been instructed by Lee to hold his advance until Jackson's arrival, lost patience and attacked alone. He sent his division, some 16,000 men, against a roughly equal number of Federal troops dug into strong positions behind Beaver Dam Creek. These Federal troops included the men of Garrett's 9th Pennsylvania Reserves regiment.

Earlier that morning, Union pickets had detected some movement of the enemy forces. In response, General Porter had ordered his troops to take up position.

"Best finish up, boys. We've work to do," said the 9th's colonel as he hurried past the men of Garrett's mess eating breakfast outside their tent. The men exchanged a quick look and bolted their remaining corn mush and coffee.

The Pennsylvania Reserves deployed in a long line of defense beginning in a wooded area along the upper Mechanicsville road northeast of the town and extending southward along the eastern side of Beaver Dam Creek. The 9th Pennsylvania dug in on the extreme left of the Union line where the creek met the Chickahominy. Sixteen heavy guns were situated behind them higher on the hill and another Reserves regiment, the 11th Pennsylvania, waited in reserve behind the artillery. Their position was an advantageous one, for Beaver Dam Creek was a small stream with marshy edges and steep, wooded banks. To attack, the Rebels would have to descend the steep bank on the northwestern side of the creek and wade through the water in clear view and range of the dug-in Union troops and artillery on the opposite side.

Garrett and the men of the Pittsburgh Rifles spent the morning piling up log and brush breastworks to protect themselves from enemy fire. About noon, sporadic shooting could be heard from the northwest as the Rebel forces began to drive in the Union pickets stationed in and near the town of Mechanicsville. As the hours wore on, the approaching gunfire, now punctuated by artillery, increased in intensity.

Garrett knelt behind a large log, with Rawlie on his left and Caleb on his right, and watched for the first appearance of the enemy. Of all the things he hated about soldiering, the waiting was the worst.

Finally, at about 3:00 p.m., Rebel troops emerged from the trees on the opposite bank. At the order to advance, they began marching in butternut lines down the hillside to the creek.

"Here they come, boys!" yelled an officer from the 12th Pennsylvania, positioned off to Garrett's right. "Get ready!"

The hillside bristled with rifles aimed at the approaching Confederate troops.

As soon as the Rebels came within range, the Union artillery opened up with a thunderous roar. Sulfurous gray smoke obscured the blue sky. Forced to slow as they reached the swampy creek bed, the Rebels became easy targets for the Federal troops entrenched on the other side. The infantry fire became steady all along the Union line.

"Goddamn," yelled Rawlie as he placed a new cartridge into the breech block of his Sharps rifle. "It's like shooting fish in a barrel."

Just then, a bullet smacked into the log breastwork just inches from his face. Wood splinters sliced the air. Decidedly paler, Rawlie raised his rifle and returned fire.

Garrett crouched down behind his own breastworks to reload. Suddenly, Rawlie called out to him.

"Hey, look!"

Garrett turned his head just in time to see Thaddeus Minter, without his rifle, sprinting to the rear for all he was worth.

"Looks like that ankle's feeling better," said Rawlie. "Whooeee! Just look at him skedaddle."

Shaking their heads, he and Garrett turned back to the deadly business at hand.

For three hours, the men of the Pennsylvania Reserves kept up a steady fire across Beaver Dam Creek. Again and again the Rebels launched disjointed assaults in an attempt to break through, but were thrown back by a combination of rifle fire and artillery.

Around 6:00 p.m., Joe suddenly paused in the midst of reloading.

"Hey! Do you hear that?" He poked his head up over the top of the piled earth and brush in front of him.

"Damn it, Joe! Keep your head down before you get it blown off," barked Rawlie.

"No, listen!" said Joe.

Garrett cocked his head. There. He heard it, too. In the slight lulls between the crack of the muskets and the roar of the cannons, there came a swelling of sound, low and rising. He peered through the drifting smoke - and froze. What appeared to be an entire brigade of Confederate soldiers was marching in line after gray line down the opposite bank in a last all-out frontal assault aimed directly at the position held by the 9th Pennsylvania Reserves.

"Oh my God," said Garrett. "There must be thousands of them."

Just then, the Rebels received the command to charge. Garrett felt his bowels loosen as the huge mass of men emitted a blood-curdling yell and stormed the Union defenses.

All along the line, the Federal soldiers increased their fire; cursing, yelling, their sweaty faces blue/black with powder from their cartridges. Cannon shot and shell screamed and whistled overhead in both directions. Geysers of dirt and pieces of men flew into the air. The deadly spray from Union canisters opened great holes in the Rebel lines, but these gaps were quickly filled by the overwhelming number of enemy troops.

Like one possessed, Garrett loaded and fired his weapon, faster, faster, the adrenaline pumping through his body. In the smoke and confusion, it was impossible to tell if he actually hit anyone, but equally impossible to believe that anyone could survive the hail of bullets. Yet, still the Rebels came on, closer and closer to the Union left flank.

At last, the call went out for reinforcements. The 7th Pennsylvania rushed up in support, along with a crack rifle company from the 11th Pennsylvania. With their firepower added to the regiments already in the line, the Rebel drive on the Union left slowed, then faltered. Finally, the Confederates began to fall back.

As night descended, the fighting slowed all along the line until only sporadic gunfire could be heard. Barns, houses, and haystacks set ablaze by artillery fire now lit the battlefield and cast a garish light on the bodies of the dead and wounded scattered about the ground like grotesque broken dolls. The artillery continued to duel until past 9:00 p.m. and filled the night with roaring sound and bursts of rocketing, exploding light.

Under cover of darkness, the Confederates finally withdrew. The repeated frontal assaults had been a disaster, resulting in the loss of almost 1,500 Rebel soldiers killed, wounded, or missing. The Union Fifth corps, by virtue of their superior tactical position, lost fewer than 300 men.

When the cannon fire finally stopped, the deafening thunder of shot and shell was replaced by the pitiful moans and pleas of the wounded on both sides. Garrett slumped to the ground behind his breastworks, too exhausted to even raise his hands to his ears to block out the sound of men crying out for water, mother, and home.

"Poor bastards," muttered Leonard as he stared out over the gruesome, writhing landscape.

During the night, more ammunition was passed out to the exhausted troops. The men remained in their entrenchments and slept fitfully on their guns.

At about 4:00 a.m., Garrett was jolted awake.

"Garrett. Garrett!" hissed Rawlie. "Didn't you hear the captain? Come on. We've got to go."

Garrett grabbed his rifle and stumbled after Rawlie in the dark. The Pittsburgh Rifles and two other companies of the 9th Pennsylvania Reserves regiment had been ordered to defend the approach to a bridge spanning Beaver Dam Creek at a place known as Ellerson's Mill. Not long after they settled into the rifle pits overlooking the creek, flashes of gunfire revealed the location of a small enemy force attempting to cross. In the dim predawn light, the Rebel troops repeatedly attempted to gain the bridge, but Garrett and his comrades were able to keep them at bay.

Around 7:00 a.m., the exhausted men of the three 9th Pennsylvania Reserves companies at Ellerson's Mill were ordered to fall back and rejoin their regiment. With one eye on the Rebels still visible across the creek, the men scrambled out of the rifle pits and up the hillside. Garrett hoped they would have a chance to grab something to eat before the start of the general advance on Richmond. He was thinking even some salt pork might taste good about now, when he saw Caleb come to a sudden stop at the top of the hill and lower his rifle to his side. Fearing the Rebs had come around behind them, Garrett rushed to his aid, only to be brought to an abrupt halt by the same sight that had stunned Caleb.

There in the distance, the entire Pennsylvania Reserves division was marching off to the south, apparently in retreat.

"Good God! Where are they going?" demanded Caleb. The men of Company A gathered around with their mouths open in astonishment.

"Lieutenant," called Garrett to a nearby officer, "what's going on?"

"The entire Fifth Corps has been ordered to withdraw," the officer answered, unable to keep the disgust from his voice. "We're to provide the rear guard."

"Maybe someone ought to tell headquarters that we won the fight yesterday," said Rawlie. "We should be advancing."

"We have our orders, soldier," snapped the lieutenant. He turned and strode away.

"Who the hell is running this army?" asked Garrett.

Leonard spat a large wad of tobacco onto the ground. "I stopped trying to figure that out a long time ago."

The Pennsylvania Reserves spent the next few hours exchanging fire with the pursuing enemy in broad daylight along four miles of narrow roads churned to deep mud by the divisions that had preceded them. Their efforts enabled the rest of Porter's Fifth Corps to reach a new defensive position at a place called Gaines' Mill in relative safety. When, at last, the Pennsylvania Reserves caught up with the rest of the Fifth Corps, they were posted in reserve in the rear to get some much needed rest.

Garrett trudged over to the ammunition wagon where an ordinance sergeant was distributing cartridges and caps. Despite the fact that more ammunition had been issued following the fight at Beaver Dam Creek, Garrett had used all but two cartridges in guarding the bridge at Ellerson's Mill and covering the Fifth Corps' retreat. As he waited at the wagon to be re-supplied, his gaze fell on some empty wooden ammunition cases stacked beside the wagon. Stenciled on the lids were the words: *From Allegheny Arsenal.* The reminder of home elicited a tired smile.

"I need a full load," he told the ordinance sergeant. The man handed him four bundles of bullet cartridges and percussion caps. Garrett removed the two storage trays from his cartridge box and packed them until he again had the full complement of forty cartridges. Then he slipped the tins back into the cartridge box at his hip. He was loading his cap box when Frank came up beside him.

"Did you hear?" said Frank as he reached for a bundle of cartridges from the sergeant. "Lieutenant Percy's been wounded."

"Bad?"

"Bad enough. Shot twice, once through the shoulder, once in the neck. They think he's going to make it though."

"I hope so," said Garrett. "Morgan Percy's a good man."

"Well, if the surgeons don't kill him, he'll be back in Pittsburgh before any of us." Frank closed the flap on his own cartridge box. "Uh, Garrett. One more thing. That little contraband you were teaching to read."

"Canary?"

Frank nodded. "Fella from Company F told me he got killed last night. Artillery shell hit behind the lines. Thought you'd want to know." He patted Garrett on the shoulder and shuffled off in search of a soft spot for a nap.

Garrett leaned against the side of the ammunition wagon. He could see the young boy's face, the light in his eyes, the determined expression. Gone. Just like that. Garrett chided himself for being so foolish as to think war had rules; that the killing and dying would be done by those in uniform. Bullets and shells did not distinguish between the guilty and the innocent, the good and the bad. The killing was random, senseless. And with each death, the reasons for it were becoming harder and harder to justify.

Garrett trudged back to his company and tried to ignore the questions that swirled in his head.

* * *

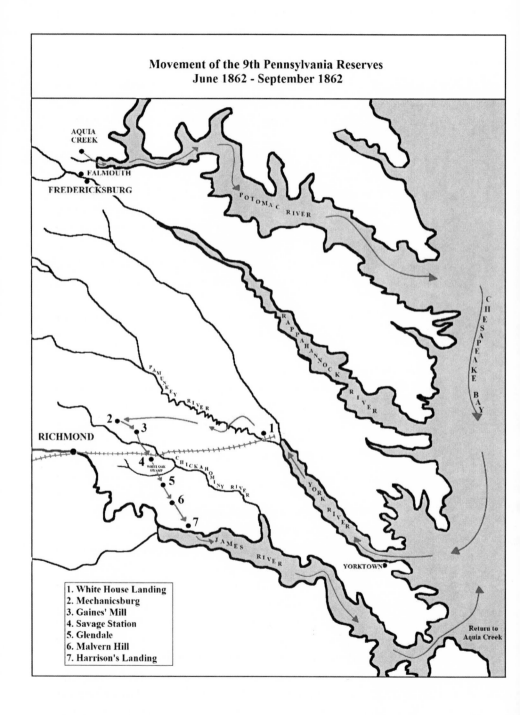

Movement of the 9th Pennsylvania Reserves
June 1862 - September 1862

1. White House Landing
2. Mechanicsburg
3. Gaines' Mill
4. Savage Station
5. Glendale
6. Malvern Hill
7. Harrison's Landing

At Gaines' Mill on June 27th, Porter's Fifth Corps took up a strong defensive position on a relatively open hillside behind a marshy creek known as Boatswain's Creek, just north of the Chickahominy River. General Porter placed three horizontal lines of infantry ascending the hillside, with the artillery positioned at the crest. Again, the men threw up breastworks of felled trees and earth. Similar to the situation at Beaver Dam Creek, any attacking Rebels would first have to descend an open field on the opposite hillside, cross the narrow stream at the bottom – which was in many areas bordered by thick swamp – climb a snake fence, and fight their way up the hill, directly in the face of Union artillery and musket fire.

A frontal attack under such circumstances would almost certainly result in very high casualty figures for the Confederates. But, now that Jackson's troops had at last caught up with the main part of the offensive, the Rebels held the advantage in numbers – 60,000 Confederate soldiers versus the Union's 30,000. General Lee felt that, with a well-organized attack, their superior numbers would carry the day.

Once more, however, the Rebel battle plan suffered from a lack of coordination. The attack on the center of the Union lines waged for hours without the expected support on the left and right flanks. Wave after wave of Confederate troops charged down the hill and slogged through the marsh and underbrush at the edge of the creek, only to be largely wiped out by Porter's artillery and infantry. Still they came on and, by sheer numbers, even managed to breech the Union lines in a few places. Finally, the struggling Federal troops had to call up the reserves to bolster these weak spots in their defense.

From the far side of the disputed hill, Garrett, his messmates, and the rest of the Pennsylvania Reserves had been listening to the roar of the artillery and the almost ceaseless rattle of the musket fire. They weren't surprised, therefore, when they received the call to fall in. The men hurried into column and set off at the quick step to plug any holes in the lines of those troops already engaged.

Despite having to struggle through a swampy ravine under enemy fire, the 9th Pennsylvania Reserves soon reached their assigned position at the center of the Fifth Corps battle line. The two regiments already there were under heavy attack. Through the thick battle smoke, Garrett could see the ground was littered with the dead and wounded of both armies, and the condition of the bodies attested to the fierceness of the shifting battle. Many of the men had their heads bashed in by musket butts, while others had been skewered by bayonets. Swallowing hard,

Garrett gripped his rifle and took his position alongside his fellow soldiers.

No sooner had the 9th Pennsylvania arrived, but their entire section of the Union line received the order to charge. With loud shouts and screams, the Federals dashed down the hill, bayonets at the ready, and drove the surprised Rebels before them. In their excitement, however, the 9th Pennsylvania and the two regiments with them advanced too far in pursuit of the retreating enemy. The Rebels counter-charged, attacking on the flank, and the three Union regiments were forced to make a hasty retreat to the relative safety of the second line of breastworks on the hill. Garrett and Caleb spied each other through the smoke and together hurdled an entrenchment made of a fallen oak tree, brush, and hastily thrown-up earth. They tucked in behind it and resumed firing at the approaching enemy.

Suddenly, a shell burst at the base of their breastwork. There was an enormous flash and Garrett found himself somersaulting through a cloud of smoke, dirt, and splintered wood. He landed with a heavy thud and his head smacked hard into the ground. The sounds of battle were reduced to a low drone, punctuated by the thumping percussion of shells hitting the earth. As his senses slowly returned, he rolled over onto his stomach and spit the dirt from his mouth. Blood dripped from a gash across his cheekbone and made muddy crimson rivulets down his face. Wiping the grit from his eyes, he raised his head to find Caleb sprawled on his back a few feet away. Caleb's left leg was turned at an awkward angle and a foot-long piece of splintered wood, like a jagged stake, protruded from his stomach.

"Caleb! Caleb!" cried Garrett, but he couldn't hear himself over the thunder of the cannons. He crawled on his belly to where Caleb lay with his dirt-covered face contorted in pain. Caleb's hands, gripping the base of the stick, were covered in blood.

"Caleb! Can you hear me?" Garrett shouted directly into his face. Caleb's eyes showed a flicker of recognition. His lips moved and Garrett pressed his ear to Caleb's mouth.

"It hurts," Caleb whispered.

"Don't worry. I'll get you out of here." Desperately, Garrett looked around for someone to help move his injured friend. But the battle was becoming even hotter, and every man not already wounded was fully engaged in holding off the enemy. Garrett turned back to Caleb. He hoped his eyes did not reveal the panic he felt.

"Caleb, I'm going to have to move you. You'll get shot for sure if you stay here."

With bullets whizzing by in all directions, Garrett came around behind his friend and grabbed him underneath the shoulders. Caleb shrieked in agony as Garrett dragged him in fits and starts across the uneven ground to the cover of another breastwork. Two Union soldiers lay dead on its uphill side. Garrett laid Caleb down as close to the base of the breastwork as he could. He removed his own jacket and placed it beneath Caleb's head. After a moment's hesitation, Garrett dragged the bodies of the two soldiers to Caleb's side and propped them up to form a protective shield. Caleb reached up and grabbed Garrett's shirt.

"Don't leave me here," he pleaded.

"I won't," said Garrett, slinging his haversack over his shoulder, "but I've got to return to the line. I'll come back for you as soon as I can. I promise." Caleb nodded, but his eyes were filled with fear. "You just hang on. Do you hear me?" said Garrett. "Hang on!"

Garrett retrieved his rifle from the ground a few yards away and, with a last glance at his wounded friend, dashed back to the ever more ragged, second line of breastworks where the rest of the regiment was attempting to fight off yet another Rebel assault. He dove in next to a wide-eyed private from Company C who was frantically trying to reload his rifle.

"Where's the rest of the army?" shouted the young man as the bullets whizzed over their heads. "Where's the goddamn reinforcements?"

With no answer to give or time in which to give it, Garrett could only aim his rifle at the enemy and keep firing.

The Union troops managed to drive the Rebels back once more, but it was clear the numerical supremacy of the Confederate forces was beginning to tell on the weary Federals.

Around 6:30 p.m., General Lee was finally able to coordinate his various brigades and launch the concerted attack he had been hoping for all day. The Rebels charged the center of the Union line in overwhelming numbers and, despite horrific losses from Union artillery and infantry volleys, advanced to within ten yards of the Federal lines. There, beneath heavy fire, the determined Confederates formed in ranks and unleashed a deadly volley that decimated the first line of Union troops. The line broke and the screaming Rebels pressed on up the hill.

From his position in the second line of defense half way up the slope, Garrett saw the retreating Federal troops streaming toward him. They bolted over and past the lines of the 9th Pennsylvania and carried much of the regiment with them in their panic.

Determined to go out fighting, Garrett raised his rifle and took aim at one of the hundreds of screaming Confederates bearing down on his position.

Suddenly, over the din of battle, he heard the faint call of a bugle sounding retreat.

"Fall back! Fall back!" yelled a Union colonel, swinging his sword in the air to draw the attention of the men.

Garrett hesitated. What about Caleb?

All around him, Union soldiers were running, climbing, scrambling up the slope. Despite their panic, they were careful to stay to the side of the belching fire of the Union artillery that was attempting to hold off the pursuing Rebels with shot, canister, and shell.

A fleeing soldier paused next to Garrett and yanked on his arm. "Come on!" he yelled before bolting up the hill.

Garrett took a last look at the fast approaching Rebels, now so close he could read the CSA stamped on their belt plates. With tears in his eyes, he turned and sprinted after the rest of his regiment.

CHAPTER 16

THE SURVIVING MEMBERS OF THE Union Fifth Corps trudged south through the darkness in a long ghostly line. Spent and demoralized, they mourned the loss of 6,800 of their fellow Union soldiers and wondered why help had taken so long to arrive.

As Lee had predicted, General McClellan's concern about the number of Rebel troops he faced in front of Richmond had made him unwillingly to significantly diminish the size of his force to aid the desperate Union troops battling at Gaines Mill.

Finally, in late afternoon, McClellan had sent 6,000 men north across the Chickahominy – just enough and just in time to prevent a total rout. These last-minute reinforcements held off the Rebels long enough to allow the battered Fifth Corps to limp across the river to the relative safety of the south side. Having lost 9,000 of their own men in victory, the Confederates had broken off the fight when night descended.

Now, as Garrett waded through the shallow swamps bordering the river, he was haunted by the image of Caleb lying alone on the hillside, waiting for him to return. The weight of Garrett's guilt made it hard for him to breathe. But what else could I have done? he agonized. A moment's more hesitation and he, too, would have been killed or captured. Distraught, he reached to pat the pocket of his coat where he kept the leatherette case containing Clara's picture. Only then did he remember that his coat was back on the hillside – with Caleb. Doubly bereft, he hung his head and a tear traced a line down his bloody, gunpowdered cheek.

Suddenly, an explosion lit the sky behind them.

"Is that the Reb artillery?" asked Joe. The whites of his eyes were illuminated by the glow.

"Naw," said Frank. "That's just our engineers blowing the bridge so the Rebs don't catch up with us."

The men slogged on as darkness descended once more.

In the pre-dawn hours of the 28th, the Pennsylvania Reserves finally halted in some empty farm fields along the roadside. Ordered to fall out, the soldiers slumped to the ground where they stood, too exhausted to even set up tents. Many laid on the damp grass and mud without even a blanket to cover them.

A rising tumult awakened them before reveille. The bulk of the Army of the Potomac, all 69,000 men, was already in motion on the roads all around them.

The Confederate victory at Gaines' Mill had convinced General McClellan to abandon any immediate plans to march on Richmond. Now, more than 5,000 wagons, 2,500 cattle, the siege train, and regiment after regiment of troops had been pulled from their positions in front of the Rebel capital and were snaking their way south on the few narrow, muddy roads leading through the rain-flooded area know as White Oak Swamp.

Their destination was the new headquarters of the Army of the Potomac at Harrison's Landing, situated in relative safety on the banks of the James River.

The exhausted 9th Pennsylvania Reserves sat on the soggy ground and watched the Army of the Potomac execute what McClellan termed a "change of base," but what to them looked like a massive retreat.

"Where do you think we're headed now?" asked Joe, his long arms resting on his bent knees.

"I don't know, but I hope it's not far," said Rawlie. "I don't think I've ever been this tired." He stretched his aching limbs toward the hasty campfire they had built.

"God, I'm hungry," said Joe. He eyed the huge herd of Union cattle weaving its way down the road under the direction of the drovers. "I swear I could eat one of those steers raw. Anybody got anything to eat? My haversack's back on that hillside somewhere."

Garrett reached into his own bag and pulled out two filthy pieces of hardtack. Leonard contributed some strips of dried beef and Frank began brewing up some coffee. Even such limited, questionable fare looked good to the famished men who had barely eaten in over two days. They sat chewing slowly while they watched the endless parade of men and supplies disappear down the road.

"Any word on Caleb?" asked Frank as a line of ambulances rattled by.

"Some of the fellows said they thought they saw him carried off the field," said Garrett, "but they weren't sure."

"Do you think he'll make it?" asked Joe.

Garrett shrugged. "He was pretty bad off," he muttered.

The men finished their meal in silence.

In a field near where Garrett and his messmates ate their meager breakfast, eighteen batteries of reserve artillery stood waiting to be moved, artillery that was crucial to the defense of the retreating army. McCall's Pennsylvania Reserves division was ordered to escort this artillery three miles south to the train depot at Savage Station, then on through White Oak Swamp to a position near the village of Glendale. The guns, caissons, ammunition trains, and battery wagons of this reserve artillery added up to over three hundred vehicles. When added to McCall's own wagons, artillery, and transports, the wagon train extended over seven miles in length. To guard this unwieldy snake, McCall placed the Reserves regiments at intervals throughout the train with flanking parties to either side. By nightfall, the entire entourage had joined the rest of the army lurching its way south.

In the dark and the rain, Garrett could barely see the man in front of him, much less any attacking Rebels that might appear in the thick, swampy woods to either side of the narrow road. Periodically, however, the darkness was relieved by the light from the smoldering ruins of vast amounts of provisions, ammunition, wagons, and tents that had been piled into great bonfires on either side of the roadway. These supplies had been intended for use in the attack on Richmond, but McClellan, with a nervous eye on the pursuing Rebels, had ordered them torched so as not to slow the Union army's march to Harrison's Landing. He had also given orders that any un-evacuated supplies at White House Landing be burned to keep them out of enemy hands. As the Union soldiers marched south on the night of June 28th, 1862, they could see the glow of that huge conflagration in the northeastern sky.

Garrett's stomach growled with hunger as he tramped along with his regiment. Despite the rubber poncho he wore, he was soaked with a combination of rain and sweat. The mud sucked at his feet and made each step an exercise in balance. Already Leonard had fallen and barely escaped being run over by an artillery caisson. Heads down and subdued, the Pennsylvania Reserves division and the artillery train entrusted to it plodded through the night. Garrett thought the whole outfit resembled a wet, beaten dog.

In the early hours of the next morning, Sunday, June 29th, the exhausted, muddy, hungry men of the Pennsylvania Reserves division finally caught up with the rest of the Army of the Potomac at Savage Station. The dawn revealed an army in disarray.

"Oh, my God," said Garrett, rising slowly from the spot where he had laid down just a few hours before. His messmates, too, stared about in disbelief at the enormous scene of chaos and suffering.

The fields and woods for acres around the train depot were crammed with wagons, ambulances, animals, and soldiers huddled in dispirited groups. Officers and orderlies, on foot and on horseback, hurried throughout the camp to deliver orders to the various division and brigade commanders. The air crackled with rumors about the certain approach of Rebel troops, and men listened for the first sound of gunfire.

Most distressing, however, was the plight of the wounded. Every tent, house, barn, or upright structure in the area had been commandeered to shelter the two to three thousand suffering, dying men arriving in a continuous stream of ambulances from the Seven Pines/Fair Oaks, Mechanicsburg, and Gaines' Mill battlefields. The overflow was laid in the fields and woods, where the dampness of the night's rain, and now the steaming heat of the morning sun, added to their discomfort. Their moans and cries provided a painful undercurrent to the rattling din of so large a massing of troops.

At the station itself, a train that had been transporting the wounded to White House Landing for evacuation stood waiting, fully loaded with its pitiful cargo. The telegraph line between Savage Station and White House Landing had stopped working the day before, a clear indication the Rebels had reached the railroad and cut the line. Still, the wounded men resisted attempts to remove them from the sweltering trains in desperate hope they would yet be taken to White House Landing for evacuation to Washington by ship.

"I'm going to see if I can find Caleb," said Garrett.

"How're you going to find him in this mess?" said Frank. "There must be thousands of wounded here." He paused. "We don't even know if he made it this far."

Garrett's face darkened. "I've got to try."

Leonard stood up and pulled on the still damp sack coat he had been using as a pillow. "I'll help."

"We all will," said Rawlie. Joe and Frank nodded.

The men split up to cover as much ground as possible. Garrett began in a nearby section of woods. He picked his way carefully among the wounded that were lying in what little shade was afforded by the trees. Soldiers from other regiments were also searching for friends and messmates. Orderlies dashed back and forth, carrying the injured to one of the makeshift hospital tents, but there were far too many men needing attention. Many of the poor souls lay where they had been placed days before, with their injuries untended, little or nothing to eat or drink, and so weak they were unable to brush away the flies that settled on their festering wounds. The stench of decaying flesh hung heavy in the humid air and Garrett fought back the bile that rose in his throat. Here and there, a form lay still, gone to eternal life with no one to ease his passage. The more fortunate ones had an identifying note pinned to their blouse or tucked into a pocket so their loved ones might eventually be notified of their deaths.

"Water. Please. Is anybody there? Please. Some water."

The plea came from a private propped in a sitting position against a tree. A filthy bandage was wrapped around his head and both eyes, and his beard was matted with blood and mud. His pants below the knees were in tatters, and the legs beneath them so riddled with grapeshot they looked and smelled like spoiled meat. Garrett stopped and knelt by his side.

"Here you go, soldier," he said and raised his own canteen to the man's lips. The soldier closed his trembling hands around Garrett's as he sucked at the water. When he finished, the man breathed a heavy sigh.

"Thank you, friend," he said. "God bless you." As Garrett rose to go, the soldier pulled at his sleeve. "Wait. Can you tell me what's happening? I was wounded two days ago and no one seems to know what's going on. Are we any closer to Richmond? Are we going to take Richmond?"

Tears welled in Garrett's eyes as he looked down on the mangled young man.

"Yes," he said with as much conviction as he could muster. "We've got the Rebs on the run. We'll be in Richmond soon."

A smile flickered across the man's cracked lips and his body seemed to relax.

"Good. Good," was all he said.

Garrett patted the man's shoulder and hurried away.

For what seemed like hours, Garrett peered into the faces of the wounded, their visages in suffering so similar that he began to wonder if he would even recognize Caleb if he did find him. His heart leapt each time he spied a soldier with red hair, but each time he was disappointed.

Garrett came upon a chaplain kneeling over the body of a dead soldier. From the stole around his neck, Garrett realized he was a Catholic priest.

"Reverend?" said Garrett as the man stood from giving a final blessing.

The priest turned to him. The lines of weariness and care were raked so deeply into the man's cheeks that his face seemed to be melting into his gray beard.

"I'm looking for a friend of mine. A soldier from the 9th Pennsylvania Reserves. Private Caleb Layton. He was wounded at Gaines' Mill."

The priest shook his head. "I'm sorry, son. There are so many soldiers." He paused. "But, I think there's a group that was brought in from Gaines' Mill just beyond the surgeon's tent over there." He pointed to a large, white walled tent beneath the shelter of some trees.

"Thank you, Rev ... uh ... Father."

"Good luck, my son."

Garrett hurried past the surgeon's tent and turned his head from the large mound of amputated limbs, hands, and feet piled beside it. As the priest had said, another group of wounded men lay in the open in the adjoining field.

"Were you men shot near Gaines' Mill?" Garrett inquired as he stepped among their prone bodies. Those who could, responded in the affirmative. "I'm looking for Caleb Layton, of the 9th Pennsylvania Reserves. Has any one seen him? Red hair. He'd have been brought in about the same time as you."

"No. Sorry, soldier," came the reply each time.

Garrett continued to search as the sun rose higher in the sky, its rays beating down on the helpless, wounded men. At last he came to the edge of the field. He looked back over its gruesome crop and hung his head at the enormity of the suffering.

Slowly, Garrett made his way back the way he had come. He came to the tree where he had given the soldier water and found the man slumped to the side, dead. Garrett hoped his lie had eased the man's last moments.

When Garrett met up with his messmates, their pale drawn faces mirrored his own. They looked at him questioningly. Garrett shook his head.

"There's still a chance he's in a hospital somewhere," said Joe.

"I shouldn't have left him," muttered Garrett.

"It's not your fault, Garrett," said Frank. "There was nothing you could do."

"You don't understand," said Garrett in a choked voice. "I promised him I'd come back. I promised."

Leonard put a knobby hand on Garrett's shoulder. "Son, one thing I learned in Mexico – promises don't mean shit in war." Garrett and the others looked at him in surprise. Leonard shrugged. "That's where I got this," he said, pointing to the scar on his face. "And where I left my best friend, in some godforsaken sandpit." His eyes took on a faraway look. "You make a choice. The only one you can." He looked at Garrett solemnly. "And then you learn to live with it."

Leonard bent down and picked up his rifle. "Come on. Time to go."

"They're not bringing them with us, you know," said Rawlie. Anger clipped his words.

"What do you mean?" asked Garrett.

"I overheard a couple of the officers talking. Little Mac's decided the only way the army can get to the James ahead of the Rebels is to leave the wounded behind."

As one, the men looked out over the acres of wounded lying all around Savage Station.

"My God," whispered Joe.

"I've seen it before," said Frank. "Sacrifice the wounded or lose the whole army."

"But, they're leaving a rearguard behind to protect them, aren't they?" asked Joe.

"They're to protect the army's retreat," said Frank. "They'll leave, too, once the army's safely away."

"But, what will happen to the wounded?" asked Garrett.

"The Rebs'll take them prisoner," said Leonard.

"Most of the men I saw wouldn't survive prison," said Garrett.

The little group fell silent.

"Do you think they know?" asked Joe after a moment.

"Not yet," said Rawlie. "But they will soon."

Sure enough, as wagons and troops continued to file down the road to the south, it became apparent to all that no provision had been made to move the wounded. Word they were to be left behind swept through their agonized ranks. The moans and outcries became louder, and those who could, struggled to their feet and attempted to rejoin their regiments. The majority, however, were left to their fate. A few brave surgeons and chaplains elected to stay with them, with the knowledge that they, too, would fall into the hands of the enemy.

"Company A! Fall in!"

Grim and stricken, the Pittsburgh Rifles fell into line with their regiment and joined the rest of the Pennsylvania Reserves division alongside the artillery train. On command, they marched south from Savage Station and struggled to block out the wails of the wounded left behind.

By late afternoon on June 29th, the Pennsylvania Reserves had delivered the artillery train to an area of solid ground south of White Oak Swamp. They were relieved of escort duty and ordered to resume their march.

"Where we headed now?" asked Joe, shifting his rifle on his shoulder.

"Away from whatever's goin' on back there," said Rawlie, jerking his head in the direction of Savage Station.

The sounds of artillery and rifle fire had followed them throughout the afternoon as the Union rearguard fought a fierce battle to delay the Rebels pursuing the main Union force. Suddenly, a louder explosion caused the soldiers' heads to snap around.

"There goes the bridge over White Oak Creek," said Frank. "That should slow the Rebs down some."

But General Lee pressed on, determined to stop McClellan before he could reach the safety of the Union gunboats on the James River. Lee knew that, due to the densely wooded terrain, the southward straining Army of the Potomac would be forced to divide up and travel on a series of three parallel roads – the New Market, Charles City, and Quaker Roads. If the Rebel forces could overpower the rearguard before the main Union body could reassemble where the three roads came together near the village of Glendale, they would be able to split the wings of the Army of the Potomac and beat them in detail.

General Porter's Fifth Corps, to which the Pennsylvania Reserves were still officially attached, was ordered to head for the James River via the Quaker Road. Unfortunately, the guides and the military maps did not agree on the location of this road and, in the dark of night, the various branches of the Fifth Corps became confused and tangled.

While the commanders attempted to sort out the mix-up, General Porter directed the Pennsylvania Reserves division to encamp by the side of the road until morning. Exhausted from five days of constant fighting and marching, the Reserves huddled around their campfires and watched in amusement as the other Fifth Corps divisions marched and counter-marched past them in their quest for the right road.

"There they go again," said Rawlie as a regiment they had seen earlier passed by again, headed in the opposite direction. "Those boys are going to be mighty tired come morning."

"Looks like Porter's finally decided on a direction, though," said Frank.

The men sipped at their dwindling coffee rations as they watched the last of Porter's troops disappear down the road. Soon, the road was empty and plunged in darkness.

"Wait a minute," said Garrett. "If Porter's going that way, who's behind us?"

The men sat in silence as the grim realization sunk in.

"Aw, shit," said Rawlie. "The whole goddamn Rebel army's behind us and we're stuck bringing up the rear again."

* * *

On the morning of June 30th, General McCall received orders from General McClellan that the Pennsylvania Reserves, along with six other Federal divisions that now made up the rearguard of the army, were to take up positions north and west of the crossroads at Glendale. The order included no coordinated battle plan, but only a request that they resist the Rebels until the main body of the Union army could reunite and proceed to the safety of the James River. The seven rearguard divisions set up as best they could along the three pivotal roadways and prepared to meet the enemy.

Garrett and the 7,000 remaining men of McCall's Pennsylvania Reserves division were deployed in a westerly facing, thin line of battle straddling the New Market Road from Richmond and some adjoining farm fields belonging to a man named Frayser. This open area was surrounded by a thick forest of sedge pines. McCall placed his artillery batteries in front with the infantry behind in double line of battle.

The 9th Pennsylvania was placed in the very center of the Pennsylvania Reserves division's line in support of Cooper's battery. Another Union division took up position behind them in reserve. Garrett and his fellow soldiers loaded their rifles, faced in the direction of Richmond, and waited. As the hours ticked by beneath an increasingly hot sun, however, the men began to slump with fatigue. The cannoneers of Cooper's battery lounged at their posts. The drivers dismounted and lay on the shady side of their horses. Garrett and Rawlie picked out a grassy spot, sat back to back, arms on knees, and attempted to grab some sleep.

Finally, around 2:30 p.m., the rumble of artillery fire could be heard in the north. The Pennsylvania Reserves leapt to their feet and straightened their ranks. Not long after, Confederate cannon, positioned directly down the New Market Road to the west, also opened up. These shots were immediately answered by the Union artillery, and a brief duel ensued over the men's heads. Minutes later, the Reserves' line tensed as their own pickets began emerging from the woods and fields ahead, the men driven in by the approaching Confederate troops.

Garrett stood with his regiment at *shoulder arms* and felt a surge of adrenalin wipe away the exhaustion of the past six days. He glanced at the men around him in Company A – Rawlie, his nonchalant expression belied by the intense look in his eyes; Frank, with the cool concentration of a veteran; Leonard dispassionately chewing a twist of tobacco; and Joe, his Adam's apple jumping nervously. Garrett felt a sudden outpouring of emotion for these brave, ordinary men who had shared with him the awful loneliness, boredom, and horror of war. He said a silent prayer for their safety and turned his attention forward once more.

"What time is it?" asked Frank without taking his eyes from the field. Leonard, next to him in line, pulled out his pocket watch.

"About 3:00 p.m.," he said.

"Good a time as any," said Frank.

Moments later, troops in gray and butternut could be seen advancing up the New Market Road. The Union artillery opened up once more and the enemy infantry spread out. With their superior numbers, the Rebels swarmed out of the woods and across the open fields to attack on the left, center, and right in waves. The Union batteries, supported by their own infantry, kept up a steady fire, but still the enemy came on, at points advancing so close as to engage the Federals with bayonets.

The fighting in front of Garrett and his comrades was some of the fiercest they had yet encountered. Cooper's battery in the center was repeatedly attacked, but each charge was repulsed by the combined fire of the artillery and the 9th Pennsylvania Reserves regiment behind it. More than once, the 9th Pennsylvania succeeded in pushing the Rebels back to their second line of infantry, but the influx of additional enemy troops eventually forced the Union troops back over the ground they had gained. The enemy was determined and, despite a steady barrage of Union grape shot and canister that opened huge gaps in their lines, they kept advancing, sometimes to the very mouth of the Federal cannons.

As the 9th Pennsylvania fought a seesaw battle in the center, the exposed left flank of the Reserves was also under heavy siege. The enemy continually attacked it in heavy force in hopes of turning it and, thereby, collapsing the whole line. Around 7:00 p.m., an urgent call went out for Union reinforcements.

"9th Pennsylvania," shouted the colonel over the fracas. "At the double-quick!"

The men of Garrett's regiment hurried into formation and trotted along behind the hotly engaged Union line until they reached the beleaguered Reserves attempting to hold the far left in a stand of woods.

"Plug the holes! Plug the holes, men," shouted the officers.

Garrett dropped to one knee between a crumpled body and a young man doggedly loading his rifle with a bloody hand missing a finger. Intermittent shafts of smoke-filled light illuminated the forest as Garrett took aim on the shadowy line of the closing enemy soldiers.

"Ready! Aim! Fire!"

The 9th Pennsylvania released a flaming volley that slowed and then halted the Rebel advance. With bullets zipping by his ears, Garrett reloaded.

"Pour it into 'em, boys!" urged the officers, and the men fired as quickly as they could reload. The Rebel line began to waver and fall back.

Garrett knew time had no meaning on the battlefield, but it seemed like only minutes before the 9th Pennsylvania was ordered to return to their original position in the center. The men formed in ranks and marched off the way they had come. Suddenly, a wounded Union soldier lurched toward them through the woods.

"The Rebs have captured Cooper's guns!" he gasped, holding onto a tree for support.

"Like hell, they have," answered the 9th Pennsylvania's colonel. He raised his saber in the air.

"9th Pennsylvania!" he shouted over the roar of battle. "Fix bayonets! Forward! Charge!"

Screaming like demons, Garrett and the men of his regiment burst from the woods to find the Rebels swarming the lightly defended guns of Cooper's battery. Shooting, clubbing, and bayoneting the artillerists, they were in the very process of turning the cannons to fire on the returning men of the 9th. The enraged Pennsylvanians rushed the battery before the enemy could finish loading and, with bayonets, knives, and pistols, attempted to retake the big guns.

Out of the mayhem, a young Confederate soldier, his blue eyes wild beneath a gunpowder mask, rushed at Garrett with bayonet raised. Garrett deflected the blade with the butt of his rifle and crashed his knee into the boy's stomach. Grunting, the youth doubled over and Garrett thrust his own bayonet into the young man's side. As the boy screamed in pain, Garrett heard rather than saw something coming at his head. He ducked just in time to dodge a musket stock swung with great force. Instinctively, Garrett tackled his new assailant, driving the man backward. The Rebel slammed into the barrel of one of the cannons, the impact causing the rifle to fly from his hands. Garrett scrambled for his own gun, which was still lodged in the boy's gut. He yanked it free, turned, and fired at point blank range into the charging enemy soldier's face. The man catapulted backward, still clutching a knife in his hand.

Garrett staggered forward. Panting, he stared down at the bloody hole where the man's face used to be, then over at the young boy crumpled on the ground. He waited to feel something - horror, satisfaction, revenge - but nothing came. Expressionless, Garrett raised his rifle and plunged back into the fight.

There was no denying ownership of the killing now. The air was filled with shouts and screams, the clang of bayonet on bayonet, and the thwack of muskets smashing into bone. Here and there, men fired their guns, but the fighting was mainly hand to hand, with each man looking directly into the face of his enemy as he fought a desperate battle for life.

Finally, the Rebels broke and ran for the shelter of the woods. Wild with fury, the men of the 9th Pennsylvania pursued them across the field and into the trees. They fired at the retreating Confederates and clubbed and stabbed the stragglers. The color bearer of the 10th Alabama fell, mortally wounded, and a man from the 9th Pennsylvania swept up the prized Rebel standard and carried it back to the Union lines.

Fearing the enraged men would continue straight into the main body of the Confederate army, the officers of the 9th Pennsylvania recalled the regiment to their original position in defense of Cooper's battery. Meanwhile, other nearby Pennsylvania Reserves regiments had also reformed and resumed their positions. The exhausted men dressed their thinning lines and prepared to meet a Rebel countercharge.

With the blade of his bayonet still wet with blood, Garrett stood panting beside the survivors of his winded and battered regiment. He knew they couldn't hold out much longer. After more than four hours of fighting against superior numbers, McCall's division was beginning to give way. Portions of the line had been shattered and retreated, while other beleaguered regiments and fragments of regiments had regrouped and fought on. As the light of day began to fade, Garrett steeled himself for a final fight.

Suddenly, a tremendous roar came from the woods to the left and rear of their position. A large body of armed men swarmed through the trees and headed directly for the Pennsylvania Reserves.

"My God," exclaimed Frank, in line next to Garrett. "What is that?"

For a heart-stopping moment, Garrett watched as the brigade of men drew closer. Finally, their standard emerged from the dusk and the battle smoke – a green flag emblazoned with a golden harp; alongside it, another flag bearing the stars and stripes.

"It's the Irish Brigade!" cheered the men of the Pennsylvania Reserves. "Huzzah! Huzzah!"

An officer of the Irish Brigade trotted up to the nearest Pennsylvania Reserves colonel.

"Colonel, your troops are relieved. You may retire."

Overcome, the Pennsylvanian could only grasp the man's arm and nod.

The men of the Irish Brigade trotted past the exhausted Pennsylvania Reserves and took up position. In the face of murderous artillery and musket fire, they mounted a charge that pushed the Confederates back into the woods once more.

As the sound of firing moved away, Garrett leaned against the wheel of one of Cooper's cannons to steady his shaky legs. Outnumbered almost three to one, the Pennsylvania Reserves had borne the brunt of the Battle of Glendale, and the killing field in front of him attested to that fact. The ground was littered with dead and wounded men and horses, shattered pieces of artillery, broken and abandoned rifles, canteens, and haversacks. As Garrett watched, Union survivors streaked with sweat, blood, and gun powder hurried forward through the fading light to help their comrades off the field. They knew the Rebels weren't far away and were certain to come again.

Seated on the ground a few yards in front of him, Garrett spied a man cradling a fellow soldier in his arms. The man's back was to Garrett and his hatless head was bent over the half-seen body. With his heart in his throat, Garrett shuffled toward the familiar form. The seated solder was Rawlie. Lying in his arms, his legs splayed awkwardly, was Joe.

"Goddamn it," crooned Rawlie softly. "I told you to keep your head down, didn't I? Didn't I tell you to keep your head down?"

Joe's head rested in the crook of Rawlie's arm. His sightless eyes stared at the sky. In the center of Joe's head was a bullet hole so neat and round it almost didn't look real. Just a small trickle of drying blood trailed from the hole to his ear, but Rawlie's coat sleeve, where the back of Joe's head rested, was drenched with blood.

Garrett dropped to one knee. "Rawlie," he said gently. "Rawlie."

Rawlie looked up at him, as if surprised to see him there. Then, with an exasperated half-smile, he shook his head. "I told him to keep his head down."

Garrett's eyes filled with tears. He brushed them away with his own blood-spattered sleeve.

"Rawlie," he repeated, "we gotta go. The Rebs are coming. We're being pulled back."

"I can't leave him here."

"You have to. Our boys will take care of him when the fight's over. Come on."

Already, the crackle of musket fire could be heard approaching once more.

Rawlie looked down at Joe's face. Tenderly, he closed the sightless eyes. Then slowly, as if loath to wake him, Rawlie slid his legs out from under Joe's body and laid him on the ground. With the sound of battle moving ever closer, he arranged Joe's gawky limbs into repose, the legs straightened, the hands folded over his chest.

Rawlie stood for a moment and stared down at his friend. Then, with eyes like hard flint, he picked up his rifle, turned, and walked away.

CHAPTER 17

GRANDMOTHER BLAKE SAT IN HER wheelchair in front of the parlor window and peered down the street with a sour expression on her face.

"Look at them. Just look at them," she growled. "Every day, praying and chanting."

"Mother, come away from the window," sighed Mrs. Ambrose as she dusted the furniture in a futile battle with the soot that drifted in on every breeze. "There's no sense in upsetting yourself."

The old woman brushed away her suggestion with an impatient flick of her hand. "Things aren't bad enough, with poor George gone to the hereafter and Peter God-knows-where. Now the Catholics have to build one of their churches practically across the street!"

Grandmother Blake had been almost apoplectic since the 22nd of June when a priest dressed in white vestments had led a procession down Butler Street, past Allen Street, to the vacant lot between Lawrence Alley and Wainwright Street to lay the cornerstone for the new St. Augustine's Catholic Church. Since that Sunday almost two weeks ago, she had talked of little else, and her ire was rekindled anytime she saw people visiting the site.

"You mark my words," said Grandmother Blake, "next thing you know, we'll be surrounded by Paddies and Papists."

"I wouldn't worry too much, Mother," said Mrs. Ambrose. "The way this war is going, it will be a long time before they can raise the money to actually build a church."

For over a week, the newspapers had carried reports of the fighting on the Peninsula, and the news, so hopeful in the spring, was increasingly bad. At great loss of life and materials, the Union army had been repulsed from the very doorstep of Richmond and was now being pushed down the length of the Peninsula by a determined Rebel force.

Clara knew Garrett's regiment was in the midst of the heaviest fighting. And there was still no word from Dr. Ambrose, who was with the 27th Pennsylvania in northern Virginia. Desperate for news, she had taken to riding the streetcar into Pittsburgh twice a day to scan the casualty lists and check the post office for letters.

"Here comes Clara," Grandmother Blake announced. She made a disapproving clucking sound. "Laura, you simply must speak to that girl about her deportment. She's much too old to be running in the streets."

"Mother!" gasped Clara as she burst in the door waving an envelope. "A letter! A letter from Father!"

"Oh, thank God," said Mrs. Ambrose. She took the grimy envelope from Clara and tore it open. After reading a few lines, her face went pale.

"Mama? What is it?" Clara reached for her mother's hand. It was ice cold. Without a word, her mother handed her the letter.

June 10, 1862

Dear Loved Ones:

Do not be alarmed when you read this note. I am in reasonably good health and out of harm's way, for the moment.

Yesterday, in a fierce battle that took place around the town of Cross Keys, Virginia, in the valley of the Shenandoah River, the Rebel army overtook our position, including the field hospital. Along with a number of wounded soldiers who couldn't be moved, I was taken prisoner. They have treated me well enough, giving me such rations as they themselves have. I am assured of being released soon, as both armies have agreed to consider members of the medical corps as noncombatants. Still, I can't say exactly when I will return, as there are so many wounded men here to care for, Union and Confederate.

The honorable officers of the Rebel medical corps allowed me to get this note off to you so you would not worry, but I will probably not be able to write to you again until after my release. Until then, take care of each other. I will be in touch with you as soon as possible.

> *All my love,*
> *Peter*

"Oh, Mama," said Clara.

Mrs. Ambrose raised terrified eyes to her daughter. "This letter was written almost a month ago. Why haven't we heard anything else? Why haven't they let him go?"

"I don't know, Mama," said Clara. "I imagine it's difficult to get a letter through enemy lines. For all we know, Father could already be released and safe in a Union camp."

"Then why hasn't he contacted us?" asked Mrs. Ambrose in a trembling voice.

"I don't know," repeated Clara, "but I'll find out."

* * *

Early the next morning, Clara stood across the street from the local recruiting office. A large banner over the doorway urged, *Come In Out Of The Draft*, and a goodly number of men milled about outside, apparently trying, like her, to gather the courage to go in.

In expectation of the North's imminent capture of the Rebel capital at Richmond, most Federal recruiting offices had been closed by order of the Secretary of State in April of 1861. As a result of McClellan's failed Peninsula Campaign, however, the recruiting offices were hastily reopened. Lincoln sent out a call for 300,000 more three-year volunteers in July of 1862, which would be followed by a call for an additional 300,000 nine-month volunteers in August. But, the increasing casualty toll from the battlefields was having a significant dampening effect on the patriotic fervor of those men not in uniform, and these quotas were proving difficult to fill.

To spur recruitment, the Federal government took a two-pronged approach. A bounty would be paid in advance to any man who volunteered to serve. In case that enticement didn't work, however, the legislature passed a law defining the state militia as all able-bodied men between the ages of eighteen and forty-five, and empowered the president to call the militia into service if the most recent quota for volunteers was not met. Men *recruited* in this way would not receive a bounty.

This combination of carrot and stick appeared to be working, for Clara could see the recruiting office was filled with men who apparently had decided it was better to volunteer and receive a bounty than receive nothing in a quasi-draft.

Clara took a deep breath, gathered up her skirts, and hurried across the dusty street. In the doorway of the recruiting office, she paused, ignoring the curious looks of the men. There was a long line of volunteers waiting in front of a desk at which a young lieutenant was busy taking down names and information. Employing her sweetest smile, Clara strode to the front of the line.

"Excuse me, Sir," she said. "I need to speak to the officer in charge."

The lieutenant scrambled to his feet.

"Yes, Miss. May I ask the nature of your request?" His eyes traveled from her face, down to her bosom, and back. Clara didn't care. He could look all he wanted if it meant she could obtain some information about her father.

"I'm trying to locate my father, Major Peter Ambrose. He's a surgeon with the 27th Pennsylvania Volunteers. He was recently captured by the Confederates in the Shenandoah Valley and is supposed to have been exchanged. Only, no one's heard from him in some time. I need to find out where he is."

"I'm sorry, Miss, but I'm afraid we can't help you. This office has no power to obtain that kind of information."

Clara pressed her lips into a pretty pout. "But, surely your colonel would know someone who might be able to help me. Perhaps send a telegraphed message on my behalf?"

The young soldier seemed sincerely moved by both her distress and her flirting, but he shook his head.

"I'd like to help you, Miss, really I would. But you have no idea how many people come in here every day trying to locate loved ones. We have neither the authority nor the manpower to look into it. And the telegraph is reserved for military communications only. It's against regulations to use it for any other purpose. It'd mean my job."

Just then, the door behind the lieutenant opened and hearty laughter erupted from the inner office. Two officers of high rank emerged, flanking a well-dressed man in a top hat. They stopped and shook his hand vigorously.

"Glad to do business with you, Mr. Gliddon. And thank you for the fine cigars."

"It's the least I could do," said Edgar with a bow. As he straightened, he saw Clara standing at the desk. His look of surprise was quickly replaced by one of nonchalance.

"Why, Miss Ambrose. Come to enlist, have you?"

He was taken aback when Clara rushed to his side.

"It's my father," she blurted out without even saying hello. "We just received word he was captured by the Rebels at the beginning of June. He got a letter through to us saying they were planning to release him, but we've heard nothing since. Mother is undone, and I …." Her voice caught. She composed herself and glanced from the lieutenant to the two officers standing behind Edgar. "I'm having difficulty finding anyone willing to help me."

Edgar resisted the urge to reach out and wipe the lines of worry from her upturned face. He turned to the lieutenant behind the desk.

"Get me a piece of paper and a pen," he said in a tone that brooked no refusal.

"Yes, sir," replied the young officer.

Edgar guided Clara to a small table in the corner, out of earshot.

"Give me all the information you have on your father," he said as he sat in the chair opposite her. "His division, brigade, and regiment, when and where he was captured, and by whom, if you know it. Anything at all that might help locate him."

Quickly, Clara wrote down everything she could remember.

"What are you going to do?" she asked as she handed Edgar the sheet of paper.

Edgar smiled. "The officers here can't help you. They have no authority or influence outside this immediate area. But, my *lucrative position*, as you are so fond of putting it, gives me access to some highly-placed individuals in both the military and the government. If your father can be found, I will find him."

Clara's eyes filled with tears. "Thank you, Mr. Gliddon."

"You are quite welcome, my dear Miss Ambrose." Edgar reached out and placed his hand on hers.

She did not remove it.

Annie hurried into the darkened church and closed the door behind her. She was relieved to find the place empty. This morning, only five days after finding Gabriel's name on the casualty list from the battle of Gaines' Mill, Garrett's letter had arrived informing her of Joe's death at the battle of Glendale. The grief unleashed by this latest news stunned her with its intensity. Loath to become the subject of gossip or pity, she had struggled to hide her tears from her friends and coworkers.

Dipping her hand in the holy water font, she made her way to the nave to the right of the altar and knelt before the statue of the Blessed Mother. The lights from the votive candles danced and blurred before her brimming eyes. She bowed her head and opened her heart.

Why? she asked as the anguish and anger spilled over. Why? Wasn't it enough that her brothers had been taken; first Daniel and now Gabriel? Wasn't it enough that her ma and da were crushed by grief over the sons they had lost, and worry over the two that remained in harm's way? Did Joe have to die, too?

She remembered that last day at the train station in Pittsburgh. Clutching the note he had sent, she had rushed there in hopes of finding him before the 9th Pennsylvania boarded the cars for Washington. She saw him before he saw her, his head above those of the other soldiers. He was searching the crowd with a worried expression. The joy that came over his face when at last he spotted her made her heart leap. He pushed his way through the throng to her side. They stood very close so as to be heard over the hiss of the train and the shouts of the departing soldiers.

"I was so afraid I wouldn't see you again," he said.

"I'm here," she said, out of breath from running. "I'm here."

With so much to be said, they both suddenly were struck dumb. Staring up at him, Annie realized how dear the sight of him had become to her, all the more dear for his leaving.

A bugle sounding assembly jolted them from their trance. Joe grabbed her by the hands and looked deep into her eyes.

"I wanted to tell you … to ask you …." He took a deep breath. "Annie Burke, will you wait for me?" His face was grim with the courage it had taken him to ask the question.

She answered without hesitation.

"I will, Joseph."

He took her in his arms and she stood on tiptoe to meet his kiss, a kiss that was filled with longing and promise.

She hadn't told anyone about that day; not her parents, not even Clara. She had held her vow close to her heart, afraid that to speak it aloud might extinguish the flame that had begun to burn. Had he returned, would that love have continued to grow? Now she would never know. And she wept for the death of that possibility, along with the universal tragedy of a young man's life cut short.

If only she could make some sense of it, she thought. If only she knew the reason for all the suffering that had occurred. Annie raised her tear-stained face to the statue. The image gave no answers, but she saw her own sorrow mirrored in the pocked plaster countenance of the saint.

Garrett leaned his back against a wooden crate on the dock at Harrison's Landing and balanced a sheet of writing paper on the knapsack in his lap. The August heat was oppressive and he watched with envy as a white gull with black-tipped wings rode a current of air amid the masts and stacks of the sailing boats and steamers waiting at dockside. These vessels were part of the flotilla of ships that, daily, were transporting McClellan's dispirited army back up the Chesapeake Bay and Potomac River to Washington.

After the Battle of Glendale in which Joe was killed, the Union army had made one last stand at a place called Malvern Hill, a sixty-foot high hill flanked by deep ravines. Despite the Federals' obviously superior defensive position atop this steep incline, the Rebels staged yet another frontal attack in hopes of overwhelming them by sheer numbers. But again, miscommunication among Lee's generals caused the attacks to occur piecemeal. Most of the Rebel troops were cut down by Union artillery before they even came under fire by the infantry.

Despite the disproportionate losses by the Confederate army – 5,300 casualties to the Union's 3,200 – McClellan did not follow up this victory, either. Instead, he used the time it bought him to complete his move to Harrison's Landing. Then, while his army waited in relative safety beneath the protective firepower of the gunboats on the James River, he petitioned Lincoln for 50,000 additional troops with which to launch a new campaign.

By the first of August, Garrett and the men of the 9th Pennsylvania Reserves had been at Harrison's Landing for almost a month. The senseless waiting after the senseless fighting had Garrett in a particularly dark mood. When the gull he was watching suddenly wheeled away, he returned to the letter he was writing to Clara.

> *We were so close to Richmond, only a few miles away. Now we sit here and cower from the Rebels. We fought well and we lost so many good men – Joe, probably Caleb – for what?*
>
> *President Lincoln was here on the 8th of July, I suppose to see for himself what had become of his army. He met with Little Mac, and word is neither of them looked very happy afterwards. There are even rumors that McClellan may be relieved of command. In any event, the decision has been made to return the entire army to the outskirts of Washington. They're loading some of the troops on transports even as I write. The 9th has been at the tail end of this retreat since we left Mechanicsville. I imagine we'll probably be the last ones out of here, as well.*
>
> *Still, I know I shouldn't complain. So many of our boys will never see home again. And there are so many wounded. They're piled up on the docks and lie about in every open area. Their suffering is a pity to behold. Of the soldiers that are not wounded, nearly one quarter are sick from the months spent in the heat and damp of this cursed Peninsula. My own regiment is reduced to less than four hundred men.*
>
> *Clara, don't ever let anyone tell you there is glory in war. The things I've seen – and done – over the last few weeks can only be described as horrific, if they can be described at all. I still believe the war had to be fought, but there's no glory in it. It's a senseless, random waste of lives. Sometimes I just want to walk away from it all, lay down my arms, and come home to you. But, I could not do that to my comrades – or myself. I pray God will give me the strength to do my duty and will grant me the divine favor of returning home safely to you.*
>
> *But, I wonder, when I do come back, will you still want the man I have become?*

Clara lowered the sheet of paper to her lap. She had wept with relief when Garrett's letter finally arrived, but the tone of his words frightened her. She had never heard him like this, so filled with doubt, so despairing. But, then, his mood mirrored that of the North as a whole. The people had monitored the disintegration of the Army of the Potomac's march on Richmond in the press, and were confused and angered by what appeared to be McClellan's inability to lead his army to victory. The spirit of the country, so high in the spring, had plummeted.

One need go no farther than downtown Pittsburgh to see the tangible evidence of the Union army's difficulties. Every day the steamboats and trains arrived, filled with the dead and wounded from battlefields in the south and the west. More and more mothers, wives, and daughters walked the streets clothed in shades of mourning, living proof of the personal toll the war was exacting.

Clara sighed. The whole world seemed to be coming apart. George, Joe, and two of the Burke boys were dead, her father missing, and now, even Garrett – strong, steady, idealistic Garrett – seemed to have lost faith in the Union cause. Yet, the war continued with no end in sight. She, too, said a quick prayer to God for strength.

Clara trudged up the front walk to the house. The bundle of foodstuffs she was bringing home from the grocer was much smaller than she had hoped and she was at a loss to figure out how they would make it to the end of the month. She needed to come up with some way to supplement their income, and soon.

Once inside the relative coolness of the front hall, she set her bags down on the table. She removed her black crepe-trimmed bonnet and wiped her brow on the long, lawn cuff of her dress. It was depressing enough to be dressed in mourning, shrouded in black from head to toe, but the dark colors absorbed the heat of the August day like a sponge. Well, she thought, at least she didn't have to worry about the Pittsburgh soot spoiling her clothes. She was immediately ashamed. How dare she joke when her sister was heartbroken over George's death. Still, she thought, if she didn't laugh, she would cry. And, once started, she feared she might not stop.

"Clara! Clara!" Helen came running out of the parlor, the tortured mask she had worn since George's death lifted. "He's coming home! He's coming home!"

"Who?"

"Father! We just got a message from Mr. Gliddon. He was released a few weeks ago and is being sent home on medical furlough."

"Medical furlough? Is he all right?"

"The note says he's recovering from a touch of camp fever, whatever that is. But, he'll be here at the end of the week. Isn't it wonderful?"

In the parlor, Clara's mother was weeping with joy while little J.B. ran around her skirts in uncomprehending excitement. Even Grandmother Blake looked genuinely pleased at the prospect of having her son-in-law home at last.

The next Friday, Clara and Mrs. Ambrose stood fidgeting at the Penn Street station as the troop train pulled alongside the platform. Clara was touched to see the effort her mother had put into adorning her mourning clothes in as attractive a way as possible for her husband.

Soldiers began to leap from the train even before it came to a full stop. They rushed into the arms of waiting family members or hurried off to find them. Then the sick and wounded began to detrain, many of them holding tight to the arms of fellow soldiers.

"Where is he? Where is he?" fretted Mrs. Ambrose as even this group of soldiers began to thin.

Farther down the track, the doors of the last three cars stood open. A detail of soldiers was carefully unloading stretchers bearing the more severely injured.

"Maybe he's helping the wounded," said Clara. She and her mother hurried down the platform to the open door of the first of the cars.

"Step aside, please, Madam," said an orderly as he reached up to grab the poles at one end of a stretcher being eased from the train.

"Oh, my," said Mrs. Ambrose, holding her hand to her mouth. Wounded men, many of them missing arms and legs, or with their heads wrapped in heavy bandages, were being transferred from the train to waiting wagons for transport to hospitals. Here and there, family members stood weeping as what was left of their sons, husbands, and fathers was carried off the train.

Clara stepped closer to the car and peered inside at the triple tiers of litters that hung from the sides of the car.

"Can I help you, Miss?" asked a young officer, coming up behind her.

"Yes, I hope so. I'm looking for my father, Major Ambrose. He's a surgeon. He's supposed to be on this train."

"Major Ambrose? Yes. They should be bringing him off any minute, now."

"Bringing him off?" said Clara.

Just then, two soldiers carrying a man on a stretcher appeared in the doorway. The man was gaunt beneath his thin blanket and his features stood out prominently from his face. The gray of his complexion matched the gray in his beard, but his pale eyes twinkled ever so slightly when he spied Clara.

"Clara," he said softly.

"Father? Oh, Father!"

Clara fell upon him, her tears anointing his cheek. A loud cry behind her caused her to lift her head just in time to see her mother slump to the floor of the platform.

With his brows knit in concentration, Dr. Todd emerged from Dr. Ambrose's room. Mrs. Ambrose led him downstairs to the parlor where Clara and Helen waited.

"I'm glad you're all here," said the doctor as he closed the parlor doors behind him. "I've examined your husband carefully, Mrs. Ambrose, and have reached a conclusion in which he concurs. The so-called camp fever from which he suffers is actually typhoid fever. Frankly, given his age, it's remarkable he's survived this long. I've seen many a man, younger and stronger than he, succumb to this type of disease."

"But, there's treatment?" said Mrs. Ambrose.

"There are various treatments recommended – alum, bleeding, opium, calomel – each with varying success. But, I believe the most effective treatment is a good diet, rest, and quiet."

"For how long?" asked Clara.

"It's hard to say. Months, at least. And you should know he may never regain his full health."

Helen gave a small whimper. Clara put her arm around her.

"I wish I could give you better news," said Doctor Todd, picking up his black bag. "But, then, absent some unforeseen difficulty, he does appear to be out of immediate danger. That, at least, is something for which to be thankful."

"Yes, of course," said Mrs. Ambrose. "It's everything. Thank you, Doctor."

"Let me see you to the door," said Clara. Once they were out of her mother's hearing, she tugged at the man's sleeve. "Doctor Todd, are you saying my father may never be able to work again?"

"Miss Ambrose, let me be blunt. Your father continued to treat the sick at that prison hospital long after he should have been bedridden himself. By all rights, he should have died. If he is ever able to practice again – and it's doubtful – it will not be for a very long time. I'm sorry."

"Thank you, Doctor," she managed. She closed the door behind him and rested her head against it. Her poor father. His work was his life. He would be heartbroken if he knew. Well, they just wouldn't tell him, she decided. Perhaps he would prove Doctor Todd wrong.

But, it wasn't just her father's physical and emotional state that troubled Clara. Financially, the family was on the brink of disaster. Their savings were almost gone and as mercenary as it sounded, without her father's income the family could not survive. They had barely been making ends meet as it was and now there would be the additional costs of the medicine and care her father would require. As the widow of a soldier killed in the service of his country, Helen had applied to receive George's military pension. But she had been informed it could be months or even years until she received any payment. Their father's claim would take at least that long. How were they going to manage in the meantime?

Clara lingered in the hallway. She didn't want to return to the parlor and the needy, questioning eyes of her mother and sister until she had formulated some plan. There had to be something she could do, some way to keep the family going.

Suddenly, she felt a terrible sense of foreboding, of a malicious prophecy coming true. No, she thought, banishing the thought from her mind. There had to be some other way. There had to be.

But, how?

CHAPTER 18

ON AUGUST 16TH, 1862, THE 9th Pennsylvania Reserves regiment boarded the ships that would take them back up the Chesapeake Bay and the Potomac River to Aquia Creek. As Garrett predicted, they were one of the last groups to depart Harrison's Landing. Although they were happy to leave the Peninsula behind, the men were discouraged to be returning to the very place they had left two months ago with nothing to show for their efforts but a greatly reduced force. Of the 9,500 men of the Pennsylvania Reserves division that had sailed to the Peninsula in June of 1862, only about 6,000 battle weary veterans now climbed the gangplanks to return to northern Virginia.

The Reserves were returning to a newly reorganized army. As rumored, an exasperated Lincoln had relieved McClellan of command of the Army of the Potomac and ordered him to return it to northern Virginia where it would be rolled into the Army of Virginia under General John Pope's overall command.

While the Army of the Potomac slowly evacuated the Peninsula, Lee was not idle. Once certain McClellan had abandoned any plan to attack Richmond, Lee sent his army north in a planned offensive against Pope's Army of Virginia. From mid-July and throughout the month of August, the Confederates harassed Pope's army in a number of small battles and raids. A frustrated General Pope sent out an urgent call to the returning Army of the Potomac for help.

The response he received was less than enthusiastic. McClellan and many of his generals, unhappy at having to serve under Pope, delayed at the docks in Alexandria, Virginia, while McClellan argued that he, McClellan, was better used in the defense of Washington. Pope, he said, could "get out of his scrape by himself."

One of the few exceptions to this military foot dragging was the Pennsylvania Reserves division. Immediately upon receiving Pope's call for reinforcements, General John Reynolds, who had replaced General McCall as commander of the division after McCall was captured at the Battle of Glendale, led the Pennsylvania Reserves on a five-day forced march to Manassas, where the Army of Virginia was about to engage the enemy.

"Where we headed in such a hurry?" asked Rawlie as they pushed their way northwest. "I haven't had a decent meal since before we left the Peninsula."

"The general says we move, we move," said Frank.

Having disembarked at Aquia Creek only three days before, the men had little time to stock up on supplies. Soon, their rations were depleted and they resorted to eating green fruit and herbs found along the way. Chewing on a handful of dandelion leaves, Garrett was amazed at how the human body could continue to function with so little food. Time was of the essence, however, for it appeared the battle had already begun near the site of the old Bull Run battlefield.

The hard-marching Pennsylvania Reserves division reached the scene of the first clash on August 29th too late to participate in any significant fighting. They were instructed to take up position on the extreme left of the Union line and prepare for action in the morning.

By company, the exhausted men clustered around a commissary wagon that was handing out rations of hardtack and salt pork.

"Nice of you Pennsylvania boys to show up," said a soldier dressed in the blue braided jacket, sash, and billowy red pants of the 5th New York Zouaves. "Don't know that we're gonna be needin' you, though. Pope trapped old Stonewall's boys behind a railroad grade this mornin'. Poured it into 'em good. By midday, they'd 'bout had it and started pullin' back. " He smirked. "Tomorrow, we're gonna send 'em back to Richmond with their tails twixt their legs." He finished filling his own haversack, tipped his cap, and headed back to his own company.

Garrett and Rawlie exchanged looks.

"If we made that march for nothing …." grumbled Rawlie.

"After that damn Peninsula, 'nothing' would suit me just fine," said Leonard.

As the men slept on their arms that night, Rawlie leaned over to Garrett.

"Aren't we awfully close to where we saw those graves last spring?" he whispered.

"Looks like it," said Garrett.

"Damn," said Rawlie softly.

The next morning, General Pope renewed his attack. He sent row after row of Union troops against the center of Jackson's line. From their position on the left, the men of the Pennsylvania Reserves division could hear the sound of this fierce fighting to the north. Confederate resistance was strong and by late afternoon the call went out for Union reinforcements. Despite reports that Longstreet had arrived in force and was massing on the Union's left flank, an unconvinced General Pope ordered the Pennsylvania Reserves to leave the left and come to the support of the faltering attack.

At approximately 6:00 p.m., not long after the Pennsylvania Reserves had vacated their position and hurried north to aid the Union thrust in the center, Confederate General Longstreet, who had, in fact, arrived the previous day, launched his assault. He sent all five of his divisions, some 30,000 men, smashing into the now-weakened left flank of the Union line, effectively annihilating the 1,100 men of the two Zouave regiments – the 5th and the 10th New York – who had been left behind to defend it.

Longstreet's men then swept northeast with the intent of overpowering the Union forces before they could cross Bull Run Creek. Their progress was slowed by the hasty return of the Pennsylvania Reserves division and parts of other Union corps. Over the next hour and a half, the Federal troops fought a desperate rearguard action. They finally stopped the Rebel advance at Henry House Hill, the site of so much fighting at the First Battle of Bull Run.

Twilight was descending as the sounds of the firing faded away, at last. Breathing heavily, Garrett turned to find Rawlie, Frank, and Leonard still beside him in the regiment's ragged battle line. They nodded back at him and the relief in their exhausted, powder-streaked faces mirrored his own. Garrett looked out over the darkening battlefield. The number of dead and wounded of both armies would have shocked him earlier in the war. Now, however, he felt only an overwhelming sense of sadness and waste. And anger. They had been ill-used this day. Their generals had failed them, and far too many soldiers had paid the ultimate price for that failure.

As night fell, Pope hurried his battered Army of Virginia east, closer to the safety of the defenses around Washington. A final attempt by Jackson's forces to circle north and get behind the retreating Federal army was thwarted when an outnumbered Federal rearguard, fighting at night in a fierce thunderstorm, managed to stop the Rebels at a place near Chantilly, Virginia, known as Ox Hill. Only the unyielding bravery of these Union troops prevented a repeat of the rout that had marked the First Battle of Bull Run.

The exhausted Confederate army pursued them no further.

Sunrise on September 2nd, 1862, found the 9th Pennsylvania Reserves regiment camped on Upton Hill near Arlington Heights on the outskirts of Washington. The men of the Pittsburgh Rifles brooded around their campfire. The Union army had suffered its second defeat to the Confederates on the battlefield of Bull Run. Now the men waited, worn out and demoralized, for what would come next.

"This is the same goddamned place we left six months ago," grumbled Rawlie.

Garrett realized he was right. They were only a few miles from Camp Pierpoint, the site of the Reserves' bivouac the previous winter.

"Yeah, but there were a lot more of us then," said Frank.

Approximately 652 men of the Pennsylvania Reserves division had been killed, wounded, or missing in the Second Battle of Bull Run, which left an effective force of just over 5,000 men. The total casualties for both the Union and the Confederate armies in this battle were 25,000 men – five times the number of killed, wounded, or missing in the First Battle of Bull Run. Unconceivable losses a year ago, they were becoming shockingly commonplace as the meat grinder of the Civil War continued to churn.

As the men of the 9th Pennsylvania waited on Upton Hill for orders, the mail wagon miraculously arrived. A letter was never more cherished than the one that arrived for Garrett from Clara that day. He took it back to read by the fire. Wanting to savor the moment, he first poured himself a cup of coffee and crumbled some hardtack into it. Within moments, the weevils floated to the top. Garrett skimmed them off with the side of his finger, took a long sip, and opened the letter. It was dated almost three weeks earlier, the very day they had left the Peninsula. At least, Garrett thought with chagrin, Clara would not have known of this latest defeat when she wrote it.

August 16, 1862

Dearest Garrett,

Father was returned to us yesterday. They carried him off the train on a stretcher. He contracted something they called "camp fever" while working in a Rebel hospital. He is much reduced in body from his ordeal, but not in spirit. We are so happy to have him home, although the doctors tell us it will be a long convalescence. Mother does not leave his side and even Grandmother Blake is solicitous of his needs.

We are managing as well as can be expected. I know our hardships are nothing as compared to those you endure. Although we are far from the fighting, we see the signs everywhere. Day and night, the streets are filled with soldiers awaiting transport, but the very trains and steamers that will bear them off to war must first be offloaded of their cargo of sick and wounded soldiers returning from the Army of the Cumberland and the Army of the Potomac. I understand now why Father was so unmoved by the brash parades that accompanied the outbreak of the war. He knew what was coming.

    I am sorry to sound so grim. There are certainly many light moments in our lives. J.B. is walking and into everything. He delights in grabbing onto Grandmother's wheelchair and pushing her along, which drives her to distraction. The Burke family has turned their home into a boarding house to make ends meet and seem to be making a go of it. Annie tells me entertaining stories of the girls with whom she works at the Arsenal. How she can keep such a positive outlook in the face of all she has lost, I don't know, but I admire her greatly for it. If her Joe had survived Glendale, but you had not, I do not know that I could be so generous of spirit.

    And I – I am well physically, but missing you with all my heart. I'm hoping you're now close to Washington and away from the constant danger that threatened you on the Peninsula. I gaze at the picture in the locket you gave me until I fear the image will be worn away. And I remember the promise symbolized by the lilac sprig. I give you my promise, too, dearest Garrett. Please know that I shall love you forever, no matter what has happened or what is to come.

Clara

    Garrett reread the letter carefully. Clara's declaration of love soothed his heart, almost as if she had taken him in her arms. And he was happy to hear Dr. Ambrose had survived his camp fever. Garrett knew many men who had not. But, he could tell things were not well in the Ambrose home, more from what Clara didn't say than from what she did. Clara, always so indomitable, seemed … despondent. Fragile.

    Suddenly, a shout went up from the company next to them. A young soldier came running down the ragged tent row.

    "Did you hear? Did you hear?" he shouted.

    "No. What?"

    "McClellan's back. Lincoln kicked Pope out and brought back Little Mac." He galloped off to spread the news.

    "I swear," said Leonard. "This army changes commanders more than I change my underdrawers."

    Frank snorted. "That's not saying much."

    Lincoln had made a difficult choice. Despite McClellan's failure to fight on the Peninsula, and what some called his treasonous inaction at the Second Battle of Bull Run, Lincoln realized McClellan was the only man who could breathe life into the demoralized Union army.

The simple fact was McClellan made the men feel like soldiers; they loved him for it, and would follow where he led. In placing McClellan back in command of the army, Lincoln explained to his detractors, "We must use what tools we have."

McClellan promptly set about reorganizing the army. He integrated the Army of Virginia back into a reorganized Army of the Potomac, and quickly absorbed the new regiments that had been raised during Lincoln's July and August calls for volunteers. The Pennsylvania Reserves division now found themselves assigned to the First Corps under General Joseph Hooker.

What the Union soldiers didn't realize was that McClellan's reinstatement as commander of the Army of the Potomac was initiated, not so much because of McClellan's skill, but because of Pope's ineptitude. And because, once again, General Lee was on the move.

Clara spent the week following her father's return making the rounds of the banks in Pittsburgh and Allegheny City. Though many of the bank officers acknowledged her father's dedicated service to the community and to the country, none of them were willing to extend credit to the Ambrose family "under the current circumstances." Her search for work as a nurse, teacher, or even a clerk was equally fruitless. At each place she inquired, her request was greeted with mild shock and amusement, and she was turned away with the polite explanation that they were not in the habit of hiring women. Trudging home after her fourteenth rejection, Clara had to admit she was out of options.

Clara arranged the meeting for early afternoon the following Monday, a time when she knew Helen would be out with J.B. and Grandmother Blake for their daily walk, and her mother would be reading to her father in his room. She watched out the window for the carriage and opened the door before the bell rang.

"Thank you for coming," said Clara. "Please, join me in the parlor."

Edgar, amused at her formal tone and her haste, followed her into the room. He raised a questioning eyebrow when she closed the pocket doors behind them.

"I want to be sure we're not disturbed," she explained. "What I have to say is for your ears alone."

"I'm intrigued," said Edgar.

Clara took a seat in her mother's chair and folded her hands. Edgar sat across from her.

"First, I wanted to thank you once again for helping to locate my father," said Clara. "I don't think he would have survived much longer in captivity. Your intervention may very well have saved his life."

"I'm just glad some of my military contacts came through," said Edgar.

"And, it was most kind of you to send Dr. Todd over to care for him," Clara continued. "As you know, my mother is very particular about doctors and ... well, he, too, was the answer to a prayer."

"Again, I was happy to be of service."

Clara paused and shifted in her seat. Edgar waited.

"After all you've done, it's difficult for me to ask you this ...." Clara took a deep breath. "But, I'm afraid we need your help once more."

"Oh?" said Edgar.

"According to Dr. Todd, my father's condition is very serious. He expects him to recover, but perhaps not completely, and not for a very long time."

"I'm sorry to hear that," said Edgar, his face a study in concern. He, of course, knew all of this from his discussion with Dr. Todd, just as he knew from his friends in the business community of Clara's unsuccessful attempts at finding employment. However, he waited patiently for her to make her case.

"As I know you are aware, Mr. Gliddon, my family's financial condition has gotten progressively worse over the course of the war, due in part to the unpredictability of both my brother-in-law's and my father's military pay. Now that it appears Father will not be returning to work for the near future, it falls upon me to find another way to meet my family's economic needs." Clara hesitated. "So, I wanted to present you with a proposition."

"Oh?" said Edgar. Victory was so close he could taste it.

Clara drew herself up tall. "I would like to ask you for a loan."

"I beg your pardon?"

"A loan," repeated Clara. "Just to tide us over until Father regains his health, or until the military pensions come in. I would pay you back, of course, at a rate of interest better than you could get through any bank. Granted, it may take some time, but I promise you, I will make good on the debt. You have my word."

"A loan?" said Edgar. "You're serious."

"Very," said Clara.

Edgar stood and walked over to the fireplace. His shoulders began to shake with laughter.

"I fail to see what is so amusing," said Clara in affront.

"You," said Edgar. He turned to face her. "You are amusing in the extreme. Do you really think I want money from you? I have money."

"I'm afraid that's all I have to offer," said Clara.

Edgar's smile faded. "We both know that's not true."

Clara felt a flutter of fear, but she kept her expression impassive.

Edgar folded his arms. "Miss Ambrose, I'm curious. You know me. I've been very clear about my intentions. And my expectations. What made you think I would ever agree to such an *impersonal* arrangement?"

Clara bowed her head for a moment. When she looked up at him, her heart was in her eyes.

"I was hoping to appeal to your better nature," she said.

Only years of bluffing at industry bargaining tables enabled Edgar to maintain his composure. That she thought him capable of such self-lessness surprised and touched him. No one had thought him possessed of such goodness for a very long time. It almost made him want to justify her faith in him. But, if he did – if he gave her what she asked with no strings attached; relinquished the only power he had over her – what guarantee had he that she would come to him of her own free will?

The smile he gave her was more self-deprecating than cruel. "Ah, now, there's where you've made your mistake. You see, my dear, I have no better nature."

Clara's crestfallen look hurt more than he anticipated. He turned toward the mantle and made a show of smoothing his hair in the looking glass above it. "There is, of course, another solution," he said. "One that appears acceptable – even desirable – to everyone but you."

Clara lowered her head. Edgar watched her reflection and thought he saw her hands tremble.

"No, Mr. Gliddon," she said, looking up at last. Her eyes were clear and determined. "I have made you the only offer I can."

He was stunned by the depth of his disappointment, almost as if he had taken a physical blow. Yet the wound to his ego was nothing compared to the wound to his heart. And as her decision hung in the air between them, he realized, with sudden clarity, that in his effort to win Clara, he had actually allowed himself to fall in love with her. Had loved and had been rejected. He could almost laugh at himself had the pain not been so acute. He struggled to maintain his composure. Finally, he turned to face her.

"Then I'm afraid, Miss Ambrose, without more … incentive, I will be unable to aid you or your family. Now, or in the future."

Clara jutted her chin. "Then I shall just have to find another way."

"What other way?" Edgar jeered, his anger rising. "You've already discovered no bank will accept such ridiculous terms. No reputable concern will hire you. And your father's friends are all poverty-stricken immigrants or penniless abolitionists. Face reality, Miss Ambrose. I am the only one who can help you." He paused. "And you know my terms."

The two locked eyes as the clock on the mantel ticked away the seconds. Finally, Clara stood.

"Your terms are unacceptable, Mr. Gliddon. I'm sorry to have wasted your time." She turned to leave.

"Has he asked you to marry him?"

Clara froze. Slowly, she turned back around. Edgar stood with one elbow resting on the mantel; his expression, like his voice, was sardonic.

"I beg your pardon?" she said.

"Mr. Cameron," said Edgar. "Has he proposed marriage?"

"That is none of your business," sputtered Clara.

"Then I can only assume he has not. So, you would risk your father's life and possibly your family's, to save yourself for a man who has not even asked you to marry him. A man who may never ask you to marry him, even if he does come back."

"Garrett will come back," said Clara. "He promised me. Just as he promised me his love."

Edgar scoffed. "He has no control over the first promise, my dear. And you have no control over the second."

Clara's eyes flashed with anger. "Mr. Gliddon, I no longer wish to discuss this with you." She turned on her heel. Edgar was across the room in a flash. He grabbed her by the shoulders and spun her around, his face thunderous.

"I will not be dismissed by you, Miss Ambrose," he growled. "For two years I have waited for you to grow up. I've put up with your slights and insults, even endured your pathetic schoolgirl crush on your boy soldier. But, I'm done wasting my time. If you will not come to me of your own accord, even after all I've done for you and your family, I shall take matters into my own hands."

He grabbed her about the waist and pulled her to him roughly. Before she could protest, he covered her mouth with his. His tongue forced her lips apart and Clara thought she would choke on the taste of cigars and desire.

"How dare you!" she cried, pushing him away. She raised her arm to slap him, but he caught her by the wrist. What she saw in his eyes made her sick with fear. Desperately, she sought a way to defuse the situation.

"Mr. Gliddon," she said as fought back her panic, "my father and mother are both right upstairs."

His smile was feral. "Your father is too weak to get out of bed and your mother would never think of intruding. I'm everything she's ever wanted for you."

"I could have you arrested."

"You could try. But whom do you think they'd believe? A well-respected pillar of the community, or a desperate young woman, fallen on hard times, crying rape to force a monetary settlement. Really, Miss Ambrose, it's the oldest ploy in the world. And, even if anyone did believe you, your reputation would be destroyed. There's not a respectable man in the country who would have you after such a scandal. And, I dare say that includes the saintly Mr. Cameron. So, you see, I will have you willingly or unwillingly. But I will have you."

Clara's astonishment momentarily stayed her fear. "I had no idea you could sink to such depths."

Edgar smiled. "I told you a long time ago, Miss Ambrose. I always get what I want."

Clara made a move to run from the room, but he retained his hold on her wrist and yanked her back.

"Let me go!" she cried, pushing at him with all her strength.

But Edgar put one arm around her waist and the other behind her head. Grabbing a fistful of her hair, he pulled her head back and smothered her mouth with his. He pushed her onto the divan and fell on top of her, pinning her with his weight. She felt his hands moving over her body, down her neck to her bosom, fumbling at the crinolines beneath her hoop. She tried to struggle, but realized in rising horror that she could not control him, could not stop him.

"Mr. Gliddon!" cried a loud voice.

Startled, Edgar pushed himself up on his hands. There, in the doorway, stood Mrs. Ambrose. She held her husband's Colt revolver pointed directly at his head. The color drained from Edgar's face.

"Sir," she said with an icy calm, "you will release my daughter and leave this house at once."

"Mrs. Ambrose," said Edgar, hastily getting to his feet, "allow me to explain. This is not as it appears. It was just youthful passion; a momentary lapse of judgment."

Clara, red-faced and teary-eyed, leapt from the couch and attempted to straighten her disheveled clothing.

Mrs. Ambrose seemed not to hear him. "My daughter tried to warn me about you, Mr. Gliddon, but I wouldn't listen. You, Sir, are a scoundrel of the worst kind."

Edgar smoothed his hair and straightened his jacket.

"See here, my good woman …."

"You are mistaken, Mr. Gliddon," interrupted Mrs. Ambrose. Her voice was cold and steady. "I am not a 'good woman.' I am a mother protecting her child. And, rest assured, if you ever go near my daughter again, I will blow your head off."

"You ungrateful witch," Edgar snapped. "How dare you threaten me!" He took a step toward Mrs. Ambrose, but stopped abruptly when she pulled back the hammer of the revolver.

"I said, leave this house. Now!" Her eyes never left Edgar's face.

Edgar hesitated, uncertain as to just what this obviously unstable woman might do. "You will regret this," he growled finally. Without even glancing at Clara, he strode out of the room. A moment later, the front door slammed.

"Oh, Mama," sobbed Clara. She rushed to her mother's side.

"Quick," said Mrs. Ambrose with the gun still trained on the door. "Check to see if he's gone."

Clara hurried to the front window and peeked out the curtain. Edgar's carriage was just pulling away.

"He's gone," said Clara.

"Thank God," said Mrs. Ambrose. She lowered the heavy pistol with a shaky hand. "I didn't know how to load it."

"There are no bullets in the gun?" said Clara, incredulous.

Her mother shook her head.

"Oh, Mama," said Clara. Laughing and weeping, she collapsed into her mother's arms. Her mother held her and stroked her hair for a long time.

Edgar stormed into his office only to find James Percy seated in one of the chairs. He had his feet up on the desk and was smoking one of Edgar's expensive cigars.

"Get your goddamn shoes off my desk, Percy," snarled Edgar.

"My, my. We *are* in a foul temper," said James. "Don't tell me the war is over?"

Edgar walked behind his desk and shoved aside some papers. "What do you want? I'm a busy man."

"Yes, you are, so I'll come right to the point." James leaned forward. "I understand Gliddon Iron Works has just signed a contract with the government for an additional two million feet of iron rails."

Edgar raised an eyebrow. "My, your spies have been busy, James. The ink's barely dry on that one."

James smiled. "You're not the only one who has people in high places. I also understand the government wants those rails immediately, if not sooner."

"So?"

"So ...," James pointed at Edgar with his cigar, "you're going to need a lot more coal, in a hurry, to fuel your increased production. I'm here to tell you that the Percy Coal Company is prepared to provide that coal to you for just a slight increase over our previously contracted price." He took a long puff and waited for Edgar's response.

Edgar turned toward the window of his office and gazed down the Allegheny to where it met the Monongahela at the point in downtown Pittsburgh. All along the shoreline of the river, factories churned and flared. Skies blackened by smoke reflected the orange glow of the furnaces, as if the core of the earth itself had burst open in a hundred places to spew molten lava to the heavens. The scene exactly matched his mood. He turned back to Percy and smiled.

"James, you are a shrewd man, but not shrewd enough. Do you really think I would put myself in a position to be blackmailed by you, or anyone else?" Edgar lifted the lid of his wood and brass humidor, selected a cigar, and let the lid slam shut. He lit his cigar with deliberate care, noting with satisfaction that the smug look on James' face had been replaced by one of apprehension. Edgar blew a lazy smoke ring into the air. "I have already contracted with two coal companies – competitors of yours, I believe – that will provide me all the fuel necessary to meet my government contracts. At three-quarters of the cost I currently pay the Percy Coal Company, I might add."

"That's not true," said James. "I would have heard of it."

"But, you didn't," said Edgar. He blew another smoke ring. "Really, James. You need to get some better informants. Still, I'm glad you came here today. You saved me the trouble of having to contact you to let you know the services of the Percy Coal Company will no longer be required."

James sat up in his chair. "You can't do that, Gliddon. We have a contract."

"Then I guess you'll just have to take me to court. Hopefully, you'll be able to stay in business until that long drawn-out process is completed. The last time I had lunch with my friends in the judiciary, they told me there was a frightful backlog."

James leaned forward. A light sheen of sweat had broken out on his upper lip.

"Listen, Edgar. Perhaps I have been a bit ... overreaching. The Percy Coal Company needs this contract. You know Gliddon Iron Works is the major part of our business."

"Yes, I do," said Edgar.

"Then, please, I'm asking you, as a friend. I'll do anything."

Edgar snorted. "A friend?" He waited, savoring the man's discomfort. After his humiliation at the Ambrose home, it felt good to strike out at someone. Although the one he really wanted to strike at was beyond his reach. Were it not for that impecunious do-gooder, Cameron, Clara would have been his long ago. He remembered Cameron's words the day he leaned into Edgar's carriage: *She prefers me.* He tasted acid in his mouth. Short of joining the Rebel army and shooting him, himself, there was no way he could get to Cameron. Or, was there?

Edgar smiled and turned to the ashen-faced Percy.

"Actually, James, there is something you can do for me." He walked over to the office door and closed it.

CHAPTER 19

ON THE NIGHT OF SEPTEMBER 4, 1862, the victorious Confederate Army of Northern Virginia, under the command of General Robert E. Lee, began its invasion of the North. Rebel hopes were high as the troops crossed the Potomac River at White's Ford and entered the fertile countryside of Maryland. They saw themselves as liberators of this border slave state and anticipated a warm welcome, as well as a much-needed influx of volunteers and supplies. The regimental bands struck up *Maryland, My Maryland* as they approached the towns and hamlets. But the people of western Maryland were decidedly less secession-minded than those of the tidewater area to the east, and the Confederates were disappointed to find most doors shut to them. Even those Marylanders who welcomed the Rebels were somewhat reserved, fearing the retribution of their Unionist neighbors.

The people's response was further inhibited by the physical appearance of the Rebel army. These soldiers did not look the part of the conquering heroes they had heard and read about. These men were lean and hungry from endless days of marching and fighting. Their filthy uniforms were in tatters and many were barefoot. More than one Maryland lady covered her nose with her handkerchief at the smell emanating from their ranks, and those would-be Rebels who had been considering joining up now thought twice. Pro-Union people were likewise shocked that these emaciated scarecrows were the ones who had so soundly and repeatedly defeated their boys in blue.

Increasingly disillusioned at their reception, the Confederate army marched on. The soldiers fed and clothed themselves from the bounty of the State of Maryland and paid for the food, animals, and goods with Confederate script. On September 7th, they entered the city of Frederick, Maryland, and promptly bought every pair of shoes in town.

Panic swept the North. Rumors flew that Lee was headed to Philadelphia, Baltimore, or Harrisburg. Washington, fearful Lee would yet turn and march on the capital itself, clamored for McClellan to take action. On the same day that Lee reached Frederick, McClellan's newly-reorganized Army of the Potomac left Washington in slow and cautious pursuit. They covered just six miles a day.

The Confederate invasion of Maryland had a direct impact on the leadership of the Pennsylvania Reserves. Governor Curtin of Pennsylvania, concerned about the Rebel presence so close to his state's border, requested the return of General John Reynolds to organize the state militia for the defense of the Commonwealth. Despite McClellan's opposition, the administration acquiesced and ordered Reynolds back to Pennsylvania. General George Meade was named to replace him as the commander of the Pennsylvania Reserves division.

The announcement was made to the men at morning roll call. Standing at attention, Rawlie muttered out of the corner of his mouth, "Hey, Leonard. Time to change your underwear again."

The old soldier's expression did not alter, but a relieved smile spread across Garrett's face. It was the first joke Rawlie had made since Joe's death.

Under their new commanding general, the Pennsylvania Reserves broke camp and joined the Union army's march north into Maryland. As they traveled up the Baltimore & Washington turnpike, their reception differed greatly from that received by the Confederates. All along the hot, dusty road, Union flags flew as Marylanders cheered their protectors. Farmers stopped at their labors to wave their hats, and their wives and children ran out to the road to give the soldiers cool water and fresh fruit. In the towns, it seemed everyone was cheering, waving the Stars and Stripes, and singing along as the regimental bands played *The Battle Cry of Freedom* and *The Girl I Left Behind Me*.

"Well, this is more like it," said Rawlie after a pretty girl in a flowered bonnet presented him with an apple and a quick kiss on the cheek. "This is the way to welcome the brave soldiers of the Union army."

"Don't get too high on yourself," said Leonard. "I heard the girls have even been kissing McClellan's horse."

"You know," mused Garrett, "after all the time we spent in Virginia, I'd almost forgotten what it was like to have people on your side."

"Well, this is one hell of a reminder," said Frank as he looked up at the open windows filled with joyous townspeople.

The massed drummers and fifers in front of the regiment struck up *The Battle Cry of Freedom* one more time, and the men of the 9th Pennsylvania Reserves marched to the music with a spring in their step and a renewed faith in their mission.

But as the Federal columns advanced northward, they did so under the watchful eye of General J. E. B. Stuart's Confederate cavalry. Based on the information received from Stuart, Lee devised a daring plan.

The Confederate march into Maryland had isolated the Federal garrison at Harper's Ferry, Virginia. This Federal stronghold, manned by some 10,500 Union troops, was a threat to Lee's supply line through the Shenandoah Valley. In addition, its well-stocked storehouses of supplies and ammunition presented a tantalizing target for the starving

Confederate army. Given McClellan's snail-like progress, Lee felt confident he could split his forces, send one branch to capture the Federal garrison, and still reunite his army before McClellan caught up with him.

On September 9th, Lee issued Special Orders 191, outlining his plan for his generals. The next day, the Rebel army began to move out of Frederick.

On September 13th, the leading edge of the Union army reached Frederick. They received a tumultuous welcome. McClellan, basking in the adulation of the crowd, ordered the army to halt while the supply trains caught up with the main body. The soldiers of the Army of the Potomac set up bivouac on the farms and fields surrounding the town, the very same ground so recently vacated by the Confederate Army of Northern Virginia. And at this point, Providence intervened.

Two soldiers of the 27th Indiana Volunteer regiment, sitting down to rest along a pasture fence outside of Frederick, discovered a piece of paper wrapped around three cigars. That piece of paper proved to be a copy of Special Orders 191, General Lee's detailed instructions to his generals revealing his plan to temporarily divide his forces.

McClellan was ecstatic at the find. At noon on September 13th, he sent a telegraph to President Lincoln in Washington: "I have the plans of the Rebels and will catch them in their own trap."

Yet, it was not until the next morning that the first of the Union troops set off west along the National Road toward South Mountain in pursuit of Lee's divided army – almost eighteen hours after Special Orders 191 were discovered.

Lee, waiting in the valley on the west side of South Mountain for news of the successful capture of Harper's Ferry, was surprised to learn of the Union army's unprecedentedly rapid approach. He ordered Major General D. H. Hill to defend the passes leading over South Mountain for as long as possible. This would enable the rest of the Rebel army to reunite and retreat west across the Potomac River to the safety of Virginia.

South Mountain was not a peak, but actually a long ridge that extended fifty miles from the Potomac River, north into Pennsylvania. There were two main passes over the mountain: Turner's Gap, where the National Road from Frederick crossed on its way to the town of Boonsboro at the western base of the mountain, and Crampton's Gap, six miles to the south. Hill's Confederates positioned themselves along the ridge, sighted their artillery for the approaches to the mountain, and waited for the arrival of the Union army.

In a long, trailing dust cloud, the men of the Pennsylvania Reserves, now part of the Third Brigade of Meade's Third Division of General Hooker's First Corps, marched along the National Road towards the town of Middletown. Garrett gazed up at the blue-gray outline of South Mountain looming ever larger in the distance. The day was hot, but the rolling countryside was beautiful; still green in mid-September with the reds and golds of autumn just beginning to touch the fields and hillsides.

At about 1:00 p.m., approximately two and a half miles west of Middletown, the First Corps halted on the banks of Catoctin Creek to await further orders. As soon as the men were released from their ranks, they scrambled to get water and wood for their cook fires. Garrett and Frank were assigned the task of refilling their mess's canteens. They threw themselves down by the edge of the stream and plunged their grimy faces in the cool water. With full canteens, they returned to the spot where they had stacked their rifles just as Leonard and Rawlie came over the rise of a pasture. They were carrying some kindling and what appeared to be a fence rail.

"Here, boys," said Rawlie, dropping the rail on the ground. "This oughta keep the fire burning."

"I hope that was the top rail," said Frank. "Orders came down that's all we're allowed to take."

"It was the top rail by the time I got there," said Rawlie. Leonard nodded in solemn agreement. Their sense of duty satisfied, the men started a fire with the kindling and began feeding the rail into it.

As they sat and drank their coffee, they could hear the steady boom of artillery and the faint clackety-clack of gunfire from the west. They watched as a growing cloud of smoke obscured the upper reaches of South Mountain.

"Sure sounds like somebody's catchin' hell," said Leonard as he took another sip from his battered cup.

"Who's up there?" asked Frank.

"Reno's Ninth Corps, I think," said Garrett.

"Think we'll be goin' in?" asked Rawlie.

"I expect so," said Frank.

Just after 2:00 p.m., the order came to march. Quickly, the Reserves doused their fires and gathered up their rifles. As they hurried through the heat and dust, ever closer to the mountain, the rattle of musketry was plainly audible between the short pauses in the artillery barrages.

The road rose steadily upward and the men, already damp with sweat from the warmth of the day, began to perspire freely from exertion and the nervous anticipation of battle.

As they ascended the eastern slope of the mountain, the soldiers frequently had to step aside to allow for the passage of ambulances heading down to the makeshift hospitals in Middletown and Frederick. They could hear the moans and cries of the wounded as the wagons jolted over the rough road, and noted the grisly trail of blood that dripped from the wagon beds to mark their passing. Grimly, the men marched on, the talk and laughter of the morning gone.

Finally, around 3:00 p.m., Hooker's First Corps reached the little hamlet of Bolivar, part way up the eastern side of the mountain. The ground here was rocky, steep, and divided into areas of pasture and heavy timber. The men could see small scattered brush fires, caused by sparks from the muskets, burning in the woods to their front.

The Pennsylvania Reserves were sent to the right along the small dirt Mount Tabor Road. This movement drew the attention of a Confederate battery positioned on the fifteen hundred foot crest of the mountain. The battery misjudged the range, however, and Garrett barely flinched as the cannon balls whistled harmlessly overhead. A Federal battery situated on a ridge farther down the mountain sent back an answering barrage.

Beneath this canopy of shot and shell, the Reserves continued their march until they reached a dirt track known as the Frosttown Road. Here, they deployed in line of battle, facing up the mountain, with the First Brigade on the right, the Third Brigade, including the 9th Pennsylvania Reserves regiment, in the center, and the Second Brigade on the left. The men of the 13th Pennsylvania Reserves regiment – the Bucktails – were lined up as skirmishers in front of the entire division.

The men stood shoulder to shoulder, rifles ready, awaiting the order to advance. Far to their left, the battle that had started early that morning continued with the rifle fire punctuated by the booming, screaming cannon. Sulfurous smoke drifted over the field and alternately hid and revealed the rival artillery batteries and columns of marching men in blue and gray.

Garrett's eyes swept the hillside in front of him for the places most likely to provide cover for the enemy. This part of the mountainside was mostly under cultivation or pasture, but it was dotted with large rocks and boulders, and the occasional stone wall. The ground was rugged, dipping and rising, but becoming ever steeper as it approached the crest of the mountain. A curved ravine cut through the open ground on a roughly east to west diagonal. Bordering this ravine on the downhill side was a cornfield and a small group of farm buildings. Beyond the ravine was another stone wall. Most ominous, however, was the rectangular wooded section halfway up the mountainside.

"That's where I'd be," muttered Rawlie, jerking his head in the direction of the stand of woods. "Tucked right behind a tree."

At approximately 4:30 p.m., the order was given to advance.

"Battalion!" shouted the colonel of the 13th Pennsylvania Reserves. "As skirmishers! On the center file! Take intervals! March!"

The Bucktails stepped off and spread out in front of the whole division.

The echoed commands of officers all along the line followed almost immediately.

"Right shoulder, shift! Arms! Forward! March!"

The three brigades of the Pennsylvania Reserves division advanced in double lines of battle and followed the skirmishers up the mountainside.

Almost immediately, the Bucktails came under heavy fire from sharpshooters from the 5th Alabama who lay waiting in the very woods Garrett and Rawlie had noted just moments before. A number of Union skirmishers fell dead or wounded. The remainder was forced to take cover or fall back to the main line.

"Close it up, boys!" shouted the Union officers over the bursts of artillery fire. "Quickly! Quickly!"

The Federal soldiers closed ranks and continued their advance. The blue lines swayed and bent as the men climbed through the rocks, swales, and underbrush. The Alabamans fired again and dropped almost thirty Federal soldiers. Still the Union troops came on and answered with a deadly volley of their own. They forced the Rebel sharpshooters to withdraw farther up the mountain, where they joined their comrades in their stronghold position behind the stone wall on the uphill side of the ravine.

Directly in front of Garrett's regiment, some skirmishers from the 3rd Alabama lay down a deadly fire from the shelter of the farm buildings in front of the ravine. Over the cacophony of musket fire and artillery, the 9th's colonel shouted to his men to take cover. The men scurried forward to reach the safety of some trees and a stone wall just downhill from the buildings.

"Come on!" yelled Garrett to the soldier next to him. He turned just in time to see the man's lower jaw completely shot away by a shell fragment. The man stared at Garrett in surprise, a gaping hole where his mouth had been. Then he fell away down the mountain.

Move! Garrett's mind screamed. *Move!* He scrambled on and dove behind the stone wall while the bullets whizzed overhead and ricocheted off the stones in front of him. Sweating profusely, he hunkered down with the rest of his regiment and waited for orders.

"Men, we must take that house," shouted the colonel over the crash of the artillery. "Attention, Battalion! Fire on my command. Ready! Aim! Fire!"

The men of the 9th Pennsylvania took aim at the flashes of musket fire and the darting shapes that appeared at the windows of the farmhouse. After twenty heated minutes, the 10th and 11th Pennsylvania Reserves arrived in support. The three regiments were able to surround the building and direct a devastating fire on the dwindling ranks of the enemy. Finally, what was left of the 3rd Alabama surrendered – just fifteen men, including their badly wounded colonel. Garrett stood and watched as a detail from the 9th escorted the prisoners down the mountain. He was struck by how young, how normal, how like him the enemy looked.

"Come on, Garrett," said Rawlie. "We're not done, yet."

The next objective to be taken was the stone wall farther up the hill on the far side of the ravine. The Rebels held a strong position there and the commander of the Third Brigade was determined to drive them from it. On his command, the 9th, 11th, and 12th Pennsylvania began fighting their way across the ravine toward the stone wall.

From the protection of a large boulder, Garrett paused to take aim at a Rebel soldier whose head was just visible over the top of the wall. He squeezed the trigger and the man lurched backward. Garrett reached into his ammunition pouch for another cartridge. It was almost empty.

"Hey, Rawlie," he shouted over the din of battle. "How many bullets you got left?"

Rawlie, firing from behind a slight rise, paused to check his cartridge box. "Not many," he yelled back.

A few yards away, Garrett spied a Union soldier crumpled behind a rock outcropping. With bullets whizzing by his ears, Garrett slid over to the body.

"Sorry, soldier," he said as he unhooked the dead man's cartridge and cap boxes, "but I need these a hell of a lot more than you do." At the last second, Garrett also took the Colt revolver from the man's waist belt and tucked it into his own.

All across the field, the men of the 9th Pennsylvania were taking ammunition from the fallen to supplement their rapidly dwindling supplies. Thus rearmed, they continued, ever so slowly, to drive the Rebels up the mountain.

Finally, as evening approached, the First Brigade of General Rickett's division arrived to relieve the men of the Pennsylvania Reserves. Exhausted, Garrett and his comrades stumbled down the mountain to regroup. When they reached the relative safety of the rear lines, they were ordered to refill their cartridge boxes from the supply wagons. Garrett waited in line and watched the battle play out on the mountainside. In the fading light, the flashes of gunpowder looked like fireflies on a summer's night. Only these fireflies were lethal.

Suddenly, Garrett heard a faint cry from far up the mountain.

"They're running! They're running!"

Sure enough, the Rebels were retreating, pulling back over the top of South Mountain. The cheering of the Union troops rolled down the hillside and was immediately swelled by the huzzahs of the men around him.

As Garrett raised his arm to join in the cheering, he became aware of a sharp stinging sensation in his left arm. He looked down to find a bullet had torn away a piece of his sack coat and shirt, and left an angry red furrow in the skin of his bicep.

Leonard came up beside him as he was examining the wound. "Pretty damn lucky to get out of that mess with just that little scrape."

Garrett nodded. "Pretty damn lucky."

In what became known as the Battle of South Mountain, ten percent of Meade's Pennsylvania Reserves division was killed, wounded, or missing. The 9th Pennsylvania Reserves regiment lost ten enlisted men killed, one officer wounded, and thirty-two enlisted men wounded. Garrett felt fortunate, indeed, to have suffered only a slight wound.

Despite their apparent victory, the Union troops spent a cold, hungry night on South Mountain. Still concerned about the size and location of the Rebel force, McClellan had forbidden the lighting of cook fires, and additional rations had not yet been brought up. The men ate what little food they had with them and huddled together for warmth. Their discomfort was greatly eased, however, by the knowledge that they had at last triumphed in battle. In the morning, they would pursue the fleeing Rebels. And for the first time in a long time, they felt they could defeat them.

Garrett spread his rubber poncho on the ground and wrapped himself in his blanket against the cool night air. The adrenalin had left his body and his limbs were heavy with exhaustion.

Suddenly, an officer loomed over him in the darkness.

"Sleeping on the job, Private Cameron?"

"Lieutenant Percy!" Garrett scrambled to his feet. His salute was accompanied by a broad smile. "I didn't know you were back."

"Just caught up with the army this afternoon," said Morgan.

"How are the shoulder and neck?"

"A little stiff," said Morgan, "but serviceable. They took pretty good care of me in the hospital. Believe it or not, I ended up in the Western Pennsylvania Hospital overlooking our old parade grounds at Camp Wilkins." He glanced around at the soldiers bivouacked nearby and frowned. "The 9th is looking mighty thin."

"After the Peninsula, Second Bull Run, and today's battle, there's only about two hundred of us left," said Garrett.

"God almighty," whispered Morgan.

Garrett nodded. "So, how are things at home?"

"Chaotic," said Morgan. "The town is crawling with soldiers, coming and going by train and steamboat, and the foundries are working twenty-four hours a day. The whole city is one giant factory churning out men and munitions."

"That must make your brother, James, happy."

"Not too much makes my brother happy," said Morgan. "Say, I saw the Ward sisters while I was in the hospital. They asked to be remembered to you. They were visiting the wounded men, if you can imagine such a thing."

Garrett chuckled at the thought of prim and proper Lucinda and Maria Ward dealing with the sights and smells of the sick and wounded. "That is hard to imagine. But then, the war changes people, doesn't it?"

"Yes, it does," agreed Morgan.

"Did you happen to see Miss Ambrose during the time you were home?" asked Garrett with unconvincing nonchalance.

Morgan hesitated. "Just once, a few weeks ago. She was at the hospital looking for work as a nurse. I don't think she had any luck, though."

"Too bad," said Garrett. "She's always wanted to do something like that to help with the war."

Morgan gave him a strange look. "Actually, I think it was more than that. She put a brave face on it, but my understanding is her family's practically destitute. You know her brother-in-law was killed?" Garrett nodded. "And when Dr. Ambrose came back from the Valley in such bad shape and needing special medical treatment … well, I guess that's why she agreed to marry Gliddon."

Garrett's face fell. "What?"

"Yes. Edgar Gliddon. The big mill owner." Morgan stopped. "Oh, God, Garrett. I assumed you knew."

"Who told you that?" said Garrett, his voice tight.

"My brother, right before I left to come back. Gliddon's a close friend of his." At the stricken look on Garrett's face, he attempted to soften the news. "Listen, the way I heard it, it's more a financial arrangement than a marriage. And, given her family's situation, it doesn't sound like she had much choice."

"Your brother is mistaken," said Garrett. "Miss Ambrose would never marry Edgar Gliddon … for any reason."

Morgan shifted uncomfortably. "Look, Garrett, I'm really sorry. I thought you knew or I wouldn't have said anything." He paused awkwardly. "Well, I just wanted to check on the boys and say hello. I'd better be getting back." With a last sympathetic look, Morgan strode off in the direction of the officers' tents.

Garrett watched him go with fear tugging at his heart. Clara's most recent letters had indicated her family was struggling, but certainly not to the extent she would be driven to do something so desperate. Still, if her family and her father's life were at stake …. No. It was unthinkable. Clara would never do that.

Garrett lay down on the ground once more. He knew he should get some rest before they set off in pursuit of the Rebels in the morning, but Morgan Percy's words kept running through his head. The last letter Garrett had received from Clara, the one in which she had sounded so dejected, had been dated almost a month ago. He had received nothing since. Had her letters just failed to catch up with the advancing Union army? Or had she stopped writing to him, afraid to tell him of the Faustian choice she had made? If only he could go to her, make sure she was all right. But, he knew he would never be granted a furlough now in the midst of a major campaign.

Garrett tossed and turned the rest of that dark night. He felt more helpless than he had at any time since he had joined the army.

The men of the Army of the Potomac went to sleep the night of September 14, 1862, thinking they had won a decisive victory. They had no way of knowing the Battle of South Mountain had been merely a delaying action, fought by fewer than 14,000 Confederates against an attacking Union force of 28,000, with the goal of buying General Lee time to regroup his fragmented army. From that standpoint, the battle had been a strategic success for the Rebels. Their sacrifice had bought their leader thirteen precious hours.

* * *

The 9th Pennsylvania awoke to thick fog the next morning. Despite the poor visibility, it was soon confirmed the Rebels had, indeed, abandoned South Mountain. Following a hasty breakfast, the Union army began its pursuit.

The Federal soldiers returned to the National Road, marched over the mountain and down the other side to the town of Boonsboro at the foot of the western slope. The morning mist burned off under a hot sun and was replaced by the ever-present dust cloud of an army on the move. But, so elated were the men over their recent victory, there was very little grumbling. The soldiers talked and laughed and happily jeered the Rebel prisoners being taken to the rear.

As the army entered Boonsboro, the streets and windows were filled with cheering, flag-waving Unionists, the same people who had fearfully watched the retreating Rebels stream through their town the night before. Along both sides of the roadway, women blew kisses and held up babies so that, in later years, they could say they saw the victorious Union army march through.

A few miles southwest of Boonsboro, in the line of march along the turnpike that ran from Boonsboro to the town of Sharpsburg, the First Corps, including the 9th Pennsylvania Reserves, was ordered to halt and await further orders.

"What a difference a day makes, eh, boys?" said Frank, resting on his elbow as he lay in the grass by the side of the road. "I haven't felt this good about this army since Dranesville."

"I just hope we can catch up with those Rebs," said Rawlie. "The way they were running, they're probably half way to Richmond by now."

Leonard nodded in agreement. Only Garrett had no comment.

Suddenly, a cheer went up from the regiments behind them to the east; faint at first, but rolling toward them like a wave. A group of officers came galloping into view along the roadway. The approaching stand of colors declared it to be none other than the little Napoleon, himself, General George B. McClellan. The sight of the beloved general atop his little black horse raised the spirits of the men even more. They got to their feet and waved their hats, and the "huzzahs" that greeted the general and his party could be heard all the way back to Boonsboro.

"God bless you, General!" shouted one of the men.

"The 9th Pennsylvania is with you!"

"We got'em on the run now, General!"

"On to Richmond!"

But, the Rebels were not running. Having just learned of the surrender of the Union garrison at Harper's Ferry and the imminent return of the Rebel forces engaged there, General Lee had stopped, turned, and positioned his army along a ridge just east of the town of Sharpsburg. The Confederate army was preparing to stand and fight.

CHAPTER 20

CLARA SAT AT THE KITCHEN table and watched her mother stir a pot of soup for their Thursday night supper. Mrs. Ambrose had stunned Clara with her courage the previous Monday when she banished Edgar Gliddon from the house at gunpoint. Even more remarkable had been her reaction when Clara had tearfully tried to explain what happened.

"Clara, you owe me no explanations," her mother had said. "I'm just sorry it took me so long to see Edgar Gliddon for the evil man he is."

Happy as she was to have her mother on her side, at last, Clara couldn't help but remember the glimpse she'd had of Edgar's face in the parlor mirror; the desolate look that preceded his violent attack. She suspected he had loved her in his own way and, distorted though that love might have been, it gave her no joy to have inflicted such pain.

"More weak than evil, I think, Mama," Clara murmured.

Her mother stared at her in astonishment. "How can you defend him after what he tried to do?"

"I'm not," said Clara. "He was horrible … is horrible. But a part of me can't help but pity him. For all his riches, he has nothing, and no one." She sighed and straightened her shoulders. "One thing's for certain, marriage to him would certainly have solved our money problems."

Mrs. Ambrose put her arm around her daughter. "Oh, Clara. I was wrong, so wrong, to ever encourage you to marry someone you didn't love. A marriage based on love is life's greatest joy. It can survive anything. A marriage based on anything else … well, it's not a marriage at all."

Clara reveled in the unaccustomed warmth of her mother's approval. "But, Mama," she said after a moment, "what are we going to do?"

Mrs. Ambrose hugged her close. "Why don't you let me worry about that for a change?"

Over the next two days, Clara had watched in amazement as her mother swallowed her pride and visited the butcher, the grocer, the druggist, and the coal man – anyone with whom they had dealings – and arranged for credit or delayed payments. She sold her ermine cape and hat, the silver tea set she had received as a wedding gift, and all of her jewelry, except her wedding band. And she informed a surprised Helen they would be taking in sewing. But, her efforts were a temporary solution at best.

Now, as Mrs. Ambrose hunched over the stove in her plain black bombazine dress, Clara realized with a shudder that her mother was beginning to resemble Grandmother Blake. Clara knew she needed to do something.

"Mama?"

"Yes, dear," her mother replied absently. Clara took a deep breath.

"I've decided to apply for a job at the Arsenal." Before Mrs. Ambrose could respond, Clara hurried on. "I know we talked about this before and you were very much against it, but our situation has changed. Despite all the sacrifices you've made, we still don't have enough money to keep the household going. And no one else will give a job to a woman. I know the Arsenal is still hiring. And the pay is good. I think it would be a big help, at least until we see if … when Father can return to work."

Mrs. Ambrose was silent for a long time. "You'd be working with those Irish girls?" she said at last.

Clara sighed. Her mother's transformation had not been total.

"Yes."

There was another long pause. Mrs. Ambrose stared into the soup pot as if the answer lay hidden among the limp carrots.

"Well, I suppose we all must do what we must," she said finally. "Still, I think it best we not mention this to your father … in his condition."

"All right, Mama," said Clara.

"So, when would you start?"

"Just as soon as I can," said Clara. "I could go over first thing tomorrow to inquire."

Her mother nodded. "I'll wake you early in the morning."

"Come in!"

Clara opened the door to the Arsenal office to find a thin young lieutenant working on a stack of papers at a battered desk. He did not look up when Clara entered, but motioned her into the room.

"Yes?" he barked at last.

Clara cleared her throat. "Sir, I'm here to apply for a job."

At her lack of an accent, the man raised his head. His look of surprise deepened when he beheld the beautiful woman in front of him. Her dress was expensive, if a bit worn, and her expression was that of one accustomed to getting her way. He rose to his feet.

"Please. Won't you sit down, Miss …?" He indicated one of the two chairs in front of the desk.

"Ambrose. And no, thank you. I'm here to apply for a job," Clara repeated. "Rolling cartridges. I understand you're hiring women?"

"Well, yes. We are," he said, bemused. "But, most of the girls and women we hire here are … well, they're not … not of your social standing."

"You mean most of them are poor Irish," said Clara.

"Well, yes. Recent immigrants, uneducated, accustomed to manual labor. I don't think someone of your evident breeding and education would find this type of situation to your liking."

"Lieutenant," said Clara, "my own situation makes it imperative that I work."

The lieutenant had already taken note of her mourning attire and the absence of a wedding ring on her finger.

"May I ask for whom it is you mourn?" he said.

"My sister's husband was with the 46th Pennsylvania. He was killed three months ago in the Shenandoah Valley."

"My condolences," he said. "But have you no husband of your own; no father or brother who can care for you?"

"No. I'm not married and I have only the one sister. My father was a surgeon in the Union army, but he was captured and imprisoned by the Confederates. He has recently returned to us, but is quite ill. When my brother-in-law died, he left my sister with a young child to support. And there are my mother and grandmother to care for, as well. So, Lieutenant, as you can see, I need this job."

"Miss Ambrose, you have had a hard time of it, without a doubt," said the man. "And you have my sympathies. But the local population was relatively scandalized when we began employing working-class girls here at the Arsenal. Imagine the uproar if we were to start hiring doctors' daughters."

"Lieutenant, I fail to see the difference."

"Perhaps, but the good ladies of Pittsburgh will not."

"So, what you're saying is, I'm too high class to work, but not too high class to starve," said Clara.

The lieutenant stared at her a moment. He noted the determined look in her eyes and the stubborn set of her delicate chin. Finally, he reached into his desk drawer and pulled out a sheet of paper.

"I'm only doing this because of your family's dedicated service to the Union." He turned the paper around to face her. "I'll need you to sign this sheet in order to work here. Put your mark … I mean, your signature on this line here."

"And I'd like to be assigned to Room 14, if that's possible," said Clara. "I understand there's a vacancy there." Annie had supplied this information in hopes the two young women would end up working together.

The lieutenant shook his head in disbelief. "As you wish, Miss Ambrose." He made a notation on the sheet.

Clara hurried to sign her name before he could change his mind. The lieutenant scribbled his signature at the bottom.

"Well, Miss Ambrose," he said, handing her the paper, "be here Monday morning at 7:30 a.m. and report to Room 14. That's in the smaller laboratory building in the upper Arsenal grounds. Give that pass to the foreman, Mr. Geary. He'll show you what you need to do."

"Thank you, Lieutenant," said Clara. She extended her hand. He took it and bowed.

"You're welcome, Miss Ambrose. I only hope neither of us lives to regret this."

At 7:15 a.m. on Monday, September 1, 1862, Clara entered the kitchen where her mother was serving breakfast to Grandmother Blake.

"Well, I'm ready to go," she announced. At Annie's suggestion, and in keeping with the strictures of permissible mourning attire, she had dressed in her simplest dark linen dress, with a black collar and cuffs, and her most modest hoop. Her thick hair was captured in a hairnet.

"Go? Go where?" asked her grandmother.

"You remember, Mama," said Mrs. Ambrose. "Today is Clara's first day of work at the Arsenal. She's going to roll cartridges for the war."

"Roll cartridges?! Why, Laura, how can you allow such a thing? What will people think?" She frowned at her granddaughter. "Clara, proper young ladies do not engage in such activities. It's unseemly. Besides, you're in mourning for your brother-in-law. It would be disrespectful for you to be seen ... *cavorting* with working girls."

"I'm hardly cavorting, Grandmother," said Clara as she pulled on her gloves. "And as for engaging in such activities, somebody better engage in them or our boys will be fighting this war with empty rifles. Besides, we need the money." She bent and kissed the perplexed old woman on the top of her white-capped head. "I'll see you for supper, Mama." Clara kissed her mother on the cheek and hurried out the front door into the late summer morning.

"Well! I never!" exclaimed Grandmother Blake. She pulled her shawl more tightly around her shoulders. "I don't know what's come over the young women these days. Tramping about the streets alone, not observing the proper mourning period, working in factories. It's shocking. Just shocking."

"The war, Mama," her daughter replied in a tired voice as she spooned out another bowl of porridge to take up to her husband. "The war's come over people. And I don't think any of us will ever be the same."

Although the Allegheny Arsenal was only two blocks from the Ambrose home, the combination of Clara's heavy mourning clothes, her nervousness, and the heat of the summer day caused her to perspire. Once across Pike Street, she paused in the shade of the Arsenal wall to wipe her forehead with a handkerchief.

The Allegheny Arsenal grounds extended from Penn Street on the south all the way north to the Allegheny River, and was bounded by Pike and Covington Streets on the southwest and northeast, respectively. The site had originally been chosen because of its proximity to the iron and coal producing region around Pittsburgh and to the nearby river transportation. Now, almost fifty years later, it was also conveniently located less than two miles from the Fort Pitt Foundry, where most of the cannon and cannon balls stored at the Arsenal were manufactured.

Butler Street bisected the Arsenal and divided it into a lower and an upper section. The lower half, between the river and Butler Street, contained the officers' quarters, barracks, armory, smithy, carriage shop, machine shop, paint shop, accoutrement shop, and the house of the post commander, Colonel John Symington. There were also two carriage sheds, three timber sheds, a three-story stone military storehouse, and the three-story main magazine of arms with its one hundred and twenty-foot high, forty-foot square tower.

The upper section of the Arsenal, uphill from Butler Street, included a large brick storehouse, stables, a small pond, a large main laboratory building, a number of smaller laboratory buildings, and three powder magazines with storage capacity for 1,300 barrels of gunpowder.

The majority of the girls and women assigned to roll cartridges at the Arsenal worked in the main laboratory building, a sixty-foot by forty-foot, one-story wood frame building shaped like an E, with covered porches around the inside. Just to the east of it was a smaller laboratory, also wood frame, which housed additional workrooms, as well as the engine room. Between the two laboratories there was a small wooden building used as a cloakroom by the workers. In all, there were fourteen workrooms in this laboratory complex, housing one hundred and seventy-six workers. All but twenty-five of the workers were girls and young women, and the majority of them were engaged in tying, pinching, and bundling cartridges and firing caps.

A stream of these young female workers was entering the gate to the upper Arsenal. Clara noticed in dismay that most of them were wearing light-colored, plain, or small-print cotton dresses, without crinolines or, apparently, even corsets. Biting her lip, Clara tucked away her handkerchief and followed them. She showed her pass to the guard, who studied it with a surprised expression. Baffled, he directed her up the hill to the smaller one-story wooden laboratory building that housed Room 14.

"This war gets stranger and stranger," he muttered as he watched her go, the sight of her swaying hoop skirt a pleasant respite from his monotonous guard duty.

Clara paused at the entrance to Room 14. Most of the other twenty-three girls assigned to that workroom were already seated on benches at two long wooden tables on which sat a stack of cartridge papers, measures of gun powder, trays of minie balls, and spools of yellow cord for tying off the top of the cartridges The girls stopped their chatter and gaped at the stylish young woman in the doorway. Clara could have cried with relief when she saw Annie's familiar face smiling at her encouragingly. Just then, the foreman approached.

"Can I help you, Miss?" he said to the pretty young lady who had obviously lost her way.

"Yes, Sir. I've been instructed to report to you to begin work today." She handed him her pass.

Taken aback, he studied the paper carefully. "Well, yes. That is what it says. And you are Miss Ambrose?"

"Yes, Sir."

"Well," he sputtered again, "I guess you may take a seat over there. I'll have one of the other girls instruct you in your duties."

"I'd be glad to help her, Mr. Geary," said Annie. She indicated an empty seat next to her that she had been carefully guarding.

"Thank you, Miss Burke. You may sit there, Miss Ambrose."

Clara slid onto the bench next to her friend. Annie gave her hand a little squeeze.

"Now, here's what we do," said Annie. "The girls in the big storehouse, down near Butler Street, form the paper cartridge cylinders. They send them up here for us to fill with powder and bullets. Then we tie them off, pinch, and bundle."

Clara gave her a confused look. Annie smiled.

"Let's just start you off with pinchin' and bundlin' the firin' caps," said Annie. "Once you've mastered that, I'll show you how to load the minie balls and powder into the cartridges."

Annie showed Clara how to tie off the end of a paper cartridge, fill it with a stack of firing caps, then fold and pinch off the end of the bundle to keep the caps in tight. Clara watched closely, and attempted to match her speed and precision. The result was less than satisfactory.

"Don't worry," said Annie. "You'll get the hang of it soon enough. Before long, you'll be as fast as me."

Clara sincerely doubted it. She took another rolled cartridge paper and was attempting to fill it with a load of caps when her fingers slipped and sent the caps spilling all over the table in front of her. The girls across the table giggled.

"Oh, Annie," said one, "your lady friend seems to be gettin' a bit flustered. You'd best get a fan and tend to her before she faints dead away."

"Shut your gob, Bridget Kennedy," said Annie. "Seems to me I recall when you first started, you packed an entire box with cartridges with no bullets in 'em. Wouldn't that have been a fine surprise for some poor soldier?"

Bridget glowered at Annie.

"It's all right, Annie," said Clara under her breath.

"Ah, she's a stupid cow, that one," muttered Annie. "Slowest worker in the place, and she has the nerve to criticize you. And on your first day, at that. If she knew you could've married one of the richest men in Pittsburgh, she'd be the one to faint."

"Annie!" said Clara. "I told you that in strictest confidence."

"And, I shall keep your confidence," said Annie. "Still, I do wish you'd let me have some of me brothers' friends pay Mr. Gliddon a little nighttime visit."

Clara shook her head. "I just want to forget it ever happened."

"As you wish," said Annie as she folded the top of a cartridge paper. "But, if you change your mind …."

Clara smiled.

The girls worked steadily all morning before breaking for dinner. Clara and Annie ate together beneath the shade of a tree on the Arsenal lawn. The other girls sat talking and laughing in small groups nearby. Occasionally, they would glance in Clara's direction, and the resulting asides were met with giggles and shushes.

"Don't pay them any mind," said Annie. "Most of them have never been around quality. They see your clothes and your manners, and they figure ...."

"They figure I won't be able to handle the work," Clara finished for her. Annie nodded. "Well, I guess I'll just have to prove them wrong."

But, as the afternoon wore on, Clara began to doubt she would ever be able to do the job as well as the young women around her. The Arsenal girls sped through stacks of cartridge papers, their nimble fingers flying as they rolled, tied, poured, pinched, and bundled. Even the younger girls, some only eleven or twelve, had no trouble keeping up and seemed unfazed by the prowling Mr. Geary, who peered over their shoulders and muttered about quotas.

At the end of the day, Clara stood on the wooden porch just outside the workroom. Her neck and shoulders were stiff and her fingers cramped. She looked down at her hands. Already rough and calloused from months of housework, the hours of pinching, tying, and bundling had left them red and chapped. She had never thought herself to be a vain person, but, contemplating the condition of her hands, she suddenly felt very sorry for herself.

Annie joined her on the porch.

"You all right?" she asked.

"My back hurts, my eyes are bleary, and my fingers ache," said Clara.

Annie laughed. "Sounds about right. Don't worry. It gets easier."

As they talked, they had to move out of the way of a young man sweeping up the powder that had spilled along the porch walkway during the workday. When he reached the end of the porch, he hesitated, glanced over at the girls, and reluctantly went to fetch a dustpan. He swept up the powder and deposited it in the barrel at the end of the porch.

"I'm going to sleep well tonight," said Clara as she and Annie began walking downhill to the Butler Street gate.

"You'll get used to it," said Annie. "Besides, you always said you wanted to do somethin' more for the war effort than just knit socks."

"That's true," said Clara. "But I guess my mother was right – 'Be careful what you wish for.'"

Annie smiled ruefully. "It's sorry I am for the misfortunes that made it necessary for you to have to work here, Clara. But, I'm glad, for me own sake, that you are."

"So am I," said Clara.

The two friends hugged goodbye and hurried off to their separate homes where more chores awaited them.

By the end of her second week at the Arsenal – the second week of

September – Clara was growing more accustomed to her duties. Her speed at tying and bundling had improved greatly, and her fingers no longer cramped. The day she managed to produce and pack the third largest number of cartridges of any girl in the room, even Bridget Kennedy nodded her head in approval.

Once it became evident Clara was willing to work just as hard as everyone else, the girls in the shop warmed up to her. They were mostly recent Irish immigrants, poor and with limited education, but they were smart and funny, and much less constrained by social convention than the girls Clara had known at the Pittsburgh Female Academy. Clara found she enjoyed their frankness and somewhat bawdy humor immensely.

What Clara liked most about working at the Arsenal, however, was the feeling she was doing something worthwhile, not only for her family, but for the soldiers fighting the war. And, most particularly, for Garrett. She had written him of her new job, but her last six letters to him had gone unanswered. From the newspapers, she knew his regiment had taken part in the recent Union debacle at Bull Run – mercifully, his name had not appeared on the casualty lists – and that the army had been on the move ever since. It was unlikely he had received her letters, much less had the time to write back. But still, she worried and waited – and wondered.

The fancy black carriage with the green trim turned from Penn Street onto Butler Street and headed for the Allegheny Arsenal. On his way to an early morning meeting, Edgar Gliddon sat in the back and glared out the window. Each time he made the trip to and from the Arsenal from his offices in Allegheny City, he had, of necessity, to pass the Ambrose's street. Each time, he relived the ignominy of his last encounter with Clara and her mother. Clara's final rejection of him had turned his feelings of affection to bitterness, and he spent much of his time mulling over ways to exact his revenge on her, her family, and her lover.

Suddenly, he spied Clara on the sidewalk up ahead, her graceful walk distinctive, even from the back. His heart constricted. Signaling to his driver to slow, he followed her from a distance. He watched in astonishment as she turned into the upper gate of the Arsenal and was greeted by a trio of common working girls. One of them he recognized as Clara's repulsive Irish girlfriend. Clara and the other girls joined a line of young women heading up the hill to one of the laboratory buildings.

My, God, he thought. She was working as a common laborer. He could not believe she would rather debase herself in that way than accept his proposal of marriage. His anger boiled up once more. Well, she was sadly mistaken if she thought she had bested him. He would make her sorry she had spurned him. She would beg him to take her back.

He banged on the roof of the carriage. "Driver! I've changed my mind. Take me back to my office."

Gathering her skirts in one hand, Clara made her way through the tall grass and brambles to the shade of a sycamore tree standing guard over the riverbank below the Arsenal. She tramped around in a circle to mat down a small area in which to sit. Spreading out her skirts, she sat and rested her dinner pail in her lap. With only her head visible over the top of the wild grasses, she watched in relative seclusion as the sparkling water of the Allegheny River rolled by on its way to Pittsburgh.

Clara had declined Annie's offer to join her and the other girls for the mid-day meal by making up a story about an errand to be run. Usually she did not indulge herself in these moments. She kept as busy as possible so that the time would pass more quickly. But her heart ached for Garrett and, every now and then, she needed these times alone.

Reaching into the neckline of her blouse, she pulled out the locket he had given her. She opened it and gazed at Garrett's picture for the thousandth time. The sunlight through the swaying leaves cast dappled light on his handsome features, endearingly stern in his uniform. She fingered the bit of lilac pressed into the other side.

Oh, Garrett, she thought as her eyes filled with tears. When will you come back to me? Will you come back to me? Each time word came of another battle, she stood trembling before the casualty lists outside the newspaper office. The relief she felt when his name was not there was always short-lived.

Almost as bad as finding his name on the list would be the knowledge that, unbeknownst to her, he had been dead or wounded, or missing for days. She would have been going about her life, talking, eating, laughing with friends, while he lay wounded in some hospital, taken prisoner by the Rebels, or buried in some faraway grave. She had heard stories of people long-married who knew the very moment when one or the other was in trouble or injured; lovers who, though separated, actually experienced each other's pain. She wondered, was their love like that? Would she know if Garrett was hurt, or ... worse? At times, like now, when his letters were inexplicably delayed, she would close her eyes and try to clear her mind so his thoughts might reach her. She tried to feel what he felt and communicate telepathically over the miles. But she felt nothing; no sense of connection or special knowledge; just unbearable loneliness.

Even worse, the long silence awakened whispers of doubt. She hated that she could not still Edgar's voice inside her head. But she knew it was because he had asked the question she dared not ask herself – why hadn't Garrett proposed to her before he left? Weeping softly, Clara hugged her knees to her chest and rocked slowly back and forth.

How long she stayed like that, she wasn't sure, but she knew she had better get back to work if she didn't want her pay docked. Wiping her eyes and nose with her handkerchief, she opened her dinner pail and tossed the uneaten contents into the weeds for the animals. She stood, brushed the grass and dirt from her skirt, and hurried back up the hill toward the Arsenal.

As Clara neared the smaller laboratory building, she was overtaken by one of the large wagons that delivered gunpowder to the laboratories each day. The dray's load of iron-ringed barrels, stamped *Dupont*, shimmied from side to side as it bounced over the stone roadway. Clara stepped aside as it rumbled past, and covered her nose and mouth with her handkerchief against the cloud of dust and fine powder the wagon kicked up in its wake, a cloud that gradually settled into the cracks between the stones.

CHAPTER 21

THE WESTERN MARYLAND TOWN OF Sharpsburg stood at the intersection of the Hagerstown Turnpike and the Boonsboro Turnpike in a green valley between Antietam Creek and the Potomac River. A small but prosperous country town, Sharpsburg was surrounded by rolling, rich farmland interspersed with limestone outcroppings and dense woodlots. North of town, the land was under cultivation by the predominately German farmers of the area. South of town, the landscape became more rugged, with wooded hills and ravines dropping down one hundred and fifty feet to Antietam Creek. Now, in mid-September, the fields and orchards were as yet only partially harvested and the cornfields were full of ripened corn with stalks standing head high.

The Hagerstown Turnpike entered Sharpsburg from the north and followed a low ridge that ran roughly north-south, just east of the town. On either side of this ridge, the land sloped away to Antietam Creek, a mile to the east, and to the Potomac River, three miles to the west.

Early on the morning of September 15, 1862, the day after the Union victory at South Mountain, General Lee positioned his 18,000 available troops in a defensive line along this ridge and turned east to face McClellan's pursuing army. All the while, Lee kept a watchful eye on the road from the south and awaited the arrival of reinforcements from Harper's Ferry, seventeen miles away.

That same afternoon, Union troops began arriving from the northeast via the Boonsboro Pike. McClellan had expected Lee to continue to move toward the safety of Virginia just over the Potomac River and was surprised to find the Rebel army arrayed on the ridge in front of Sharpsburg. Even by his habitually inflated calculations, McClellan knew the Confederates did not have the manpower to match the 80,000 Federal troops McClellan had at his disposal. Furthermore, he knew Lee had not had time to reunite his army and was beyond immediate help from his forces at Harper's Ferry. Yet, there Lee stood, with his infantry spread out in a thin, four-mile line of battle, while his batteries kept up a harassing fire at any Federals that came within range. McClellan knew it had to be a bluff. And, yet....

McClellan ordered the Union troops to halt on the east side of Antietam Creek while he mulled over this new turn of events. He used the time to bring up his batteries and supply trains so as to be completely ready to face whatever lay ahead of him. He decided tomorrow would be soon enough to decide upon a course of action.

From the opposing hillside, Lee watched the gathering sea of blue, and waited.

A heavy ground fog blanketed the fields and valleys around Antietam Creek on the morning of Tuesday, September 16th, and obscured the massing of the two great armies, barely two and a half miles apart. The men, blue and gray, readied themselves for the coming battle. But as the morning wore on, hot and still, with nothing more than the sporadic exchange of cannon fire, they settled into resting mode and spent the day griping about their generals and the interminable wait.

The men of the 9th Pennsylvania Reserves, along with the rest of the First Corps, sat and lay about on either side of the road from Keedysville, on the far side of a hill just east of the creek out of sight of the probing enemy cannon. They passed the time by dozing, reading from small pocket bibles, or writing letters to loved ones.

Garrett sat on a small rock outcropping a little way from the rest of the company. He chewed on a piece of grass as he watched the 80,000 men of the Army of the Potomac pour into the Antietam Valley. Their blue lines stretched across the fields and to the upper reaches of South Mountain. Infantry, cannon, cavalry, all were in attendance, with more arriving every hour. No enemy could stand against such a force, thought Garrett. And the presence of one soldier, more or less, would make no difference in the outcome of the battle to come.

Suddenly, a shadow fell across the ground. Garrett whipped around.

"What's the matter?" said Rawlie. "Think a Reb was sneaking up on you?"

Garrett shrugged. "Just a little jumpy, I guess."

Rawlie joined him on the rock outcropping. "Looks like it's gonna be a big one," he said as he looked out over the gathering force.

"Yeah," Garrett nodded, "it does."

Rawlie took off his battered cap and wiped his forehead on his sleeve. "You've been kinda quiet lately," he said. "You all right?"

"Yeah," said Garrett. "It's just …." He stopped. He dare not give voice to his thoughts; not even to Rawlie. "Guess I'm just a little … scared."

"Me, too," said Rawlie. "I've spent every day in this goddamn army either scared to death or bored to death."

Garrett nodded.

"You ever think about it?" said Rawlie after a few moments. "Dying, I mean."

"Sometimes," said Garrett. "Figure there's not a lot I can do about it though."

Rawlie snickered. "That's true. But I can't help but wonder … what really happens when you die? All the boys we've known. Are they just gone? Or are they still out there somewhere?"

Garrett glanced over at Rawlie. He seemed to be searching the grassy swales for a familiar form; listening for a voice on the breeze.

"I think they're still out there," said Garrett. "Just in a different way. A better way, if you can believe the preachers."

Rawlie looked unconvinced.

"Actually," said Rawlie, "I'm not afraid of being dead. It's just the getting killed I'm not particularly looking forward to. And I'd hate to have to leave before I find out how this all turns out. It'd be kinda like leaving a play before you get to see the ending."

"Well," said Garrett as he watched a growing dust cloud that signaled more troops arriving from the northeast, "if this keeps shaping up the way it is, it's going to be one hell of a performance."

As the Union troops assembled in the east, the majority of the Rebel brigades Lee had sent to capture Harper's Ferry began staggering in from the southwest. Their forced march brought the total Confederate forces facing McClellan to more than 25,000. Only A. P. Hill's division of approximately 3,300 men, assigned the task of securing the garrison and paroling the captured Union troops, remained behind at Harper's Ferry.

General McClellan spent most of that Tuesday preparing his army to fight. He reconnoitered the ground and the enemy strength, searched for fords, and assembled his ammunition and supply trains. He wanted to have his entire army around him, every available man fed, rested, armed and in position, and every possible move of the battle planned down to the last detail, before he was willing to move against an enemy he was now convinced was at least his equal in numbers and supplies. Lee was content to wait him out, for every hour brought closer the possibility of additional reinforcement from A.P. Hill's troops at Harper's Ferry.

Finally, at about 2:00 p.m. on the afternoon of the 16th, McClellan ordered Hooker's First Corps to cross Antietam Creek and take up position opposite the Confederate left flank. Meade's Pennsylvania Reserves division, along with James B. Rickett's Second division, was to cross at the Upper Bridge where the road from Keedysville crossed the stream. At the same time, General Abner Doubleday's division was to ford the stream at Pry's Mill, a quarter mile to the south. All three divisions would bivouac astride the Hagerstown Turnpike a few miles north of Sharpsburg, just north of a stand of woods that would become known as the North Woods. Within two hours, the First Corps was on the march.

The 9th Pennsylvania took its place in line and tramped across the arched stone Upper Bridge spanning Antietam Creek. At this spot, the south-flowing creek was about thirty feet wide and relatively shallow. Garrett thought it quite a pretty little stream. Large trees lined its banks and threw cool shadows across the edges of the bubbling water. The vegetation and the bends in the creek prevented him from seeing the men of Doubleday's division he knew to be wading across a ford not far downstream. Even on this hot day, he did not envy them their wet pants and brogans.

Near a sunken log on the far side, a small painted turtle poked its striped head out of the water, spied the marching troops, and disappeared beneath the surface as quickly as he appeared. Garrett was reminded of carefree boyhood afternoons spent catching turtles and crayfish on the banks of the Chemung River in western New York ... so long ago.

"Probably a Rebel scout," quipped Frank, who had also observed the little reptile.

Once across the creek, the column turned northwest. They marched through farm fields and pastures, and past another stand of woods just to their south. Lee's scouts had been monitoring Hooker's progress and, as the Pennsylvania Reserves marched past these woods, soon to become known as the East Woods, gunfire erupted from a division of Confederates hidden there. Garrett and the men of the 9th Pennsylvania found themselves on the side of the Union advance farthest from the Rebel attack.

"Who's over there?" asked Garrett.

"Part of the First Brigade and the Bucktails, I think," said Rawlie. "Sounds like they disturbed some of our Confederate friends."

The sound of the fighting intensified and was augmented by the thunder of supporting artillery from each side. The Pennsylvania Reserves units closest to the East Woods provided flank protection for the rest of the First Corps while it continued toward its destination. This was not a full-scale attack, however, and as darkness fell, the rifle and artillery fire slowed and finally stopped.

"Was that it?" asked a green private from Company B as the rumble of the cannons faded away.

"Nah," said Leonard, "that was just a little teaser. Real fight comes tomorrow."

Hooker's First Corps bivouacked out of sight of the Rebel troops just north of the North Woods on land belonging to a farmer named J. Poffenberger. General Hooker and his officers set up headquarters in the Poffenberger house while the troops bedded down in the yard, the fields, and throughout the woods. The 9th Pennsylvania settled in for the night in a low depression in a field just east of the Hagerstown Pike at the northern edge of the North Woods. They looked forward to a hot meal and the warmth of a campfire, but the order came down from General McClellan that no fires were to be lit so as not to draw enemy fire to their position.

"Shit. It's not like they don't know where we are," complained Rawlie as he laid his rubber poncho on the ground near his messmates. "They watched us march here in broad daylight."

Leonard pulled a handful of coffee beans out of his haversack and began chewing them. "Yup. McClellan's pretty much shown Lee exactly where we plan to attack. The Rebs'll be waitin' for us come mornin'."

"You don't think much of Little Mac, do you, Leonard?" said Garrett.

"The way I see it," said Leonard, "he spends all his time gettin' ready to fight and precious little time fightin'."

"I disagree," said Frank. "I think he just cares more about the men than Pope or Halleck. He's more careful about when and where he sends them out to fight. That's why the men love him."

"Maybe," said Leonard. "But seems to me he's more interested in being popular than in winnin' this war. And the longer this war drags on, the more men are gonna die." He lay down and pulled his blanket around himself, signaling the end of the discussion.

The low murmur of voices quieted as the regiment settled in for a cold, anxious night. Though a few hardy souls slept, most of the men on both sides of the fight dozed fitfully amid the popping of picket fire and the occasional artillery burst. The night had a fractured, nightmarish quality, filled with foreboding at what the dawn might bring. The very countryside seemed to hold its breath, waiting.

Around midnight it began to rain, a little at first, then steadily. Before long, the soldiers, Yankee and Rebel alike, were soaked to the skin. Garrett shivered in his damp blanket and tried to ignore the voices in his head – Edgar Gliddon's threatening promise to "watch over" Clara while he was away; Clara's troubling letter in which she promised to love him "no matter what has happened or what is to come;" Morgan Percy's report of Clara's engagement to Edgar. Garrett couldn't conceive of Clara willingly agreeing to marry Edgar. But, what if something awful had happened, something beyond her control? Garrett knew from personal experience that, despite the best intentions, "Promises don't mean shit in war." And, he believed Edgar to be capable of almost any villainy to get what he wanted.

Garrett rolled over. The anxiety and longing to go to Clara was almost unbearable. But, duty demanded he stay where he was. Or did it? What if Leonard was right? What if tomorrow's battle meant only that inept generals would send more good men to the slaughter? Did his duty to his country require that he die for nothing?

The thoughts swirled in Garrett's mind. He tried to shut them out and steel himself for the battle he knew would begin at first light. But, his fear of the coming fight paled in comparison to the fear his beloved was slipping from his grasp. And there was nothing he could do to stop it.

Unable to stand it any longer, Garrett sat up. The motion roused Rawlie.

"Where you off to?" he mumbled.

Garrett hesitated. "The sinks."

"Be careful," said Rawlie. "Lots of nervous pickets out there. Ours and theirs."

Garrett reached over and picked up the revolver he had taken from the dead soldier on South Mountain.

"I'll be careful," he said and tucked the pistol into his waist belt.

Stepping over the sleeping bodies of his fellow soldiers, Garrett made his way to the edge of his regiment's campsite. The rainy night was dark and, as he neared the Hagerstown Pike, he could just make out the tall wooden post and rail fences that lined both sides of the road. Unbuttoning his pants, he relieved himself against one of the posts and stared up the dirt road to where it disappeared in the darkness. Just thirteen miles north up that road was the town of Hagerstown, Maryland; another seven miles beyond that, the Pennsylvania line. A man could cover that much ground in a day or so. A driven man, much faster.

Garrett never made a conscious decision to leave. He just started walking, moving north, alongside the Hagerstown Pike. To his right and straddling the road up ahead, he could hear the rain-muffled sounds of the various regimental camps of the Union army as they restlessly waited out the night. He realized his greatest danger lay in being discovered by his own troops. He would need to work his way west and skirt the Union lines until he could turn north once more. He slipped through the rails of the fence, crossed the Hagerstown Pike, and ducked through the fence on the other side. Running in a crouch, he hurried toward the dim shape of a rock outcropping. He stopped there, his breath sounding loud in his ears. The terrain seemed to urge him on, offering boulders, swells, and hollows to hide his progress. He scurried from place to place with the patter of the rain covering the sound of his movement. In the darkness, the outlines of cornfields and wood-lots loomed. He reached an area of open pasture and felt the ground begin to rise beneath his feet. Feeling he must surely have outflanked the Union forces by now, he stopped beside the cover of some low bushes to rest.

Suddenly, he heard the jangling of a horse's bit, nearby and coming closer. He dropped to his belly and hugged the damp ground. Reaching for the pistol in his belt, he slowly turned his head in the direction of the sound.

A lone rider emerged from the fog and rain, the thud of his horse's hooves barely audible on the soft, soaked earth. Garrett could tell little about the man except that he wore a large hat and rode with the ease and erect posture of one accustomed to long hours in the saddle. Although the man was no more than five yards away, the rainy night shielded Garrett, and neither rider nor horse seemed to sense his presence.

Just when Garrett thought he had escaped detection, the horse halted abruptly and snorted, head up, ears pricked.

"General!" A man on foot appeared out of the darkness. He saluted when he reached the rider's side. "General Stuart," he repeated in the soft tones of Virginia.

"What is it, Corporal?" asked the rider.

"Sir. A message from General Jackson."

My God, thought Garrett. Could it be? Somehow, in the dark of the Maryland countryside, he had stumbled upon legendary cavalry officer, General J. E. B. Stuart, the eyes and ears of the entire Confederate army. Garrett's hand tightened on his revolver.

"Go on, Corporal," said Stuart.

"General Jackson wishes to speak to you at once, Sir. He asks that I accompany you to his headquarters."

Garrett had a split second to act. From such close range, it would only take one shot. He could eliminate one of the most important men in the Confederate command, and, undoubtedly, deal a serious blow to the Rebel battle plan. Perhaps enough to tip the scales in favor of the Federals. But, he reasoned, even if he managed to elude the Confederate soldiers he now realized were all around him in the dark, the noise would alert the Union troops, who would most likely shoot him as he tried to return to his own lines. Either way, he would never get home to Clara.

"Lead the way, Corporal," said General Stuart.

The young man set off at a trot and General Stuart spurred his horse to follow. Within moments, the two of them were enveloped by the darkness.

Lying in the wet grass, Garrett began to tremble as the shameful realization hit him. He was a coward. He had put himself and his own needs above his duty to his country; even worse, above the lives of his fellow soldiers. At this most crucial of moments, he had let them down. They deserved better. So did Clara.

He pressed his face to the earth and wept.

After what seemed like hours, Garrett slowly pulled himself up from the ground. He began to retrace his steps, zigzagging through the dark and the fog. He prayed that the miracle that had allowed him to venture undetected through both armies' lines would protect him on his return. Any moment, he expected a bullet to find him. He almost wished it.

Finally, Garrett saw the outline of the fence lining the Hagerstown Pike. He ducked beneath it, crossed the dirt road, and followed the eastern fence line until he came to the 9th Pennsylvania's bivouac area. Damp and shaken, he trudged back to his blanket.

"You all right?" asked Rawlie. "You were gone a long time."

"Yeah," mumbled Garrett as he lay down once more, "I got a little lost."

Rawlie gave him a long look. "Well, I'm glad you found your way back."

Garrett did not answer. Guilt-ridden, he lay awake in the dark. As the minutes passed, however, his self-recrimination turned to resolve. He could not undo his craven failure to act, but at least he could stick by his comrades and see this through to the end. He would do his duty, no matter the personal sacrifice. He would just have to trust in Clara's promise to love him forever – and pray that forever did not come with the dawn.

With this new resolve came a kind of peace. Garrett pulled his blanket around his shoulders and slept. But it seemed in no time at all, Rawlie was shaking him awake.

"Garrett. Get up. We got picket duty."

Garrett lurched to his feet and grabbed his rifle. The cold grimy hardtack he had eaten for supper felt like lead in his stomach and he fought back a wave of nausea. Dodging bushes and tree limbs, he followed his company into the blackness of the North Woods until he reached the southern edge. He took up position behind a large red oak tree and attempted to peer through the darkness. The moon was hidden by clouds, making it difficult to get the lay of the land. He knew the East Woods, from which much of the afternoon's harassing fire had come, was somewhere off to his left, just to the southeast. Directly in front of him there was open pasture and what appeared to be the indistinct shapes of an orchard. The occasional flash of rifle fire from Confederate pickets came from a third stand of woods – the West Woods – which ran along the west side of the Hagerstown Pike, southwest of his position. In the silence between shots, Garrett could clearly hear the taunts of the pickets from across the dark farm fields.

Garrett's head was bobbing with fatigue when suddenly, he heard a faint crackling and scratching to his left. He spun with rifle raised only to find Frank scribbling on a small piece of paper propped on his bent knee.

"Geez, Frank," said Garrett, "you scared me half to death. What the hell are you doing?"

"Writing down my name and company," said Frank as he stood and stuffed the paper into the pocket of his sack coat. "Just in case," he added with a shrug.

Garrett nodded.

The rain stopped just before daybreak. Garrett, stiff and cold, leaned against a tree and listened to the slow drip-drip of water from the leaves. As the sky behind South Mountain began to lighten, the contours of the landscape emerged from the gloom. The ground fog moved silently across the fields and crouched in the swales and depressions. He gave an involuntary shiver. He had a sense he might not survive the coming battle. He thought of his father and how sad he would be to learn of his son's death. He hoped he would be comforted by the fact he had died for his country. But most of all, Garrett thought of Clara. How he wished he could see her one more time, look into her eyes and hold her in his arms. He wished he could tell her how much he loved her. Remembering her instruction, he closed his eyes and pressed his hand to his heart.

Just after 5:00 a.m. that Wednesday morning of September 17, 1862, the First Corps commander, Major General Joseph Hooker, rode up to the picket line on a large white horse. Flanked by a group of officers and aides, he reined to a halt abreast of Garrett's position. Hooker was tall and clean-shaven with piercing blue eyes and brown hair and sideburns that were feathered with gray. He chewed on an unlit cigar as he peered through the gray half-light at the vista Garrett had been staring at since the night before. His horse stood quietly, but dark gray blotches

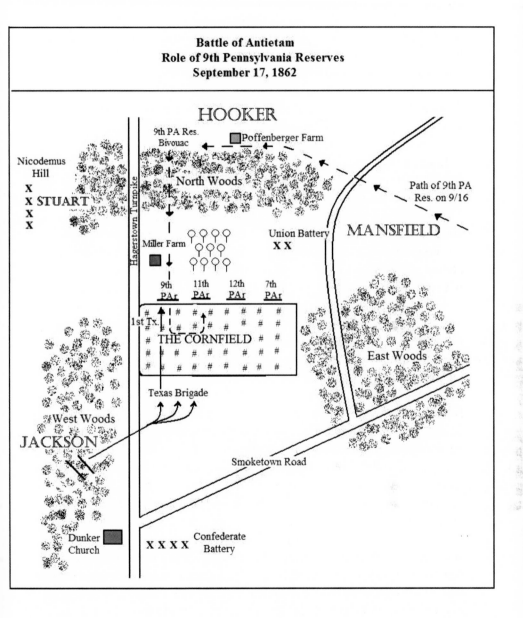

of sweat stained the animal's coat, and its ears flicked back and forth nervously.

Barely a hundred yards southwest of where Hooker sat on his horse, the blurred shapes of the house and outbuildings of a well-ordered farm began to appear out of the mist. The farm, which straddled the Hagerstown Pike, belonged to the Miller family, but the family had wisely fled with as much of their livestock as they could gather to get out of the way of the two great armies.

"Careful, General," said one of the Union pickets. "We seen some skirmishers lurking around those buildings and trees over there." He jerked his head in the direction of the Miller farm and the West Woods.

"Thank you, Private," said Hooker.

Directly in front of Hooker, to the east of the Hagerstown Pike and the farmhouse, was an open area with a small orchard and a plowed field. To the south of the field, a wooden fence marked the northernmost edge of a thirty-acre cornfield where a wall of standing corn, seven feet tall, extended from the Pike to the edge of the East Woods. By the end of the day, this acreage would become known simply and infamously as The Cornfield.

From left to right, Hooker scanned the undulating ground from the East Woods to the open field and orchard with The Cornfield just beyond, to the dark mass of the West Woods, which extended south along the west side of the Hagerstown Pike. Near the bottom of the West Woods, on a long raised plateau that ran nearly perpendicular to the Pike, a small white building glowed faintly in the pre-dawn light. This was a church belonging to the German Baptist Brethren, called *Dunkers* by the people for their custom of baptism by total immersion. To the east of this church on the same plateau, Hooker could just make out four batteries of Confederate artillery and the dim outline of Confederate infantry. He pointed toward the Dunker Church with his cigar.

"Men, that white building will be our rallying point. Have your regiments fall in and prepare."

Hooker reined his horse around and, followed by his aides, returned to the Poffenberger farm to give his instructions to the rest of his officers. Garrett, Frank, and the other Pittsburgh Rifles fell into line and marched north out of the woods to rejoin the rest of the 9th Pennsylvania regiment at the site of the previous night's bivouac.

Hooker's battle plan for the First Corps that day was designed to turn the Rebel army's left flank. Doubleday's division would move south on either side of the Hagerstown Pike, through the Miller barnyard and orchard, and the west side of The Cornfield, to the West Woods. Rick-etts division would advance through the East Woods and the eastern side of The Cornfield. Meade's Pennsylvania Reserves division would wait in reserve in the center. Orders went out and the 8,600 men of the First Corps began to form in line of battle. The 9th Pennsylvania Reserves took up position just inside the southern edge of the North Woods, close to the Hagerstown Pike.

Facing Hooker were 7,700 Confederates, under the command of Stonewall Jackson, formed in a line of battle approximately three-quar-ters of a mile long. The thick vegetation and uneven ground prevented Hooker from seeing that Jackson had placed one brigade in a battle line just south of the East Woods, another brigade in the pasture just to the south of The Cornfield, and four more Rebel brigades in and just to the east of the West Woods. Four additional Confederate brigades waited in reserve behind them. A line of Confederate artillery, the one Hooker had spied through the morning fog, occupied the ridge next to the Dunker Church.

Perhaps most deadly, however, were the fourteen Rebel cannons positioned on an area of high ground on the Nicodemus farm just west of the Miller farm. This was the very place where Garrett had stumbled into General J. E. B. Stuart the night before. These guns, made up of General Stuart's horse artillery and three regular batteries, were in a perfect position to direct enfilade fire on the Federal columns as soon as they stepped off from the Poffenberger farm and the North Woods.

As the officers' calls to form battle lines faded away, the men of the two armies stood in ghostly ranks in the gray and fog of morning. All was in readiness. There was a momentary pause, a last gathering of breath, of courage. Then, at approximately 6:00 a.m., Hooker gave the order to advance.

The Union skirmishers headed out first. With rifles in hand, they emerged from the North Woods and moved south across the Miller fields and orchard. Immediately, the Confederate artillery on Nicode-mus Hill opened fire and was quickly supported by the Rebel batteries on the plateau near the Dunker Church. Union artillery positioned on a ridge on the Poffenberger farm, just north of the North Woods, answered, as did the long-range guns on the high ground two miles to the east of Antietam Creek.

While the artillery dueled, the main body of the Union First Corps infantry began its advance. In long blue lines, the men of Doubleday's and Rickett's divisions moved south along the Hagerstown Pike and across the plowed fields of the Poffenberger farm. As these troops cleared the southern edge of the North Woods, they came under a lethal enfilading fire from the Confederate artillery on Nicodemus Hill. Scores of men were leveled by the shot and shell that ricocheted and exploded through their ranks. Thirteen men of the famed western Iron Brigade were wiped out by a single shell.

Despite this furious barrage, the Union troops continued on, closing ranks to fill the holes left by those felled by artillery shells or by the incessant small arms fire coming from Confederate soldiers hidden in the West and East Woods. The Federals pressed on through the fields and orchards of the Miller farm, and through the East Woods, to the wooden rail fence that marked the northern edge of The Cornfield. At the same time, Union artillery units galloped forward and set up in the field east of the Miller orchard. These batteries, in addition to dueling with the Confederate artillery near the Dunker Church, aimed a few canister shots into The Cornfield to chase out any Rebels that might be hiding there.

As soon as their own artillery had cleared the way, the Federal soldiers advanced into the head-high corn. They held their ranks as best they could, dodging the cornstalks and marching over and around dead and wounded Rebels, while minie balls hissed through the air and cannon balls from both armies whistled and crashed about them.

As the blue-clad soldiers appeared at the southern edge of the corn, the line of Confederate soldiers who had been waiting behind the rail fence at the northern edge of the next pasture suddenly rose up and opened fire. The first line of Union troops fell almost to the man, dead or wounded, lying in rows just as they had stood. The second line stepped over them to return the deadly volley. As fast as they could reload, the two enemies kept up their lethal fire from devastatingly close range, with murderous results for both.

In the eastern part of The Cornfield, a command breakdown in Rickett's Second and Third Brigades thwarted plans for a coordinated attack and temporarily left the First Brigade to carry the battle alone. The men fought valiantly, but after heavy losses, and with their ammunition almost exhausted and no reinforcements in sight, what was left of the First Brigade retreated back north through the corn. Again, their progress was slowed by having to step over the growing number of bodies. Only now, many of the dead and wounded were their own comrades.

By this time, the command problems of Rickett's Second Brigade had been resolved, and the unit rushed forward into the battle. The

Union troops fought their way into the corn, their shouts and cries almost primal as they clashed with the pursuing Confederates. Supported by an aggressive Union battery that managed to set up on a rise in The Cornfield, they halted the Rebel advance and pushed them to the south once more.

Meanwhile, the men of Doubleday's division were hotly engaged on both sides of the Hagerstown turnpike. Like Rickett's First Brigade to the east, the first line of the 2nd and 6th Wisconsin, advancing through the western side of The Cornfield, had been mowed down by three regiments of Rebel troops lying in wait at the southern edge of the corn. Shaken but determined, the Wisconsin regiments closed ranks and began blazing away at the enemy at close range. When reinforcements arrived from the 84th New York Zouave regiment, the three Union regiments managed to drive the Confederates back. The Federal momentum was halted, however, when two more Rebel brigades counterattacked from the direction of the West Woods. These Rebels, themselves, fell victim to a deadly crossfire of Union artillery and small arms. The battle line continued to sway as each side threw more and more men into the fight.

In fact, The Cornfield would change hands at least nine times during the course of that morning, each side charging through the broken, blood-stained stubble, only to be driven back by the renewed efforts of the other. The opposing armies were like two fighters throwing and taking punch after punch; each bloodied, neither entirely triumphant nor entirely defeated. On both sides, whole divisions were reduced to brigades; brigades to regiments. By battle's end, the ground would be littered with the dead and wounded, helpless witnesses to the battle that raged back and forth over the top of them; the once head-high corn almost entirely flattened by the crush of fallen bodies, the storm of bullets, and the artillery and canister shots.

While the Union's lead divisions battled, Garrett and the rest of the 9th Pennsylvania Reserves waited in reserve in the North Woods on the side nearest the Hagerstown Pike. Rifles primed, they flinched and ducked as artillery rounds shattered the tree limbs overhead and small arms fire clipped the leaves, thwacked into tree trunks, or found an unlucky victim. Despite the increasing daylight, gray smoke from the cannons mingled with the ground fog and made it almost impossible to see. The seemingly endless crackle of gunfire and the scream and crash of the artillery barrages combined into one incessant roar. Still, shouted commands, yells, and cries carried back to them on the wind, the words unclear, but the desperation unmistakable. Most chilling were the screams of men killing and being killed.

"God, I hate this waiting," said Frank, kneeling to Garrett's left. He spat on the ground. Garrett was impressed the man could summon the moisture. His own mouth was as dry as dust.

"I can't see a damn thing," said Rawlie. "Can you tell what's happening?"

Leonard shook his head. "Nothing good."

In addition to the firing going on in front of them, the 9th Pennsylvania could hear the sharp staccato of musket fire off to the left from the direction of the East Woods. The firing was intermittent at first, then almost continuous, indicating an intense battle was underway at the eastern edge of The Cornfield, as well.

"That'd be Rickett's men," said Garrett. "God help them."

"God help us all," said Frank.

As the battle in front of them intensified, the men of the 9th Pennsylvania continued to wait in the semi-protection of the North Woods. Gripping their rifles, they fidgeted, cursed, and prayed, not knowing whether their fellow soldiers were driving the enemy before them, or would soon come running through the tall corn, back toward the Union lines, fleeing for their lives.

Finally, after almost an hour of agonized waiting, the 9th Pennsylvania was ordered forward to take up positions at the fence at the northern edge of The Cornfield, on the side closest to the Hagerstown Pike. At the quick step, they marched across the open field adjacent to the Miller farmhouse, their ranks snaking over bodies and around wrecked artillery units. Garrett watched in amazement as an artillery mount, its stomach ripped open by a shell and its intestines dragging, galloped through the nearby orchard in a desperate attempt to keep up with its harness-mates who were pulling a caisson to a new position.

When they reached The Cornfield, the men of the 9th found portions of the fence already blown apart by artillery blasts or knocked down by the regiments that had preceded them. Soldiers, dead and dying, Union and Rebel, lay on the ground on either side of the fence line. The men dismantled what was left of the fence, and piled the posts and rails into as much of a protective shield as they could.

Directly in front of Garrett's position, a dead Union soldier hung over the topmost rail. His body was riddled with bullets from counterattacking Rebels who thought he was still defending his position.

"Rawlie! Give me a hand," cried Garrett.

Together, the two of them hoisted the soldier off the rail and laid his body on the ground. Working swiftly, they took apart the fence and stacked the wood into a crude breastwork. Then they knelt beside the rest of the regiment, rested the muzzles of their guns on the topmost rails, and waited for the order to attack.

Here, at the edge of The Cornfield, the world was noise and smoke. Shells and canisters screamed and exploded sending bits of dirt, cornstalks, and men into the air. The rifle and musket fire were continuous, the powder flashing and the bullets whizzing like angry bees. Men yelled, screamed, and laughed maniacally as they fought, sometimes hand to hand. Rifle barrels showed briefly over the tops of the corn as new units moved into position, and attempted to hold or advance the line of battle. The fighting surged one way and then the other.

Crouching at the fence, Garrett ducked as yet another cannonball screamed overhead, closer this time. Through the sulfurous smoke he glimpsed battle flags, both Union and Confederate, falling, rising, then falling again. He patted the cartridge box on his belt and wiped his sweaty hands on his pants before clutching his rifle once again.

Garrett felt rather than saw the tide of the battle turn. The roar of the struggle that had been moving slightly away to the south turned north and grew louder. Ghostly forms began to approach through the gray smoke and what was left of The Cornfield. Some were running, some crawling, and some carrying others. Garrett and Rawlie exchanged a look.

"Hold steady," shouted a Union officer. "They're our men."

Soon, the tattered blue uniforms became visible as what was left of the 2nd and 6th Wisconsin and parts of other regiments struggled out of The Cornfield. Garrett also caught a glimpse of the distinctive white blouse and red pants of a Union Zouave unit. The horror of the battle was etched on the retreating men's powder-blackened faces. Close behind them, in mad pursuit, were the 226 men of the 1st Texas regiment, their blood-curdling Rebel yell barely audible over the thundering cauldron that was The Cornfield.

The Texas Brigade, including the 1st Texas regiment, had been held in reserve behind the Confederate lines that morning in order to give them time to eat their first meal in three days. But, when the Union forces succeeded in pushing the Confederate troops back toward the Dunker Church, the Rebel commander put out a desperate call for reinforcements. The Texas Brigade answered, leaving their breakfast cooking on the fires.

Enraged by this last indignity, the Texans threw themselves into the fight with unbridled ferocity. Lining up with the 1st Texas regiment closest to the Hagerstown Road, the Texas Brigade surged across the field just south of The Cornfield and drove the Union troops before them into the corn. But the 1st Texas, in their excitement at having the Yankees on the run, continued on into The Cornfield. Yelling and screaming, they advanced one hundred and fifty yards ahead of the rest of the brigade – directly into the waiting guns of the 9th Pennsylvania Reserves.

The men of the 9th Pennsylvania waited while the last of the retreating Union soldiers ran or dragged themselves through their lines.

"They're right behind us," yelled one of the Wisconsin boys.

Desperately, Garrett searched for the enemy through the clouds of gunpowder.

"Watch for their legs beneath the smoke," shouted the captain.

Sure enough, in just a few moments, Garrett saw the butternut clad legs of the enemy hurrying towards them. Above the smoke and the scattered stands of corn, he glimpsed their flag – blue, red, and white with one lone white star. He closed one eye and took aim at the spot where he expected the Rebels to emerge. Just as the first of the Texans became visible, he heard the order.

"Fire!"

The 9th Pennsylvania let loose a tremendous volley, almost simultaneously with a barrage from the Federal batteries positioned in the Miller orchard. In the resulting firestorm of shot, flame, and smoke, the first row of the 1st Texas regiment simply vanished. The second line of the 1st Texas, stunned by the ferocity of the fire, faltered … but only momentarily. Once more they pressed forward and opened fire on both the 9th Pennsylvania and the artillerists in the field behind them.

With the Texans bearing down on him, Garrett fired and reloaded like a madman. At one point, the Rebels seemed to be breaching the Federal line to his left, but a second line of Union infantry was pushed into position and the Texans began to fall back through the corn.

As soon as it was determined the Texans were retreating, the 9th Pennsylvania set off in pursuit. They loaded and fired as they went, stepping over bodies, blue and gray. Garrett added his own voice to the roar of advancing men, but could not hear himself over the din of battle. In the smoke and confusion, he quickly lost track of the soldiers who had been next to him at the fence. He thought he saw Rawlie over to his right, stopping to reload his rifle, but he couldn't be sure in the screaming rush. Keeping his eyes on the regimental colors so as not to completely lose his way, Garrett continued to fire at the fleeing forms in front of him.

Suddenly, a shell exploded to his right and the men that had been running abreast of him vanished. Garrett stumbled and sprawled flat just as a bullet whizzed over his head. Glancing behind him, he saw he had tripped over a severed leg, its owner nowhere to be seen. Garrett scrambled to his feet and ran on. For a second, he caught sight of Leonard, his eyes wild as he ran through the smoke with bayonet raised. But, where was Frank? And Rawlie? Dodging bloody, bent corn stalks, Garrett continued on, his progress slowed by the bodies, haversacks, canteens, and rifles that were the debris of battle.

Finally, just ahead of him, Garrett spotted his regiment's color guard. The flag bearer was waving the banner to rally the troops. Garrett hurried toward him. Suddenly, the air turned to fire as remnants of the 1st Texas turned and directed a thunderous volley at the pursuing Federals. The 9th Pennsylvania Reserves color guard was shot down to the man. A soldier near the severely wounded flag bearer threw down his rifle, grabbed the colors, and raised them aloft. Almost immediately, the man's body convulsed as three Rebel bullets found their mark and sent him crashing to the ground. Yet another soldier of the 9th Pennsylvania rushed forward, snatched up the banner, and raised it high. Within moments, a minie ball in the shoulder sent him spinning away. By this time, the forward motion of the Reserves had slowed. The men began to hesitate, halt, then walk backwards as they fired, the momentum of the battle having reversed itself once more.

"Forward, men! Forward!" Another brave soldier had taken up the fallen regimental banner and was waving it frantically. Garrett, pausing to reload, was close enough to see the passion in the young man's eyes. That look of passion changed to one of dull surprise as a minie ball pierced the man's forehead. Garrett dropped his rifle and lunged forward, seizing the colors just as the flag bearer slumped to the ground.

Garrett looked up at the banner above him. The blue cloth and gold fringe were shredded by bullets and blackened by smoke, a testament to the intensity of the fighting. With no rifle in hand, he knew he was defenseless. But the importance of this flag – to him and the men with him - drove such thoughts from his mind. Now it was his voice shouting, urging the men on. The Union soldiers nearest him paused in their retreat and fixed their eyes on the swaying banner. Garrett began pressing forward through the smoke in the direction of the enemy. The Rebels were sweeping through the corn once more, toward the stalled Federal advance. Garrett could see their shadowy figures approaching, the flash of their rifles, the sound of that infernal Rebel yell. He knew they were coming for him – for him and Rawlie and Frank and Leonard. But, they would not carry the day, he thought, breaking into a run. They would not.

Suddenly, Garrett found himself flat on his back, slammed to the ground as if kicked by a mule. There was no pain, just an odd tingling in his shoulder and a roaring in his ears. Men were running by him, over him. He saw rather than heard them shout and the thunder of battle seemed to come from far away, like sounds under water. He lay there and watched, mesmerized, as thin gunpowder clouds passed overhead, alternately hiding and revealing a hot sun. After a while, beneath the battle sounds, he heard men moaning and crying out for water. Some of them seemed very near.

Garrett had no idea how long he lay there, but he eventually became aware of soldiers running over him once more, first in one direction, then another. Suddenly, he felt a heavy weight on his chest. He struggled to breathe, thrashing his head from side to side.

That's when he saw her. A woman, indistinct, moving between dark shapes on the ground, stopping, moving again. He tried to reach out to her.

"Clara," he whispered through cracked lips. "Clara."

CHAPTER 22

Casualty Reports From Union Victory At South Mountain, Maryland!

AT 7:20 A.M. ON THE morning of Wednesday, September 17, 1862, Clara stood outside the *Pittsburgh Gazette* building and read the latest telegraphed war reports pinned up on the bulletin board. She had arisen extra early so as to have time to travel into Pittsburgh to check the casualty lists before work. Holding her breath, she ran her finger down the names of killed and wounded.

"Thank God," she whispered when Garrett's name was not among those listed. She turned and began threading her way through the crowd to catch the omnibus back to Lawrenceville.

Suddenly, she felt an odd tingling sensation spread through her body. There was a roaring in her ears, and the people and carriages in front of her began to swim before her eyes. The sounds of the city seem to come from far away, like sounds under water. Swaying, she reached her hand out to the side of a nearby building to steady herself.

"Here, Miss. Are you all right?" inquired an older gentleman, seeing her distress.

"Oh. Yes, Sir," said Clara. "It's just the heat. I'll be fine."

The older man, who was wearing a wool topcoat against the morning chill, gave her a quizzical look. "If you're sure, then." He gave her a last glance before continuing down the street.

The dizzy spell passed within a few moments. Admonishing herself for having rushed out without eating breakfast, Clara hurried to Penn Street and leapt aboard the Citizen's Passenger Railway Car just before it pulled away. She plunked down in an empty seat in the back and stared blindly out the window. Despite her relief at not finding Garrett's name on the casualty list, she couldn't shake the feeling of unease that had been growing over the past few days.

At the end of the line near the closed Camp Wilkins, Clara exited the car and began walking as quickly as decorum allowed. Although there were plans to extend the rail line along Butler Street into Lawrenceville, at the moment she had to travel the remaining mile and a quarter to the Arsenal on foot. She arrived at the Butler Street gate at four minutes before eight and joined the thinning crowd of girls and men climbing the roadway to their workstations in the upper Arsenal. Most turned off at the large brick storehouse just inside the gate. Others, like her, continued on to the laboratory buildings farther up the hill. Despite the coolness of the morning, the sun climbing in a clear blue sky promised a warm day.

Over one thousand people were employed at the Arsenal in this, the second year of the war, with more being hired every day to meet the Union army's demand for cartridges, artillery shells, cartridge boxes, caps, belts, saddles, harnesses, and all the other accoutrements of war. With the recent escalation of the fighting in Maryland, the activity at the Arsenal had increased accordingly. A steady stream of wagons loaded with kegs of powder clattered back and forth from the powder magazines to the laboratory buildings to keep the workers supplied with the deadly ingredients needed to assemble the cartridges and shells. More wagons carried the finished munitions to the warehouses for storage, or rumbled out the gate to begin the process of delivering the arms to the soldiers at the seat of war. Clara felt a sense of pride to be engaged in this important work.

As she neared the laboratory buildings that morning, Clara spied Louella Brody, the twelve-year-old daughter of one of her father's patients, up ahead on the roadway. Mr. Brody had enlisted at the start of the war and his family was struggling. The Brodys had been very grateful when Clara managed to obtain a job for Louella at the Arsenal.

"Louella!" Clara called, waving.

The young girl turned and her freckled face broke into a broad smile.

"Hello, Miss Clara."

"So," said Clara, falling into step with the younger girl, "how has work been going?"

"Wonderfully," said Louella. "The supervisor says I'm a very fast learner. This past week, I haven't had to redo any of my cartridges. And today, I get my first pay."

"Your mother will be so proud," said Clara. "You're such a help to her."

Louella beamed.

The two of them entered the small wooden cloakroom building between the main laboratory building and the smaller laboratory building just to the east. They hung their shawls on the last two vacant hooks.

"I'd better hurry," said Louella as she tied a bright red kerchief around her hair to protect it from the dusty work. "I don't want to be late."

"Have a good day," Clara called after her.

With a smile, she watched the young girl skip across the yard, leap up onto the porch, and disappear into Room 13 of the smaller laboratory building. Clara followed at a more dignified pace.

As usual, Mr. Geary stood on the wooden porch just outside the doorway of Room 14. He squinted at his pocket watch as the last of the girls scurried by. A stickler for punctuality, he delighted in docking their pay if they were even a minute late. Clara nodded to him politely as she passed and noted his look of disappointment when he confirmed she was on time. She entered the room to find Annie already seated at one of the long wooden tables.

"I was afraid you might not make it," said Annie as Clara took her place on the bench beside her.

"So was I," Clara replied, arranging her hoop skirt around her legs. She wished she could just wear a petticoat like most of the other girls, but the hoop was one convention upon which her mother insisted. "I went to read the casualty lists outside the *Pittsburgh Gazette*."

Annie's eyes grew large. There had been no word from her brothers in weeks.

"None of them were listed," was all Clara was able to say before Mr. Geary took his place at the front of the room.

"Ladies, let's begin," he said.

The twenty-four girls in Room 14 set to work. On that Wednesday morning, they were assigned the task of assembling .54 caliber rifle cartridges and .71 caliber rifled musket cartridges, as were the girls in most of the other workrooms of the Arsenal laboratories that day. In addition, a few of the workrooms were engaged in filling artillery shells with gun powder for use in ten-pounder and twelve-pounder Parrot guns.

After two and a half weeks of working at the Arsenal, Clara was accustomed to the order of the work day. The work was repetitive, but ideally suited to the girls' small dexterous fingers. On this particular day, she, Annie, and ten of the other girls in Room 14 worked as pinchers; the other twelve as bundlers. The paper cartridge cylinders, pre-assembled by the three hundred girls and boys who worked in the storehouse building down the hill near Butler Street, were delivered to the workrooms before the start of the day. The pinchers would make a powder tube by tying off the bottom of a cylinder with a thread and pouring in a carefully measured amount of gunpowder. A minie ball was then inserted, pointed end down, into a second, outer tube, followed by the powder tube. The entire cartridge was then folded down in such a way that the ball and powder stayed secure until the soldier bit off the top of the cartridge paper prior to loading his rifle.

The bundlers would take ten of these finished cartridges, along with one cartridge filled with percussion caps, and bundle them together in a small package wrapped in water-resistant brown paper. They would affix a label identifying each package as a product of the Allegheny Arsenal and tie the entire bundle with twine. Each soldier was issued four of these bundles, or forty rounds, which they kept in two water-proof tins in their cartridge boxes.

By 8:30 a.m., the excited chatter that typified the start of the work day had quieted. The girls settled into their routine and spoke only occasionally as they bent to their tasks.

"So, Clara. Have you heard from your boyo?" asked May Ryan who was seated across the table.

"Not recently," replied Clara. "But his regiment is on the move, so the mail tends to be fairly unreliable."

"Well, when you do, tell him to take care," said May. "I've been read-in' the star charts. There's great trouble ahead. Fire and death."

"That's sacrilege, May Ryan. And well you know it," said Katy Lyn-don, making the Sign of the Cross as she reached for another bundle of cartridges. "Only God knows what the future holds."

"Sure and didn't God put the stars in their place?" May replied. "I'm just sayin', there's somethin' big comin'. You'll see."

"Predictin' fire and death durin' a war. It's a grand prophet you are, May," said Annie. She pinched another cartridge closed and leaned over to Clara. "Don't pay her any mind. She's a great believer in superstition. Last week it was tea leaves."

Clara managed to smile, but the uneasy feeling intensified.

Edgar Gliddon paused on the front stoop of the large Greek Revival house belonging to the post commander of the Allegheny Arsenal. A fine day, he thought as he looked out over the bustle of the lower Arse-nal. A fine day, indeed.

His meeting with Commander Symington had been most produc-tive. Given the extent of the Gliddon Iron Works' contracts with the Allegheny Arsenal, it had been a small matter to get him to agree that hir-ing a doctor's daughter to work at the Arsenal was a public relations mis-take that would needlessly inflame the sensibilities of Pittsburgh society, many of whose members were already upset over the fact that female work-ers, albeit Irish ones, were being employed in place of boys. The comman-der had assured him Clara would be notified at the end of the day that her services were no longer required. With that action taken, the Ambrose family would lose their last means of steady income.

Edgar smirked. Watching Clara and her family sink into poverty would be sweet revenge for their treatment of him. And if, with any luck, Morgan Percy had unwittingly delivered the news of Clara and Edgar's alleged engagement to the hapless Mr. Cameron, as Edgar hoped, any concomitant suffering on Cameron's part would be a bonus.

He pulled out his pocket watch. 1:58 p.m. Just enough time to ride out to the mill and check on things before meeting some colleagues for an early supper at his club. With a self-satisfied smile, he descended the porch steps and strode south toward the Butler Street gate where his carriage and driver waited.

The wagoner rolled the last barrel of gunpowder on its end to its usual place at the end of the porch outside Room 14 of the smaller laboratory building. Straightening, he removed his filthy hat and began fanning himself. He had unloaded a total of ten barrels of gunpowder outside the various workrooms of this and the main laboratory building, and his back was killing him. Now, he had only to pick up the empty cylinder boxes stacked outside Room 14 and deliver them back to the lower storehouse, and he could take his break.

Just then, a young man came around the end of the main laboratory building fifty feet away.

"Hey, Frick," he shouted to the wagoner, "I still need you to pick up those cylinder boxes outside of Number 1 before you go."

"I'll be there in a minute," barked Frick, jamming his hat back on his head. He loaded the boxes from Room 14 into the wagon, climbed aboard, and clucked to his two-horse team. The wagon rattled over the new stone road that ran along the southern, open end of the E-shaped main laboratory building. When he reached the porch outside workroom Number 1 – the room at the southwest corner of the building – he reined the horses to a halt. The three barrels of gunpowder he had unloaded earlier stood at the end of the porch. One of them had its lid off. Just beyond the barrels, the young man stood waiting next to a stack of empty cartridge boxes piled outside the workroom door.

"Hurry up, boy," Frick said as he glanced at his pocket watch. "It's almost 2:00 p.m., and I've not even had my dinner, yet."

One of the carthorses stomped his ironclad hoof on the stone roadway as if he, too, was eager to return to the comfort of a cool barn and a full feed bag.

The young man bent down to pick up the stack of cylinder boxes. As he turned back toward the wagon, he spied a wisp of smoke, then a small flame rising from the roadway near the dray horse's back hoof.

His shouted warning never had time to leave his lips.

Just before 2:00 p.m., Mr. Geary entered Room 14.

"All right, girls. Pay day. This side of the tables first."

The eleven girls on the near side of the room rose from their work and followed the foreman out the door. The paymaster had set up his table in front of the small cloakroom building between their laboratory and the main laboratory building. The girls chatted as they waited in line to receive their drafts and speculated how they might spend their hard-earned money. The remaining thirteen girls, Annie and Clara included, lingered at their tables or went out onto the porch to wait their turn.

"I'm so glad it's finally pay day," said Annie, stretching as she stood up from her table. "I'm goin' to buy a new petticoat. I know it's dear, but this one I'm wearin' is practically in shreds." She raised the hem of her dress as proof. "What about you, Clara?"

Before Clara could answer, a loud explosion rent the air like a cannon being fired at close range. Almost immediately, they could hear the sound of girls screaming.

"God in heaven! What was that?" cried Annie.

Clara leapt from her chair and rushed to the window. The other girls quickly crowded around her. Smoke was billowing from the far corner of the main laboratory building.

"The laboratory's on fire," shrieked one of the girls. Her cry was taken up by the others, panicked by the tremendous danger posed by fire in a place filled with gunpowder and ammunition.

"Quickly!" shouted Clara. "We must get out!"

The girls from Room 14 needed no urging. They stampeded out the door, colliding with each other as they squeezed through the narrow opening.

"Ladies! Don't push!" Clara implored as she attempted to control the panic that seized the girls, but the scene outside the door was too much. In addition to the smoke, flames were now visible coming from the main laboratory, and terrified, screaming girls were pouring out of the other workrooms.

"It's the Rebels!" yelled one. "They're blowing up the Arsenal!"

Her allegation only increased the general panic, as did the sight of two girls stumbling out of Room Number 1 with their clothing on fire.

"Come on," said Annie, grabbing Clara's hand. "We must get away from the buildin's." The two girls leapt from the porch and began running down the hill toward the Butler Street gate.

Suddenly, a second, much larger explosion slammed them both to the ground. Dazed, they lay there for a few moments. When, slowly, Clara managed to pull herself to her feet, she could only stare in horror at the carnage around her.

The second explosion had blown the roof off the main laboratory building and hurled people, ammunition, and pieces of the structure high into the air. The ground around Clara and Annie was littered with charred bodies and body parts, burning shards of wood, exploded and unexploded shells, torn clothing, fragments of dinner baskets, steel bands from hoop skirts, minie balls, melted lead, and the occasional odd shoe. Much of this same debris hung from the surrounding tree limbs. Weeping and retching, girls covered in blood were running from the ruins of the building, some with their hair and clothing on fire; others with the very clothes torn from their bodies by the force of the blast. As they ran, shells ignited by the explosions and the fire continued to burst. The resulting noise and deadly shrapnel added to the chaos and destruction.

"God have mercy on us." Annie, bleeding from her forehead, had pulled herself to her knees, only to discover the dead body of a young girl on the ground next to her. There were only two mangled stumps where the girl's legs used to be. "God have mercy on us all," Annie repeated.

As unspeakable wreckage continued to rain down on them, Clara snapped to her senses. She grabbed Annie by the waist and dragged her to her feet.

"Come on, Annie! We must keep going!" Leaning on each other for support, the two girls rejoined the frantic mob fleeing down the hill toward safety.

Just ahead, at the bottom of the hill near the Butler Street gate, Annie and Clara could see people milling about the two-story storehouse building. The blast had shattered the windows of the building, and the frightened workers had jammed into the stairs and doorways in their desperation to escape. Finding the stairways clogged with people, the girls on the upper floors were attempting to climb out the second-story windows. Some men and soldiers, having come on the run from the lower Arsenal at the sound of the first explosion, were trying to help them evacuate the building. Others were racing up the hill toward the main laboratory in hopes of rescuing the girls trapped in the burning wreckage.

As the men ran past them, Clara glanced over her shoulder to find the smaller laboratory building they had just vacated was now also on fire. A young girl, her face and clothes blackened and burned, was trying to climb out of the window of Room 13. The girl sat straddling the windowsill – half in and half out; frozen in fear – even as the flames from inside the room licked at the opening. Through the smoke, Clara could just see the bit of bright red cloth that bound the girl's hair.

"Oh, my God," said Clara. She let go of Annie's waist and shoved her in the direction of the Butler Street gate. "Run, Annie!" she commanded, her blue eyes earnest in her smoke-blackened face. "Run!"

Clara turned and raced back up the hill.

"Clara, no!" screamed Annie as Clara disappeared into the smoke.

Suddenly, up the hill to the right, the heat of the fire ignited another shell. Annie cowered as dirt and hot metal rained down. As the air cleared, she hesitated for just a moment. Then, fighting her fear and her common sense, she began pushing her way back up the hill against the stampede of terrified girls still attempting to flee the upper Arsenal.

Suddenly, someone grabbed her by the shoulders and spun her around.

"Where is she?" shouted Edgar Gliddon. His face was covered with sweat and his eyes were wild. When she didn't answer immediately, he shook her. "Where is she? Where's Clara?"

"She ran back to help," sobbed Annie, pointing to the smaller laboratory building. "Stop her! Oh, please, stop her!"

"Oh, God," muttered Edgar as smoke and flames poured from the building. "The little fool." He released Annie and sprinted toward the laboratory.

The third explosion knocked Annie to the ground once more. For a moment, everything went black. A searing pain in her left hand and arm pulled her back to consciousness. As she struggled to her knees, Annie realized, as if watching herself from far away, that she was on fire.

CHAPTER 23

THE FAINT SMELL OF LILACS reached him first, the familiar scent that announced her presence like a soft, cool breeze and lingered after she had gone. He turned and saw her standing there in her blue gown. Smiling, she beckoned to him. He stretched out his hand, but her image, just out of reach, began to waver and fade.

Suddenly, the sweet fragrance was replaced by an indescribable stench of blood, viscera, vomit, and ether. The air was filled with shouts and groans. He realized, in dull surprise, that some of the sounds were coming from him.

"Hey, orderly. This guy's comin' to," said a voice near his left ear. Garrett turned his head in the direction of the sound. His eyelids felt like dead weights, but he forced them open to find a soldier lying on the ground next to him. He was staring at Garrett with the one good eye not covered by the filthy, bloody bandage around his head.

A thin man wearing Union blue pants and a sweat-soaked shirt with the sleeves rolled up came and bent over Garrett.

"Don't move, soldier. You've lost a lot of blood. Minie ball near took your shoulder off."

Garrett searched his memory. He recalled charging forward, the flag in his hands, then looking up through the smoke at a blue sky. But his mind was as sluggish as his tongue.

"How...?" he finally managed.

"You were found on the battlefield by Miss Barton. You know her?"

"Miss ... Barton?"

"Miss Clara Barton. The female nurse. You were calling her name. Good thing, too. There was a dead Reb draped over you. She never would've seen you if you hadn't called out like that. Most likely, you'd have bled to death. She bandaged your shoulder and got some soldiers to carry you to the field hospital. That's where you are now."

Though to do so sent a shooting pain behind his eyes, Garrett lifted his head to take in the scene around him. He appeared to be in some kind of barn and was lying on a makeshift stretcher made of two fence posts stuck through an army coat. All around him were the wounded and dying, some eerily quiet, others moaning and crying out in pain. Harried, tired-looking men flitted among the sufferers, checking on one here, removing a dead soldier there. Garrett looked down at the dirty, blood-soaked bandage that bound his right shoulder and instinctively reached for it.

"Don't you touch that, now," warned the orderly. "The doctor said you gotta keep pressure on that wound. You're one of the lucky ones. We ran out of real bandages a while ago. Hold on while I see if I can get the doctor."

As the orderly hurried away, Garrett took a closer look at the injured men around him. The man was right. Many of the soldiers' wounds were bound by strips of cloth torn from their own or someone else's uniform. In dismay, he realized some of the makeshift bandages were actually bloody cornstalks, a macabre memento from the field in which the soldiers had fallen.

A strange rasping sound, like someone sawing wood, drew his attention to the far corner of the room. Garrett turned just in time to see a steward carry a severed arm away from the prone form of a soldier lying on an operating table made by laying one of the barn doors atop two barrels. The steward tossed the arm out one of the barn windows and hurried back to aid the surgeon, who was busily scraping the bone and suturing the skin over the end of the remaining stump. All around on the dirt floor, wide-eyed men, awaiting their turn, watched in horror.

Suddenly, an older man wearing a bloody, pus-stained apron loomed over him.

"What've we got?"

"Shoulder wound, Doctor," the orderly recited. "He was brought in about three o'clock this afternoon. He's one of the ones Miss Barton found."

The doctor, his face lined and heavy with exhaustion, merely nodded.

"Roll him onto his left side."

Even that slight movement caused Garrett to grimace in pain. The doctor unwrapped the filthy bandage from Garrett's shoulder to reveal a dark oozing wound just under his clavicle and a slightly larger exit wound at the back of his shoulder.

"Now, this is going to hurt some," said the doctor. With no further warning, he inserted the index finger of his right hand into the entry hole, and the index finger of his left hand into the exit wound. He probed until the two fingers touched. Garrett screamed in pain. He was afraid he might faint.

"Good," said the doctor, withdrawing his bloody fingers and wiping them on his apron. "I don't feel any fragments. The bullet must have just missed the bone. Lost a lot of blood, though. Orderly, re-bandage this shoulder. Use the sleeve of his shirt. When you're done, put him under the trees with the others for transport."

Looking down on Garrett's sheet-white face, the doctor suddenly seemed to see him for the first time. "What's your name, son?" he said in a kinder tone.

"Garrett," he replied through gritted teeth. "Garrett Cameron. Company A, 9th Pennsylvania Reserves."

"Well, Garrett, don't you worry. We're going to move you to the brigade hospital now. They'll take good care of you there. Absent any infection, you should be just fine. Good luck." He turned back to the orderly. "Hurry up, here. We've got plenty more coming in."

Once Garrett's shoulder was bandaged, two soldiers came and lifted his stretcher. The pain he experienced as they carried him to the ambulance caused him to pass out, but not before he glimpsed the pile of amputated arms and legs outside the door of the barn-turned-hospital, or the lines of corpses that made a somber honor guard for the wounded being carried in and out.

"Where do you want this one, Sister?" asked the soldier at the head of the stretcher as he paused in the doorway of Ward A.

"In that next bed, please," the nun instructed without looking up.

The bearers made their way between the double rows of cots that stretched from one end of the long wooden building to the other, laid the stretcher on the floor next to the available bed, and lifted the unconscious soldier onto the mattress. Given the vast numbers of wounded they had carried and had yet to carry into the hospital that day, they were surprisingly gentle, but still the young man moaned in pain. With a nod to the nun, they left to retrieve the next patient from the waiting ambulance.

Sister Catherine made a last check of the bandage around the leg stump of the man she was tending, then turned to examine the new soldier. The man's right shoulder was bound in a filthy bandage made from someone's shirtsleeve, and blood seeped through the cloth from the underlying wound. She knew the wound needed to be cleaned as soon as possible and a fresh bandage applied, but by army regulation, she was required to wait for the doctor to examine the patient. Given the number of wounded arriving in Frederick each hour, that could take some time. She sighed in frustration.

Well, at least she could make the man more presentable. She took a rag and wet it from the pitcher of water on the small table beside the bed. Poised to wipe the dirt and sweat from his face, she suddenly stopped and her face went as pale as that of the young soldier before her. The strong jaw and high cheekbones. The straight, full brows.

Even the hair, though filthy and matted with blood, appeared to be the right shade of brown. The resemblance to her only brother, Andrew, dead these past fifteen years, was uncanny. She almost expected him to open his eyes and say, "Hi, Cat," with that crooked grin of his. As if hearing her thoughts, the young man's eyes fluttered open. He stared at her, unseeing, before drifting back into unconsciousness. She noted with relief his eyes were brown, not blue. Making the Sign of the Cross, she began to wipe the blood from the young man's face with trembling hands.

When Garrett awoke, it was quiet. The air smelled of soap and quinine. He was lying in a clean bed in what appeared to be a wooden barracks, just one of at least fifty occupied cots that were lined up on either side of a narrow aisle. All around him were men in various stages of recuperation, many missing an arm or leg; most silent, a few moaning softly. He was very thirsty and his shoulder felt as if it was on fire. Looking down at it, he saw that a clean cotton bandage had replaced the one made from his shirt, though a large yellow-and-pink-tinged stain had seeped through the material.

Garrett turned his head to find a matronly woman mopping the forehead of a patient two beds down. She wore a dark blue dress with a large white collar, and her hair was completely concealed by an odd-looking, severely starched hat that perched on her head like a large white bird, extending its wings.

"Ma'am?" he called hoarsely.

She looked up in surprise.

"Well, it's about time you woke up," she said, hurrying to his bedside. Up close, she looked younger, perhaps no more than thirty. She had a round face and intelligent, deep set blue eyes. Without asking, she poured a cup of water from the pitcher at his bedside and helped him lean forward to drink. The effort was painful and he fell back, exhausted.

"There, now," she said in a business-like tone. "How are you feeling?"

"I've been better," he said, managing a weak smile. "Where am I?"

"You're in Ward A of General Hospital #1 in Frederick, Maryland. They brought you in the day before yesterday, along with at least a couple of thousand others."

"What happened? With the battle?"

"We can talk about that later. I'm going to get the doctor."

Within minutes, a nondescript man wearing a major's gold oak leaves on his blue uniform accompanied the nurse back into the ward.

"Let's see what we have here," the man said without introduction.

Garrett grimaced as the doctor peeled away the dressing and began to poke and prod at the wound. Garrett's shoulder looked angry and red, and thick yellow matter oozed from the hole torn by the minie ball.

"Hmph," the doctor grunted in approval. "A great deal of laudable pus. That's a good sign. We had to go in and remove a few bullet fragments and bone spiculae the field surgeon missed, but I feel confident we got them all. Time will tell how much mobility you retain in that shoulder." He straightened. "Change his dressing and get him started on a good strong broth." In response to the nurse's cold stare, he added, "If you would, please, Sister."

"Yes, Doctor."

The man hurried away.

"You're a nun," said Garrett. Now he understood the odd dress and headpiece, and the feverish dreams he had been having about giant white cranes.

"Yes. I'm Sister Catherine Bateau, of the Daughters of Charity." At the look on Garrett's face, she snickered. "Don't worry. I won't bite. Try to rest now, while I go fetch some clean bandages and something for you to eat."

When she returned, Garrett managed to swallow a few spoonfuls of broth.

Sister," he said, plucking at her sleeve as she prepared to leave, "can you tell me now? Did we beat them?"

"There's plenty of time to discuss that when you're feeling better."

"Please. I have to know." His eyes searched hers for some clue.

Sister Catherine contemplated the desperate young man before her. She sat down in the wooden chair next to his bed and leaned forward so as not to be overheard by the other patients.

"The newspapers are calling it a Union victory," she said in a quiet voice. "Lee was successfully driven out of Maryland, although some people are already grumbling because McClellan didn't follow and defeat him once and for all. Still, the invasion was stopped. But, at a horrible cost. There were so many killed and wounded, on both sides. Over twenty thousand, they estimate. Every house and serviceable building between here and Sharpsburg is filled with wounded. Many are even being sent to Washington." Her eyes dimmed as she looked over the rows of patients. "Such a horrible cost," she repeated softly.

Even after what he had seen on the Peninsula, Garrett's mind could not conceive of such numbers of dead and wounded. He only knew the slaughter and horror around his small corner of the battlefield had been like nothing he had ever seen before ... or ever hoped to see again.

Suddenly, his eyes flew open. The newspapers! Surely word of a battle of this magnitude would have reached Pittsburgh by now. The official casualty lists would take days if not weeks to compile. Clara would be worried sick, not knowing if he lived or died. He had to get word to her.

"Sister, could you write a letter for me? I need to send it right away."

"Certainly." She rose and went to the cabinet at the end of the aisle and returned with pen, ink, and a piece of paper.

"I assume this is to be sent to Clara?"

"How did you know?" he said in surprise.

The nun's stern face softened for just a moment. "You've been calling for her off and on for the last two days. Go ahead." She wrote while Garrett dictated:

> September 19, 1862
>
> *Miss Clara Ambrose*
> *Allen Street*
> *Lawrenceville, Pennsylvania*
>
> *Dearest Clara,*
> *I'm writing to let you know I am alive and well. I received a slight wound in a battle near Antietam Creek, but am receiving good care in the hospital. A nurse is writing this letter for me. Write to me as soon as possible, care of Ward A, General Hospital #1, Frederick, Maryland.*
>
> > *All my love,*
> > *Garrett*

"A 'slight wound'?" said Sister Catherine. "Well, I can understand how you wouldn't want to worry her."

"Could you mail the letter for me, Sister? I had some stamps in my haversack ...." He looked around for some sign of his belongings.

Sister Catherine put up her hand.

"Don't worry. I'll take care of it. I warn you, though. With all the confusion surrounding the battle, you may have a difficult time getting anything out or in."

* * *

Brandishing his rifle, Garrett ran through choking clouds of smoke, past falling banners, broken cornstalks, and the powder-blackened faces of his fellow soldiers. The rattle of musketry and the roar of the cannon filled his ears so that he saw rather than heard the screams of the fallen. Still, he kept fighting his way toward the light. Gradually, the sounds of battle faded and gave way to the low drone of voices and the clink-clink of spoons against bowls. He opened his eyes and remembered where he was. Soaked with sweat, he struggled to clear his mind and his vision.

From the angle of the sunlight coming through the windows of the ward, he figured it must be late afternoon. He turned his head to find the soldier in the bed next to his watching him. The man's dark hair fringed the bandage that covered his forehead.

"The dreams are the hardest," said the soldier in an accent that reminded Garrett of Annie Burke.

"What?" Garrett croaked through cracked lips.

"The dreams," the soldier repeated. "I could tell from the sounds you was makin'. Don't worry. We all have 'em." He gestured to the ward in general. "Name's Johnny Lynch. 69th New York."

"The Irish Brigade," said Garrett with admiration.

Johnny nodded. "You?"

"Garrett Cameron. 9th Pennsylvania Reserves. You boys did some fine work on the Peninsula."

"As did yourselves." Johnny motioned to Garrett's shoulder. "Where was you when you got hit?"

"In a cornfield near the Hagerstown Pike."

"Bad business, that," said Johnny.

"What about you?" said Garrett.

"I got mine tryin' to take that damned sunken road to the south and east of where you were. And wasn't the Rebs just sittin' there waitin' for us? Lost nearly half our men. Got me twice, in the head and the side." He drew back the covers to reveal his bandage-wrapped midsection. There was a dark, oozing stain on the side closest to Garrett. "But, take it, we did. And when we was finished, the dead was piled up so deep you coulda walked the length of the road and never touched the ground." For a moment, his eyes grew dark and distant, as if seeing the horror anew. "But then, I don't know that we had it worse than you, or Burnside's boys tryin' to take the lower bridge over the creek. Some of them as was in it told me they was sittin' ducks for the Georgia boys up on the bluff."

Garrett, whose understanding of the battle had been limited to the area in which the Pittsburgh Rifles had fought, began to get an inkling of the breadth of the daylong battle at Antietam Creek and the unthinkable loss of life that had occurred. He wondered what had happened to Rawlie, Frank, and Leonard.

"Did we win?" Garrett asked.

"Depends on who you talk to," said Johnny. "But, I do know General Lee and his boys skedaddled back over the Potomac to Virginia. That's certainly a victory of sorts. Wish we'd finished 'em off, though." He winced as he shifted position in the bed.

"Where're you from, Cameron?" he asked when the pain subsided.

"Pittsburgh. You?"

"Brooklyn, New York. Sure wish I was back there now. Haven't seen me family in over a year. Got a sweetheart there, too." He smiled. "We're goin' to get married as soon as I finish me enlistment. Looks like that may be a little sooner than I thought."

Just then, Sister Catherine arrived with a pitcher of fresh water.

"Well, Mr. Cameron," she said, "it's good to see you awake. I see Mr. Lynch has been keeping you company."

"Saints be praised, if it isn't Sister Catherine, our own Angel of Mercy, wings and all. And how are you this fine day, Sister?" said Johnny.

"Don't try to sweet talk me, Private Lynch," said the sister. "You'll get out of that bed when the doctor says so, and not before. How's the head?"

"Grand, grand. I'm on the mend."

"And your side?"

"Practically healed."

"Uh huh. Let's just take a look, shall we?" Sister Catherine pulled back the blanket and peered at Lynch's bandage with its weeping wound. Garrett caught the subtle change in her expression. "Well, since I need to change the dressing anyway, why don't I just have the doctor take a look at it?"

She turned to Garrett. "And you, Mr. Cameron. How are you feeling?"

"Better," he said. "Tired."

"I don't wonder, with Mr. Lynch bending your ear."

"Ah, Sister, you've hurt me worse than any Rebel bullet ever could," said Johnny with his hand to his heart.

"Somehow, I think you'll recover," said Sister Catherine. "Now, lie still until the doctor gets here." Her gentle look belied her gruff tone.

"She's a good one, that one," said Johnny as she disappeared in search of the doctor. "I don't know that I've seen her rest since I've been here."

* * *

The next morning, Garrett awoke to find the bed next to him empty and stripped of its blanket and sheets.

"Orderly," he called to the disabled soldier assigned to the ward. "Orderly!"

The man set down the bandage he was rolling and limped to Garrett's bedside.

"What happened to Johnny?" asked Garrett.

"Who?"

"Johnny Lynch. He was right there. In that bed."

"Oh, him. They took him out this morning."

"Took him out?"

"Yeah. He died in the middle of the night. Hospital fever."

"B-But ...," Garrett sputtered. "But, he was fine yesterday."

The orderly shrugged. "I've seen it a thousand times. Fellow looks like he's getting better, then, all of a sudden, bang. He's gone. No one knows what causes it, but once they get it, they rarely survive." He shrugged again. "Sorry."

As the orderly returned to his duties, Garrett stared at the empty bed. Poor Johnny. To have come through the battle with all it horrors, then die like this .... Obviously, being in the hospital presented almost as many dangers as the battlefield. One way or another, Garrett vowed to get out of there. And soon.

Over the course of that day and the next, Garrett felt his strength slowly return. As his wakeful periods grew longer, he watched Sister Catherine care for the injured men. She tended not just their wounds, but soothed and comforted their spirits. She would read to them, pray with them, write letters for them, listen to their stories of home and family, or just sit quietly by their sides when they were frightened. It seemed no matter when he awoke, day or night, she was there.

When the sister brought him his supper that evening, he ventured a question.

"Sister Catherine, how did you end up here, taking care of all these soldiers?"

"A number of us came down from the Motherhouse in Emmetsburg, Maryland, last June when President Lincoln put out the call for nurses." She gave a small sigh. "I fear we underestimated just how much we'd be needed, however." She spooned a bit of warm broth and brought it to his lips.

"And where did you learn nursing? In the nun house?"

Sister Catherine suppressed a smile. "Actually, I learned about medicine from my father. He was a doctor in Philadelphia. A good one.

When I joined the Daughters of Charity, I was able to use that knowledge to help others."

"I've been watching you," said Garrett. "You're good at it."

"I'm but the Lord's instrument," she said simply. "I exist to do His will."

Her words seemed to trigger something in Garrett. His expression darkened. "And what of the rest of us?" he asked, motioning to the mangled, wounded soldiers in the beds around him. "Are we God's instruments? Is this His will?"

Sister Catherine looked at Garrett with understanding. "I cannot pretend to know why God would allow such evil and suffering to exist. I simply choose to believe there is a reason for all this, a higher purpose that will be made known in God's own time."

"Forgive me, Sister, but I don't think much of a God who would allow the things to happen I've seen happen."

His words did not seem to shock her. "Faith is never easy, Private Cameron," she said. "We are all tested. And we must all find our own answers." She watched the internal struggle play across his face, and her heart ached for the pain and confusion she saw there. "But, you don't need to find them today," she added gently. "You rest now ... Private Cameron."

She turned away so he wouldn't see her face redden. She had almost called him Andrew.

A few hours later, as the ward was settling in for the night, a familiar voice pulled Garrett from his sleep.

"Cameron? Garrett!"

Garrett's eyes fluttered open. There, in the lamplight, was Rawlie. His eyes were bright with tears.

"God, it's good to see you," said Rawlie. "I've been looking everywhere for you." He nodded toward Garrett's shoulder. "How are you?"

Garrett shrugged, a movement that made him wince. "Passable. How did you find me?"

"Lieutenant Percy gave me a pass. We're bivouacked not too far from here. I've been searching for you off and on for three days. It's a miracle I found you. Every town for miles around is one giant hospital. I was just about to head back to camp, but something made me decide to check one more ward."

"How are the boys?" asked Garrett.

Rawlie's face sagged. "We lost close to half the regiment, killed or wounded. There're still some that aren't accounted for. I'm hoping they're just lying in some hospital somewhere, like you."

"Did Frank make it?"

"Looks like it. Lost a leg, though. They took him down to one of the hospitals in Washington. That's all I know."

"And Leonard?"

Rawlie snorted. "You can't kill that old buzzard. He's scratched up a little, but he's fine. He'll be pleased to hear you made it."

Garrett's smile faded. "Worst fight I've ever seen."

Rawlie nodded. "Think they'll send you back to Pittsburgh?"

"Don't know. Depends on how the shoulder heals, I guess."

Rawlie hung his head. "I know I should hope you get out for good, but frankly, if you don't come back ... well, this army just wouldn't be any fun."

Garrett grinned. "Well, I can't see you boys winning the war without me."

"That's a fact," said Rawlie. He patted Garrett's leg. "I'd better go. The nun who let me in here said I could only stay a few minutes, and she didn't look like anyone I'd want to cross. You take care now. I'll let the boys know you're down here loafin'." He turned to go.

"Rawlie?"

"Yeah."

"Can you do me a favor? I need to get word back to Miss Ambrose that I'm all right. I've sent one letter, but with all the confusion ...."

"I'll try, Garrett. Might be a little tough though. Between the battle down here and the explosion up there, the mails are a mess."

"What explosion?"

"That's right. You wouldn't have heard. There was some kind of explosion at the Allegheny Arsenal. Killed some of the girls working there. I don't know too many details. There wasn't much about it in the newspapers around here, what with all the news about the battle."

Garrett's heart constricted. "Miss Burke – Miss Ambrose's friend – she works at the Arsenal. I hope she's all right."

"I'm sure she is," soothed Rawlie. "You know how rumors exaggerate. Anyway, I'll send off a letter to Miss Ambrose for you. Tell her what a beat you are."

"Thanks, Rawlie," said Garrett. "And you take care of yourself until I can get back there to do it for you."

Rawlie winked and was gone.

Despite the doctor's confidence and the sister's gentle care, Garrett began to feel increasingly poor as the night wore on. By the next morning, the area around his wound was swollen and suppurated. He spiked a high fever and began slipping in and out of consciousness. He thought he heard Sister Catherine and the doctor mumble something about *hospital fever*, but he couldn't hear them very well because he was running through The Cornfield again, shells exploding around him, trying to keep up with the rest of the Pittsburgh Rifles. Suddenly, he lost sight of his company in the battle smoke. He kept hearing voices, his father's, his mother's, calling his name, but he couldn't find them. Then he was on a dance floor with Clara, twirling and twirling, until the room spun out of control and she was torn from his arms. Every now and then he became aware of a searing heat on his shoulder or a cup being held to his lips. Finally, after twenty-four hours of delirium, he fell into a deep slumber.

"What day is it?"

Sister Catherine, who had been changing sheets on the bed next to Garrett's, jumped.

"You're back," she said. She placed her hand on Garrett's forehead and smiled. "And your fever has broken."

Checking to be sure the ward was empty of medical personnel, she quickly undid the bandage on his shoulder and peered at the wound.

"Yes, it's looking much better," she said, replacing the bandage. "When your fever started, the doctor said we should just let things run their course." The disdain was plain in her voice. "But I was pretty sure that course was headed right to the grave. So, I tried an old remedy of my father's. A hot steaming herb poultice applied every hour. It's supposed to draw out the poison. And, I do believe it worked."

"Thank you," Garrett whispered. He did feel better, if exhausted. His shoulder was still sore, but the stabbing pain and burning were gone.

"What day is it?" he repeated.

"Tuesday morning, September 23rd."

The 23rd. Six days since the battle. Sister Catherine saw the question in his eyes.

"No, I'm sorry. No letter for you, yet. But I told you, it's hard to get word through just now. It will come. Now, you rest. You gave us quite a scare."

Garrett's eyes fluttered closed and his breathing slowed. Within seconds, he was asleep. Sister Catherine bent over the bed. Her face softened as she stared down at him. Watching that almost-familiar face fight for life had taken her back to that dark time when she watched, helpless, as her own mother, father, and lastly, her brother, succumbed to typhus, leaving her alone and afraid at fifteen. Sister bowed her head and said a quick prayer of thanksgiving that at least this young life had been spared.

Just before supper, a commotion at the end of the ward wakened Garrett from his sleep. A number of orderlies and ambulatory patients were huddled around a hospital steward holding a newspaper.

"I don't get it. Read it again," demanded one of the wounded.

"A Proclamation," read the steward in a loud voice. "Whereas on the 22nd day of September, A.D. 1862, a proclamation was issued by the President of the United States ...."

"Get to the main part," urged another soldier. The steward scanned the paper, then resumed.

" ... on the 1st day of January, A.D. 1863, all persons held as slaves within any State or designated part of a State the people whereof shall then be in rebellion against the United States shall be then, thenceforward, and forever free; ...."

"Well, I'll be goddamned," said one of the orderlies.

"What does it mean?" asked a one-legged soldier on crutches.

"It means," said the steward, "Lincoln has freed the slaves."

"Nah, it only frees slaves in the states that are in rebellion," said another orderly.

"Maybe, but I guarantee that's just the first step."

A soldier seated on one of the cots shook his head slowly from side to side. "You mean I got my arm blown off just to free a bunch of darkies?"

"You got your arm blown off to ensure that all men are entitled to freedom," said a soldier from the 15th Massachusetts.

"Not me," said another. "I joined this fight to keep the Union together. That's all."

As the arguing continued, Garrett leaned back on his pillow. So, at last, it had been said aloud. They were fighting, not just to preserve their country, but to end slavery. He sighed. It gave the horrible things he had witnessed a moral justification they had lacked before. It placed everything on a higher plane. Freedom – for all men. Perhaps, he thought grudgingly, God has a plan, after all.

For two more days Garrett lay in bed and slowly regained strength. But every time he fell asleep, he dreamed the same dream – Clara, her face streaked with tears, was reaching out for him, but something kept pulling her farther and farther away. Something was wrong. He felt it in his very soul.

The next day, when there was still no word from Clara, Garrett swung his legs over the edge of his cot, waited for the room to stop spinning, and reached for his boots. Sister Catherine rushed to his side.

"And just where do you think you're going?"

"It's been seven days since I sent that letter. I should've heard something by now."

"Private Cameron, you must be patient. I told you things were very confused after the battle. There was probably just a delay in receiving the message, that's all."

"Maybe, but Clara would surely have read about the battle in the newspaper by now. You don't know her. If she thought there was a chance I was wounded, she'd have come here by now, searched every town, every tent, every ward until she found me. There's something wrong. I know it. I keep having these dreams …." He stopped.

"What kind of dreams?"

"You're going to think I'm crazy."

Sister Catherine just stared at him, waiting.

"Ever since I was shot," he said, "I keep dreaming about Clara."

Sister Catherine smiled. "Well, that's only natural. You're hurt and in a strange place. You miss her."

"No, it's not that. She appears to me. The first time was on the battlefield. Now, every time I close my eyes, she calls to me. She's crying and reaching out for me, but I always wake up before I can get to her." His troubled expression changed to one of resolve. "I can't wait any longer. I've got to get home." He attempted to stand up. The sister grabbed his good arm as he began to sway.

"Private, you get back in this bed right now. You're in no condition to go anywhere. Even if you were, you'd need a medical furlough signed by the doctor, and with all the wounded, that could take some time to obtain."

"Then I won't wait for the furlough," he said.

"You don't mean that."

"I do. I have to get to Clara. I have to let her know I'm all right. Make sure she's all right. Once I've done that, I'll come back and rejoin my regiment."

"They'll shoot you for a deserter."

"Only if they catch me."

Sister Catherine stared into Garrett's unflinching eyes.

"Let me see what I can do," she said. "Promise me you won't move from this cot until I get back."

* * *

"Doctor Robert Weir, Surgeon in Charge of General Hospital #1, was seated at his desk in his office in one of the two stone buildings that had comprised the original Hessian Barracks built just south of the city of Frederick during the Revolutionary War. When Sister Catherine was escorted into the room, he stood and bowed.

"Ah, Sister Catherine. To what do I owe the pleasure of a visit this time?"

Doctor Weir, like most of the all-male medical establishment, had been skeptical of the presence of these Daughters of Charity in the hospital wards of the Army of the Potomac. But he had since learned the value of these gentle healers, both in raising morale and decreasing mortality rates. He had also come to admire their courage.

When the Union hospital in Frederick was hastily evacuated just prior to the arrival of the invading Confederate forces on September 6th, the Sisters had remained behind to care for those patients who could not be moved. They cared for the soldiers, both Union and Confederate, while at the same time keeping the Union surgeons' instruments and valuables hidden until the Union Army regained control of the city on September 13th.

Sister Catherine, in particular, had earned the grudging respect of the doctors and hospital stewards by insisting on the highest level of care and cleanliness for *her* patients. Her complaints to Doctor Weir were frequent, but never without basis.

"Good morning, Doctor," said Sister Catherine. "I would like to speak to you about a patient currently under my care in Ward A."

"Please," he said and motioned to a chair in front of his desk.

"The man's name is Garrett Cameron, a private with the 9th Pennsylvania Reserves, wounded in the recent fighting near Antietam Creek. He needs an immediate medical furlough."

"Sister, you know that is within the purview of the surgeon in charge."

"Yes, Doctor, but I do not believe the surgeon in charge would be willing to grant him a furlough at this time."

"Why not? What is the nature of the man's injury?"

"A shoulder wound. He lost a great deal of blood, initially, and has since suffered an infection and high fever. He appears to have passed the crisis point, but he's still quite weak."

"What is his prognosis?"

"With rest and proper medical attention, he should achieve close to a full physical recovery."

"Then, I'm sure the surgeon will grant the furlough just as soon as it is safe to do so."

"I'm afraid that won't be soon enough," said Sister Catherine. "There are ... extenuating circumstances."

"What sort of *extenuating circumstances*?"

"Doctor, Private Cameron underwent a horrific ordeal during the battle. Severely wounded, he lay for hours on the battlefield beneath the body of a slain Confederate soldier, while all around him his fellows lay dead and dying. He believes that, as he lay there, passing in and out of consciousness, his sweetheart appeared to him. In fact, only because he called out her name in his delirium was he discovered before he bled to death.

"Once transported here, he endured the questionable attendance of one of your less capable surgeons, subsequently suffering an infection and fever that had him close to death. Again he called out to this young woman, over and over. I heard him, myself, while I sat at his bedside. Upon awakening, he told me she had appeared to him again, and he fears she is in danger. With all the chaos following this latest battle, his attempts to contact her have failed. As a result, he is greatly distressed and growing more agitated each day. I fear, unless he is able to contact her, he will do something rash."

Dr. Weir frowned. "Sister, do you mean to tell me this young man is planning to desert?"

"I'm not telling you any such thing," she replied evenly. "I'm just telling you that in my opinion, in this individual situation, an immediate medical furlough is both necessary and appropriate. The man needs time for both his body and his mind to heal, something I feel he can best do at home."

"Let me get this straight. You want me to furlough a man who, by your own admission, may be too ill to travel, based solely on his belief in an apparition?"

"Many people base very strong beliefs on what others call apparitions," replied Sister Catherine pointedly.

"Of course, Sister. I didn't mean to offend. It's just that if I were to grant a medical furlough to every lovesick soldier who missed his girl, there would be no one left in this army except me - and you."

Sister Catherine raised an eyebrow. "Doctor, I don't believe this is just a lovesick soldier. There's something very ... genuine about him and very special about his bond to this young woman. He's a brave, good young man, thoroughly committed to the Union cause, who is also thoroughly convinced his beloved has been trying to contact him." She paused. "And, who are we to say that she hasn't?"

Doctor Weir raised an eyebrow. "Sister Catherine, that's hardly something I can put in my report."

"Then try this. It is your esteemed medical opinion that sending Private Cameron home to convalesce would be not only in his best interest, but in the best interest of the army in that it would return a fine soldier to fighting strength at no cost to the government, while at the same time freeing a bed and medical resources for the treatment of the hundreds of more gravely wounded soldiers that continue to stream into Frederick every day."

Doctor Weir stroked his mustache. "Sister, you would have made a fine bureaucrat."

"So, you'll grant the furlough?"

The doctor rose and walked to the window. With his hands clasped behind his back, he stared down the length of South Market Street at the seemingly unending line of ambulances still arriving from the Antietam and South Mountain battlefields.

"If this Private Cameron does manage to survive the trip home, which from your description is somewhat doubtful, what's to ensure he will return to his regiment after enjoying the … comforts of home?"

Sister frowned at the man's implication. "He has given me his word, Major Weir. And I give you mine." When he did not respond, she added, "I'd be happy to take my request directly to Doctor Letterman, if you prefer."

Doctor Weir smiled at his reflection in the window. What a tempting thought. But, no. The new Medical Director of the Union Army had enough to do untangling the mess that was the medical corps without setting Sister Catherine on him. He turned to face the determined woman. "I'm sure you would, Sister."

He returned to his desk and sat down in his chair with a thud.

"Sister," he said, rubbing his eyes with one hand, "if I grant the furlough, will you leave me alone?" He gave her a tired grin. "For a little while, at least?"

"Of course, Captain," she said. The corner of her mouth turned up ever so slightly. "For a little while."

Doctor Weir pulled a piece of paper from his desk, filled in some information, and signed it with a flourish. "Private Cameron may have his medical furlough," he said as he handed the paper to Sister Catherine. "But if he's not back here in one month, I'll see to it you're court-martialed, or whatever it is they do to nuns."

"Yes, Doctor. Thank you, Doctor."

* * *

Garrett stood in the roadway outside Ward A with his right arm in a sling and a borrowed haversack over his shoulder. Sister Catherine had located a used uniform for him – he dared not ask from where – and arranged for a wagon to take him to the station in Frederick in time to catch the train to Baltimore. Amid the chaos of wagons unloading more wounded, Garrett paused to say goodbye.

"How can I thank you, Sister, for everything you've done for me? For all the men?"

"Just find your Clara, get well, and come back to your regiment."

"I will. I promise."

"And Garrett …."

Garrett looked at Sister Catherine in surprise at her use of his given name.

"No matter what you find at home … trust in God's will."

Ignoring the whisper of foreboding in her charge, Garrett nodded. He gave the nun an awkward, one-armed hug.

"You'd better get going," blustered Sister Catherine.

Garrett shuffled over to the waiting wagon already almost filled with soldiers sporting various bandages and disfigurements. An amputee sat at the back of the wagon, his one leg hanging over the drop gate. He moved his crutch to one side to make room for Garrett, while two other men reached down to help him up. With a grimace, Garrett plunked down in the wagon bed. Beads of sweat appeared on his forehead.

"Git up," yelled the driver. The wagon lurched forward.

"Good bye, Sister. I'll never forget you," called Garrett.

"I'll pray for you," said Sister Catherine. He looked so pale and thin; she wondered if she had made a terrible mistake by interceding for him.

"Sister Catherine," Garrett shouted as the wagon turned onto the main road, "Private Lynch was right." He pointed to her headpiece. "Angel wings."

Sister pursed her lips in mock disapproval, but her eyes were bright with tears. She watched until the wagon disappeared in the dust clouds kicked up by the long line of traffic moving down the road toward Frederick, and the even longer line of wagons arriving from the battlefields.

The steward wandered the length of the hospital ward and studied the faces of the patients lying or sitting on the beds. He stopped when he reached the nun changing the linens on an empty cot.

"Ma'am," he said, with a slight bow of his head, "where's that soldier?"

"What soldier?" replied Sister Catherine without looking up. "We have a lot of soldiers here."

"The one with the shoulder wound. Cameron."

"He left this morning. Medical furlough. Why?"

"I got a letter for him."

"Oh." She straightened and stared in dismay at the paper in the man's hand. "He was waiting for that." She looked at the postmark: Lawrenceville, Pennsylvania. "Good. It's from his sweetheart."

"Well," said the steward, "I guess whatever was in the letter, she can just tell him in person, now."

CHAPTER 24

GARRETT RESTED HIS HEAD AGAINST the train window. The coolness of the glass was a welcome relief to his feverish forehead. He was exhausted and his arm throbbed with every bump and lurch of the car. At least he had managed to get a seat inside the car for the Harrisburg to Pittsburgh leg of the trip. He, along with hundreds of other soldiers, had to ride on the top of the cars for the journey from Baltimore to Harrisburg, where they were exposed to the elements and the sooty smoke streaming back from the locomotive stack. Once, succumbing to weakness and lack of sleep, he had almost slipped off the car, but was saved at the last second by the quick reflexes of the soldier next to him.

Garrett reached into his pocket and unwrapped the remains of a half loaf of soft bread, the gift of an elderly woman at the Baltimore train station who had been moved by his emaciated condition. Nibbling at the now stale crust, he watched the forested hills and unscarred green fields of western Pennsylvania pass by the window and willed the train to hurry. He closed his eyes and tried to calculate the lost days since he fell in the Cornfield. Nine days in the hospital, two on the trains. September 28th. Eleven days since the battle.

He hoped he had made the right decision by coming home. He had seen other soldiers' sweethearts, wives, and parents search for their loved ones through the rows and rows of hospital beds and tents. How tragically ironic if, while he risked life and limb to get to her, Clara was at this very moment scouring the hospitals and dressing stations in the towns around Antietam for him. No. The fates couldn't be so cruel. She had to be in Lawrenceville. She just had to be.

Garrett stood on the sidewalk in front of Clara's house and stared at the black wreath on the door. No one had answered his insistent knocking, nor was there any movement behind the closed drapes of the windows. And it was not just Clara's house. Every house in Lawrenceville seemed to be dressed in mourning. A chill ran down his spine. What could have happened? Where was everyone? Uncertain of where to go or what to do, he stood in the empty street. Just then, a constable walking his beat on Butler Street crossed the intersection at the top of Allen Street. Garrett hurried to intercept him.

"Sir, can you help me?" Garrett panted. "What's going on? Where is everyone?"

The man looked at him curiously.

"At the service at the Presbyterian Church."

"What service?"

"Didn't you hear?"

"No. I just got back to town."

"There was an explosion at the Arsenal. A big one. Killed almost eighty people, young women and girls, mostly. Horrible, sad thing. Not sure what caused it."

Rawlie had mentioned an explosion, recalled Garrett. But, eighty people?

"Here, now!" said the constable. He reached out to steady Garrett. "You all right?"

"When did this happen?" asked Garrett.

"On the afternoon of the 17th. Blew up a couple of laboratory buildings and just about everyone in them. It took a long time to identify the bodies, what bodies as were left. That's why they held off on the service 'til today. Say, where're you going?"

Garrett took off down Butler Street at a shaky trot. His shoulder ached with each step, but that was nothing compared to the fear gnawing at his heart. He turned up Pike Street and began the climb toward the Presbyterian Church. Carriages draped in black garlands and wreaths lined both sides of the street. Many of the horses wore black plumes on their bridles.

The effects of the explosion were increasingly evident here. The windows of almost all of the houses facing the Arsenal were boarded up, broken and blown in from the blast. To his left, above the stone walls of the Arsenal, he could see that many of the trees had been stripped bare of their leaves by the force of the explosion; victims of an unnatural autumn.

As he came abreast of the Pike Street gate to the Arsenal, Garrett stopped to catch his breath. He staggered across the street and peered through the opening. Crews of soldiers were at work cleaning up and hauling away the last of the rubble from the ruins of the main laboratory building. The wind carried an all too familiar smell; the smell of smoke and sulphur, burned metal and wood. And what he recognized as the smell of death. Fear gripped his heart once more.

Fighting back nausea, Garrett turned and hurried diagonally across the street to the church, just a little farther up the hill. The building's stained glass windows were also boarded up and another large black wreath hung on the entrance door. Garrett grasped the heavy iron handle with his good arm, pulled the door open, and stepped into the dimly lit vestibule. His labored breathing echoed off the walls.

In the brightly lit nave of the church, the Reverend R. Lea, the pastor, stood at the lectern in the midst of a somber, heartfelt sermon.

"*... from these, coffin after coffin was lowered to men below, who placed thirty-nine coffins side by side, filled by those whom no one could recognize, but whom the whole community adopted and honored as sisters and brethren who fell at the post of duty.*"

Garrett heard the words, but could not make sense of them. Thirty-nine coffins? He paused, swaying slightly, at the back of the church.

"*... Among those unrecognized remains were some dear to their own church for their piety and virtues. They will be missed from the house of God. Three were members of this church ...*"

Like one in a trance, Garrett began to make his way down the aisle toward the Ambrose family pew. His worn shoes made soft scuffing noises on the wooden floor.

"*'Ye know not what hour your Lord may come.' Who could have known in the morning that the day would end so sadly? ... Who could foretell what the firing of the first gun at Fort Sumter would bring about? It brought about remotely, the catastrophe of Wednesday. And who can tell what more it may bring?*"

Heads began to turn, following the soldier's slow progress.

"*... 'Watch, therefore, for ye know not what hour your Lord doth come.' So live, that whether your call shall come suddenly or find you waiting, you may hear the welcome plaudit, 'Well done, good and faithful servant, enter into the joy of thy Lord.'*"

Reverend Lea finished his sermon just as the young soldier reached the Ambrose family pew. There, four figures, shrouded in black, sat with heads bowed. Garrett felt his heart leap. He lurched forward and grabbed the end of the pew to steady himself.

"Clara?"

Four faces turned to him, four grief stricken faces – Dr. and Mrs. Ambrose, Helen ... and Annie. The last thing Garrett saw before he collapsed to the floor was Annie's anguished expression, a mixture of sorrow and guilt.

Garrett sat in the Ambrose's parlor, the cup of tea Mrs. Ambrose had prepared for him untouched on the side table. Exhausted by grief, she had retired to her room. Annie sat in the chair across from Garrett with her head bowed. Dr. Ambrose, his face gaunt and pale, stood at the mantle and tried to explain the unexplainable.

"They don't really know what caused the first explosion," he said in a voice beyond weariness. "A coroner's jury has been holding hearings to try and find out, but ...." He shrugged. "Of course, once the first explosion occurred, the powder and ammunition caught fire and led to the other explosions. The newspaper said a whole day's production was waiting at the laboratories to be removed to the magazines. Over one hundred and twenty-five thousand cartridges and one hundred seventy-five rounds of field ammunition. The force of it was tremendous, unlike anything I've ever heard in battle.

"When it was over, we searched and searched for Clara, talking to anyone we could find, examining bodies. But they were all so charred and burned ...."

Dr. Ambrose rubbed his hand across his eyes as if to erase the memory of those barely human forms. He began to sway slightly and gripped the mantle. He continued in a halting voice.

"The government provided coffins for the remains that couldn't be identified. And the Allegheny Cemetery donated a plot. They buried them the next day – thirty-nine plain black coffins, side by side, in a mass grave. We can only assume Clara was among them." His voice caught and he lowered his head. Without another word, he hobbled from the room. He paused to pat Garrett's shoulder as he passed.

Annie and Garrett sat in silence for a long time.

"It wasn't supposed to be this way," Garrett muttered at last. "It was supposed to be me."

"I'm so sorry, Mr. Cameron," said Annie, looking at him with red-rimmed eyes. "She went back to help another girl. You know how she was. And then there was another explosion ...." Annie lowered her head and instinctively covered her bandaged hand with her black-gloved one.

"Why was she even there?" asked Garrett. "She wrote me about wanting to work at the Arsenal, but said her mother forbid it. What happened?"

"The war," said Annie. "Mr. Pitcher and Dr. Ambrose were gone for so long, and their pay was never dependable. The family used up all of its savin's. Then Mr. Pitcher was killed and Dr. Ambrose captured. And when he did finally return home, he was so ill he couldn't work. The family was desperate."

"But, why didn't she tell me? I could have helped."

"She didn't want to worry you. And she felt she had no right." Annie saw a flash of remorse cross Garrett's face and hastened to reassure him. "I doubt she'd have accepted your money, anyway, proud as she was. But, finally, things got so bad ... Truth be told, I think she was happy to be workin' at the Arsenal. She felt she was doin' somethin' important for the Union. And for you."

Garrett put his head in his hands and shook it from side to side. "I'm such a fool," he muttered. "Such a fool." Suddenly, he looked up at Annie, his grief tinged with apprehension.

"Someone told me, while I was away, that Clara ... and Edgar Gliddon ...."

"No, Mr. Cameron," said Annie firmly. "Clara wanted nothin' to do with Mr. Gliddon. 'Tis true, he tried to pressure her into marryin' him, but she'd have none of it. She never loved anyone but you."

Over the past ten days, Annie thought she had cried all the tears she had to cry, but the mixture of relief and remorse in Garrett's eyes touched her anew. She dabbed at her own eyes while Garrett rose and walked to the fireplace.

"We tried to contact you after it happened," Annie continued. "Mrs. Ambrose, herself, wrote you." At the dubious look on Garrett's face, she smiled faintly. "I know. But Clara told me her mother had a change of heart since you'd left. She knew Clara loved you. And she wanted her to be happy." She sighed. "I guess you never got the letter."

Garrett shook his head. He continued to stare into the fire.

Suddenly, he whirled around. "Maybe she's not dead," he said in a voice tinged with desperation. "They can't be sure. They didn't find her body. Maybe she wandered away and is in a hospital, or someone's home, unconscious, unable to tell them who she is. It happens all the time in battle. Men listed as dead are discovered recuperating in someone's back bedroom or some far corner of a hospital tent."

Annie looked at Garrett with compassion. "No, Mr. Cameron," she said gently. "They might not have found her body, but they did find this."

Fumbling a bit, Annie pulled a carefully folded handkerchief from the pocket of her skirt. She peeled the layers of cloth back to reveal a small locket attached to a bit of broken, burnt chain. She placed the trinket in Garrett's hand.

"She never took it off, not once since the day you left. So, of course, when we found it, we knew ...." She stopped. "We all thought you should have it."

Garrett stared down at the blackened locket. With trembling fingers, he opened the clasp. On one side was the picture he had given Clara, his proud, determined expression still discernable despite the scorched edges. On the other side, a charred bit of lilac. Clara was right, he thought, his eyes filling with tears. He could smell the perfume in the smoke.

"Thank you," he whispered and snapped the locket shut. Without meeting Annie's eyes, he rose and left the room.

Seeking to find a cause and place the blame, both a coroner's inquest and a military inquiry followed the explosion at the Allegheny Arsenal. Eyewitnesses were called and extensive testimony taken, but no definitive answer was ever found. The coroner's jury attributed the accident to gross neglect on the part of the Arsenal's commander and some of his subordinates in failing to properly oversee the handling and disposal of the gunpowder. But the military tribunal, deeming the eyewitnesses' accounts implausible or contradictory, exonerated Commander Symington and found no conclusive cause for the explosion. Regardless, Symington's career was irreparably damaged. He was relieved of command of the Arsenal on November 1, 1862.

Garrett did not follow the newspaper accounts of the investigations. He did not care how or why the explosions had happened. He had seen enough of the vagaries and horrors of war to know that, even if the answers to these questions could be found, it did not change anything. Clara was dead. And he knew who, ultimately, was to blame.

Garrett stayed in Pittsburgh for three weeks while he recuperated from his wound. Both the Ward and the Ambrose families offered to take him in, but he declined. Instead, he rented a room in the Burke's boarding house and took what comfort he could from being in silent proximity to the one other person who understood what he felt; the young woman whose loss most nearly equaled his own. He emerged from his room only for meals, which he ate in silence. And, once each day, he took a long solitary walk around the stone walls of the Arsenal. For long hours, he would stare at the blackened spaces where the laboratory buildings had stood and search for something in the lingering smell of the smoke.

Annie, too, kept mostly to herself. She'd had two fingers blown off in the final explosion at the Arsenal and the skin on her left arm had been badly burned. She knew these injuries would eventually heal, but the emotional wounds ran much deeper. In silence, she agonized over her actions on that fateful day. Maybe if she had run a little faster, not hesitated those precious few moments, Clara would still be alive. Annie struggled with the question of why she had survived when her beloved friend – and so many others – had been taken. And her heart broke anew each time she saw her own misery mirrored in Garrett's eyes.

Of the many questions raised by the explosion at the Allegheny Arsenal, there was one whose answer Annie vowed to take to her grave.

Although his driver had recounted to both the police and the press how Edgar Gliddon had leapt from the carriage at the sound of the first explosion, no one knew for sure what had become of the noted industrialist. Through the weeks and months that followed, Annie kept her silence, just as she had when the newspaper first reported Edgar's disappearance and the large reward offered by his family for information of his whereabouts. Clara had not wanted to be connected to Edgar in life. By her silence, Annie would ensure that she was not connected to him in death. It was the least she could do for her friend. And for Garrett.

In late October, at the end of his medical furlough, Garrett returned to his regiment. He caught up with them in mid-November, just a few weeks before the Army of the Potomac began its move toward Fredericksburg, Virginia.

The men of the Pittsburgh Rifles found Garrett a much different man from the one they had known before Antietam. Silent and brooding, he kept mostly to himself. Even Rawlie was unable to draw him from his grief.

At the battle of Fredericksburg, and at Gettysburg the following July, Garrett fought with a reckless disregard for his own life that won him commendations for bravery, but worried and frightened his friends. In reality, only within the single-mindedness of battle did Garrett find respite from the pain of Clara's death. And the hope that a Rebel bullet might allow him to join her was never far from his mind.

On the afternoon of May 4, 1864, Garrett crouched in line of battle behind the cover of a fallen scrub oak in the thick, second growth forest known as The Wilderness, just west of Chancellorsville, Virginia. Just that morning, the Army of the Potomac, including the 9th Pennsylvania Reserves regiment, had crossed the Rapidan River and entered this godforsaken jungle. It was the same area in which General Lee had defeated the Union forces under General Hooker almost exactly a year earlier, at great cost of lives on both sides. Another such battle appeared imminent. As the sun slid toward the horizon, Garrett wondered, would tomorrow be the day? Would tomorrow be the day his torment would finally end?

As he waited in the brush for the battle to begin, Garrett gradually became aware of a sound, a low murmur of voices, moving down the line toward him. A soldier trotted over to speak to Rawlie, who was positioned next to Garrett. Rawlie turned to Garrett with a strange look on his face.

"My God," said Rawlie. "It's over."

"What?"

"Our enlistment. It's up. We've been ordered back. Garrett, we're going home."

Garrett stared at him uncomprehendingly for a long moment. Then, as simply as that, he and Rawlie picked up their rifles and headed for the rear with the rest of the 9th Pennsylvania Reserves regiment.

The few remaining members of the original 9th Pennsylvania Reserves, having completed their three-year tour of duty, returned to Pennsylvania. Traveling in reverse the path that had brought them to the fight so long ago, they traveled to Harrisburg, then on to Pittsburgh, where they were formally mustered out of Federal service on the 13th of May 1864.

But Garrett's struggle was far from over.

CHAPTER 25

ON A STEAMY AUGUST DAY in 1864, Garrett stepped down from the train onto the platform at the Pennsylvania Railroad Station in Pittsburgh. The heat and humidity reminded him of the Peninsula, and he fanned his face with his bowler hat. With the war now entering its fourth year, the station was filled with soldiers in blue on their way to and from the battlefields. Though only a few years older than most of the recruits, Garrett felt ancient, and not just because of the nagging stiffness in his right shoulder. He had none of their youthful passion for the great cause that moved them. He had seen and experienced too much.

After being mustered out of Federal service, Garrett had returned to his hometown of Elmira, New York, to try to figure out what to do with his life. Although his anger at Clara's death had spent itself in his last months in the army, it had left behind a numbing emptiness, broken only by an immobilizing grief that struck without warning. His concerned father urged him to resume his studies in hopes that the intellectual stimulation would pull him from his despair. After three months of fractious indolence, and with no real alternative, Garrett agreed. He returned to Pittsburgh – the site of his greatest happiness and greatest sorrow – to resume the study of law.

Garrett had not been back to Pittsburgh since returning to his regiment the month after Clara's death. During the intervening two years, much of what had connected him to the city was gone. The Ambrose family, including Helen and J.B., had left Lawrenceville in March of 1864. Although Dr. Ambrose never regained his full health, he did recover to the extent that he could manage a small practice. Following Grandmother Blake's death in the winter of 1863, he accepted a position in a small town in central Pennsylvania where the air was better for his health and where the stone walls of the Allegheny Arsenal did not loom over the family's daily lives, a constant reminder of the tragic death of their beloved daughter and sister.

Frank and Leonard had both stayed in the army. Frank, minus his leg, was working in the Quartermaster's Office in Washington. Leonard and some of the other surviving members of the original

Pittsburgh Rifles had decided to see the war through to its end, and re-enlisted with Company K of the 190th Pennsylvania Volunteers.

Rawlie, like Garrett, had had enough. While still in Elmira, Garrett had received a letter from him announcing his decision to go to California. Rawlie urged Garrett to come along. The thought of leaving everything behind and starting anew was tempting, but Garrett turned him down. Unwilling to look backward, Garrett was unable to look forward. His full concentration was taken up with just surviving each day. So, he had bid his closest friend a sad farewell.

Now, standing on the train platform amid the bustling crowd of soldiers, Garrett felt like the sole player left in a morbid game; the last one seated at a once crowded table. He wondered if he had been unwise to come back.

"Carriage, Sir?"

Startled, Garrett stared at the hackney driver standing by the edge of the platform.

"Do you need a carriage, Sir?" the man repeated.

"Oh. Yes," said Garrett. He handed the man his bag and climbed into the back of the buggy.

"Where to?"

Garrett hesitated for only a moment. "St. Mary's Street in Lawrenceville."

Despite a sincere invitation from his godfather, Garrett could not bear to go back to live with the Ward family in Allegheny City. Too much had happened; too much had changed. Instead, he took a room once more in the Burke's boardinghouse. He felt more at home there, partially because of the kindness they had extended to him while he had been recuperating from his wound, and partially because they, too, had suffered great loss during the war. With the Burkes, there would be no need to explain his sudden absences or long periods of silence. Mr. and Mrs. Burke greeted him with open arms and gave him his old room. More important, they gave him his privacy.

Annie was still living with her parents. She had never returned to her job at the Arsenal. Even had she been able to do the work with her mangled fingers, the memories were just too terrible. Instead, she helped her parents run the boardinghouse, grateful to lose herself in the mundane duties of cooking and cleaning. Occasionally, one of the young male boarders would attempt to catch her eye or engage her in conversation, but Annie steadfastly refused all overtures. She had lost too many people to risk loving – and losing – anyone else.

Garrett dealt with his sorrow by immersing himself in his studies. Time and again, he turned down the social invitations of the Ward sisters and other former friends until, at last, they stopped asking. The teas and lectures, even those in support of the war, seemed so frivolous to him now; so a part of the world *before*. He spent his days at the office or in court, and returned to the boardinghouse only to sleep or take his meals, always sitting at the table alone with a law book in front of him.

As the weeks passed, Garrett and Annie maintained their separate orbits within the life of the boardinghouse. They exchanged polite pleasantries, but the tragedy that bound them also kept them at arms length. Each was to the other a precious connection and a painful reminder of a loved one lost.

Garrett was admitted to the bar in January of 1865. He rented a one-room office in a small building on Fisk Street in Lawrenceville and hung out his shingle. Standing on the sidewalk, he stared up at the newly painted sign: *Garrett E. Cameron, Esquire*. He waited to feel a swell of pride at the attainment of this hard-won goal. But he felt nothing.

Garrett had abandoned his original grand dream of championing the rights of the oppressed and the disenfranchised against the powerful and the unjust. Instead, he established a quiet legal practice dealing in minor business transactions and simple wills. His work was blessedly routine, undemanding. Even so, there were times when just the effort of getting through a day was almost more than he could bear.

Garrett stared out the window of the Citizens Passenger Railway car as it rumbled down Penn Street toward Lawrenceville. He had spent most of the day in court and was glad to be outside in the spring sunshine. Despite the worsening smog that shrouded the city as a result of the war-driven increase in the number of foundries and mills, the April air held a bit of sweetness, more so as they neared the less polluted air of Lawrenceville. He looked south toward Herron Hill and searched for that hint of color, but it was too early. The lilacs would not be blooming yet.

Suddenly, he heard a commotion in the street up ahead. A large crowd was gathered around a red-faced man standing on the corner of Taylor and Penn, almost alongside the opening to the grounds of old Camp Wilkins.

"It's over! It's over!" the man was yelling as the street car passed. He was waving a telegram in the air. "The war is over!"

His cry was taken up by people all along the street. The excited cheering moved toward and over Garrett like a wave. The news raced ahead of the streetcar, and the residents of Lawrenceville rushed into the streets. They shouted, prayed, and wept in joy and disbelief that the long agony was over.

The report of Lee's surrender at Appomattox Courthouse, Virginia, on April 9, 1865, was greeted with the same rejoicing throughout the North. Church bells rang and bands played *The Battle Hymn of the Republic* over and over, while tears ran down the cheeks of the musicians.

Garrett, in contrast, felt only a sense of relief that the killing was over. He alighted from the streetcar and threaded his way through the throngs of people, down St. Mary's Street to the Burke house. To his surprise, Annie was seated on the front stoop.

"Well, I suppose you've heard," he said, sitting down next to her.

"I'd of had to be deaf not to," she said with a wan smile. Garrett watched with her as cheering, flag-waving people on foot, on horseback, and in carriages galloped up and down the street in front of the house.

"So, I guess your brothers will be coming home," said Garrett.

"Yes, at last," said Annie. She shook her head slowly. "It's hard to believe. Four long years. And we thought it would be over in a few months."

"We were very naïve," said Garrett, "as individuals and as a nation. We had no idea what war would mean. Or what it would cost." He stared unseeing at the commotion in the street. "Life has turned out much differently than I imagined," he said, almost in a whisper.

Annie lowered her head. To Garrett's surprise, a tear trickled down her cheek.

"Miss Burke! What's wrong?"

"It's my fault," said Annie, her voice quavering.

"What?"

"The way things turned out. It's my fault." Two and a half years of repressed guilt tumbled from her lips. "I couldn't tell you. I was too ashamed. The day of the explosion, when Clara ran back to save that little girl ... I could have stopped her. Run after her. But, I was afraid. I hesitated. And then ...." She bit her lip before she said too much.

"And if you hadn't hesitated, do you truly think it would have made any difference?" Garrett admonished her gently. "No. You know as well as I do that when Clara set her mind on something, there was nothing you, me, or anyone else could do to change it. The only thing that would have happened is you both would have been killed."

"Maybe that would have been better," muttered Annie.

Garrett frowned. "Don't say that."

"No, 'tis true. She should be here now, not me. The two of you were meant to be together, and now she's gone. I blame meself." She hung her head. "And I've always felt a part of you blamed me, too."

"Blamed *you*?" said Garrett in astonishment. "Nothing could be further from the truth. If anyone's to blame, it's me. She wouldn't even have been at the Arsenal if it hadn't been for me. If I'd proposed to her before I left, she would've turned to me for help. I wanted to. I did. But, I thought I was being noble, leaving her free to marry if …." He shook his head. "It doesn't matter why I did it. What matters is, I just left her here, alone. Now my punishment is to spend the rest of my life without her."

The noise in the street filled the silence that followed. Annie, confronted with the surprising revelation of Garrett's self recrimination, wrestled with a new thought. Finally, she looked over at him through reddened eyes.

"What if we're both wrong?" she ventured. "What if … no one is to blame?"

Garrett stared at her, his expression growing hard. "What are you saying? Clara's death was just an accident? A random bit of bad luck?" He gave a bitter laugh. "And Joe, Caleb, and your brothers? Even little Canary? They were all just in the wrong place at the wrong time? No. There has to be some reason for all this, some purpose, or else it's all just … meaningless. The whole war. The whole goddamned world." His eyes filled with angry tears, the first he had shed in a long time.

Annie longed to reach out to comfort him. Instead, she gazed out over the crowds celebrating in the streets of Lawrenceville. "Perhaps there is a reason," she said quietly. "Some higher plan we just don't understand."

Garrett snorted derisively. "Some plan. Take away the people we love – good, innocent people – and leave us behind to mourn and suffer. Why? Why would a just God do that?"

Annie shrugged. "I don't know. I pray I will, one day. But there has to be a reason. Otherwise, 'twould be as you said – they all died for nothin'. And I can't … I won't accept that."

"So, you choose to pretend," said Garrett.

Annie gave him a solemn look. "I choose to believe."

Garrett shook his head slowly. "I don't know what I believe anymore. Without Clara …." His voice caught. "I miss her so much. How can I go on without her?"

Annie gave him a look filled with the understanding of one facing her own long journey down a seemingly empty road.

"Just the way you have been," she said gently. "One day at a time; one day after the other."

Garrett shook his head. "I haven't your courage. Or your faith."

"You're wrong," said Annie. "After such a loss, it takes the greatest courage just to go on livin'. And that's not possible without at least some faith that there's somethin' to go on livin' for."

Garrett did not respond, but he reached out and took her mangled hand in his.

As spring turned into summer, the soldiers began to return from the war – tired, wounded; some physically, some spiritually. Annie's brother, Liam, returned with a neck wound that would trouble him the rest of his life; her brother, Francis, without a scratch. Still, all who had fought in the great Civil War had been changed by the experience, an experience truly understood only by those who had also endured it.

Almost immediately, veterans groups began to spring up. Men who had been comrades on the battlefield continued that kinship at memorial events, parades, and veterans' meetings. As the years passed, even those men on opposing sides of the fight found a measure of peace in their shared history and their mutual participation in the defining event of their lives.

Garrett never joined any of the veterans' organizations or took part in their commemorations. He never returned to the Antietam or Gettysburg battlefields for any of the anniversaries or tributes. For his life had not been changed there, but on a sloping hillside alongside the Allegheny River in Lawrenceville. His only acknowledgement of his years spent in the service was his faithful correspondence with Sister Catherine Bateau of the Daughters of Charity, now back at the Motherhouse in Maryland. Instead, he clung to the safety and predictability of the life he had established for himself in Lawrenceville. The sameness of the routine and its well-established parameters lent a shape, if not a purpose to his days.

As the months passed, however, Garrett found himself drawn to spending more and more time with Annie. Their encounters in the hallways or dining room of the boardinghouse changed from brief greetings to shy conversations. Garrett began to alter his routine ever so slightly. He would come out onto the back porch to smoke his pipe when he knew Annie would be hanging laundry in the yard, or time his walk home from work to coincide with her return from the market.

The occasional shared meal at the Burke house turned into after-supper walks by the river. Sometimes they talked; sometimes they just strolled along in silence. Two damaged souls, forever changed by the war, they drew upon each other for strength and gave each other the forgiveness they could not give themselves. It was with Garrett that Annie was finally able to lower the protective wall she had built around her heart. And it was with Annie that Garrett laughed, truly laughed, for the first time since Clara's death. The Burke family watched in silent hope. They took care not to do or say anything that might disturb the tentative reaching of these two fragile hearts.

As their unacknowledged courtship continued, Garrett began escorting Annie up the long hill to St. Mary's Church each Sunday for morning Mass. He never attended the service himself, but would be there, waiting outside, to walk her home when it ended.

On a warm spring morning in the spring of 1866, the bells calling the worshipers to Mass were already tolling when Annie and Garrett reached the front walkway of the church.

"I'd best hurry," said Annie. "I don't want Father Gibb to be scoldin' me from the pulpit." She turned to Garrett. "As always, I thank you for the company, Mr. Cameron. I ...." She stopped when she saw the strange expression on his face.

"Miss Burke," said Garrett, shifting his weight, "do you think it would be all right if I went inside with you today?"

Annie struggled to hide her surprise. A breeze from the river ruffled the dark veil on her hat as she looked up at Garrett.

"Yes, Mr. Cameron," she said as evenly as she could manage. "I think that would be entirely all right."

From that day on, each Sunday and holy day, Garrett would sit in the flickering candlelight at the back of the church during Mass. He would follow along with the English translation of the Latin words and music in the missal and listen to the Gospel. He paid particular attention to the sacrifice commemorated in the Consecration and to the promise of the triumph of life over death contained in the Eucharist. Annie never questioned Garrett about his attendance or pressed him about his intentions. She just sat quietly at his side each week and sent her own conflicted prayers up to heaven.

Finally, in the fall, Garrett announced he had decided to convert to Catholicism. He received formal instruction from Father Gibb and was baptized in June of the following year, 1867. Sister Catherine received special permission from the Mother Superior to attend the ceremony.

The Burke family held a small reception for Garrett at the board-inghouse following the administering of the sacrament at St. Mary's. As the festivities wound down and the guests began to leave, Sister Catherine found Garrett standing alone on the front porch. He was staring out into the shadows of the early evening.

"So, how do you feel?" she said as she joined him at the porch railing.

Garrett looked at her and smiled. Sister Catherine was a little thinner than he remembered her being at Frederick; a little wearier. But her blue eyes were just as piercing. And just as kind.

"Like I've found something I've been searching for for a long time," said Garrett. "And I have you to thank."

Sister Catherine smiled. "No, no. I'm just one of many people and events that God put into your life to bring you to this day." She looked back at the house. "She's quite a remarkable young woman, you know."

Garrett turned and observed the tableau framed in the lighted parlor window. Mr. and Mrs. Burke were talking and laughing with Father Gibb by the fire while Annie, in the foreground, cleared away the tea tray. Suddenly, reacting to something the priest said, her face broke into a radiant, dimpled smile.

"Yes, she is," said Garrett. "She lost so much in the war, so many people she loved. Not to mention her own injuries. And yet, she was never bitter. I couldn't understand that. I was so angry and adrift in the years after Clara died. But, the more time I spent around Miss Burke ... well, I just had to find out where such a slip of a girl derived such strength."

"I could tell she'd made quite an impression on you. Your letters were full of her."

"Were they?" said Garrett. "Well, she saw me through a very dark time." Suddenly, he looked alarmed. "I hope you don't think she was the reason for my conversion."

"Not the sole reason, no," said Sister Catherine. "But the Lord uses many instruments to guide us to Him." She smiled. "And there's no law that says some of them can't be quite pleasant."

Garrett looked sheepish. "Well, I would be lying if I told you I hadn't thought about what else my conversion might mean; the impediment it would remove."

Sister Catherine could have sworn she saw him blush, even in the failing light.

"So," she said after a moment, "when are you going to ask her?"

Suddenly, Garrett looked as young and vulnerable as he had the first time she saw him in the hospital in Frederick. "Do you really think she'd have me?"

Sister Catherine sighed. As with most young lovers, the depth of Garrett and Annie's attraction to each other was obvious to everyone but themselves. "Well, you'll never know if you don't ask."

Annie stood beneath the shade of the trees in the Allegheny Cemetery and stared at the stone obelisk marking the burial site of the unidentified victims of the explosion. Her eyes filled with tears as she read down the inscribed list of names and, for a moment, she feared she might be sick. So many names. So many friends, gone forever.

She had only come to this place twice before; once, when the bodies – or what was left of them – were buried the day after the explosion; the second time, with Clara's parents when the obelisk was dedicated in 1863. Otherwise, she had stayed away. The memories were just too strong, too wrenching. But, today she felt duty bound to come.

Focusing on a name near the top of the stone, Annie squared her shoulders.

"Clara." Her voice sounded jarring to her ears and she glanced around to be sure she was still alone in the graveyard before continuing. "Clara. It's me. Annie. I know I've not been by to visit. I … I just couldn't. But now … now there's somethin' I need to tell you. Somethin' I hope you'll understand." She realized she was shaking and took a deep breath to steady herself. "Garrett has asked me to marry him."

She waited, half expecting to hear some kind of response; a ghostly reprimand or a crash of thunder. But all she heard was birdsong and the soft whoosh of the wind through the oak and sycamore trees.

"I've not given him me answer. I told him I needed some time to think. But, the truth of it is … I love him. I don't know how or when it happened. But, it did." Saying the words aloud, Annie felt something akin to the guilt one felt in the confessional, but without the blessed prospect of absolution. "I don't know if he feels the same way, but I do believe he cares. And I know he'll be a good and faithful husband. Just as I know he's never stopped lovin' you. Neither of us has ever stopped …." Her voice broke and the tears she had been fighting slipped down her cheeks. "But, Clara, we have to go on. For whatever reason, we're still here. We're still alive. Aren't we entitled to some happiness?" she pleaded, her voice rising. "Aren't I?"

Annie covered her face with her hands and wept as competing emotions tore at her heart. When at last she looked up at the silent stone, her eyes were filled with a trembling resolve.

"So," she said, jutting her chin ever so slightly. "'Tis what I came to tell you."

She nodded her head in punctuation and turned to go. But not before making one last vow to her friend.

"I'll take good care of him, Clara," she whispered over her shoulder. "I promise."

Then Annie gathered her skirts in her hands and fled down the hill toward home.

Garrett Cameron and Annie Burke were married in October of 1867 at St. Mary's Catholic Church in Lawrenceville. Their lives quickly settled into a comfortable rhythm, a soothing predictability after the turmoil of the war years. In the little bedroom of their newly purchased house on Bellefontaine Street, Garrett would rise each morning, dress in his suit, and walk down Butler Street to his office. Annie took care of their home. Their days were filled with the joy of small things – evening walks, Sunday Mass and dinner with family, quiet nights spent in each others' arms. They, like the country, were eager to leave the pain and privation of the past behind and build a new peaceful life together.

As the years passed, their marriage was blessed with four children, whom they named Daniel, Rawlie, Gabriel, and Catherine. Garrett and Annie delighted in each and every one of them. They, whose dreams had been so irreparably changed by the war, were now content to provide the foundation for the dreams of a new generation. Their children, in turn, gave them eleven grandchildren. And as they lay in bed each night, Garrett and Annie spoke in wonder of how the improbable union of their two small lives had caused ever-expanding ripples to spread across the surface of the future.

They couldn't escape life's sorrows altogether, of course. Annie's parents died, only a few months apart, in the fall and winter of 1875. And one rainy spring day in 1891, Garrett received a letter from the Mother Superior of the Daughters of Charity, informing him of the sudden and unexpected death of Sister Catherine Bateau at the Motherhouse in Emmetsburg. But, to cope with these losses, Garrett and Annie now had the comfort of leaning on each other.

In fact, all who knew Mr. and Mrs. Garrett Cameron remarked on their uncommon devotion to one another. Their marriage seemed perfect; blessed. Still, once each spring, when the lilacs bloomed, Garrett would come to Annie with flowers in his hands.

"I'm going to take a little walk," he would say. And she would nod.

The electric trolley car stopped in front of the massive stone gate of the Allegheny Cemetery on Butler Street. Gripping the side of the railing tightly, Garrett hobbled down the steps.

"You have a good day, now, Mr. Cameron," said the motorman.

Garrett waved his thanks and watched as the passenger car rumbled away. He supposed the electric cars were more efficient – cleaner and faster – but he missed the charm of the old horse-drawn car that used to travel the length of Butler Street.

He paused to look up at the castle-like entrance gate to the cemetery. For almost fifty years he had been making this trip. It hardly seemed possible. Despite the aches and pains, and the cane he now needed to help steady his steps, he did not think of himself as an old man. But, at seventy-seven years old, he supposed he was. To be sure, his mind was showing the effects of age. People and things from long ago came to memory with such clarity, while the names and details of yesterday danced out of reach.

He shuffled through the gate, turned to the right, and followed the dirt road up the hill to Section 17. He stopped twice to catch his breath and let the familiar pain in his chest subside. Finally, he saw it up ahead, the stone obelisk marking the site of the mass grave of the unidentified victims of the explosion at the Allegheny Arsenal. Reaching it, he removed his hat.

"The lilacs are particularly beautiful this year, Clara," he said, and stooped to lay the blooms at the base of the monument. With difficulty, he straightened. Then, although he knew it by heart, he read aloud the inscription that had been placed on the stone at its dedication in 1863:

> *Tread softly. This is consecrated dust. Forty-five pure patriotic victims lie here. A sacrifice to freedom and civil liberty. A horrid memento to a most wicked rebellion. Patriots! These are patriots' graves, friends of humble, honest toil. These were your peers. Fervent affection kindled these hearts, honest industry employed these hands, widows' and orphans' tears have watered the ground. Female beauty and manhood's vigor commingle here. Identified by man, known by Him who is the resurrection and the life, to be made known and loved again when the morning cometh.*

When he had finished reading, Garrett found her name among those listed and gently ran his fingers along the weathered indentations of the letters carved into the stone.

"Until next year," he said with a nod.

A soft breeze off the river whispered in the leaves of the trees overhead. Garrett smiled. He turned and headed back down the hill, back to the life he and Annie had built from the ashes.

EPILOGUE

Lawrenceville, Pennsylvania
May 1915

ANNIE JOLTED AWAKE. THE AIR blowing in the window, so fresh and welcome, had turned cold. She shivered and stood to lower the sash.

"Annie."

The sound of his voice startled her.

"Garrett. You're awake." She hurried to his bedside.

"Have been for some time. I was watching you. What were you dreaming about?"

Annie lowered her eyes for a fraction of a second. "Nothin'."

Garrett smiled. "Annie, you always were a terrible liar."

She shrugged. "Just some old memories."

"Happy ones, I hope."

Garrett frowned when she didn't respond.

"What is it, Annie?" he said. "What's troubling you?"

She took a deep breath. "Garrett, why did you marry me?"

He smiled. "Annie, we've been married almost fifty years. You're asking me this, now?"

She nodded.

"Come here," he said, reaching out his hand. She drew closer and sat in the chair by the side of the bed.

"Where is this coming from?" he asked.

"I just never knew why you married me."

"Because I loved you. Still do," he teased. When she didn't reply, he frowned again. "You do believe me, don't you?"

"I've just always been afraid ... afraid you settled for me. That I was second choice." She paused. "I wasn't Clara."

"Oh, Annie." Garrett's faded brown eyes filled with tears. He stared at her for a long time. Then he began to speak, his breath coming in short gulps.

"It's true, when Clara died, I wanted to die, too. Tried to, in fact." He glanced away for a moment and the dark smoke of a dozen battlefields drifted across his face. He looked back at her with a self-deprecating grin. "But it appeared the entire Rebel army had lost its aim. Still, I was dead just the same. Dead inside.

"After the war, I came back to Pittsburgh mainly because I couldn't think of where else to go. I thought at first I was drawn to you because you were the only one who understood how I felt, you who were so close to her. And maybe it was that, in the beginning. But, as time went on, I realized it was much more. After all the horror and death of those years, you showed me life still held goodness and beauty and meaning. I fell in love with your courage and your faith. I fell in love with you. You gave me something I never thought I'd have again – a second chance at love."

Annie stared into his eyes and saw in them no reserve, no part or past that didn't belong to her. She bowed her head and the tears flowed unchecked down her face.

"Oh, Garrett," she whispered, "I've been such a fool."

"No, no," he soothed. "Never that. You have been my dear sweet Annie. Loving and steadfast – to me and to Clara. And all these years, you've allowed me to honor her. Allowed an old man to honor a young man's memory." He smiled. "Oh, Annie, don't you know? Clara was my first love. The love of my youth. But you, my darling girl," he said, reaching up to cup her face with a trembling hand, "you have been the love of my life. God forgive me if I haven't shown you that."

Annie smiled through her tears. "You have, Garrett. You have. But lovely 'tis to hear you say it."

He took her hand and pressed it to his lips.

"I think I'll rest now. Good night, Annie. I'll see you in the morning."

Annie continued to hold his hand. She watched the rise and fall of his chest become slower and slower. His eyes moved restlessly beneath closed lids. Suddenly, they stopped. He gasped, once, twice, and his hand in hers became unbearably light. With tears running down her face, Annie smoothed a few gray hairs on his head.

"'When the mornin' cometh,' Garrett, me love," she said, and pressed her cheek to his.

AUTHOR'S BIO

Mary Frailey Calland was born in Elmira, New York, and has always had a love of writing and history. She has a B.A. in American Studies from the University of Notre Dame and a Juris Doctor from Notre Dame Law School. Her books focus on American history as experienced, not by the famous, but by the common people of the period. Her previous works include the historical novel, *Barefoot In The Stubble Fields*. Mary lives with her husband, Dean, in Pittsburgh, Pennsylvania. Visit her website at www.maryfraileycalland.com.

CPSIA information can be obtained at www.ICGtesting.com
Printed in the USA
BVOW041947101111

275830BV00001B/22/P